Kathryn Freeman started her ~~career~~ as a pharmacist but soon realised ~~that~~ handwriting wasn't for her. In 20~~~~ ~~she~~ left the world of pharmaceutical science to begin life as a self-employed writer.

She lives with two teenage boys and a husband who asks every Valentine's Day whether he has to bother buying a card again this year (yes, he does) so the romance in her life is all in her head.

www.kathrynfreeman.co.uk

X x.com/KathrynFreeman1
f facebook.com/kathrynfreeman

Also by Kathryn Freeman

The New Guy

Up Close and Personal

Strictly Come Dating

Mr Right Across the Street

The Beach Reads Book Club

The Italian Job

Nobody Puts Romcoms In the Corner

Was It Good For You?

THANK YOU, NEXT

KATHRYN FREEMAN

One More Chapter
a division of HarperCollins*Publishers*
1 London Bridge Street
London SE1 9GF
www.harpercollins.co.uk
HarperCollins*Publishers*
Macken House, 39/40 Mayor Street Upper,
Dublin 1, D01 C9W8, Ireland

This paperback edition 2024
First published in Great Britain in ebook format
by HarperCollins*Publishers* 2024

1

Copyright © Kathryn Freeman 2024
Kathryn Freeman asserts the moral right to be identified
as the author of this work

A catalogue record of this book is available from the British Library

ISBN: 978-0-00-856037-9

This novel is entirely a work of fiction. The names, characters and incidents portrayed in it are the work of the author's imagination. Any resemblance to actual persons, living or dead, events or localities is entirely coincidental.

Printed and bound in the UK using 100% Renewable Electricity
by CPI Group (UK) Ltd

All rights reserved. No part of this publication may be reproduced, stored in a retrieval system, or transmitted, in any form or by any means, electronic, mechanical, photocopying, recording or otherwise, without the prior permission of the publishers.

Chapter One

Molly glanced around her open plan kitchen/living area. Subdued lighting: check. Pizza ready to go in the oven, nibbles on the coffee table, wine bottle and glasses out: check, check, check. TV on the right channel: check. All she needed now was Duncan...

The doorbell sounded and she laughed. Yet another reason she and Duncan were a perfect match – like her, he was always on time.

'Hey, babe.' He wrapped his burly arms around her. As an online personal trainer, he was ridiculously fit. She wasn't quite in that league – okay, she definitely wasn't in that league – but she did work out with him twice a week. Mainly because he insisted on it, so he could film them as he tested out new routines. But she would ... almost certainly ... work out more if she had the time.

'Hey, yourself.' She waved him towards the kitchen. 'If you go and pour the wine, I'll pop the pizza in the oven.'

'Thin crust, yeah?' He asked as he unscrewed the wine bottle. 'And you got the vegetarian one with no cheese?'

'Of course.' She glanced down at the vegan pizza sitting ready on the tray, and felt a pang of longing for pepperoni. But processed meat was bad for her, as was the tasty thick crust and the gooey mozzarella that ran down your chin. So now she ate the same pizza as Duncan, which was much healthier.

Slipping it into the oven, she set the timer and went to snuggle up to him on the sofa. 'Here you go.' He handed her a small glass of red wine before pouring another for himself.

Saturdays were the best days, and not just for what they were about to watch on the TV. It was alcohol day. She totally bought into Duncan's healthy living lifestyle. Of course it made sense to take care with what she ate and drank, and to exercise. She could vividly remember the first time he'd asked her to try out one of his routines. Talk about embarrassing. Not just the tomato face and the inability to breathe, but the wobbles the lycra hadn't managed to disguise. After that, it had been a no-brainer to follow the diet and exercise plan he'd created for her. It didn't mean there wasn't a teeny, tiny part of her that still wanted to slob now and again.

And to drink more than once a week.

She'd also occasionally like a few crisps, she acknowledged as she listened to him talk about his day. Swerving the carrots she'd carefully peeled and sliced, she grabbed an olive, which at least had some taste.

When he'd finished relating his tale of how the check-out guy in the supermarket had recognised him and asked for an autograph, Duncan shot her a grin. 'Speaking of celebrities, I can't wait to see how that mouthy couple have got on tonight. If I were the bloke, I'd have bolted at the altar.'

And this was why she didn't mind the healthy snacks, or the vegan pizza. How many other men would be as excited as she was about watching dating shows? Her mind flashed back to the last guy she'd fallen for. Ben would rather have swum through a crocodile-infested lake, after running through a burning building.

Immediately she pushed the thought of him away. It had taken far too long to get over a man she'd only known for two glorious, whirlwind, yet ultimately devastating months, but the important point was that she *had* got over him. Thanks to Duncan.

Duncan cleared his throat, jolting her out of her thoughts. 'Speaking of altars…'

Her heart thumped. Oh my God, was he going to *propose*? 'Yes?' It came out as a squeak, she was so excited.

'Shit, no, I'm not about to ask you to marry me.' A panicked look crossed his face. 'Not that I'm against the idea. I mean, I think it could be on the cards for us, yes? But that's not what … bummer.' He sighed and took her hand. 'Now what I was going to say will be a real let down.'

'No, it's okay.' She tried to laugh, though inside she was dying from embarrassment. She was so stupid. 'Of course you weren't going to propose. I mean, if you were…' *Stop it!* 'I mean big if, obviously, and not necessarily to me, but if you were going to propose to some lucky person one day, you'd do it properly.' Swallowing down her tears, she forced another laugh. 'You wouldn't just blurt it out in front of the TV.'

'Hey.' He rubbed a thumb gently over her knuckles. 'I want to get married one day, you know that. We've talked about how my mum wants those grandkids.' He gave her a sweet kiss. 'Just not today, yeah?'

Her smile felt lopsided, but the embarrassment was receding, along with some of the disappointment. This wasn't a *no*; it was a *not yet*. 'So what were you going to tell me?'

'Ah, well.' Was it her imagination or was he avoiding her

eyes? 'I've been asked if I want to take part in that show where they date for four weeks and then have to choose whether to marry or not at the altar. You know the one—'

'*The One.*'

'That's it.' A grin broke out across his face. 'One of our faves, isn't it?'

Molly blinked. 'Yes, but … can you repeat what you said, because I thought I heard that you'd been asked to take part?'

He laughed. 'I know, it's nuts, right? I figured contestants applied to go on the show, but apparently sometimes these reality shows use social media to find people they reckon have got the right look or personality.'

'And they asked you? I mean, the producers of *The One* actually asked you to be on their frigging show?' Part of her was excited for him, but part of her… 'They know you're in a relationship, right?'

Again he avoided her eyes, nodding towards the TV where the opening credits of *Married at First Sight* were playing, the familiar theme tune echoing around the room. 'Can we shelve this chat, babe? It's about to start.'

'Sure, yes.' The timer sounded and she jumped to her feet to grab the pizza out of the oven.

But as she settled down to watch the fallout from the previous evening's dinner party – what an episode *that* had been – she couldn't focus. She wanted to laugh at the mouthy couple as they had a full-blown shouting match, neither listening to the other. To cringe at the pair who looked all sorts of wrong for each other as they ate their breakfast in a stilted silence. But her head wouldn't budge from the conversation with Duncan.

When it came to the adverts, she was ready to explode. 'What did you say to them?'

Duncan dragged his gaze from the TV screen to frown at her. 'Say to who?'

'The producers of *The One*. What did you say when they asked if you wanted to take part?'

He let out a heavy sigh. 'What do you think I said? You know how much exposure it would give me, being on the show. No way could I turn it down.'

'But...' Her head was starting to spin. 'You'd be paired with another woman. Go on dates with her.'

'Sure, but only for the show.' His fingers curled round her chin, blue eyes finding hers. 'Come on, you know how I feel about you. Just think of this as ... work. Yeah, that's what it is. The chance for me to advertise myself on a major TV show, and for free. Imagine how many new followers I could get out of it.'

As she stared at his animated face, Molly felt a stab of guilt. She was being selfish. This was a huge opportunity and she should be happy for him. But. 'What do I tell my family, my mates? They all watch the show and they're going to have questions about why my boyfriend is on it claiming he's looking for love when...' – she swallowed, feeling a burn of tears – 'when I thought he'd already found it.'

'Of course I have.' His eyes strayed towards the TV where the adverts were coming to an end. 'But I've got to go back to being single for a bit.'

Her heart began to thump. 'What are you saying? You're *dumping* me?'

'That's not the word I'd use, but I can't be in a relationship if I'm going to do the show, you know that.' He glanced sideways at her and his brow furrowed. 'Hey, come on, don't look at me like that. It's only temporary, babe. Just business, right?'

'But you're dumping me.' The slice of pizza she'd eaten began to work its way back. Shit, she was going to be sick. Lurching to her feet, she ran to the bathroom. There she clutched at the basin, forcing herself to breathe. This was okay. She wasn't being skewered again. Unlike the last time she'd been blindsided, she knew exactly why Duncan was ending things. It's not like he'd given her the glib 'it's not you, it's me' bullshit.

'Hey, babe, please come out.' Duncan shouted through the closed door. 'This is daft. You know I love you. I've just got to think of my career for a bit, that's all.'

Sucking in a deep breath, she pushed open the door. 'I know you do, and I'm sorry. It's just, well, it's quite a shock.'

'But you get it, yes?' His eyes searched hers before bending to give her a quick kiss. 'I need you to get it, because I'm not sure I can go on the show if you're not behind it.'

This was a test of their relationship, that was all. And if she wasn't prepared to support his career, what sort of partner did that make her? 'It's fine, I understand.' The emotion she was trying to push into a box kept trying to escape and she felt her eyes sting. 'Just don't fall for whoever you're partnered with.'

He dropped another kiss on her mouth. 'How can I when I know I've got you waiting for me when I get out?'

'Easy to say now.' Her voice caught as her mind scrambled ahead. 'Matchmakers and some computer algorithm are going to find the perfect woman to pair you with.' Oh God, she'd forgotten the show ending. 'You could get *married* to her.'

'Hey, babe, stop this. Of course I'm not going to marry whoever they pair me up with.' He held her shoulders and gave her a little shake. 'How are they going to find me a more perfect woman? We're soulmates, yeah?'

'Looks like we're about to find out.' Confusion, hurt, fear that she was about to lose him ... it all churned inside her and she stepped away from his hold. 'I think it's best if you go home. Good luck in the show. For once, I'm going to give it a miss.'

'Molly, come on, try to be a bit more positive. This is a chance for me to really grow my personal training business while appearing on our favourite show. You know how much I need it to be successful so I can support my future wife and all those kids I'm hoping for,' he added with a crooked smile. 'I thought you'd be *happy* for me.' He snatched at his coat, disappointment etched across his handsome features. 'I'll call you tomorrow when you've calmed down and started to see sense.'

The door shut behind him, and as she heard his footsteps trail away, she slid to the floor and sunk her head into her hands. Up until now, Duncan had always made her feel loved, cherished. The once daily flower deliveries might have been cut back to monthly, but they still happened. As did their dress-up Friday dates. Even after a year together, he still booked a fancy restaurant for them and put on a suit, or a shirt and those black trousers he looked so good in – the ones that stretched tight across his muscular thighs.

The tears stopped flowing and as her heart returned to its normal beat, she realised she was overreacting. Duncan loved her. He'd told her that, repeatedly. He was only going on the show to grow his business so he could support the family he planned. The one he'd hinted he wanted with *her*.

Yet the unease refused to budge, prodding and poking at the corners of her mind like an unwanted guest trying to regain entry. Duncan might not be going on the show to find a new partner, but he would be matched with one. And if that person turned out to be a more perfect fit for him than she was?

She'd be left in the one place she feared more than anything else. Alone.

Chapter Two

Three weeks later

Molly hated her job, but she loved the three women she worked with, who were currently looking at her expectantly.

'Come on, Moll, don't keep us in suspense.' Ava waved her sandwich at her. 'You promised us a picnic in the park *and* something juicy. Besides the melon,' she added with an ironic smile. 'So far you've only delivered on the picnic.'

Molly had asked them if they wanted to go to the park for lunch. Something they tried to do a lot in the summer because it provided a welcome escape from the drab four walls of their office.

'Okay.' She sucked in a deep breath, still giddy over the call she'd had that morning. 'You know Duncan and I split up—'

'Because Dunc the Hunk was asked to go on that dating show,' Penny filled in for her. 'And you're happy for him, but secretly you're also really miserable 'cos you're scared he's going to fall for whoever he's matched with, though we all know he's never going to find anyone better than you.'

'Aw, thank you.' Molly smiled at her friend. 'So anyway, the thing is, this assistant producer from the show, Rachel, phoned me this morning and asked if I'd be interested in going on, too.'

'OMG.' Even Emma, the quietest of their group, had her hand over her mouth.

'Why you?' Ava demanded. 'What did she say?'

'They found out Duncan used to date me and thought it would add a dramatic twist to the show to get me to go on it. You know, feuding exes.' She gave them a sly smile. 'Or the possibility of second chances.'

'So you're going to be partnered with him?' Ava gushed.

'Well, it's not guaranteed, but from the way she kept going on about adding some tension to the couple dynamics, it's pretty obvious they'll put us together.'

'Do you think that's what he'll want though?' Emma asked, her expression full of concern.

It was the question Molly had wrestled with, and still didn't have an answer. 'I don't know, but the way I see it, I can leave him to go on the show and get matched with someone they believe would be a perfect fit for him. Potentially fall for them. Marry them.' A lump rose into her throat and she swallowed it down. 'Or I can use this opportunity to take fate into my own hands and join him. Fight for him.' She pointed down at her body. 'I've lost weight since he started me on this health and exercise trip and I look the best I've ever done. Maybe this is my chance to prove that we really are meant to be together. I mean we've talked of getting married, but it's always been something that might happen in the future. Now it's going to be there, at the end of the four weeks.' Her pulse kicked up a gear. 'A real option.'

'But what happens if you're not matched together?' Emma asked softly. 'It could be really hard for you to be in the same house as him and watch while he dates someone else.'

'I know.' Unconsciously she rubbed at the place on her chest, over her heart. 'But I really think Duncan and I are meant to be, you know? What did you call us, Penny?'

'Two peas in a pod.'

'Exactly. So the odds are good that we'll get matched together. And even if we're not, there'll be a chance to swop after two weeks.' She pushed the doubts to one side and focussed on the end goal. 'By the end of the show we could actually be husband and wife.' The thought was enough to stir the butterflies in her belly.

'You'd say *I do* to him?' Ava asked. 'For real?'

'You know I would.' Molly glanced curiously over at Ava. 'What is it with you and marriage? Why are you so against it?'

'I'm not against it,' Ava protested. 'I just don't see why you're so keen on it. Why tie yourself down to one guy?'

'Because he's perfect for me. Because I can't imagine ever wanting anyone else.' Briefly the image of a guy with dark hair, model good looks and a devastating smile flashed across her mind, but she shook it away. That experience only went to prove how right for her Duncan was. A man who actually talked about his feelings, who opened up to her.

'But you can still have perfect-for-you Duncan without actually having to marry him,' Ava insisted.

'Could I? Or would he only be on loan to me. Ready to be loaned to someone else the moment he'd had enough.' Her heart twisted and Molly stared down at her half-eaten sandwich. She sounded insecure and needy, which she hated, but her friends would never understand how important that piece of paper was to her. The legal promise that she was not going to be abandoned on a whim. 'Besides he wants to get married, too. His parents are kind of religious and he's the only child. They keep hinting at him that it's time he settled down and started a family.'

A hand curled around her arm and she looked up to find Penny smiling kindly at her. 'We're getting ahead of ourselves here. All we know for certain is you're going to be on your favourite TV show and so is Duncan. That's enough freaking excitement for one afternoon.'

'You're right.' Molly let the reality of that sink in. 'I was a basket case when Rachel asked me. I couldn't stop babbling, telling her how honoured I was, how I was sure they'd match me with The One because I totally believed in the show and was thrilled to get the chance to marry my soulmate. I bet she has me down as a total goofball.' A thought occurred to her 'Oh my God, I'm going to have to ask for a leave of absence from work. I wonder if they'll give it to me?'

'If they don't, just leave.' Ava shrugged. 'Fuck 'em, fuck the job. You hate it anyway.'

'I do.' That curl of excitement started again in her belly. 'This is going to be mega. A month away from work, staying in a posh mansion with Duncan and going on lots of fun dates with him.' There was just one potential fly in the ointment. 'I wonder what Duncan will think when he sees me?'

'He definitely doesn't know you're joining him?' Emma asked.

'He phoned me the day after we split and said he needed a clean break to clear his head before he went on the show so I've not been in contact with him since. Rachel said they weren't going to tell anyone we'd dated, not the viewers or the contestants, because they want it to come out naturally so they get a proper reaction on film.' It was hard not to feel panicked when she thought of what his reaction could be. 'By the time we meet up it will have been over two months since we parted ways.'

Would he be happy to see her? Or would he see it as her interfering with his gig, his chance to shine in front of the cameras? Maybe his chance to find someone better to marry and have his kids?

Emma must have read her fear because she slipped her arms around Molly. 'Hey, if he really loves you, he'll be thrilled to see you. And if he's not, then it's best to find out now. Who knows, between this fancy dating algorithm the show always bangs on about, and the professional matchmakers, you might find yourself partnered with someone even more perfect for you.'

Emma was trying to help, so Molly kept quiet, but the truth was, even if more perfect existed, she wasn't interested. She wanted Duncan. He was the one who'd helped put the broken pieces of her heart back together and made her believe in love again. Duncan also wanted what she wanted. Marriage, stability. A family.

Chapter Three

One month later

Ben was lying on the beach, under an umbrella, the gentle breeze from the sea helping to keep his body at that perfect temperature where all of his muscles felt loose and languid. Similar to after sex, he thought, though he could barely remember that far back.

Speaking of sex, there was a woman in a hot red bikini with her back to him, walking down towards the sea, long red hair cascading down her back. Hips swaying seductively. She halted at the water's edge. Was she going to turn around? Give him a chance to see if that perfect behind was matched by a knock out face?

Wait, didn't he recognise that bum? The hair…

The shrill ringing of his doorbell catapulted him out of his dream and he sat up with a start, looking around him. Not on the beach then. He'd fallen asleep on his damn sofa.

'Ben.' The annoying voice of his sister sounded through the door. 'I know you're in there. I called your assistant and she said you'd gone home. Something about you being tired, you sad git.'

He rubbed his sleep-blurred eyes with the heels of his hands. 'Go away.'

'You know that won't work with me. Get off your backside and let me in.'

He could argue – he usually did. But these last few months had sucked all the energy out of him. With a deep sigh he heaved himself to his feet and padded over to open the door.

Rachel studied him from head to foot. 'Bloody hell, you look like shit.'

'And you look beautiful as always.' He bent to kiss her cheek.

'Don't think flattery is going to get you back into my good books.' She swept inside and went straight through to the kitchen where she started to make herself a drink. 'I phoned you twice yesterday. And messaged you so much my fingers ached.'

'Tea.'

She swirled round to stare at him. 'What?'

'Presume you weren't just making yourself a drink.'

She huffed, but dug into the jar for a teabag. 'A please wouldn't hurt.'

'You woke me up. I'm feeling cranky.'

'You're always cranky.'

Because that was probably true – and certainly had been of the last few months – he walked over and planted a kiss on the top of her head. 'But you love me anyway.'

'I suppose.'

She twisted her head to glance at him, and something flashed in her eyes that sent alarm bells ringing. 'What's with that look?'

'What look?' She gave him a breezy smile and handed over a steaming mug of tea.

'You know what I mean. It was…' – he snapped his fingers together as the word struck him – 'calculating. Like you know something I don't. Something I probably don't even want to know.'

She let out a dismissive sound and went to sit on his huge – and apparently comfortable enough to fall asleep on – grey sofa. 'Shouldn't we be drinking champagne now instead of tea?'

It took him a moment to realise what she meant. 'I'll save the celebration for when I'm not so knackered. I'd be felled like a daisy after one glass.'

'But you're rich now.' She gave him another careful study. 'And passably handsome, when you've not gone without sleep for months.'

He exhaled heavily, knowing her too well. 'Just say what you came here to say.'

'Right, okay. No small talk, straight down to business. Got it.' He knew it was bad when she pushed to her feet. 'I was thinking, now you've finally sold your company, you have some time on your hands for a change.'

He narrowed his eyes. 'After I've tied up the remaining loose ends I'm looking forward to a break from what has been an exhausting period of my life, yes.' Setting up the company, running it, then selling it. The last few years had been full on, the last couple of months totally manic.

Rachel nodded enthusiastically. 'A break, that's exactly what you need. Time away from here in new surroundings. The chance to do something different.'

He decided it was time to cut the obvious bullshit. 'What do you want?'

'God, why do you always fast forward to the end. I'm trying to lure you in gently.'

'And I'm trying to end this conversation so I can get back to the part where I'm asleep.'

She rolled her big brown eyes and came to sit next to him. 'When was the last time you went out on a date?'

'A date. Christ.' He hung his head, rubbing at the tension in the back of his neck. 'Is that what this is about? You want to set me up?' He suddenly remembered what she'd asked him to do a few days ago. 'Is this why you got me to fill in that questionnaire? The one you told me was a prototype that you needed to validate?'

'Not exactly.' She prodded him. 'Back to the question. Can you even remember the last woman you properly dated?'

'You know damn well who it was,' he retorted. 'And why I haven't dated since.'

That wasn't quite true. He'd had a few glorious weeks of madness when he'd dated a woman he shouldn't have done. Someone he hadn't told Rachel about at the time because he'd known she'd worry, say it was too soon. Yet when this woman had literally almost fallen into his lap, he'd been unable to resist her. What harm a little slice of heaven, he'd told himself. A respite from the hell he'd been living through? He could still picture the wide smile, long red hair, emerald green eyes. The quirky clothes, the way she wore jewellery to match her mood. Still remember her ability to say in a hundred words what he could say in five. Her unfiltered talking without thinking. The way she'd made him laugh, turning the dullest day into one so bright, he'd never wanted it to end.

But of course it had to.

'God, Ben, Helena was three years ago.' Rachel's voice broke through his trip down memory lane. 'I'd assumed you were just doing your usual trick of not telling me all the juicy stuff. I never for one minute thought there *wasn't* any juicy stuff.'

'What's your point?' he asked abruptly, anxious to move the conversation on.

'My point is you've buried yourself in work the last few years. But now you've sold the company, and it's time to put your head back above the parapet. Start thinking about what you want out of life.'

'Let me guess. That includes a partner.'

'You're trying to tell me you don't want that?'

Feeling restless, he got to his feet. 'If I do, I'm quite capable of finding myself one.'

'Of course you are.' The soothing tone made him suspicious. Rachel was never compliant; she was as stubborn as he was.

'Then we're in agreement. So if that's all you came to say...'

'Okay, okay.' She looked up at him, an entreaty in the hazel eyes that were so similar to his. 'I'm in a bind, and I need you to help me out of it.'

Warily he sat back on the sofa. 'What sort of bind?'

'A work bind.'

Relief washed through him. Work, he could handle. He might not be an expert on producing TV shows, but business was business. 'You need me to go through a report? Write you a strategy document? Test out another questionnaire?'

She swallowed. 'I need you to take part in the next series of *The One*.'

'You ... *what*?'

'We're all ready to go live next week. The contestants have been paired up, we've filmed their intros and, well...' – her eyes shone with enthusiasm – 'you get a real sense of how it's going to go down when you start to get to know the people taking part and I'm so excited about this one. I think it's going to be the best series yet. At least I did, until one of the guys pulled out two days ago, leaving us, and the gorgeous woman we'd picked for him, high and dry.'

He'd only taken in every other word, but it was enough. *More* than enough. 'No.'

Her face fell, all that shining enthusiasm suddenly extinguished. 'I'm desperate, Ben. We don't have time to go through the whole matchmaking process again, and though we have a few people on reserve, none of them are right for this lovely lady. Then I realised the guy who pulled out was similar to you in terms of personality so I got you to fill in our profiling questionnaire—'

'*That* was what I was doing?'

A hint of pink tinged her cheeks. 'Okay, okay, so I cheated a bit but you'd never have done it if I'd told you the truth. And guess what, my gut feel was right. Felix and Stephanie agree you're a perfect match for her. Even more so than the other guy.'

'Who the hell are Felix and Stephanie?'

'You remember, you met them at the Christmas bash. They're the relationship experts. And when I say experts, I mean it; so you should be thrilled that they think your pairing is the most likely to be successful.' Her eyes pleaded with him. 'Honestly, this woman is so excited to be going on the show, there's no way we can let her down. She wants to find her soulmate, like they all do, and *The One* is also her favourite TV show. Can you believe that?'

He didn't have the energy for this. With a sigh, Ben slumped back against the sofa. 'What I'm struggling to believe is that you think a perfect match for me is someone who loves to watch a bunch of publicity seeking airheads take part in a dubious dating experience under the guise of finding true love.' It was too harsh. He realised the moment he saw her expression harden.

'That's not fair. I didn't tell you how stupid your idea was to start a business renting private spaces out for events.'

'My bank balance suggests it wasn't stupid,' he countered dryly. Because he saw the tension behind her annoyance, he reached to squeeze her hand. 'I'm sorry, that was an asinine comment.'

'It was.' She sniffed. 'I'm proud of our track record. We've had ten couples marry each other on the show since we started, and three more who married afterwards.'

And how many regretted it? He swallowed the words down, aware he'd already pissed his sister off. 'Come on, Rach, I'm the last person you should be inviting onto your show. Especially if you're pairing me with someone keen to find their soulmate.' His fingers itched to mime quotation marks around the word. 'There must be another solution.'

She sighed, and he knew he was in serious trouble when her eyes began to glisten. His sister didn't cry. She straightened her back, took in a breath and got on with whatever life had thrown at her. 'We could match her with someone clearly unsuitable, which goes against the heart of what we're trying to do. The only other solution is for her to drop out and us to go ahead filming with one less couple, which would seriously limit the amount of decent footage we'd get. We're committed to a TV schedule of daily episodes and though it's not live, we only have a day to edit it down to a show, so we really need the right balance of people. Especially as we've got a month of air time to fill—'

'A month?' He repeated numbly. 'I'd have to commit to this

for four weeks? Can't I duck out after the first few days and say we tried and it didn't work?'

'Have you ever watched the show your sister works on?'

He felt a prick of shame. She'd spent a lot of time talking to him about his business, yet he'd not bothered to show her the same courtesy. 'Remind me.'

She gave him a shrewd look. 'Okay, so you've probably *forgotten* that our top matched couples go to stay in Happily Ever After Towers…'

'You've got to be kidding me.'

'As I'm sure you *remember*,' she continued, ignoring his mutterings, 'HEA Towers is a luxurious stately home in the Chalfonts with a gym, swimming pool, tennis court … basically everything you could possibly want in five-star accommodation. And our couples live there for a month with nothing to do but take part in a few activities and enjoy their surroundings. It's the perfect place for an exhausted single guy to take a break,' she added pointedly.

'Perfect except for the cameras and the enforced dating.'

'We don't have hidden cameras,' she countered. 'You'll know when you're being filmed because the camera will be obvious or you'll see the crew.'

'But there will be cameras. Plural. And I'll have to date this woman in front of them.' God help him, he wasn't even sure he was ready to date again.

'Yes.' She let out a long, slow breath, her shoulders slumping. 'Look, I know this isn't you. I know you'll hate talking in front of the cameras, hate the thought of anyone trying to pair you up, hate the group activities like cooking and quiz games, oh and giving up your phone—'

'You're not helping your cause.'

'I know.' She gave him a tremulous smile. 'Probably won't

help if I tell you that at the end of the month you have to plan your wedding.'

His eyes bulged. *'My wedding?'*

'Yes, but obviously you can say no.' She paused, swallowed. 'When you're both at the altar.'

He baulked. He couldn't do this. It had everything he hated. Lack of privacy, forced social situations … planning a wedding, for fuck's sake. She knew how he felt about marriage.

But then he looked at his sister. The tears she was valiantly keeping in check. 'Is there anything I won't hate about it?'

She let out a strangled laugh. 'Let me see. I think you'll really like the woman you'll be paired with. If we're wrong though and you don't get on, you get the chance to ditch her for someone else after two weeks. And in the remaining two weeks the viewers are in charge. They can vote for you to swop partners. Or even vote you off the show.'

'So, if I make a terrible partner, which we both know is highly probable, I could only be forfeiting two and a bit weeks of my life?'

'Yes.' Rachel burst out into laughter. 'Oh God, I know this is your idea of hell but you'd be doing me such a huge favour. Not to mention getting me loads of brownie points with my boss. Plus, you never know, you might even enjoy it. Your match is loads of fun and it's about time you had some of that.'

He couldn't believe he was seriously contemplating this. 'Do I get my own room?'

'Yes.'

'With no cameras in it?'

'Absolutely. I told you, we don't have hidden cameras. You'll know when we're filming you. The show isn't about gossip and lurching from partner to partner. It's about building real relationships that could end in marriage. Though obviously that's totally down to the couples involved and absolutely not compulsory,' she added quickly.

Okay. He took in a deep breath, let it out slowly. Repeated the exercise. The only things he had planned for the next month were to sleep, relax and think about what to do next. He could probably do all of that in the ridiculously named HEA Towers. 'Fine. I'll do it.'

The beaming smile on Rachel's face, the joy, the gratitude … he made a mental note to record it in his databank and play it back the first time a camera was shoved in his face.

Chapter Four

Molly's knee bounced up and down in excitement as the limo – yes, she was in a frigging chauffeur- driven limo, like some celebrity – turned into the long, sweeping drive of HEA Towers. And God, it looked every bit as impressive as it did on the TV. Her eyes boggled as the sleek black Mercedes carried her closer and closer towards what looked like a mini castle, two towers rising dramatically against the blue sky. Scrunching across the gravel, they rounded a fountain ... seriously, was that Aphrodite, Goddess of Love, water cascading out of her outstretched hand?

And holy moly, even the two bay trees set on either side of the entrance were carefully styled into love hearts.

She bet Duncan freaked out when he saw it.

Her heart tugged and Molly steeled herself not to cry. Please God he'd be happy to see her. When it came to judging how people felt about her, she knew her track record was abysmal, but even she couldn't have got the last year all wrong. Could she? They fit together, like ... she'd say fish and chips but Duncan would hate that. Avocado and poached egg, maybe. Oatmeal and blueberries.

Hopefully the relationship experts responsible for doing the match ups had seen that, too.

Her phone buzzed with a message, her last for a while, she thought ruefully as she'd have to hand her mobile over as soon as she stepped inside. When she glanced down, she saw it was from her mum. Strictly, her second mum, but the first she tried very hard not to think about.

Good luck sweetie. We'll be routing for you. Mum and Dad xx

Tears pricked her eyes. It was fair to say that both her adopted parents had been wary of her going on *The One* when she'd first mentioned it.

'I don't like the idea of the show producers using you,' her mum had complained when she'd told her about Rachel wanting Duncan's ex-girlfriend on the show to add some drama.

Molly had tried to explain that actually she was the one doing the using – she was using the show to be with Duncan again.

The man she believed loved her and wanted to marry her.

Of course there had been a time she'd believed that of Ben, so it *was* entirely possible she'd got Duncan all wrong...

Breathe, Molly, breathe.

She pushed the air past the pain in her chest. At least by the end of the month, she would know.

They came to a stop and the driver walked round the car to open the door for her. As she stepped out of the limo, her heart jumped into her throat.

'Welcome to HEA Towers!'

She had a second to wonder what the gravel was going to do to her strappy heels before she was dazzled by the smiles from the production team lined up to greet her. As if she was frigging royalty, she thought with a silent squeal. Some of the faces she recognised, like Rachel, the pocket dynamo of an assistant producer. And Natalie, the larger-than-life show host who she'd not met in person but felt she knew from the telly.

She shook their hands in a daze, heart thumping against her ribs as she was led through the grand entrance hall and into an oak-panelled drawing room.

There, a crowd of women shrieked and leapt up to greet her.

Faces and names became a blur as she was introduced to the other female contestants on the show.

'This is really happening.' A bouncy blonde, Molly thought she was called Jasmine, did a little dance. 'It's like the best thing, ever.'

'I can't wait to see who I've been matched with.' Maya, a gorgeous woman with dark brown skin, smiled playfully. 'Hope he's hot.'

'You and me both.' Chloe flicked her dark, poker straight hair over her shoulders.

'The good news is, you're all going to find out very soon.' Rachel's authoritative voice carried across the room as they all fell silent. 'Now, I'm going to hand over to your host, Natalie, who'll tell you how this part of the evening is going to work.'

As the cameras focussed on her, Natalie whooped and clapped her hands together, her plus-sized body shimmering in sequins. 'Well, my lovelies, welcome to HEA Towers. The place where, in four weeks' time, we hope some of you, maybe all of you, will be saying *I do* to the man of your dreams.' Molly glanced at the other girls and they all shared a giddy grin. 'So are you all excited to see who you've been matched with?'

There was a collective scream of *yes!*

'This series we're making a few little changes from how we did things last season, beginning with the reveal.' Natalie paused, her gaze resting on each of them in turn. 'The main dining room has been set up in tables for two, spaced far enough away from each other that it will feel like an intimate dining experience. After the initial meet and greet here, where you'll see all the guys you'll be living under the same roof with for the next month, you ladies are going to be taken to the dining room and invited to sit down at a table. And then we'll blindfold you.' There was a collective gasp, and Natalie chuckled. 'I know, it sounds a bit kinky, doesn't it, but trust me, this is going to make the evening more fun, and more intense. Without sight, your other senses will become more important. Take your meal, for example. You'll be able to focus on the taste and the aroma.'

Molly burst out laughing. 'I'm not sure any of us will be focussing on the food tonight.'

Natalie beamed. 'I hear you girl, I hear you. That guy who'll be joining you at your table though, your match? You won't be able to see him, but you'll notice the timbre of his voice. His smell. If he's wearing expensive cologne or he's the soap and water type.'

'Oooh, what about touch? Can we touch him?' Jasmine did another jig.

Natalie roared with laughter. 'Go for it, though obviously both parties need to be willing. Oh and just in case you're worried, he'll be blindfolded too, so you're both in this together.' She paused, gaze skimming the room, ramping up the anticipation. 'Are you ready to meet the male line up?

Because right now they're standing outside this door, and I can tell you, they're chomping at the bit to meet you.'

With a flair for the dramatic, Natalie marched over to the door and threw it open. Molly's heart skipped a beat when she caught sight of Duncan striding in first. He looked handsome in his suit, big shoulders straining the seams.

Jasmine whistled. 'Please let him be mine.'

Unlucky, he's mine.

Duncan's eyes flew open when he clocked her, his expression almost comically shocked. Molly flicked him a quick grin, turning away quickly before the cameras saw them.

The first time she'd met Duncan had been in a crowded bar after matching with him on a dating app. It had been a bit awkward to be honest, the place too noisy for proper conversation. Tonight was a chance to have their first time all over again, but with the romance of an elegant setting, the mystique of a blindfold. And the thrill of knowing they were on their favourite TV show.

'Forget Mr Muscles, I'm digging Mr Tall, Dark and Totally Delicious.' Beside her, Chloe licked her lips. Molly turned to see who she was fussing over.

And froze.

No, it couldn't be. The man she knew, the one who looked the spitting image of the one who'd just strode confidently into the room as if he was on a flaming model shoot, would never, even if hell had frozen over, appear on a show like this.

But then his eyes collided with hers, and her heart almost exploded out of her chest. Acting on pure impulse, uncaring of the camera crew, of everyone in the room except the man who'd once left her so utterly devastated it had taken years to get over, she marched up to him and threw the contents of her glass in his face.

Ben inhaled sharply, staring at her for a few beats as champagne slowly dripped down his sharp cheeks, his square jaw. Then, with all the calm control she lacked, he carefully picked up a nearby napkin and wiped it away. 'Feel better?'

Anger, hurt, loss, the emotions swirled inside her, causing her hands to shake. 'Not even close.'

How mortifying, how devastating, that seeing him again brought everything she thought she'd buried, flooding back to the surface. Yet he seemed so utterly unaffected by her.

'Molly?' Rachel marched over, giving her a concerned look. 'Is everything okay?'

'No.' Heart thumping, she glared back at Ben. 'I need to get some air. I'll leave him to explain why he's wearing my drink. It's the least he can do.'

She wanted to sashay out of the room with her head held high and enough sway to her hips to make Ben wonder why he'd decided to discard her after eight of the most intense, passionate weeks of her life. Sadly her legs felt like leftover spaghetti, and as she staggered towards the door she nudged at a table of drinks, causing the untouched glasses of champagne to topple over. 'Oh bugger. I'm sorry.'

Ben, who'd managed to get another dousing, picked up the napkin again. 'Good to see some things don't change.' He gave her a half smile. 'Going out with you was never dull.'

Being so close to him again, that quirk of his full lips, the tall, athletic body, the eyes that held a person spellbound yet rarely told them what he was thinking. All in front of not just an audience of contestants, but a camera crew recording her meltdown to show to a wider TV audience. It was too much. She turned and fled from the room, finding sanctuary in the ladies across the hallway.

For a few minutes she stared at herself in the mirror,

dragging deep breaths into her lungs and willing her emotions to calm.

'Molly?'

She startled at the knock on the door. 'Duncan?'

'You okay?'

Dashing over, she threw it open and wrapped her arms around him. 'Oh my God, I'm so glad to see you.'

'Hey, hey.' He soothed a hand down her back. 'Not complaining, but what on earth are you doing here, babe?'

'They know I'm your ex and they invited me on the show.' At the warmth of his touch her heart began to settle. 'I figure they're going to match us together, you know, the two exes, so I thought why not? This way we don't have to be apart and you don't have to pretend to get on with someone else.' She tried to smile, but her lips weren't working properly, like they knew she was on the verge of tears again. 'You can pretend to fall for me all over again.'

'Yeah, well, I won't be pretending. You know I love you.' He eased back a little, his expression uncertain. 'But what if we *don't* get matched?'

'Stick or ditch, remember? We get a chance to change partners at two weeks.'

'Okay.' He let out a rough exhale. 'Not being funny, but I'm doing this to increase my following, so I can't come across as a dick. If we don't get paired, I've got to be nice to the woman I'm with, yeah?'

Her stomach twisted at the thought of him spending time with someone else, but she nodded. 'I know.'

'The guy you threw your drink over?' He smoothed a hand down her hair in a way that made her feel cherished. 'Who was that?'

'My ex.'

His eyebrows scrunched together in a frown. 'The one who screwed you over?'

She did not want to talk about Ben. 'Yep.'

'Jesus. Better hope you don't get paired with him, at least.' He paused, gave her a small smile. 'Let's keep it quiet that we dated. I don't want to end up as the second arsehole ex to get a drink thrown in their face.'

'You're not an arsehole. You might have ditched me, but I know why.'

He gave her a sweet kiss. 'Thanks, babe. But still, I want to keep the viewers on side.' He glanced down at his watch and winced. 'Sorry, babe, I've gotta go. I told them I was going for a slash, but guys don't take this long. They'll be bringing out a search party soon and I don't want to get caught in the ladies.' He planted a quick kiss on her mouth. 'Hope to see you sitting opposite me when I take off my blindfold.'

Chapter Five

As Ben wiped champagne off him for a second time, he noticed Rachel motion the cameras towards the other couples before directing her fierce gaze on him.

'Upsetting a woman within the first two minutes is a new low, even by your standards.'

Ben gave his sister a loaded look. 'Do I need to remind you that I don't want to be here?'

'No, but I thought you'd be able to pretend to be a decent guy looking for love. At least for my sake.' She blew out a breath. 'What did you say to her?'

'I didn't get a chance to say anything.' He took a sip of his champagne – at least some of it would go down his throat – and tried to settle himself. Molly was fire; he was ice. It was part of why they'd been so explosive together. And part of why he'd had to hit the pause button on them. It didn't mean he'd not been sucker punched at seeing her.

Just meant he was better at hiding it.

'Ben.' His sister's sharp command brought him out of his head. 'Please explain why one of my contestants – my most smiley, happy contestant – threw her drink over you and then fled to the ladies.'

'Molly and I used to date.' Rachel's jaw dropped, and as she muttered something that sounded a lot like *holy fuck*, a burst of hope shot through him. 'Is that going to be a problem?'

'Of course not. Not a problem, definitely not a problem.' She sounded like she was trying to convince herself. 'Why didn't I know about her?'

'Because we didn't see each other for very long.'

Her eyes narrowed. 'There's something you're not telling me. Was it a one-night stand?'

'No.' He swallowed, avoiding her eyes. 'It happened three years ago.'

Her forehead scrunched as she mentally worked back. Then her expression softened. 'How long after Helena?'

His throat locked up. 'Not long enough.'

She winced. 'Let me guess. You broke Molly's heart.'

He didn't think he had. Hurt her a little, yes, and he'd hated himself for it. But eight weeks shouldn't have been long enough to cause any permanent damage.

It also shouldn't have been long enough for him to still remember how easily she'd slotted into his side as they'd sat together on the sofa, her watching something awful on TV, him reading his book. Or for him to still have dreams featuring pretty redheads with flashing green eyes, a wide dimpled smile. And the most perfect rear he'd ever had the good fortune to smooth his hands over.

'There must have been some pretty powerful chemistry between the pair of you for her to be so upset after all these years,' Rachel murmured. 'And for you to be looking so shaken.'

As his reaction to Molly wasn't something he wanted his sister to witness, never mind the bloody cameras, he slipped on the mask he was usually good at keeping in place. 'I'm surprised she's here, that's all.'

'Sure. The pale face, the way your eyes keep darting towards the door she left through. It's just plain old surprise.'

His body went into full alert as Molly walked back into the room, green silk dress sliding over all those glorious curves.

'Oh boy.'

He turned to find his sister sporting a rather satisfied smirk. 'What?'

She looked again at Molly, and then back at him. 'Just thinking what dynamite TV this is going to make.'

Discomfort settled heavily in his belly. Bad enough being filmed dating a bland woman he knew he'd never be interested in, but being filmed with Molly? The idea of cameras seeing something he didn't want them to see? Involuntarily his jaw clenched. He'd keep out of her way, make sure there was minimal interaction between them.

At least that way he'd avoid further drenching.

Ben slipped into the corner as Rachel signalled to the camera crew. A moment later they followed the women out of the room, apparently to film them getting seated and blindfolded ready for their matches. The discomfort resurfaced, making his stomach turn over. Whoever his sister had convinced herself was a good match for him, was going to be heavily disappointed. He wasn't sure he was a good match for anyone, and certainly not for a woman who'd willingly applied to be on a reality dating show.

His mind swung to Molly. What had Rachel said about his match when she'd been trying to persuade him onto the show? *Gorgeous*, Molly was certainly that. *This was her favourite show.* It wasn't a stretch to imagine it. *Here to find her soulmate.*

He baulked. He could just imagine how thrilled Molly would be if she found him sitting opposite her when she took off her blindfold.

'Looks like the redhead doesn't think much of you.'

He turned to find the stocky guy with the fake tan and a suit a size too small for his bulging muscles – Duncan, he recalled – giving him a dirty look.

'I'm clearly not her type.'

The man nodded, as if that was a perfectly reasonable explanation for why he'd had a drink thrown at him.

'Hope she isn't going to do that to all of us she doesn't like the look of.' Marcus, a tall, handsome guy with deep brown skin and striking dark eyes, grinned over at him.

'I'm not worried.' James, Ben remembered. Looked like a rock star with his long straggly hair, pale white skin that hadn't seen much daylight, and a rangy body squeezed into too-tight leather trousers. 'I'm every girl's type.'

Duncan snorted. 'Hot girl like that? She's after a guy who takes good care of himself.'

By pumping iron in the gym? Ben kept the thought to himself. The best way through the next four weeks was to keep a low profile, lurk in the shadows.

Avoid anybody liable to throw a drink, or a punch.

'Gentlemen.'

He didn't know whether to be relieved or terrified when Rachel interrupted their little bonding session to announce it was time to meet their matches.

Which meant it was also time for him to be blindfolded, he remembered belatedly as Lauren, one of the assistants, approached him holding a strip of black cloth. Seriously, how much worse could this get?

'This is ridiculous,' he muttered, to which she just laughed. They'd met when he'd had to have his backstory filmed. And hadn't that been a joy, telling the camera exactly what he was looking for in his perfect woman when he wasn't even looking for a woman, never mind a perfect one.

'You're a cynic, we get it.' She put her hands on her hips and gave him a bright smile. 'But put that aside for the next four weeks and think about the opportunity being here has given you. In a few minutes you're going to meet the person a computer algorithm and dating experts have determined you've a high chance of falling in love with. Maybe even getting married to.' Lauren clasped her hands together. 'That's soooo exciting, isn't it?'

The woman positively oozed sparkle and joy. He didn't like to tell her marriage wasn't ever going to be a *maybe* for him; it was a *hard no*. 'You're clearly in the right job,' he murmured non-committedly.

'Oh I know; I love working on this show. And tonight is my favourite part, when you all get to see your match for the first time.' His vision was suddenly obscured as he felt the blindfold cover his eyes. But then she huffed out a breath as it slipped. 'Umm, can you duck down a bit? How tall are you, anyway?'

'Six three.'

'Tall, dark and handsome, huh?' She secured it tightly in place. 'Someone's about to get lucky.' The lucky women were the ones he wasn't matched to, he thought grimly, but forced a smile. 'Well then, are you ready to meet her?'

No. He wasn't ready for any of it. Hadn't been ready the last time he'd dated, three years ago and felt no readier now.

Especially not under the watchful eye of TV cameras and the scrutiny of a viewing audience ready to lambast him for every faux pas he made. And he'd make a tonne of them, he knew that from bitter experience.

An arm slid round his waist, the touch familiar. 'I know you're cursing me right now, but this might not be as awful as you think.' Rachel gave his side a quick squeeze. 'You might even meet your future wife today.'

'Not a cat in hell's chance,' he muttered.

'You do know your feelings about marriage come from a hard, cynical part of you that needs to be excised or you'll never be happy,' she hissed back.

'I'm not against love,' he felt compelled to point out. Again. 'Just the outdated practice of making it part of a legal pact.'

He heard a deep sigh. 'Fine. I get the message. You won't meet your wife today. Just, maybe, the love of your life.'

He shook his head, half irritated, half impressed. 'You don't stop, do you?'

'Why would I, when winding you up is so satisfying.' He heard the smile in her voice. 'And so easy?'

Chapter Six

Molly was sitting at her table in the dining room, blindfold on, heart racing like the clappers. It almost jumped out of her chest when she heard the scrape of the chair opposite. Following a rustle of clothing, she inhaled a wave of sophisticated, fresh-smelling aftershave that was vaguely familiar. Her stomach dropped as she realised it wasn't one Duncan used.

Maybe it was all part of his new TV image.

'Hi.' Her voice was a squeak and she cringed. Duncan probably thought he'd been matched with a mouse.

'Hi.'

What? She froze at the deep, gravelly sound. No, it couldn't be. Neither life or her favourite TV show would be that cruel. One thing for certain though. The man sitting opposite her wasn't Duncan.

'Well, fancy meeting you here, whoever you are.' It was a pretty weak joke, yet the silence that met it was surely unfair. At least she'd *tried*. 'Err, there is someone sitting opposite me still? You've not scarpered at the sound of my voice, have you?

I know it's not the sexiest, and when I'm nervous I tend to ramble on a bit, but I'm kind of hoping you're prepared to give us more of a chance. At least make it till the end of the meal.'

'Molly?'

The bottom fell out of her stomach. 'No. It can't be you.'

'I suppose that depends who you mean by *you*.'

Oh God, her mind was spinning so much she felt dizzy. '*You're* my perfect match?'

'Apparently.'

'This *is* Ben, right?' She asked, just to make absolutely sure she wasn't in the middle of some nightmare she could wake up from.

'I think we've established it's me.' The bone-dry reply was the final proof.

'What we've established is that life is really doing a number on me,' she muttered in reply, finally grateful for the blindfold so she couldn't see him smirking at her. 'I suppose you want an apology for the champagne.'

'Why? I deserved it.'

That made her pause. It was hard to justify being angry with someone when they admitted they were wrong, because then she just sounded bitter. A woman so hurt she couldn't let it go. 'I'm glad you realise it.' More silence. She tried to listen for clues. Was he jamming a hand through his hair? She remembered him doing that when he was frustrated, or annoyed.

'I never meant to hurt you.'

The rough edge to his voice sent an unwanted shiver of awareness through her. 'Well tough, you did. But I got over it,' she added quickly.

'I'm sure.'

And now she wished she could see his face. 'Are you humouring me?'

'I thought I was agreeing with you.'

Damn, he was tying her in knots. Or maybe she was the one doing the tying because he'd always unbalanced her. 'The champagne was me letting off steam. Call it three years' worth of pissed off, finally getting a chance to surface.'

'So I'm safe from further drownings?'

'That depends how much you piss me off while we're here.' She fumbled about for her wine glass, very aware her hands were shaking. Thank God he couldn't see it. 'So anyway, what *are* you doing in HEA Towers? I'd have thought a reality TV show was the last place you'd want to be.'

'Would you believe, finding true love?'

'That's a big fat no.' A plate was slid in front of her with a quietly worded 'bon appétit'. 'How are we supposed to eat when we can't even see what it is?'

'Take the blindfold off?'

She spluttered. 'You can't do that. It's cheating.'

There was another long silence, and then she heard a quiet sigh. 'You're even more stunning than I remember.'

Heart galloping, she whipped off her blindfold, only to feel pinned to her seat by a pair of mesmerising eyes. A unique shade of hazel/green/tawny/brown/whole palette of autumn colours that she'd once been utterly addicted to staring into.

But was thankfully immune to now.

Just in case her heart forgot that important detail though, she dropped her gaze to the table. 'You're not supposed to do that.'

'Compliment you?'

'Take your blindfold off.'

'But you have,' he pointed out mildly.

'Only to see if you had.' *He said you were stunning.* How was she supposed to keep hating him when he wrongfooted her like that?

Duncan. She pictured him as he'd walked into the room earlier, and her mind settled. That's who she was here for. The man who'd helped get her over the broken heart and shattered self-confidence Ben had left her with.

Frantically she glanced round the dining room, ignoring the cameras fixed in their direction.

'Who are you looking for?'

'I'm looking at the other men and trying to work out why I've been saddled with you.'

Finally she located Duncan on the other side of the room, sitting opposite … Jasmine. What the blazes did the blonde have that made her more suitable for Duncan than she was? Aside from a killer toned body.

Ben exhaled heavily. 'I realise this isn't ideal—'

'Not ideal?' She stared back at the man she'd spent an unhealthy amount of time oscillating between obsessing over and hating. Damn him for looking even better than he had three years ago. His dark hair cropped shorter, emphasising cheek bones that seemed to have sharpened with age. He was model handsome, something she'd once enjoyed, but now resented. 'Being shown to a table near the toilets isn't ideal. Having to walk a mile home in the pouring rain without a coat isn't ideal. This.' She motioned between the pair of them. 'This is a disaster.'

'I see you haven't lost your sense of proportion.'

Anger bubbled. 'And I see you haven't lost your love of sarcasm.'

Thankfully, whatever else he was about to say was halted as Rachel approached them, camera crew following behind.

'I knew some couples would cheat and take off their blindfolds,' she told them. 'But I didn't figure on it happening this soon.'

'Ben started it,' Molly blurted.

He let out a soft laugh. 'Very mature.'

Okay, maybe that wasn't one of her finer moments, but she'd always been quick to temper and he knew all the buttons to press. 'Rachel, I'm sorry but there has to be a mistake. There's no way Ben and I should be matched together.' Again her eyes found Duncan. Both he and Jasmine still had their blindfolds on, no surprise there. Duncan loved this show. He wouldn't do anything to break the rules. Jasmine was laughing and … her stomach shrivelled as she watched the blonde reach across the table to find Duncan's arm. Then slowly slide her hand up and squeeze his bicep.

'There's no mistake, Molly.' Rachel looked at her in concern. 'I know you had a rather strong reaction to seeing Ben and I'm sure the viewers would love to hear your reasons behind that. I look forward to chatting it through with you both after the meal.'

Ben exhaled heavily. 'Do we have to?'

Rachel gave him the sort of look a school head gave an unruly pupil. 'Yes, Ben, you do. Having heart-to-camera time with members of the production team is a vital part of the show. And something you signed up to when you agreed to come on.'

Molly sniggered. 'That told you.'

Ben simply stared at her, and shook his head.

She wished he wasn't so damn good-looking. Or so tall, she thought later as they were led to the interview room after a stilted meal where neither of them had said anything beyond pass me the xyz, please.

Duncan was a nice height. Taller than her, but not so tall that she didn't feel he was always looking down on her.

Ben was going to murder his sister. Yes, fine, she had gone through the contract with him; yes, he knew it was dating in front of cameras, but he'd figured he could sneak through it largely under the radar. There would be no chemistry between him and his match, no feelings involved. Just a bland few weeks of average dates, pretty much like the two his mates had tried to set him up with when he hadn't paid attention enough to say no.

But there was nothing bland or average about Molly.

And talking to the film crew about her, about them, was going to bring back a whole raft of feelings he wasn't ready to discuss in private. Never mind in front of a camera.

Rachel opened the door to a small lounge. Comfy-looking red velvet sofas, dark wood panels on the wall, a wood burning stove in the fire place, it reeked of cosy, intimate. Of lulling interviewees into a relaxed state of mind so they spewed their innermost thoughts.

His sister pointed to the largest sofa. 'You're the first pair to be interviewed as you were the first to take your blindfolds off. If you'd both like to sit down, I'll go and find Natalie and the camera crew.'

'Bloody great,' he muttered, slumping onto the sofa.

Plonking herself down as far away from him as she could get, Molly smirked. 'Not exactly your strong point this, is it?'

Even when she was looking at him with disdain, he found her way too attractive for comfort. Her hair was still glossy red, her skin had just the right amount of freckles. 'What do you mean?'

'Talking about yourself, especially about your, you know, "feelings".' She mimed air quotes. 'I, on the other hand, don't mind this bit. It's healthy to talk things through, to get grievances out in the open.'

'Grievances?'

'Yes, you know, those nasty feelings of resentment when you think you've been treated badly.'

He flinched. He'd hurt her, he understood that now, but to imply his actions had been deliberate was grossly unfair. He didn't have a chance to defend himself though, because Rachel was back, camera crew and the sequin-festooned Natalie in tow. He watched bleakly as they set up in front of them. Wide prying lens, terrifying-looking microphone. Whatever debts he might have owed his sister, their slate wouldn't just be wiped clean, it would be scrubbed and bleached after the next four weeks.

'So, Molly, honey,' Natalie began. 'I'm sure everyone is wondering why you threw your drink over poor Ben earlier.'

Molly made a sound of disgust, presumably at the show of sympathy towards him. 'Let's just say he had it owing to him. We used to date, three years ago, until he decided he'd had enough. The drink throwing was something twenty-six-year-old Molly would have loved to have done, if she'd had the chance.'

Ben had to make a conscious effort to unclench his fists. *Had enough?* Like he'd been playing with her feelings?

'And what about twenty-nine-year-old Molly?' Natalie smiled encouragingly at her. 'How does she feel being paired with her ex?'

'Like she's been cheated of the chance to find real love.' He wondered if she realised her voice caught on those last two words. 'I'm open, smiley, friendly.' She gave him a cutting glance. 'He's none of those things. No way are we a match, as our last experience together proved.'

Suddenly Ben felt the full intrusive glare of a camera on him. 'And how do you feel, Ben? Are you happy being matched with Molly?'

'Yes.'

Beside him, he was aware of Molly giving a jolt of in surprise.

'Then why on earth did you ditch her?' Natalie prompted.

His gaze flicked over Natalie's shoulder to where Rachel was standing, watching, and all those years when he'd wanted to pull her hair as a boy came flooding back to him. 'I had my reasons,' he answered tightly.

'Will you share them?'

Again he glanced at Rachel, who at least had the grace to look uncomfortable. She knew damn well he wouldn't want to talk about that time in his life. 'No.'

Beside him, Molly started to laugh, but it lacked any of the warmth he remembered. 'Why am I not surprised? Good luck getting him to tell you anything. He doesn't communicate.'

Again, he felt her words slice through him. He found it hard to articulate his feelings but that didn't mean he didn't have any. Yet along with the hurt was a heavy dose of guilt. And the oppressive weight of failure. If he'd been better at communicating, things with Helena could have turned out differently.

'Well, there certainly seems to be a lot of unresolved tension between the pair of you, so I've got a question for you both. One that's very important for the sake of the show.' Natalie's gaze swivelled from Molly to him. 'Are you prepared to give your relationship another chance?'

'Yes.' He *knew* Molly. If he could get her to forget the fact she hated him, perhaps they could enjoy each other again, like they had before. Until he'd called things off, wracked with fear, with guilt. With the overwhelming knowledge that he wasn't ready to give her what she needed.

At the very least, being paired with Molly on the show would make this whole nightmare slightly less painful. He didn't need to pretend with her. She'd already seen him at his worst.

'If I say no, does that mean I'm out of the show?'

Molly's question made him smile grimly. 'I'm the better of the two evils?'

She ignored him. 'Couldn't you swop us round instead? Give us new partners?'

Natalie looked over at Rachel, who gave a single shake of her head. Ben recognised the look on his sister's face. It was the same one she'd had when they were kids and she'd realised she'd found a way to beat him at Monopoly.

'I'm getting a firm no for that request, honey.' Natalie chuckled. 'And to be honest, I don't think our viewers would ever forgive us if we deprived them of the opportunity of more fireworks between the pair of you.'

Molly let out a dissatisfied huff. 'Then I guess I'll have to stick with Ben for two weeks.'

'That's excellent news.' Natalie beamed and behind her, Rachel signalled the end of the interview – sorry, heart-to-camera time.

Dismissed, he followed Molly out, but not before giving his sister a hard glare.

'I thought this was for a month,' he murmured.

Molly whirled round to face him. 'Do you know *anything* about the show you signed up for?'

'I know you and I will be seeing more of each other while we're here.' And despite her anger towards him, he realised he was looking forward to it. He'd meant what he'd said earlier, when she'd drowned him in champagne. Going out with her had never been dull.

'I can't avoid our dates, but I can avoid seeing you in between them.' She flicked her hair over her shoulder. 'And in two weeks I can swop partners.'

'Stick or ditch,' he murmured, reciting the awful catch phrase.

She glared at him. 'So you *are* aware of the rules.'

He was stuck in a place he felt uncomfortable, with a bunch of people he felt uncomfortable with. And the one person who could turn this hell hole into something at least bordering on pleasant, hated him. 'I'm aware that we're going to have to spend time together. Either we do that as enemies, or we find some way to be civil to each other.' He frowned, eyes searching hers for some of the warmth he'd once received. 'I remember a time we used to enjoy each other's company.'

She blinked and looked away. 'I remember that time, too.' Her face turned back towards his. 'But while I was thinking we were going to have this grand love affair, you were deciding you didn't want my company anymore.'

'That's not true.' Frustrated with how she was making it sound, he shoved his hands in his pockets. 'It wasn't a question of not wanting to be with you. More that I *couldn't* be with you. Not feeling as I did at the time.'

'It's fine. I'm not everyone's taste, I get that. It's just I expected to have a sense that you thought we weren't clicking, though that was probably stupid of me.' He watched as she swallowed, and remembered how soft her neck was. How she loved to be kissed there. How she giggled when he trailed his kisses higher, to behind her ear. 'You blindsided me, Ben, and I thought I was done being blindsided. I won't let it happen again.'

He nodded, aware nothing he could say would help improve her opinion of him. He'd had his chance, and he'd stepped away from it, too scared, too emotionally rung out to risk it. His punishment was being stuck on a TV set with a bunch of strangers and a camera crew, the only people he *wanted* to talk to either hating him, or content to see him suffer because it made good television.

Damn it, one mistake didn't make him a bad person though, he reminded himself as he trudged away in the opposite direction to Molly. Maybe the next few weeks would give him a chance to prove that to her.

If he hadn't been thrown out before that, for strangling the associate producer.

Chapter Seven

Sitting in the vast kitchen the following morning, Molly laughed as James began to juggle the eggs.

'See, told you I was an eggspert.'

Both she and Chloe, who he'd been matched with, groaned at his joke, but Marcus laughed. She'd discovered from last night's drinking games that he did that a lot. His match, Maya, was much more serious, yet Molly had a feeling if anyone could get her to lighten up, Marcus could.

Her first night in the house had been fun, though she suspected that had something to do with the relief she'd felt when Ben had excused himself. He'd been the only one not to take part in the charades evening.

'Is your partner going to join us for breakfast?' Chloe asked. 'Or is he going to spend the entire day locked away in his room?'

'How would I know? I've not seen him since dinner last night. And please don't call him my partner,' she added. 'He's just the man I've been mistakenly put with.'

'Poor sod is probably scared you're going to pour cereal

over him,' James supplied, then swore as one of the eggs splatted onto the ground.

'Guess you'll be having scrambled eggs.' The smile slid off Molly's face as Duncan entered the kitchen, his arm around Jasmine. The sight was like a kick to the stomach. His gaze found hers and he gave an apologetic shake of his head which did nothing to quell the sick feeling.

As he went to open the fridge, she wandered over to join him.

'I got matched with Ben,' she hissed. 'Can you flaming believe it?'

'I know, babe. It's a crap deal.'

'I really thought I'd get matched with you,' she mumbled, pretending to search through the yoghurts. 'Now I'm well and truly skewered. You look like you're enjoying yourself though,' she added, trying to keep the jealousy out of her voice.

'It's only for show, babe,' he whispered as he poured out two glasses of smoothie. 'We talked about that.'

She watched miserably as he handed the second glass, with great flourish, to the giggling Jasmine. 'There's a difference between not coming across as a dick, and being all over someone,' she muttered to herself.

Just then prickles raced down her spine, and when she turned to see what had caused them, her gaze collided with a pair of hazel eyes.

'Ah, so you're still here, mate.' James went over to slap Ben on the back. 'We all thought Molly had scared you off when you didn't appear last night.'

Again Ben's gaze found hers. 'Why would I be scared?'

'She's your ex, yeah?' When Ben nodded, James grinned. 'Well, let's just say I wouldn't want to go anywhere near any of my exes.'

Thank You, Next

'Maybe I'm looking forward to it.' Dressed down in faded jeans and a green T-shirt that fit just well enough to hint at the muscles of his chest, Ben sauntered into the kitchen with the quiet confidence she remembered him for. Not cocky, because that was for people who pretended to be confident when they weren't. Ben was so self-assured he didn't need to put on an act.

It was something she'd always found really sexy about him. *Found*, note. In the past tense.

His hand touched the top of her arm in greeting, light and very brief. Her body answered with an unnerving flutter deep in her belly. 'Sleep okay?'

'Err, yes.' She didn't want him being polite, or considerate. She wanted him cool and aloof so she could stay indifferent to him for the next month.

'So who dumped who?' James's gaze jumped between the pair of them.

'That's our business,' Ben replied tightly.

'He dumped me.' When Ben gave her a steely look, she shot him one back. 'Come on, we're all friends here. I don't mind these guys knowing. It's not like it bothers me anymore.'

Ben raised a dark brow. 'I have a suit in dry cleaning that suggests otherwise.'

'That was long overdue.' Avoiding his eyes, she glanced round at the group. 'I mean, this is the guy who gave every impression he was into me, but when he found out I'd booked tickets for a concert three months down the line, suddenly decided he wasn't ready for a relationship.'

She watched the muscle in Ben's jaw jump. He hated this, she knew. The intrusion into what he considered to be private territory, being forced to discuss their break up with people he didn't know. But she was angry, too. Angry at fate, putting her with him and not Duncan.

Angry at Ben for once letting her believe he was into her, then abruptly deciding he wasn't.

Angry at herself, for still being affected by him.

'If we're going to talk about this, at least let's get the facts straight,' Ben interrupted quietly. 'I didn't *dump* Molly.' His gaze raked over her face before resting on hers. 'The only part of us that wasn't right was the timing.'

Her heart bounced as those hazel eyes seared hers. She could see he was trying to make things less awkward, but she was a big girl, she could take the truth. She *wanted* the truth. She'd had enough of being lied to, even if it was well meaning.

Your mum will be back. She probably just wants a break.

The childhood memories still haunted her. Teachers and social workers trying to be kind, to reassure her she hadn't been abandoned. Yet her mother had never come back. She'd not wanted her anymore. Just like Ben hadn't. So just say that. If there was one thing worse than hope, it was false hope.

Involuntarily her gaze flew to Duncan. He caught her eye and gave her a small smile. Is that what he was doing to her now, giving her false hope? Saying he loved her, that he was only on the show to increase his followers, when really he saw it as a chance to break up with her?

Ben watched the shadows cross Molly's gorgeous face. What was she thinking? Was this still about him, *them*, or was something else making her upset? When they'd dated, he'd sometimes caught an expression that had made him want to ask what was wrong, but he was worse than useless at finding the right words.

'Well, it looks like you're going to get a second chance at screwing things up with Molly.'

Ben turned to see the personal trainer staring at him with an expression Ben couldn't identify. How did he know Duncan was a personal trainer? Because the guy hadn't stopped banging on about it yesterday when they'd been waiting for everyone to arrive. That and how he'd been chosen to go on the show – take note, he was the special one – because apparently he could turn bodies, and thus lives, around through his wildly successful exercise videos.

Ben had briefly considered thumping him. At the very least strapping some strong parcel tape over his mouth.

'Or maybe I just get a second chance,' he countered, wondering what the guy's problem was.

Molly let out a choked sound. 'Why would you want that? So you can decide it's the wrong time again, later down the line?'

He flinched. Couldn't she see how much he regretted letting her go? Or how excruciating this was, having their past played out in public. And with a camera crew in the corner of the kitchen recording every word. 'Maybe now is the *right* time.'

Surprise flickered in green eyes that had lost none of their allure. But then she blinked and looked away. 'There will never be a right time for you and me.'

An awkward silence followed her statement and when Ben looked over towards the huge table in the middle of the kitchen, he noticed everyone had stopped eating to stare at them. Like spectators to a boxing match, he thought irritably.

'But you guys have four weeks in Happy Ever After

Towers.' The blonde, he thought her name was Jasmine, thankfully broke the deathly quiet. 'Who knows what might happen? I mean, that's what we're here for, right? To find true love. The person we want to marry. And we're never gonna do that if we're not open to the idea of it.'

'Even with your ex,' Marcus supplied with another of those wide grins it was impossible not to warm to. 'I know I'm very open to getting to know *this* beautiful lady over the next four weeks,' he added smoothly as he caught sight of Maya entering the kitchen. The way she rolled her eyes suggested Marcus would need to work on his charm offensive. Dial down the cheese, up the sincerity.

They were saved any further painful relationship dissections by the entrance of Natalie, who was thankfully sequin-less today. Lauren followed quietly behind her.

'Good morning, ladies and gentlemen.' Natalie's voice boomed across the kitchen. 'Did you sleep well?'

Ben groaned inwardly as everyone yelled out their replies. It was like being at a 60s holiday camp.

'I bet you're all wondering what we've lined up for you lucky folk today. Well, this morning we're going to film you watching your partner's background stories.' Shit, he'd forgotten about that. Ben looked sideways at Molly and felt a twinge of discomfort. 'Then this afternoon we're going to take you on a trip.'

'Oooh, do we get to know where?' Jasmine clasped her hands together in a show of excitement more usually seen at awards ceremonies. Or winning lottery announcements.

'You do, honey. We're off to the Birmingham aquarium.'

'Oh.' Jasmine's face fell.

Duncan laughed and threw an arm around his date. 'That wasn't what you were expecting, was it, babe?'

Thank You, Next

Molly inhaled sharply. Puzzled, Ben shifted to look at her, and found her staring at Duncan and Jasmine with a tight expression.

Did she fancy the guy? Was she *jealous*? 'Seriously?' He muttered under his breath, but of course she heard.

Instead of answering him though, she shot him a look that said, 'Mind your own business.' Or 'Piss off.' Or possibly both.

'As you know, this show is split into two halves,' Natalie continued. 'In the first two weeks the focus is on whether you want to date the person you're with. In the second two weeks the focus is on whether you want to marry them.'

At least that was one area he and Molly would be in agreement, he thought sourly. They wouldn't want to marry each other.

'With that in mind, going round the aquarium is a fabulous opportunity to get to know the person you've been matched with.' Natalie grinned enthusiastically. 'So we ask you to stay in your pairs on the coach and when you're going round.'

'Think that means you're stuck with me,' he murmured.

Molly huffed. 'Maybe I'll feed you to the sharks.'

'Or maybe you'll remember the reasons you once went out with me.'

For a moment her expression softened, but then she stuck out her chin. 'Remembering them isn't the problem. The problem is reminding my heart not to trust you.'

Frustration burned through him, yet it was hard to defend himself when he knew he deserved her animosity. He *had* behaved badly all those years ago, so consumed by her in those first few weeks that he'd let common sense desert him. It had taken finding she'd bought those damn tickets to yank him back into his hard, cold reality. He'd failed the last woman he'd become seriously involved with. Failed in the most tragic way. He had no business continuing his relationship with Molly. She'd deserved far better than him.

Yet now fate had intervened and they were thrown together again, the attraction too sharp to ignore. Could he learn from his mistakes? Did he dare try again?

'Ben and Molly?' Lauren's voice splintered his thoughts and he looked up to find Lauren smiling brightly at them. Did she ever dial down the wattage? 'Do you want to come with me to watch your video clips?'

'If I say no?'

Lauren's smile finally faltered, but then she wagged her finger at him. 'Rachel has warned me about you.'

What had his sister been saying? 'Oh?'

'Yep,' Lauren said cheerily. 'She warned me you were at bit grumpy when it came to being interviewed, but to ignore you.'

Molly let out a strangled laugh. 'See what I have to put up with? And yet somehow the matchmakers put *us* together.'

'Maybe they know something you don't,' he argued.

'Umm, or maybe you didn't show them your true personality when they interviewed you.'

As he'd not actually been interviewed, he kept quiet. Besides, nobody knew him better than Rachel.

Lauren pushed open the door of the small lounge where they'd had their interrogation/heart-to-camera chat – depending on your point of view – yesterday, and signalled for them to sit on the sofa.

A moment later, Natalie breezed in.

'Hello, you two. As promised, we're going to play back both of your pre-show interviews and film you watching them to see your reactions.' She beamed over at him. 'I think we'll do gentleman first this time.'

A moment later he watched his face fill up the TV monitor. Automatically his body sunk further into the sofa.

'So Ben, describe your perfect woman to me,' his sister asked him on screen.

Christ, did he really have to watch this? 'I don't want perfect,' he heard himself tell her. 'I'm a long way from perfect myself.'

'Wise words,' Molly mumbled beside him.

'What would you like her to look like, then?' prompted the on-screen Rachel.

Ben squirmed and tried to bury himself deeper into the sofa. He vividly remembered his answer, which had seemed okay at the time but now, with Molly sitting next to him...

'Red hair,' his image replied. 'Green flashing eyes.'

Molly sucked in a breath.

Rachel nodded. 'And her personality?'

'Happy, I guess. Upbeat.'

As he cringed inside, the recording was stopped and Natalie gave him a satisfied smile. 'Seems you got your wish with the lovely Molly, huh? Shall we see what she was looking for in a partner?'

'Oh boy,' he heard Molly mutter.

The recording was fast forwarded to an image of Molly, sitting in what was probably her living room from the look of all the personal touches; the giant potted palm that needed water, the bookcase stuffed full of haphazardly arranged books. His heart twisted as he saw the large multi-coloured hippo print on the wall behind her. The one he remembered buying with her.

'Looks-wise, I like someone who's really fit,' on-screen Molly replied. 'You know, a hot body, all those rippling muscles.' She giggled, pretending to fan her face. 'And if you add blond hair and blue eyes, I probably won't be able to resist him.'

Ben was reasonably confident in his ability to attract women – he'd been called handsome many times, and he regularly went to the gym to keep himself in good shape. But his confidence shrivelled a little at Molly's description.

No wonder she kept looking at the personal trainer. Clearly her tastes had changed over the last three years. He wasn't just stuck with a date who hated him, but with one who fancied someone else.

The next few weeks were going to be awkward as fuck.

Chapter Eight

Sitting on the coach on their way to the aquarium, Molly gave the man next to her another side glance. She might as well have stared though, because Ben's eyes were firmly fixed on the notepad he'd brought along, which he'd write in every now and then. Phones weren't allowed, but it seems Ben had found another way not to engage with her.

As her gaze skimmed over him, a flutter in her lower belly told her what she didn't want to admit. She might now prefer blond hair and blue eyes, but broodingly handsome still worked for her, too. And it pissed her off that he could happily ignore her when she found it impossible to ignore him.

'Did you know the Birmingham aquarium has a tunnel that goes all the way round so we get to see the fish swimming above our head and below our feet? And when I say fish, I also mean sharks because they've got some of them, too, which is so cool.' He turned to look at her, giving her a narrow-eyed look from those hypnotic hazel eyes. Now she had his attention though, she wasn't sure what to do with it. 'Sharks are fish though, aren't they?' She babbled on. 'Some people think they're mammals but I'm pretty sure I heard they were fish because they breathe through gills. I wonder if we'll see some otters, too? I know they definitely aren't fish, but a lot of aquariums have otters. Ooooh, and penguins. How could I forget about them? They're my favourite, they're so funny. I really hope we get to see some penguins as well.'

He gave a small shake of his head and focussed again on his notepad. She noticed a little furrow between his eyes as he frowned and crossed out the last thing he'd written.

Annoyed at his lack of response, she nudged him with her elbow. 'What do you want to see?'

He gave her a wry glance. 'The exit?'

'Well, I can see this is going to be a really fun afternoon.' She looked around the luxury coach, listening to the babble of conversation. The lilt of laughter. Automatically her eyes found Duncan and she felt a jolt of pain as she saw him and Jasmine talking quietly to each other, his attention totally focussed on her. 'If you're going to be this uninterested on every date, why did you sign up to this show in the first place?'

He let out a deep exhale, closed the notebook and slotted it into the inside pocket of his jacket. 'I didn't.'

'Okay, that's far more believable than thinking you actively signed up to be on a TV dating show. But there's no way I buy into the producers seeking you out because how on earth would that meeting go?' She put on a different accent. 'You know what would be a real asset on our show? A guy with no social media profile who doesn't like talking to anyone, never mind cameras. Oh and who'd be totally uninterested in whoever we partnered him with.'

That little frown appeared again. 'Who said I'm uninterested?'

She waved her hand towards his jacket pocket. 'Err, you've

Thank You, Next

spent the last half an hour giving that notebook way more attention than you have me.'

'Sorry. I wasn't aware you wanted my attention.'

'I don't. Well, not in a *I want to date you again* way.' She blew out a breath, taking another moment to listen to the sounds of lively chatter. To watch Duncan give Jasmine his trademark cocky grin. 'But you were right, we're stuck together for the time being so it makes sense to try and get on.' If only to give Duncan something to think about.

Those eyes rested on hers, swirls of greens and browns that still caused her heart to jump. 'We didn't used to have to try.'

Memories of them together flooded her mind; her laughing at him trying to prove he could do whatever yoga pose she'd been trying. Him calmly staring back at her with a quiet intensity that always made her giddy. The way he'd always noticed things about her, what she wore, when she'd had her hair done.

Unable to hold his gaze, she glanced out of the window, waiting a few beats for the images to leave.

'Rays.'

Puzzled, she turned to find him sporting a crooked smile, a mix of amusement and irony that made one of his dimples pop. And her heart miss a beat. 'Sorry?'

'I'm looking forward to seeing the rays.' He gave a little shrug of his shoulders. 'Always had a soft spot for them.'

Okay, she could do this. Push all their history aside and talk to him as if they were strangers who'd been forced together on a dating show. 'Me too. It's their smile. You know, when they float over your head in the tunnel and you see them from underneath, they have this curvy mouth and eyes thing going on, and it looks like they're grinning at you. It's so cute.'

'Their eyes are on top of their head,' he pointed out. 'You're looking at their gills.'

'Well, yes, I know that.' She was sure she had. 'But it still looks like they're smiling. And it's still cute,' she added for good measure.

'It's the way they move.' He gave her a mild look. '*That's* what I like about them. They're graceful.'

'So not because they look cute and smiley then.' She smirked. 'I should have guessed that. In fact, I'm surprised you're not a fan of the sharks. They're aloof, kind of cold-looking. And that evil grin is right up your street.'

'Is that really how you remember me?' An expression crossed his face that she'd not expected. Hurt.

'Not all the time, no.' He'd not been aloof when they'd met. Sad, yes, she remembered that, but he'd made it quite clear he liked her. That he enjoyed spending time with her. And she'd thrived under his obvious interest, floating along from day to day on a cloud of blissful infatuation, rolling right along into love. Until the day she'd overstepped and planned too far ahead.

'When then? That last time we met? Because I told you, my head wasn't—'

'In the right place. It wasn't me; it was you.' She shook her head. 'Please let's not rehash all those clichés again. This is Molly and Ben take two. We've never met before and against the odds we've been matched together on a dating show. Which reminds me, you didn't really answer my question earlier. What *are* you doing on the show if you didn't apply?'

'My sister asked me to come on.' He paused, and for once looked uncomfortable. 'She works on the show.'

Molly gaped at him. 'You have a sister who works on *The One*? Why didn't I know that?'

He glanced away. 'I don't remember us talking too much about our families.'

No, she thought. Their time together had been too intense to involve others. At least that's how it had felt from her side, happy to exist in their love bubble, cushioned from everything else happening around them. Until the bubble had burst. 'Which one is she?'

'Rachel.'

'Assistant producer Rachel? The one who smiles sweetly at you and before you know it you're agreeing to everything she says.'

His lips twitched. 'That's her.'

'Wow, if she got you on here, she really is good.'

'Apparently so.' He let out a sigh. 'She was in a bind, the guy who was meant to be matched with you, pulled out.'

Molly clicked her fingers together, the pieces of the puzzle finally slotting together. 'I knew it.'

He glanced at her warily. 'Knew what?'

'That there was no way any dating algorithm or professional matchmakers would have put you and me together.'

Ben watched as something that looked a lot like relief crossed Molly's face. She was happy they hadn't been matched.

She really didn't want to be with him.

And the way her eyes kept darting to where the personal trainer was sitting three rows ahead of them, it was brutally clear who she thought her match should have been.

'Actually, I filled in the questionnaire.' When she gave him a disbelieving look, he felt compelled to add. 'Felix and

Stephanie, the relationship experts, thought we would make a good pairing. Better even than your original match. *That's* why they wanted me on the show. Not just because I'm a single male.'

Her eyes went wide. 'Did you know I was the person they were matching you with?'

'No. I wasn't given a name or a photo. I was as surprised as you to find myself sitting opposite you.' He recalled the horror in her voice when she'd realised it was him. 'But not nearly as upset.'

'Oh, come on, part of you must have been looking forward to meeting a potential love interest.'

Maybe I have. The words were on the tip of his tongue but he swallowed them. She wasn't interested, and he wasn't sure he could, or even should, go down that route again. 'Honestly, I was dreading having to spend time with a stranger, be on my best behaviour. With you, I don't have to pretend.'

She screwed up her face, her nose wrinkling in a way that made his heart trip. 'I'm not sure whether to be insulted or not.'

'I meant it as a compliment. When you're not shooting daggers at me, I enjoy your company.'

She sniffed. 'Fine.'

There was a long pause, the silence speaking volumes. *She doesn't enjoy yours*. She used to though, he thought grimly. Maybe he could persuade her to enjoy it again. 'So you know why I'm on the show. Why are you?'

'To marry my soulmate.' Her gaze once again drifted over to Duncan before darting away again. Coincidence? Or did she really think the arrogant git with the muscles could be her perfect match? 'Plus I love this show, it's my favourite. Watching couples dating, falling for each other, working out whether they want to get married ... it's addictive. You should tell your sister that. I told her when she interviewed me but she probably thought I was saying it to get in her good books. Truth is though, me and...' She hesitated. 'Me and my ex used to watch it together all the time.'

'Your ex?' He felt an unexpected twist of his gut. Of course she'd dated after him. It had been three years.

'Yeah. We split up a couple of months ago.'

'And that's when you decided to apply to go on the show?'

She glanced away from him to stare out of the window. 'Pretty much. Oh look, we're here already. Amazing what a bit of conversation can do to pass the time.'

He followed her off the coach, appreciating her back view. She was dressed more conservatively than he remembered, her clothes looking like they were off the peg rather than the bohemian creations she used to make herself, yet he couldn't help but notice how well she still filled out her jeans.

They walked side by side towards the entrance, Molly making passing comments to the others, a wave here, a quip there. A chat with Natalie, who was waiting with her microphone, ready to sniff out the unguarded remarks. Something Molly was bound to offer as that was her all over, open, spontaneous. She had a way about her that made people want to engage, be folded into her warm, happy aura. It was the reason he'd been drawn to her when they'd first met. He'd been sitting at the bar in a quiet pub, drowning his grief and guilt in alcohol, when someone had bumped into him, causing him to spill some of his drink. Irritated, he'd turned to glare at the person who'd practically landed in his lap ... and the indignation had drained away when the beautiful redhead had smiled at him. He'd barely heard her rambling apology, far too distracted by the wide curve of her mouth, the pink of her cheeks. The way her eyes had radiated warmth.

'Ooooh, look, they're feeding the penguins in ten minutes. Bagsy we do them first.'

His attention snapped back to the Molly in front of him now, green eyes glittering with that same warm enthusiasm. It was unsettling to find he was as drawn to her now as he had been then, only now his grief was dulled and as for his guilt ... maybe he could shove it into a box, lock it up tight and bury it at the back of his mind.

'We wouldn't want to miss that delight,' he murmured. Trying his best to ignore the camera crew, he placed a hand on her lower back and guided her past the others who'd stopped, presumably to work out an organised, systematic way through the aquarium.

'Exactly.' She beamed triumphantly, and his heart thumped against his ribs.

Yes, the attraction was every bit as intense. And every bit as terrifying.

The penguins did as penguins always do. They waddled, swam, swallowed down the fish in an alarming single gulp. Molly was enchanted by them, though. He could tell by her animated expressions, the way she clasped her hands. The mind-boggling torrent of facts that poured from her mouth at an impressive rate.

'Look at them go,' she breathed, watching as two penguins threw themselves into the water. 'They're one of the most streamlined animals in the world. They may look a bit dodgy on land, but when they're swimming their body is kind of tapered at both ends, so they're like a torpedo zipping through the water. I remember reading that the Gentoo penguin is the fastest. I think it goes something like twenty miles an hour which is giving it some considering how small they are.'

He wasn't required to say anything in return. Just to nod occasionally, to make eye contact so she knew he was paying attention. And he was. Maybe not so much to the facts – penguins were daft birds that smelt of fish – but he was charmed by her.

'What's next?' She asked when the penguins had hoovered up all the fish.

He glanced over at the site map, strategically placed along the walkway, a helpful guide, alongside the arrows on the pavements, to ensure the most efficient way around the aquarium.

One they were clearly going to ignore. 'By my reckoning if we head left, we'll find the otters. Then a right will bring us to the tunnel, and the sharks.'

'Excellent.' She started marching, then came to an abrupt halt. 'Wait. They were all the things I said I wanted to do.'

He frowned. 'And the problem is?'

'You were paying attention. I didn't think you were. I mean you looked like you were listening, but I didn't think you actually were.'

'Molly.' He heaved out a breath. 'When did I ever *not* listen to you? Not pay attention?'

'I ... I don't know.' He watched her throat bob as she swallowed. 'I guess I assumed, as you broke off with me, that you'd stopped being interested in me a while before that.'

Regret stung his eyes. That she'd ever thought, for one minute, that he'd grown bored of her. 'I didn't stop.' His voice felt rough, emotions embarrassingly close to the surface. 'How could I, when you're so captivating?'

Her expression went from one of amazement to disbelief in

a matter of moments. 'If I was so captivating, then why…' She turned away from him. 'Forget it. Let's go and see those otters.'

She started walking, but he was aware of her giving him furtive glances. 'Before we do the tunnel,' she said finally, after he began to worry he'd somehow got penguin poo on his face. 'We should divert to the rays.'

Her smile was tentative, almost shy, and it wrapped around his chest and gave it a soft tug. 'Is that the cute, smiley rays?'

She rolled her eyes. 'Okay, okay. You were listening. I get it.' She gave him a side glance. 'You know what's really great about the rays though? They're graceful. Apparently.'

She darted him another smile and something slithered into his chest, opening it. But then she shook her head and when she turned away, whatever it was, slunk straight back out again.

Later, he realised that feeling had been hope. He wanted another shot at a relationship with her. Even if it was under the glare of cameras and an audience. And even if he wasn't convinced he deserved it.

Chapter Nine

Molly was lying on a lounger by the pool, making the most of the warm July weather. HEA Towers was every bit as awesome as it appeared on the TV. It was like living in a high-class hotel, only with strategically set cameras. Beside her, Maya stretched out her long, slender legs, looking not only gorgeous, her rich brown skin a stunning contrast to the red bikini she wore, but elegant, too. Molly was glad she'd kept her shorts on, but seeing her short pale legs next to those of Maya's, she wished she'd worn trousers instead.

'Marcus is trying to impress you,' Molly murmured, watching as the man in question powered through the water.

Maya smiled. 'Maybe. Or maybe he's just swimming.'

Molly burst out laughing. 'I see he's got a way to go yet to win you over.'

Maya's gaze travelled towards the man in the pool. 'I like him. He's good-looking and friendly, but it's early days yet.' She gave Molly a sidelong glance. 'How about you? Must be really odd having to spend time with your ex. How did you get on yesterday?'

'It was okay, actually.' *He called you captivating.* Her heart gave an involuntary flutter at the memory. 'I think we can probably be civil to each other for the next couple of weeks, but I'll definitely be planning to swop partners.'

'Anyone in mind yet?'

Molly couldn't help but glance at the man lounging on the opposite side of the pool, his muscles glistening in the sun, thanks to the generous application of suntan oil by Jasmine. And ouch, it hurt to watch another woman running her hands over him. Hurt even more to see him look up from his prone position on the lounger and give that woman a grin. 'Maybe.'

He'd not once looked over in her direction though.

It was hard not to feel inadequate, being in daily contact with not just one, but apparently now *two* men who'd rejected her.

'Wow, you've got to love the sun, and the way it makes the men take off their shirts.' Chloe dropped down onto the lounger the other side of her, and Molly watched as her gaze skimmed first over Duncan, then over to Marcus, who was hauling himself out of the water, before finally landing on James. 'Though in the case of James, he'd have done better keeping his shirt on.'

Molly winced. 'Wow, that's harsh. And we'd be really cross if they made similar remarks about us.'

Chloe shrugged. 'I say it like it is. James is good-looking, sure, in that lean-hipped kind of way, but Marcus and Duncan are hotter, body-wise.' She scanned the pool area. 'Where's Ben? I notice he didn't join us last night, and he's not here now. You must be really pissed off with him.'

She was more … disappointed, though that was really hard to admit. There was Duncan, getting lathered up by Jasmine, and yet the man who claimed to have never stopped being interested in her, couldn't even be bothered to come out of his room to join her. Never mind rub sun tan lotion all over her pasty white body.

'It's up to him.' She forced her voice to sound casual. 'I'm not fussed what he does. It's not like we'll be heading for marriage and an all-expenses-paid honeymoon in Hawaii.'

Chloe gave her a calculating look. 'What do you think of James? 'Cos I'm thinking we could swop, you know, when we get the chance after two weeks.'

No. The word bounced immediately into her head, unsettling her for a moment until she reassured herself it wasn't the swop she was against, but the swop to James. She wanted Duncan. 'I think it's too early to know yet.'

'Umm, maybe. But for me, Ben has that whole dark, broody vibe which I really dig. James is more of a cocky bastard. Works for some girls, just not sure it's my thing.'

'What do you think of Duncan?' Molly was careful not to look at Chloe in case she gave herself away. 'Ben and I are down to cook with him and Jasmine tonight.'

Chloe gave Duncan a considering look. 'He's a bit too focussed on himself. I mean, look at him now.' Molly took the opportunity to survey her hopefully temporary ex, who'd just jumped up from the lounger and was sauntering towards the other end of the pool, flamingo pink shorts tight against his heavily muscled thighs. 'Sure, he's got a great bod,' Chloe continued, 'but seriously, dude, stop preening. It's a total turn off.'

Well, that was one less woman she had to fight off, Molly reasoned, watching as Duncan put his hands on his hips and flexed his pecs. Maybe that did look a bit show-offy, but then again, he did have a body worth showing off.

As if aware of her eyes on him, Duncan looked over and winked.

'Looks like someone is trying to impress *you*,' Maya whispered.

'Maybe he's just going for a swim,' Molly countered, waiting for the rush of pleasure. It never quite arrived though. Possibly because his wink had felt forced, like he'd known she was watching and felt he had to pacify her.

'Warning, warning. Sex on legs alert.'

At Chloe's announcement, Molly swivelled her head round. And her breath caught in her throat.

Chloe was not wrong. Not wrong at all.

With a towel thrown casually over his shoulder, Ben strolled towards them in the same confident, fluid gait that used to make her heart race. Unconsciously she placed a hand on her chest, concern niggling when she felt the scampering beat. His trunks were an unfussy plain black and he wore them with a simple grey T-shirt, tight enough to emphasise what she knew was a leanly muscled chest. Loose enough to make it clear he wasn't trying to impress. His legs were long and well defined, dusted with dark hair. A pair of green tinted shades completed a look which reeked of understated assurance. The brooding model to Duncan's bodybuilder.

Ben paused, gaze skimming the pool area. When it collided with hers, he changed course and headed towards them.

'He told me he sold his company last month,' Chloe murmured. 'Bet he's loaded. I mean, as if his sex appeal wasn't already off the charts.'

Molly frowned, irritated to realise Chloe knew something about Ben she didn't.

'Ladies.' Ben stopped a few feet away from them and slid the shades onto his head in the way of film stars. And apparently brooding ex-company owners. Though he addressed them all, his gaze was riveted on her, and her alone.

A hot flush rushed through her. 'Finally decided to leave your room?'

His jaw tightened briefly at her barbed comment, but then he smoothed his expression and gave a wry glance at the nearby camera. 'Apparently it doesn't make for good television.'

'Of course not, the viewers will want to see you. Especially the female ones.' Chloe gave him a playful look and patted the lounger next to her. 'Come and join us girls.'

His eyes locked on Molly's, perhaps asking permission, and she shrugged in what she hoped signalled her indifference. Let Chloe flirt with him. Maybe a swop with her would be okay. James might not be Duncan, but at least he wasn't a man she knew would be a mistake.

After throwing his towel onto the lounger, Ben pulled his T-shirt over his head. The single, fluid movement brought the muscled ridges of his pecs and abs directly into her sightline. Ditto the dark trail of hair that disappeared into his shorts, a trail she vividly remembered following with her fingers, her lips…

She jerked her gaze away and deliberately sought out Duncan who was now seated on the edge of the pool, feet in the water, signalling to Jasmine to come and join him.

Ben let out a silent sigh as he threw his T-shirt onto the floor. He was going to have serious words with his sister when this damn month was over. She'd lured him here on the pretext of it being the perfect place for him to take a break.

Then hounded him out of the sanctuary of his room. The one place he could relax.

He certainly couldn't do it here, by the pool, with Molly and her dynamite curves on display just the other side of Chloe. He wouldn't mind if she'd look at him now and again, show some sign that she was as affected by him as he was by her, yet all he'd received so far was a barbed comment.

And now she was staring at the guy flexing his muscles by the pool.

Ben could only hope Duncan's big head would prove too heavy for his body and topple him into the pool. Though probably the git would do a neat somersault first, and arrow in like some pro diver.

And yes, it was painful to admit that some of his judgement of the man was based on pure jealousy.

'What have you been doing holed up in your room all morning?' Chloe gave him a sly smile. 'Or shouldn't I ask?'

He dragged his focus back to the woman who *was* paying him some attention. 'Sleeping. Thinking.'

'Sounds mysterious.' Chloe batted her eyelashes. 'Thinking about what?'

He wasn't in the mood for small talk, but at least Chloe wasn't ignoring him. 'Work. What I'm going to do next.'

'You didn't make enough money with your last company?'

He had. If he was careful, he didn't need to work again. 'It's not about the money.' It never had been. In the beginning it had been for the distraction. A reason to keep going when everything inside him had wanted to close down. Later he'd enjoyed the challenge, the desire to prove he could do it.

'Hey, Ben.' Marcus waved over at him from the other side of the pool. 'Are you up for a game of water polo?'

If it meant getting away from the lure of Molly in her green bikini top and tiny denim shorts, and the pain of Chloe's questions, he thought he'd do pretty much anything. 'Sure.'

As he stood, he was aware of Chloe's eyes looking him up and down.

'Umm, I spy a sexy little tattoo.'

Instinctively he wanted to clasp his hand over the initials he'd had tattooed near his left hip.

'It's the initials of an old girlfriend,' Molly supplied, her eyes darting up to his in a way that made his chest clutch. Did she remember the first time she'd set eyes on it? The way he'd distracted her from too many questions by pulling her back up to straddle him?

Did she remember them making love for hours that night? And then again in the morning, when he'd managed to persuade her to stay in bed with him for most of the day? Did chocolate chip ice cream bring back memories of him licking it off her skin like it did for him?

'Do you have Molly's initials tattooed on you as well then?' Chloe asked unhelpfully.

Molly snorted. 'Of course he doesn't. We didn't even last long enough to plan a birthday.'

'Birthday?' He frowned over at her but she studiously avoided his eyes. It was then that he began to feel a heavy sense of dread. 'The tickets for the concert … you were planning them as a surprise for my birthday?'

'It hardly matters now.' Before he could ask anything further, she waved towards the guys in the pool. 'Looks like they're waiting for you.'

He'd never felt so dismissed. Or so deserving of it. She'd once cared enough to take note of when his birthday was, and plan a surprise for him. How had he responded when he'd come across the tickets by accident? In a knee jerk reaction caused by blind panic, he'd pulled the plug on their relationship.

As shitty as it sounded, he still stood by the decision. Molly had deserved far more than he'd had to give at the time. Yet now fate had offered him a second chance. Was he terrified he'd mess this up, too? Absolutely. But that didn't stop him looking at her, and *wanting* her. Not that it mattered, because the bridges he might have wanted to build looked like they'd already been burnt to the ground.

He darted her a final glance, but she wasn't looking his way. Instead her gaze was fixed on Duncan. The bridges weren't just burnt, he realised. She was set on a whole new direction.

Fuck that. Determinedly he marched towards the pool. No way was he going to stand aside and let her make an even bigger mistake with that arsehole than she would do with him. Ben knew his faults: too blunt, he'd been told; too black and white; cold, apparently, though he disputed that one. He liked to get the measure of someone before he let them in. Once he did though … he shook away his thoughts, unwilling to head down memory lane. Fact was, nobody had ever accused him of being arrogant.

He slipped into the pool next to Marcus. 'What are the rules?'

Marcus nodded towards the other end, where Duncan and James were standing in front of an inflatable goal. 'Throw the ball into the goal.'

'That easy huh?'

Marcus flashed him a grin. 'Piece of cake.'

Ten seconds later, Ben was nearly drowned as Duncan came hurtling towards him, swiping the ball from his hands with all the grace of a rhinoceros. And laughing in his face with all the charm of a crocodile. 'That's the trouble with you office types,' Duncan crowed. 'Too soft.'

It took him until the last minute of the game to get his own back. Marcus looked around and threw the ball to him. Fuelled by adrenaline and anger, Ben leapt into the air, caught it, then whipped it into the back of the net for the winning goal. For once, he was grateful to see the camera crew filming on the other side of the pool.

'That's the trouble with you gym bunnies,' Ben murmured to Duncan as he swam past him. 'You forget it's not all about muscle.'

Duncan laughed it off, but as his teammates gave him a high five, Ben felt a lot better than he had before he'd climbed into the pool.

Sadly, by the time he'd dragged himself out and back to the lounger, only Chloe was there to congratulate him. He had to stop himself from asking her if Molly had stayed to the end.

Chapter Ten

Molly was on her way to cook with Ben, Duncan and Jasmine. What joy. If there was one thing worse than being in a kitchen with two exes, it had to be being in a kitchen with two exes *and* a woman who clearly wanted in the pants of the one ex she didn't want to be an ex.

As she rounded the corner, she collided with someone coming in the opposite direction.

'Oh my God, sorry, I wasn't looking.'

Rachel smiled and straightened her already perfectly straight jacket. 'No worries. I don't think I was either. Are you off to cook?'

'Yep.'

'Good, I'll walk with you. The camera crew are coming along, too.' She winked. 'Maybe cooking with Ben will bring some sizzle to more than the frying pan.'

'Sorry, but that's not going to happen.'

Rachel slowed her step to peer at Molly. 'You don't feel *any* of the spark of attraction you once had with him?'

She pictured Ben earlier in the pool, his body as athletic as she remembered with its sexy dusting of dark chest hair, the muscles well defined. As he'd thumped in the winning goal, his face had come alive, bringing with it a rush of memories, *good* memories, knocking aside the hurt and reminding her of happier times. Unbalanced by them, she'd had to walk away and remind herself that doing the same thing again, and expecting a different result was the definition of insanity.

'Molly?'

She let out a long breath. 'Attraction isn't the issue.' She turned to face Rachel. 'Did you know we'd dated when you asked him to come on the show? And before you pretend to look confused, he told me he's your brother and he came on to do you a favour as my original match pulled out.'

'Ah, he confessed to being related to me, did he? Not that it's a secret,' she added quickly. 'Me being his brother just wasn't something I was going to broadcast, in case it makes the other contestants feel there's some sort of favouritism going on in how we'll edit the show. Which I can assure you there won't be, as I'm only one small cog in the production wheel. But to answer your question, we knew you used to date Duncan, which was why you were invited to take part, but we didn't realise you'd also dated Ben. It didn't come up in the research and he never mentioned you to me.'

And wow, that stung far more than it should have. 'Clearly I wasn't important enough.'

Rachel's expression softened. 'That wasn't the reason he didn't talk about you.' She paused, her gaze searching Molly's as if she was coming to some sort of decision. 'When you met, it was a difficult time for him.'

The only part of us that wasn't right was the timing. 'So he's said.'

'But you don't believe him?'

Molly shrugged. 'It doesn't really matter now. It's all water under a bridge that I won't be walking over again.'

Still, her heart let out a very solid thump when she stepped into the kitchen and found Ben already there, talking with Lauren. He'd changed out of his shorts and put on some worn denim jeans and a black polo shirt. Somehow, whether it was the confidence with which he wore them, the lean lines of the body underneath, or maybe the way the look was completed by an expensive watch circling his left wrist, his whole bearing was effortlessly stylish.

She glanced down at her denim shorts and clown fish T-shirt proclaiming *Keep Your Friends Close, Anemones Closer* that she'd bought at the aquarium yesterday. Yep, the pair of them were not a perfect match by anyone's standards.

As if aware of her scrutiny, Ben glanced over, dipping his head once in acknowledgement. It was only then she realised Duncan and Jasmine were sitting at the kitchen table behind him, Duncan in a white T-shirt that was a tight fit over his muscles and a stark contrast to his all-year tan. Again, she looked down at herself, this time at her pale legs, and the curves which she liked to think were soft, but a harsher critic could call saggy. Never mind Ben, how had she convinced herself she was a perfect match for the super-fit Duncan?

But then Duncan caught her eye and grinned. 'Hey, Molly. Dig the T-shirt.'

Feeling instantly better, she smiled back. 'Thanks.'

'On the evenings we don't have events, we've selected two couples to make a meal for everyone,' Rachel announced. 'It's a chance to see how well you work together in a pressured environment. You'll work in pairs, one pair taking care of the main course and the other the starters and dessert.'

'What are we making?' Duncan asked, a frown crossing his

face. 'Because it needs to jibe with my healthy lifestyle philosophy. As I say in my videos, fitness isn't just something you can dip in and out of.' Whether it was conscious or not, Molly wasn't sure, but Duncan angled his head towards the camera above the door. 'Fitness is a way of living, affecting not just what you do with your body, but what you put into it.'

From the corner of her eye, Molly saw Ben give a little shake of his head. 'You don't believe exercise and healthy eating is important, Ben?' She asked him tartly.

His head swivelled round to stare at her. 'I believe in a lot of things. I just don't go shouting off about them.'

'You call it shouting off; normal people call it talking about things openly.' Irritated, she turned to Rachel. 'Do I have to stick with Ben, or can we change partners for this?'

Ben inhaled sharply, but Molly ignored him. He claimed he'd never stopped being interested in her, yet by his own admission, he'd only joined her at the pool because his sister had bullied him into it. Now he was deliberately goading Duncan, and okay, maybe Duncan did go on about his fitness stuff a teeny bit too much, but that was why he'd come on the show, to promote himself and his business. *The business that would support his wife and family.*

'You can choose who you cook with,' Rachel replied, glancing between her and Ben. 'And you can also choose what you make. We'll go out and buy what you need if it's not already in the fridge.'

'Great.' Molly carefully didn't look at Duncan. 'I for one totally believe it's important to eat healthily.'

'That's not what I remember,' Ben murmured.

She glared back at him. 'People change. I've changed. And I'd love to make a low-fat dish if anyone else is up for it.'

'You're talking my language.' Duncan flicked her a grin and

rose to his feet. Then, as if he'd suddenly remembered her, he gave Jasmine a crooked smile. 'You don't mind cooking with Ben, do you, babe?'

She pouted. 'I suppose.' Easing up from her chair, she walked over to Ben and tapped a finger provocatively against his chest. 'What do you reckon, can we make something decadently sweet together?'

Ben stared down at where her finger rested against his chest, then let out a low chuckle. 'We can give it our best shot.'

Not the reaction she'd been expecting. Molly felt a clutch in her belly, and an awful realisation that she wanted to change her mind. That making a decadent dessert sounded more fun. But she couldn't let anyone see that, least of all Ben who might think it was to do with him, so she gave Duncan a playful glance. 'Low on fat but brimming with flavour.' She fluttered her eyelashes. 'And packing some heat, yes?'

Duncan grinned. 'Heat sounds good to me.'

All too aware of the cameras recording his every facial twitch, Ben forced his expression to remain neutral as he watched Molly and Duncan stand very close to each other at the stove, Molly giggling at something Duncan said. Hard to believe it was *that* funny. From what he'd seen so far, the man had the personality of a plank of wood.

Ben couldn't work out if she was deliberately trying to wind him up with her cosy chatting (mission accomplished), wind Jasmine up (he suspected also accomplished) … or if Molly genuinely enjoyed flirting with the man she'd clearly had her eye on from day one.

'Oh Duncan, stop.' Molly's voice sounded breathless. 'You're making me blush.'

Jasmine, who'd been in the process of whisking together melted chocolate and cream, stopped and glared over at the pair by the stove. 'What's he saying to you?'

Molly glanced over her shoulder. 'Nothing important.'

'Why don't I be the judge of that,' Jasmine countered, obviously not prepared to be brushed off. 'He is supposed to be *my* partner.'

Molly sighed. 'Fine. I asked if he thought the sauce was too spicy, and he dipped the spoon in and asked me to give it a lick and see. And then...' She groaned, her cheeks really flushed now. 'Probably I just have a dirty mind, but I said it was a bit hot and he said I could always try blowing it.'

'I see.' Jasmine clattered the whisk onto the work top. 'I bet that's something you're really good at huh? Blowing guys. Especially guys who belong to someone else.'

Anger fizzed through Ben, sharp and hot. 'That's enough.'

Molly's eyes flashed, telling him he wasn't the only one getting angry. 'You seriously think Duncan belongs to you after, what, two days? I went out with him for a lot longer than that.'

There was a collective gasp; the camera team, Jasmine, Duncan and yes, probably from him, too. Molly immediately clamped a hand over her mouth, looking horrified at her outburst.

Jasmine was the first to recover. 'Oh my God, first Ben, now Duncan. Is there any guy on this show you haven't fucked?'

Molly's eyes widened, her face turning from red to pasty white before crumpling in a way that made Ben's heart twist.

'Jasmine.' He put a warning hand on her arm and whispered under his breath. 'Knock it off.'

Duncan didn't seem worried by the insult to the woman he'd apparently dated. In fact, to Ben's amazement, the man chuckled. 'I know, right? So weird, Molly being here with two of her exes, though I want to make it clear Moll and I are still mates. It was all very amicable. Still, I know being on the same show as one ex has been done before, but two ... that's got to be a first, huh?'

He directed his question at Rachel, who Ben knew wouldn't be happy to be included in this little pantomime. 'As you say, it's not the first time I've seen someone matched with an ex, though it was a surprise to find Molly's dated both of you,' his sister replied carefully.

Surprise was a bloody understatement.

Jasmine sniffed. 'Seriously, what on earth do you guys see in her?'

Molly laughed bitterly. 'Clearly not very much, as both of them dumped me.'

'Not true. At least not from my end.' Ben kept his eyes firmly on Molly. 'What I saw in you then is the same as I see in you now.'

'Oh yeah, and what's that?'

Someone I think I could love. His brain froze as he felt the camera lens swivel in his direction. Fuck, he hated this. He felt vulnerable enough admitting his feelings to someone who so obviously had her eyes set on someone else, never mind doing it in public.

'Forget I asked.' Molly turned sharply away from him and went back to stirring whatever healthy ingredients were in the pan.

At least she and Duncan were no longer flirting. Yet as he saw her retreat into her shell, her interactions with everyone kept to a minimum as they all ate together on the long kitchen table a little while later, he wondered if perhaps he didn't prefer to see her flirting. At least then she'd seemed happy.

'Charades tonight,' Jasmine chirped as the four of them cleared away – apparently kitchen duties involved not just cooking the meal.

Molly flicked her gaze towards him. 'Ben will enjoy that.'

He forced a smile. 'Absolutely. One of my favourites.' No bloody way was he going to sit through that. He'd plead a headache.

Just then Rachel appeared. 'We'll finish clearing up, guys. Can you all walk down to the heart-to-camera room for a chat?'

Christ, every time he heard that name, he cringed.

And every time he stepped into it, his stomach sank to the floor.

The room had been rearranged since he'd last been in, with two small sofas replacing the one larger one. Rachel indicated for them to sit down in their couples. Their current couples. Not the couples he was starting to realise Molly wanted them to be in. As if to emphasise the point, she sat down about as far away from him as she could.

He ached to reach out to her, wrap an arm around her waist at least as a show of solidarity, of friendship, but she was obviously as upset with him as she was with Duncan and Jasmine, which gutted him.

Natalie swanned in a moment later on a cloud of pink: frilly pink blouse, bubble gum pink skirt. She took up her position and beamed over to the cameras. 'Tonight we found out that Duncan and Molly were dating prior to being accepted on this show. Quite a revelation, considering we already know Molly once dated Ben.' Yeah, a revelation he'd like to bet the producers, including his flaming sister, had neatly set up. 'I thought now was a good time to dig a bit deeper into what these couples thought, now everyone is on the same page.'

Ben caught his sister's eye and saw a flicker of concern. He had a hunch it came from the chat she'd had with him when she'd persuaded him out of his room and down to the pool this afternoon. *I've been looking at some of the footage, Ben. It's clear you still have a thing for Molly. So what the blazes are you doing hiding up here like some saddo, letting guys like Duncan hog her attention?*

It would have been helpful if she'd mentioned Duncan being Molly's fucking *ex*.

'I'm going to start with you, Duncan.' Natalie's question dragged Ben's focus back to the present. 'Why don't you tell us how you felt when you found you'd been matched with Jasmine instead of Molly?'

'Well, they're both knockouts,' Duncan replied with his usual eloquence. 'I mean, me and Molls, we only split up because I got invited onto the show.'

And the bombshells kept on coming. Snippets of the conversation he'd had with Molly on the coach floated back to him. She'd talked of splitting up with a guy only a few months ago. Of watching dating shows with him. Apparently not only had Molly dated Duncan until recently, their relationship hadn't really ended. It had just been conveniently paused while the man sought fame and fortune on the show.

As the realisation burrowed its way into his consciousness, anger and frustration burned in his gut. His chances of trying again with Molly had just shrivelled to dust.

'Can't say I was disappointed to find I was paired with this one, mind,' Duncan added, wrapping a huge paw of a hand around Jasmine's. 'I mean, look at her. What bloke in his right mind isn't going to give a relationship with this babe a real shot?'

Molly inhaled sharply and when Ben turned to look at her, the desolation on her face cut him to the quick. She had genuine feelings for Duncan. Feelings she must have believed were returned.

'And how about you, Molly?' Natalie turned her focus to their sofa, the cameras following suit. 'You told us you came on the show to find your soulmate. Did you believe that was Duncan?'

'Yes.' Her voice sounded shaky and she must have realised it because she cleared her throat. 'When Duncan ended our relationship to come on here, I was upset. Then I was invited on and I figured it was an opportunity to see if we really were meant to be together.' She smiled brightly at the camera. Too brightly. 'Plus I got to take part in my favourite show.'

Invited to come on? So this had been a fucking set up from the start, and he'd just been a pawn in the producers' ... in *his sister's* little game.

'Then you found yourself paired with Ben.'

Molly let out a heavy breath at Natalie's statement. 'Yes. I definitely wasn't expecting that.' She slid him a look. 'It was like a double whammy. I didn't get paired with the man I'd hoped to be matched with...'

'Instead you got lumbered with the last person you'd choose to spend a month with,' he filled in for her.

Molly frowned. 'That's not... Lumbered isn't the word I'd use. Well, I suppose I would have used it, or something worse when I first found out, but I've got that out of my system now.' She paused, eyes darting once more to his before focussing back on the camera. 'It's safe to say things haven't worked out as I'd have liked, which is kind of putting it mildly, considering I'm sort of living with two guys who've decided to break up with me.' Her gaze dropped to her hands. 'Maybe I'm not cut out for a relationship. For love.'

There was a wobble to her voice that made Ben's protective instincts come out in full force. 'Bollocks.'

The camera, and Natalie, turned towards him. 'What do you mean by that, Ben?'

Damn it, what happened to his famous keep shtum motto? 'Relationships, love … they're hard for everyone.' *Too personal.* Abruptly he rose to his feet. 'Excuse us, it's been a long day.' He held out his hand to Molly, willing her to take it and not just because he'd look like a total chump if she didn't.

If ever there was a person who needed to get away and lick her wounds in private for a while, it was Molly.

Chapter Eleven

Molly felt her throat constrict as she looked into Ben's eyes. Compassion wasn't a word she'd ever associated him with, but right now his gaze shimmered with it.

Not just that, but during the last awful couple of hours, he'd been the only one who seemed aware of how much she was hurting. How humiliated she felt, how upset. It wasn't just Jasmine's *anyone here you've not fucked*, comment. It was Duncan laughing it off. Duncan, the man who'd professed to love her, who'd told her this was a temporary break, and that his attention towards Jasmine was just a show. The same Duncan who'd just casually admitted on camera that he wanted to give his relationship with Jasmine a real shot.

She grasped Ben's hand tightly, absorbing the strength his gesture seemed to offer.

'Let's get some air,' he whispered as he led her down the hallway, twisting his hand so it folded around hers. Warm, reassuring.

The balmy evening hit her as they stepped outside onto the patio and she inhaled a lungful of it, relishing the quiet, the dark, feeling her muscles finally start to relax. That was when she became conscious he still held her hand, the touch lighter now, but all the more dangerous for it. She did not want to feel the tingles currently racing down her spine. Nor did she want her heart to flutter, like it was doing now.

With a tug she released her hand and began to walk towards the pool, dropping onto the nearest lounger with an unladylike flop, just before her knees betrayed her and buckled.

Ben glanced over at where the camera was situated, then deliberately put himself between her and it. 'So, you and Duncan.' His voice was low, with a husk to it suggestive of intimacy, of sitting under an inky sky, the stars twinkling above. A shiver of awareness ran through her and she wrapped her arms protectively around herself. 'How long have you been dating?'

'About a year.'

He inclined his head slowly, then dragged a lounger over and sat on the edge facing her, hands resting loosely on his thighs. His body obscured the camera and the distance between them was now so small, they could talk without being overheard. 'Do you love him?'

'Yes.'

Ben's brows drew together. 'You hesitated.'

Had she? Or was he just trying to mess with her head? 'I didn't. I definitely love him. And he loves me.' There was something about the darkness that made it feel easier to admit to her fears. And forget who she was admitting them to. 'I thought he did, anyway, but seeing him with Jasmine … that's hard. Even though I know he's only being attentive to her for the cameras. You know, so he can come across as a good guy.'

A muscle jumped in Ben's jaw. 'That man will always put himself first. You deserve better.'

Did she? She liked to believe she deserved more than a man who laughed when she was insulted, and who flirted openly with another woman right in front of her. 'What do you mean by better? A guy like you? You both strung me along.'

Ben bent his head, rubbing at the back of his neck in a gesture that spoke of frustration. When he looked back up at her, his eyes blazed. 'I understand you're hurting right now, that you don't trust a word any guy tells you, but even if you don't believe anything else I say, please believe this.' His eyes seared hers. 'Nothing about what we had was a lie. I *was* falling for you. But if we'd carried on, it would have ended badly.'

'Well, thanks for looking out for me, but from my side it ended badly anyway.'

He sighed and glanced away before seeming to come to a decision and turning that magnetic hazel gaze back on her again. 'You give your heart away too easily, Molly. Love should be earned. When we split, I hadn't earned it yet.' He nodded towards the house. 'And that man should never earn it.'

The criticism stung. 'I don't expect someone like you to ever understand the need to love. And be loved.'

His right eyebrow flew up. '*Like me?*'

'You're super-confident. Self-contained. Very secure in yourself and happy with your own company. We're not all like that.'

Laughter seemed to burst out of him, but there was no humour to it. 'If Rachel were here, she wouldn't recognise that description.'

Molly found it hard to believe, but she kept quiet, letting the silence soothe some of the raw edges from earlier. As expected, Ben didn't make any effort to break it. Instead he shifted, stretching out on the lounger, hands behind his head, acting as a pillow.

Seeing him laid out like that reminded her how *long* he was and memories of waking up next to him prodded through her consciousness. Memories she'd thought she'd permanently squished. Captivated by his looks, his dry wit, the way he'd made her feel important, not to mention the response of her body to his every touch, his heavy-lidded stare, she'd rushed headlong into sex. And it had been off the charts, a rawness to it she hadn't expected. Like he'd not just wanted her, but he'd needed her with a hunger that had bordered on desperation.

Unwanted heat pooled between her legs and she shifted on the lounger. 'We should head inside. We don't want to miss the charades.'

He gave her a crooked smile. 'Don't we?'

'Imagine how cross Rachel would be if we did.'

'I'm not scared of her,' he countered dryly.

'Well, I am. Besides, I don't want Duncan to think I'm … I don't know… hiding away from him, all upset about what he said about giving his relationship with Jasmine a shot.' When Ben said nothing, she slipped her feet onto the floor and swivelled to face him. An idea danced around her head as she skimmed her gaze over his lean body, his handsome profile. 'Maybe we could give him a taste of his own medicine.'

Ben's eyes widened, and a line formed between them as they raked over her face. 'You're asking me to flirt with you?'

Her heart began to hammer. 'Yes.'

His gaze pressed hers. 'Put my hands on you?'

Oh God, when he said it like that, all gravelly, it sounded dirty. Wicked. 'If it's appropriate, yes.'

'All so we can make Duncan jealous?'

'Yes, no... God, does that make me sound awful?' When he didn't respond, just kept staring at her with those incredible eyes, she started to fidget. 'It does – I know it does – but, and this is going to sound really sad, my ego would welcome a bit of attention right now.'

He nodded, one single, sharp incline of the head before he jumped to his feet.

She wasn't ready for the way his arm slid around her waist, drawing her closer. Making her acutely aware of the expensive cologne she remembered inhaling that first evening.

Nor was she prepared for the way he took her hand as he eased her to a stop just before they went inside, turning to face her.

She definitely wasn't ready for the words he whispered into her ear. 'Just to be clear, I won't be doing this because you've asked, or to make him jealous.' Hazel eyes glittered as they stared into hers. 'I'll be doing it because I want to.'

If he hadn't wrapped his arm back around her waist, hadn't supported her as they walked inside and towards the main living room, her knees would have given way.

Whoever invented charades, needed to be shot. At the very least, tied to a chair and forced to play the blasted game for two hours like he had. All in front of a camera.

Sitting next to him on the sofa, Molly bounced up and down. 'I've got it! *Fast and Furious*...' she trailed off as she watched Chloe hold up six fingers. 'Six!'

Ben shook his head and whispered into Molly's ear. Did he need to whisper? No. But she'd handed him an excuse to get close to her now, and he was damned if he was going to waste a single opportunity. 'How did you get that?' All he'd seen was Chloe jogging up and down on her feet, then pointing to Duncan.

Molly gave him a pitying look. 'Come on, that was easy peasy. She was running fast and furiously, plus Duncan's kind of like The Rock.' When he looked at her blankly, she added. 'You know, Dwayne Johnson, the actor who's in—'

'I know who Dwayne Johnson is.' He stared scathingly over at Duncan. 'But forgive me if I don't see any resemblance.'

She smirked at him. 'Well, Chloe did. And I did. Guess it's a woman thing.'

Unconsciously he flexed his biceps. Yep, they were still there. 'I seem to remember you once liking my body,' he murmured.

The smile slid from her face and those sparkling green eyes darted away from his. 'I seem to remember you once liking mine. Funny how easily a mind can change.'

'Molly.' How could he regain her trust? Prove that what they'd had, had been real? *You could open up to her, you dumb arse. Give her the detail behind the glib lines.* His stomach rolled at the idea. What had she said about him? Self-contained, superconfident. She had no fucking clue how insecure he was. How badly he'd fucked up in the past. How terrified he was to put his heart on the line again.

'My turn.' Molly leapt to her feet and snagged a card. With a sigh he slumped back against the sofa. He'd get another chance to talk to her. Maybe he'd find his balls by then.

His gaze strayed to Duncan, whose attention was totally focussed on Molly now, all but ignoring Jasmine as she smoothed her hand up and down his hulking thighs.

Even if Molly never trusted him again, even if he never found his balls again, he was going to make it his mission to ensure she realised she was worth far, far more than the self-absorbed personal trainer with a wandering eye.

Much to the amusement of everyone, Molly went to sit on the floor by the coffee table. Gripping both sides of the table, she reached her head back and groaned.

Immediately Duncan laughed. *'When Harry met Sally.'*

Apparently it was the right answer, because Molly grinned and high-fived him, much to Ben's annoyance.

'How did he get that?' he muttered when she came back to sit next to him.

'The orgasm scene.'

Slowly the penny dropped, but it niggled at him that Duncan was so clearly on her wavelength. When Natalie had announced the game, she'd said it was designed to see how in tune they were with each other. He'd smirked at the concept, but now the grin had been wiped off his face.

The niggle turned into a knot as Molly left to go to the loo, and Duncan rose to his feet and followed her out a few seconds later.

Nothing you can do, he told himself. But his head kept turning towards the door, and his body felt like a coiled spring, ready to pounce into action.

The minutes ticked by, and his restlessness increased. Sod it. Anyone asked, he was off to the gents.

Once out of the room, he took a left turn and headed down the corridor towards the French doors that opened onto the patio. He'd been out there with Molly, knew how seductive the moonlight could be. When he'd been sitting next to her on that lounger, he'd had to shove his hands behind his head to stop from giving in to the urge to pull her on top of him.

What he wouldn't give to feel the slide of her legs over his hips again, the heat of her as she arched her back and impaled herself on him.

Not helpful.

As he neared the doors, he heard voices.

'You're not being fair, babe.' Duncan. It was whispered, clearly to avoid being picked up by the lurking microphones, but he recognised that 'babe', employed, Ben felt certain, to soften up whoever he was talking to. 'It's not like I'm doing anything behind your back. You know why I had to split up from you, why I'm on this show. I'm going to come across as a right douche if I don't at least try with Jasmine, especially now you've told everyone we used to date.'

'I didn't mean to.' Molly, and she sounded miserable. 'It's just, the way Jasmine was making out you belonged to her. It pissed me off.'

'I know babe, but if I don't give Jasmine a go, it will look like I cynically ditched you just to get some visibility.'

Funny, because that's exactly what you did. Ben clenched his jaw in an effort not to say it out loud.

'Fine.' Guilt pricked as he heard Molly's hushed tone again. He knew he should step back. He'd be fucking livid if Duncan had listened to him and Molly talking. 'I take it you won't mind if I try again with Ben then, either.'

He froze at the sound of his name. Could he justify staying if they were talking about him?

'Seriously? You want to give that dickhead another chance after what he did to you? Remember how cut up you were, babe? I do. Took me ages to convince you to trust me.'

An image of Molly when he'd told her they should end things, pushed its way to the front of his mind. Face distraught, tears flowing down her cheeks, it was an image he'd struggled to bury over the weeks and months that had followed as he'd dragged himself out of his torment and turned his focus to business. To anything that hadn't involve feelings, or his heart. Or redheads with glittering green eyes.

'I don't need the reminder,' Molly hissed. 'But as you've so clearly pointed out, we're no longer together, so what I do isn't your concern.'

'Can't see what you ever saw in him,' Duncan muttered. 'Guy's an arrogant twat. Thinks he's a big man because he owned a business. I mean, dude, I own a business too. And I could knock him to the floor if I wanted to.'

Before he knew it, Ben was striding out onto the patio. 'I'd like to see you try,' he retorted, feeling like he had when he'd been fifteen, full of raging testosterone needing an outlet. It wasn't a good look on a thirty-year-old and he knew it.

All in full view of the sodding cameras.

Molly gaped at him. 'Have you been eavesdropping on us?'

A little bit? 'You were gone a long time. I came to check you were okay.'

'She's a damn sight more okay with me than with you,' Duncan sneered. 'You broke her heart, dickhead. You shouldn't be allowed within a million miles of her again.' He turned back to Molly. 'Remember I'm here for you, babe. Always have been, always will be.'

With one final glare at Ben, Duncan marched back inside.

The air crackled between them as silence descended. A tense, awkward silence, full of simmering anger and resentment.

'I wasn't deliberately listening in.' He exhaled heavily, shoving his hands into his pockets. 'I came out to find you.'

'What did you hear?'

Taking her arm, he led her to a spot round the corner where

he'd worked out they couldn't be seen or heard. 'Everything from "You're not being fair, *babe*."'

He wasn't sure, but he thought her lips twitched at his emphasis of the last word. 'So you heard me saying I was going to try again with you.'

He tried to keep the hope out of his voice. 'Yes.'

She nodded, and turned away to stare at the garden. 'Well, just so we're clear, I only said that to wind him up.'

That told him. 'Understood.'

'I don't want Duncan thinking he holds all the cards. If he wants to try with Jasmine, fine. But I'm not going to sit around pining for him.'

Bending his head, Ben whispered in her ear. 'You're going to give us another go instead.'

Her breath hitched and satisfaction flared through him. But then she darted away. '*Pretend* to give us a go. Don't think for one minute that I've forgiven you for what happened, or that I could ever trust you again.'

He couldn't fault her clarity. 'I've got it. I only get to pretend-date you, pretend-touch you.'

'Yes.' She jutted her chin in the air. 'Do you think you can handle it?'

He searched her eyes, finding anger, yes, but also an uncertainty that tugged at his heart. 'I can handle it,' he told her softly, gaze dropping to her soft, pink lips. 'The question is, can you?'

For a few beats the air around them hummed, and when her tongue darted out to lick those very same lips, he felt his groin tighten. But then she seemed to realise what she was doing, and stepped away from his hold before turning and heading back inside.

Chapter Twelve

Molly watched as the ball Ben released rolled smoothly down the alley and clattered into the pins.

She didn't need to look at the scattered pins to know he'd knocked them all over. Again. She just had to look at his smug face.

'It's hardly an important life skill,' she muttered as she squeezed her fingers into another ball. 'Seriously, why do they assume women have such tiny digits? No wonder you're winning. The heavy balls are so much easier to get hold of.' A muffled exclamation followed her statement and when she slid Ben a look she found him creased at the waist, his shoulders heaving up and down. 'What are you doing?'

'Nothing.' He straightened, but the corner of his mouth twitched and humour didn't just dance across his face, it positively jived across it.

Damn, she'd forgotten how breathtaking he looked when he was relaxed.

Frustrated, she shoved her hands on her hips. 'Come on, out with it.'

She watched as he visibly tried to straighten his features. 'I just wondered, as you're such an expert at handling heavy balls, if you wanted to have a go at handling mine.'

She huffed as she lugged the ball – the *bowling* ball – off the rack, refusing to be amused by him. Or charmed by the way his silent laughter lit up his face. 'Now you discover a sense of humour huh? Shame that sort of smutty innuendo is more fitting for a playground.'

He nodded. 'You're right. My apologies.'

But his eyes still twinkled, and damn, if he didn't look even more gorgeous because of it.

Resolutely she turned away from him and stomped to the foul line where she threw the ball down the alley.

It swerved straight into the gutter. Of course it bloody did. 'This is a stupid game.'

'Absolutely,' he agreed, a smile still playing around his mouth. 'A game meant for people with skinny fingers. Or who can hold heavy balls.'

She narrowed her eyes. 'If you're trying to be cute, it's not working.'

'No. I don't suppose cute was ever a look I managed.' His smile faded. 'But I did use to make you laugh.'

There was no point lying. 'Yeah, you did.'

Around them she could hear the clatter of balls, the yelp of those who'd managed a strike, the laughter of other couples as they enjoyed themselves. But silence descended between her and Ben. 'I don't want to remember how things were between us,' she said finally.

'Why not?'

'Because then I might be tempted to have all that again.'

Surprise flickered across his face and he took a step towards her. Then another until he was right up in her personal space, staring down into her eyes. Slowly his right hand reached up to cup her face. 'You *can* have it again. We both can.'

His thumb gently traced over her cheek and her heart went into overdrive, thumping against her ribs. This wasn't bloody fair. She didn't want to still have this reaction to him. She didn't want the butterflies in her belly to swoop as those hazel eyes searched hers. 'No, we can't,' she whispered. 'Because I know how it ends.' With a huge effort of will, she stepped away from his powerful force field.

He exhaled heavily, raking a hand through his short, cropped hair. It had been longer when she'd dated him. Long enough for her to bury her fingers in when they'd kissed. This short style looked more ... business-like. Sharper, to match his chiselled jaw and those striking cheekbones.

'You don't know how it ends.' There was a rough edge to his voice that sent the butterflies flapping again. 'We'd be starting from a totally different place.'

'Just because the route we take might be different, doesn't mean the outcome will be.' Unsettled, she went to sit down. 'It's your turn again. You can show the viewers your bowling prowess,' she added, waving towards the camera crew who'd started to film them.

Ben didn't even glance their way. 'Why don't I show you how to bowl, instead?'

She eyed him dubiously. 'You just want an excuse to show off.'

He smiled. 'Nope. I want to make sure next time you go ten-pin bowling, you don't end up making tacky jokes about heavy balls.'

She rolled her eyes. 'I've changed my mind. You never made me laugh.' He continued to stare at her, his mouth curving in a bewitching little smile, and her own traitorous mouth smiled back at him. 'Okay, fine. Show me your secrets, oh ten-pin bowling maestro.'

'First rule, choose the right ball.' With a gentle hand to her lower back, he eased her towards the ball rack.

'This is where we started,' she grumbled. Then felt the breath from his laughter as it tickled the back of her neck.

'Those heavy balls you can easily get hold of? The holes are too big for you. Try sliding your fingers into here.' He took her hand in his warm palm and placed it on one of the medium-weighted balls.

Suddenly she felt surrounded by him. A wall of solid heat behind her, his hand over hers, her bum nestled far too comfortably against his groin. Arousal pumped through her and she bit down on her lip to stop a groan escaping. This might be good for the cameras, for Duncan if he was looking, but it wasn't good for *her*. 'Sounds like more innuendo to me.' She jerked her head round to stare at him, but he wasn't laughing. He was gazing at her with a smouldering intensity that woke all her hormones.

It was an intensity she remembered all too vividly.

He was as aroused as she was.

'So, umm.' Jerkily she stuffed her fingers into the holes of the bowling ball. 'This is fine.'

'Are they a snug fit?' His voice, sexy enough ordinarily, had slipped down an octave and resonated through her like a rough palm sliding over sensitive skin.

'Yes.' Aggh, she sounded all scratchy. Clearing her throat, she tried again. 'It feels good.'

She groaned inwardly at her choice of words.

'It does, doesn't it,' he whispered. Then to her relief – and fine, okay, her disappointment, too – he moved away. 'Now we

Thank You, Next

have you holding the right ball, we need to get you in the right position.' This time amusement glimmered in his eyes, along with the heat.

'How long have you been working on that line?'

'What line?' He smirked. 'Wait till I tell you to roll the balls, using a specialist grip. And focus on a consistent release.'

'Oh God, stop, please.' How easy it would be to slip back into old ways, seeing him not as the enemy, but as a hugely attractive guy who made her laugh and want to kiss him. Sliding the ball back onto the rack, she made a decision. 'How about we ditch the bowling and get a beer and some wings instead?'

The moment she said the words, Ben saw Molly's face crumple. Then she shook herself and bent to pick up her jacket. 'I meant let's get a drink and some food. Whatever you want to order.'

'Beer and wings sounds great.' As they walked towards the bar, he gave her a knowing look. 'We always used to enjoy it, as I recall.'

'That was the old me.' Avoiding his eyes, she strode towards the bar. 'The new me will stick to ... sparkling water.'

'You're sure about that?' He watched as she glanced over his shoulder. Turning to follow her gaze, he saw she was staring at Duncan, who was hauling the heaviest ball off the rack, no surprise there. 'Please don't tell me Duncan is why you're refusing the ultimate combination of beer and wings.'

'Of course not. I realise how bad greasy food and alcohol is for my body.'

'I see. That's why you threw your champagne at me.'

She gave him a withering glance. 'No, that was because I wanted to see you squirm as it rolled down your face and left a sticky mess.'

Turning away from him, she gave the woman behind the bar her water order. He quickly added his beer and a sharing platter of wings before handing over his card.

'That's a lot of wings for one man,' she remarked when the platter arrived an impressive few minutes later.

'Figured you might change your mind when you saw them.' He dived in, making a show of groaning as the BBQ sauce hit his taste buds. 'Then again, you're better off sticking to the water. These are awful.' He licked his lips and reached for another one. 'Definitely awful.'

'Don't think I'm not aware what you're doing,' she grumbled.

As if there was some sort of magnet attached to the man, her eyes once again darted towards Duncan, who was lining up to take his shot. Had he shrunk all his clothes, or did he deliberately buy a size too small to show off his physique? 'What do you see when you look at him?'

Her eyes blinked in surprise. 'Aside from a really fit, handsome guy?'

'You see fit and handsome, I see a man about to rip his trousers,' he countered. 'But yes, aside from his looks.'

'He's attentive, not afraid to show his feelings. Or talk about them,' she added pointedly.

The barb pierced and pain radiated throughout his chest. He was bad at communicating. He got it. He should have learnt from his experience with Helena, but his feelings had been still too raw when he'd met Molly, and the thought of exposing them when he already felt emotionally battered, had seemed too dangerous. 'Anything else?'

Thank You, Next

She pursed her lips. 'Let me think. Duncan's thoughtful.'

'So thoughtful he broke off with you so he could come on this show?'

She gave him a hard glare. 'At least I knew why he broke off with me. He didn't just give me some lame line.'

'Lame line?' It felt as if she'd slapped him. He couldn't remember much about that time in his life – aside from two glorious months with Molly. It had all hurt too much. But he *could* remember trying desperately to find the right words to make sure she understood the fault was all on his side.

'You do realise "it's not you it's me" is a cliché for a reason?'

'That's not what I said,' he retorted, stung.

'Okay, I'm paraphrasing, but the result is the same.' When she raised her eyes to his, he was horrified to see they glistened with tears. 'You made me feel important, Ben. Then you dumped me.'

He was tired of hearing this version of what happened. 'Did I?' he replied tightly. 'I said I thought you were amazing but it wasn't the right time for me.' He exhaled heavily, memories of that awful day seeping their way back. 'I also said I wanted to keep in touch. You ignored my messages.' And boy had *that* hurt. Twice he'd messaged her in the following months. Twice the message had gone unread.

'Why would I want to read a message from a guy who eviscerated me? Who made me feel stupid and worthless?'

Anger vied with guilt. 'Because he never intended for you to feel that way. Because he wanted to stay connected with you for when it *was* the right time for him. For when he was ready.' He leant back against his chair, trying to get his spinning emotions under control. 'The way I see it, you were the one who walked out on me.'

To his astonishment, she started to laugh. 'Oooh, that's good, I like how you did that, twisting it all round so you're suddenly the good guy.'

Okay, he wasn't good. But was he really that fucking *bad*? He wanted to think he wasn't, yet what was the point of arguing any further? She believed what she wanted to believe. And anyway, none of it mattered because she was in love with someone else. Restlessly he grabbed at another wing.

'Did you really want to keep in touch?'

Her softly worded question made him pause. When he glanced up he found her watching him carefully. The vulnerability in her expression made his heart twist. 'Yes.' He made sure to look her straight in the eye. 'The connection we had, you honestly believe I didn't feel it too?'

'I wasn't sure,' she answered quietly. 'I mean I thought you did, but then you didn't want to see me again, so I figured it was all me.' Her gaze dropped to her glass. 'It galls me to say these next three words but you were right when you said I give my heart away too freely.' Slowly her eyes rose to meet his again. 'I'm going to take your advice, and make sure the next time I give it away, it's to someone who deserves it.'

'Good.' Because surely to God she didn't really think the man who'd ditched her to go on a dating show deserved *any* part of her.

But do you?

His stomach rolled, and suddenly the plate of wings lost their appeal.

Molly regarded him silently as he cleaned his fingers on the wet wipes provided. 'Is that all you're eating?'

'Seem to have lost my appetite.'

She nodded, but her gaze didn't leave the platter. 'Are they really as awful as you said?'

He schooled his expression. 'Absolutely. Worst wings, ever.'

'Maybe I could have one then.'

He had to stifle a groan as her teeth sank into her soft lower lip. 'Sorry?'

'All the tasty stuff in life is bad for us, yes? Chocolate, chips, salted peanuts, cheese, doughnuts…'

'I'm following so far,' he said dryly.

'Okay, then by the same token, the awful tasting stuff should be good for us. Or at least it can't be bad, can it?'

Keeping a straight face was becoming harder and harder. 'Sure. If you say so.'

She reached out and tentatively picked up a wing, then, as if coming to a decision, demolished it in two bites, leaving BBQ sauce all round her mouth. 'That tastes so bad.'

The desire to lick her lips clean was so strong he had to grip the chair to stop himself from jumping up. 'I did warn you.'

She grabbed another wing. 'I'll need to have a few more, just to be sure.'

Instinctively he glanced over at the lane Duncan was in. When he saw the guy looking over and watching Molly devour the wings, Ben allowed himself a smug smile.

Chapter Thirteen

It was the perfect day for a boat trip, the temperature warm, the sun out and glistening off the water. They were all on board the river cruiser currently chugging gently down the Thames towards Windsor and the afternoon's activity: an escape room. Molly had chosen to sit at the front and her heart had sunk when Duncan and Jasmine had perched themselves on the row in front. She had no interest in watching them flirt.

Thankfully James and Marcus came to join her. Maya – who Marcus admitted he still hoped to win over – opted to sit on the top deck with Chloe and some of the camera crew. It was clear James and Chloe weren't clicking, Molly suspected because they were both loud. She liked him though, and hadn't completely ruled out Chloe's suggestion of swopping. The wave of optimism she'd breezed onto the show with, that she'd end up marrying Duncan, was starting to look like a childish dream. If Duncan chose to stay with Jasmine, Molly knew she needed a plan B to get through the next few weeks. And that was definitely not B for Ben.

She cast her eye to where Duncan was chatting animatedly

with Jasmine, because that's what some men did. *Talked*. They also took every opportunity to touch the woman they fancied, she noted sourly as she watched him put his hand on Jasmine's thigh. The expected bolt of jealousy was more muted today though. It was like her brain had got so used to seeing the pair of them together, it was numb to it.

'Where's Ben?' James asked, helping himself to another coke from the ice box. 'Didn't think he'd still be doing his lone wolf act on the boat.'

'He's prowling the decks, quizzing everyone about escape rooms. "I don't go into anything I've not done before, blind",' she mimicked. 'I did point out it was meant to be fun,' she added as Marcus and James fell about laughing.

'Not sure he knows the meaning of the word,' James smirked.

'To be fair, he can be a lot of fun,' she admitted. 'He just needs to get to know you a bit more before he can relax around you.'

'How are things going with you two, then?' James probed. 'Still feel like throwing your drink over him?'

She chuckled. 'I've got over that. We're being civil now.'

In fact, somewhere between the picnic lunch (where he'd not laughed when she'd sat on the cake), the bike ride (when he'd calmly waited at the top of each hill for her) and the ice-skating (where he'd told her one session was enough for any sane person, but patiently waited while she'd had a second go) she realised she'd forgiven him for ditching her.

He'd not intended to hurt her, she could see that now, and she'd not exactly handled things well from her side either, twisting everything he'd said until she'd convinced herself he'd not cared at all. He had, just nowhere near as much as she'd cared for him.

'Wonder if you'll still be feeling civil once you're in an escape room with him?' Marcus smiled, tipping his head back to stare at the cloudless blue sky.

'There's no wondering to be had. Me and Ben locked in a small room, forced to work together against a ticking clock, is a recipe for disaster.'

James almost bent over with laughter. 'Yeah, I can see that. The pair of you bicker like an old married couple.'

'Err, no. We bicker like two people not meant to be a couple,' she corrected.

'Who aren't meant to be a couple?'

She turned to find Ben sauntering towards them. He had those shades on again, the ones that looked seriously sexy on him. His left hand was slipped nonchalantly into the pocket of his blue cargo shorts. Beneath them, his legs looked lean, and very *masculine*, she thought with a flutter in her belly.

Unconsciously her gaze darted towards Duncan, and his tanned, hairless, very muscled legs. Legs she'd always liked, yet now looked overblown, somehow. Like a caricature of how sexy legs were meant to look.

Ben came to sit beside her, slotting his long body right up against her before threading the fingers of his right hand through hers and bringing them both to rest on his thigh. Her pulse jumped as she felt the hard muscle through his shorts. And when she accidentally brushed the hairs on his legs, a slow sizzle began in the pit of her stomach.

Belatedly she remembered they were meant to be pretending to try again.

'Surely you don't mean *we* aren't meant to be a couple.' His eyes glinted provocatively, as if he knew exactly what his touch was doing. 'Our start was shaky, but look how well we're getting on now.'

She wanted to tug her hand away, but she'd been the one to insist on this pretence. 'Just because you have … one or two attributes I might like,' she settled on, horribly aware of what some of those attributes were; sexy legs, hypnotic eyes, quiet authority, powerful self-confidence. 'It doesn't mean you aren't on the whole still really annoying.'

Ben winked at Marcus and James. 'She likes me more than she wants to admit.'

It was alarming to realise he wasn't entirely wrong.

'Ah, I spy another group.'

They were interrupted by the sound of Natalie's booming voice. She was dressed in the most over the top white silk sailor suit, complete with yards of gold braid and a jaunty captain's hat. Behind her, the camera crew scampered to keep up.

'Should we pipe her on board?' Ben whispered, and Molly had to bite into her cheek to stop from laughing.

Natalie came to a stop in front of them. 'Mind if we come and join you?'

Ben let out a heavy sigh. 'Mind if I go?'

Natalie hooted with laughter. 'You're such a naughty one, Ben Knight. But you stay right there, honey. Our viewers want to hear from everyone.' Her gaze swivelled round the group. 'Well, we've nearly come to the end of the first week. How are you all finding being on the show?'

'We're having a fantastic time, aren't we, babe?' Molly turned to find Duncan had risen to his feet and, with the dutiful Jasmine in tow, was squeezing himself on the bench beside her.

On the other side of her, Ben inched closer, his grip on her hand tightening.

'Yours certainly seems to be a pairing that's working out,'

Natalie remarked to Duncan before turning her attention to Molly. 'How about you and Ben? Viewers have noticed a thawing of your relationship.'

Hard to deny it when she was acutely conscious of his body heat against her side. 'If you mean I only feel like throwing my drink over him twice a day, then you're right.'

Ben gave her a small smile. 'Progress.'

'Well, the next activity should determine exactly how much progress.' Natalie chuckled. 'There's nothing like being locked in a room together to bring out the tension between a couple.'

'I reckon we'll do just fine, don't you, babe?' Duncan winked at Jasmine. 'Escape rooms are all about communicating with each other, listening, working together. All things we've been pretty good at so far.'

Ben shifted against Molly, sending her body into hyper-awareness mode. 'I thought they were about solving puzzles and getting out as fast as possible?'

Duncan gave Ben a cocky smile. 'Guess we'll find out who's right in a few hours.'

Testosterone molecules bounced between the pair of them and Molly sighed. Somehow this had turned into a competition, and it was only going to go one way.

That phrase, wanting to pull your hair out? Ben was surprised he had any hair left.

'I told you, I asked everyone on the boat. These places usually hide objects in books.' He yanked another text book off the shelf and shook it out.

'Usually isn't always,' Molly pointed out. 'And there's fifty odd books to check. If we're trying to save time, we should go for the quickest route and check out the containers on the shelves first.'

'It's not quickest if it's wrong.' He tugged out another book. Next time someone mentioned going to an escape room, he was going to be very, very, busy.

'This is ridiculous.' She planted her hands on her hips and raised her chin. 'Will you please stop stubbornly going through all the books for a second and check inside that box on the top shelf. I've done all the others.'

'You check it.'

She let out a frustrated wail. 'I would, if I could reach the bloody thing. Oh, bugger it. I don't need you.' With a huff she dragged off her trainer and threw it at the wooden box, which toppled onto the floor, spilling its contents. Beaming, she held up the blasted key they'd spent the last five minutes looking for. 'Told you.'

That smug expression on her face? The beaming smile? He wished it didn't do weird things to his insides. 'Clearly this is a sub-par escape room.'

All cocky now, she marched over to the giant safe in the corner of the room and unlocked it. 'If you'd listened to me, it would have saved us five minutes.'

'If I'd listened to you, we wouldn't even have made it past the first clue,' he pointed out.

'That first clue was just stupid. Why have a room looking like a library, but not make the five-letter code to the combination lock, BOOKS?'

'Because in these rooms it's all about thinking laterally.' Another piece of advice he'd received on the boat. When he'd tried CRIME – because they were supposedly here to solve one – and it had worked, he figured he had this place sussed.

'Didn't work with the key, did it?' she retorted, dragging stuff out of the safe.

'That was just a hiccup.' He stared down at the supposed clues she'd uncovered. 'There's nothing helpful there.' Taking a step back, he looked round the room again. 'We're missing something. Does anything look out of place to you?'

'Err, hello.' She held up a piece of paper that had come from the safe. 'Aren't you going to help me solve this?'

'Solving the puzzles is getting us nowhere. We need to think ... bigger.' He'd built his own company, for God's sake. He could beat a cocksure personal trainer in a ruddy escape room.

'You realise we've only got five minutes left now to solve the murder?' She stared down at the paper again. 'Doesn't it make a teeny bit of sense to focus on using the time to solve a clue we've taken fifty-five minutes to find? Rather than staring at four walls?'

'Not if it isn't the right clue. What if they've all been red herrings and the right clue is staring us literally in the face?' What had the boat crew said? 'We need to look for something that shouldn't be in a library. Or that's here but looks odd.'

'You shouldn't be in the library,' she muttered. 'And you look odd. So by your logic, you're the clue.'

Miffed, he glanced down at what he was wearing. 'I don't look odd.'

'Depends on your point of view. This set is from the Agatha Christie era, so you standing here in shorts and a polo shirt looks very odd.' She glanced back at the clock. 'And you've just wasted three minutes arguing with me when we could have been solving this.'

'*I've* wasted three minutes? You're the one arguing when

you could have been helping me figure out what's out of place in here.'

With a loud exhale she stood up and waved the paper under his nose. 'Just listen to this, will you? Where are the lakes always empty, the mountains always flat, and the rivers always still?' She read out.

He shrugged. 'A map.'

Her face lit up. 'That's it! The answer to who the murderer is, is in the map book.' She stared down at all the books he'd upended looking for the last clue. 'Do you remember one of them being a map book?'

'I was looking for a key,' he reminded her sourly.

'Quickly, we need to—'

A claxon sounded, indicating the time was up, and the door on the other side creaked open.

'Well, I guess we failed. No surprise there.' Not looking at him, she stalked out of the room.

Disgusted, he stomped out after her.

He wanted to ask her what she meant by *no surprise there*, but Natalie was waiting for them with her annoying wide smile and stupidly big microphone.

'What a shame, you guys so nearly cracked it. Only one couple has managed it so far.'

His gaze strayed over Natalie's shoulder and he caught sight of Duncan and Jasmine laughing and … crap, was that a medal round the man's neck?

As if aware of him watching, Duncan turned his head, caught his eye. And winked.

The bitter feeling of defeat lay heavy in his gut.

'Where was the answer?' Molly asked.

Ben had an awful, creeping feeling that he knew.

Natalie chuckled. 'You guys were so close. It was in the

map book.'

Molly gave him an accusing look. 'I guess if we'd sussed out each other's strengths before we started, worked as a team, *listened* to one another,' she emphasised. 'We might have cracked it. Everything I bet they did.'

She looked pointedly over at Duncan and Jasmine, who were now drinking glasses of champagne, Duncan's chest so puffed up he looked like a frigate bird. And no, Ben wasn't a bird-watcher, but his parents were and he'd had a lot of bird facts thrown at him growing up.

With a sense of doom he saw the microphone slide towards him.

'Do you have anything to add, Ben?' Natalie asked.

'It's not the winning, but the taking part that matters.' He forced a smile, aware he wasn't convincing anyone. As if to prove it, Molly burst into laughter. Before she could say anything damning, he grasped her hand. 'Excuse us. We're off to drown our sorrows.'

'Not the winning, my arse. You hate to see them drinking champagne as much as I do,' she grumbled as he led them towards the café/bar.

'Champagne is overrated.'

'Only when you're taking a shower in it.' Again her gaze swung towards Duncan. 'As a drink, it's fizzy and celebratory, expensive and indulgent. Classy and—'

'Do you want a glass?'

She stared at him with wide eyes. 'You can't drink champagne when you lose. That's like … ooh, let me think. Like having a picnic on a rainy day, or throwing a party when you get sacked. Or…'

'I get the picture.' He exhaled, the disappointment – and he should not kid himself, the humiliation – ebbing away as he gazed at her animated face. In a flash he was taken back to when he'd first met her, experiencing that same sense of wonder, of everything that was hurting in his life being pushed aside through the sheer pleasure of listening to her.

'What?' She wrinkled her nose. 'Did I get something on my face from that room? Dust? Ink?'

He took the excuse and ran a thumb across her cheek. 'I'm sorry I didn't listen to you.'

Her pretty green eyes popped. 'Apology accepted.' She gave him a hesitant smile, but then her face fell. 'I'm sorry we got beaten by Duncan and Jasmine.'

He wasn't sure what was worse, the reminder that they'd lost, or the reminder that she was still totally invested in Duncan. Turning back to the bar he signalled to the bartender. 'Two bottles of lager, a bowl of chips and a plate of wings, thanks.'

'What are you doing?' she whispered, and it pissed him off that she glanced over at Duncan again.

'They get overrated champagne. We get wings, chips, beer.' The bartender slid two bottles across the bar. He picked his up and toasted Molly with it.

'I shouldn't be eating chips, or wings.' She glanced down at the bottle. 'Or drinking alcohol during the week.'

'Looks like Duncan doesn't mind breaking the rules.'

'Fine.' She took a sip, then another. And when the platter of chips and wings arrived, she was the first to dive in.

'Who are the winners now?' He remarked, picking up a chip.

She rolled her eyes, but as he watched her devour a wing a few minutes later, her mouth smeared with BBQ sauce, it did feel like he'd won.

Chapter Fourteen

Tonight was what the production team had coined Date Night. Molly had just finished giving her eyelashes a quick once over with the wonder mascara that, it turned out, wasn't that wonderful at turning short red lashes into long, dark ones, when she heard a tap on her door.

Lauren stood outside, clip board in her hand. 'Is now a good time for the chat with your parents?'

'Ooh, yes.' In her rush to get ready, she'd totally forgotten that before they went out, everyone had a scheduled video link with their family or friends. A way of giving the viewers a glimpse into what they really thought of the person they'd been matched with.

She followed Lauren down to the heart-to-camera room, and felt a ball of emotion lodge in the back of her throat as the images of her parents flickered up on the screen. She might have been unlucky with her real parents – a father who'd not even wanted to meet her, a mother who'd left her – but she'd won the lottery with her adopted ones.

'Hey there,' she greeted them, swallowing to clear the ball of emotion from her throat. 'How are you both?'

Her mum, silver hair in a neat bob and wearing a simple white top, waved a hand in the air. 'We're fine, sweetie, but we're not here to talk about us, we want to talk about you. How are you doing? We were so upset when we saw you weren't partnered with Duncan like you wanted. And then to find that man you are with was the same one who broke your heart...'

'Your mum was swearing at the television on your behalf,' her dad interrupted. 'She even cheered when you threw your drink over him.'

Molly grinned, feeling a rush of love for them both. 'It did feel good.' Then she remembered Ben telling her how he'd wanted to stay connected. 'But maybe he didn't totally deserve it.'

'So you're getting on with him now? It certainly looks like that to us, sitting on our sofa watching you.'

'Let's just say things aren't so strained. It was hard at first, but we've moved on.'

Her mum frowned, and even through the screen Molly could see the worry in her eyes. 'Do you still have feelings for him?'

Afraid of the answer, Molly hesitated. 'I still find him attractive. I mean, have you looked at the guy? I would need to be wearing that blindfold permanently not to fancy him, and even then his voice would do things to my insides.' *Remember the frigging huge stumbling block.* 'But the saying "once bitten, twice shy" exists for a reason, so don't worry. I won't fall for him again.'

'And Duncan?' Her mum pressed, her worry still visible.

'He was the reason I came on the show,' she answered

carefully, 'but he's with Jasmine now, so I guess we'll have to see how things go.'

'Well, they tell me the next time we see you will be at your wedding.' Her mum gave her a bemused look.

'I know, it's crazy right?' An involuntary shudder ran through her. Trying on dresses, choosing settings and themes … what a miserable prospect when she knew there was no chance of exchanging vows. Not if she stayed with Ben.

'We know you were hoping to marry Duncan,' her mum added softly. 'Do you still think that could happen now?'

It was a question Molly didn't have an answer to. Possibly? Yet even if they did get paired in the second half of the show, would they be able to reclaim the relationship they'd once had? Was Jasmine the only thing getting in their way, or was there another reason Molly didn't feel quite the same tug in her chest when she looked at him now?

She glanced back at her parents, saw the worry still on their faces, and smiled. 'Relax, you might be coming to my wedding, but I very much doubt I'll be saying *I do*. It will be great to see you both though. I miss you.'

They said their goodbyes and Lauren ended the connection, shouting 'Come in!' when there was a knock on the door. 'Molly's just finished.'

Molly jumped up from the sofa and turned to find Ben hovering outside the room. Shit, that tug in her chest? It was right *there*, so strong she had to place a hand over her heart to rub the spot where it ached. Why did he have to look so film-star handsome? She'd forgotten what a suit could do to him, how the charcoal grey could emphasise his dark features, the black open-necked shirt somehow make his hazel eyes even more striking.

He stepped to the side to make way for the camera crew,

who were presumably slipping out for a quick pee break, and she couldn't help but admire how poised he looked, at ease in his own skin in a way few men did.

'Have you come to talk to your mum and dad?'

He gave a slight shake of his head. 'Err, no.'

The only time he'd mentioned his parents had been when she'd asked about them, having rambled on about hers. She vividly remembered his answer. *Yes I have parents, they live in France. But I don't want to talk about them. I want to talk about you.*

God, he'd made her feel so special.

Until he'd made you feel stupid, worthless and unlovable.

Yet now she had to acknowledge some of that had been her fault, thinking the worst.

'Our parents declined the chance to be on the show.' Molly hadn't realised Rachel was here until she slid past Ben into the room. She smiled breezily at Molly but it looked forced, as if the family chat hadn't gone very well. 'We decided to be up front with the viewers about our relationship and have the chat between brother and sister instead.'

'Rachel decided,' Ben remarked, his gaze raking over Molly in a way that sent prickles skating across her skin. 'I was happy not to have the chat at all.'

'But then you'd miss the chance to have a real heart-to-heart about your feelings. You wouldn't want that, would you?' she prompted sweetly.

He raised his eyes to the ceiling, and Rachel laughed. 'She knows you well.'

It was Molly's turn to laugh. 'No way can I claim that. This guy is like a vault, his thoughts and feelings are locked up so tight. It would take a top notch, balaclava-wearing bank robber to crack it open.'

'Or perhaps just someone with the right key,' he remarked,

his gaze pinning hers with an intensity that was a direct contrast to the mild tone of his voice.

Somewhere deep in her chest, her heart gave an involuntary flutter. Was he trying to tell her something? Or was he just being *Ben*?

'Well, that was an interesting conversation,' Rachel whispered as the door closed behind Molly.

The same Molly who'd looked unbelievably stunning in a red strapless dress that showed off her pale but really fucking sexy shoulders.

'Interesting how?' He asked, playing dumb. Like he hadn't just admitted he wanted to open up to Molly. To prise apart his heart and let her in.

Rachel shook her head at him. 'I work with matchmakers, Ben. I help produce a show where we aim to find people their future wife or husband. Add that to the fact I've known you all of your thirty years, and I think it's safe to say I can tell when you're falling for someone.'

No. He didn't want her to be right. He definitely didn't want others thinking the same – the other contestants, the crew, the viewers. Molly. His gut churned. Admitting he liked her, that he wanted to get to know her again, even though she was more interested in getting back with Duncan, was fucking tough enough. He couldn't bear the thought of her knowing he was trailing around her like a lovesick puppy, desperate to impress, to get her to look in his direction.

And what if Duncan knew it, too? It wasn't a stretch to picture him laughing with Molly over it when the two of them met in secret, which he tried not to believe was happening but sometimes woke up in a cold sweat thinking about.

'This is what you like to do, isn't it?' To disguise his fear, he went on the attack. 'Set people up, play with their emotions so your viewing figures go up? You must have been thrilled to find you had a love triangle.' Anger from a few days ago bubbled to the surface. 'Why didn't you tell me Duncan and Molly were exes?'

Rachel huffed out a breath. 'Okay, I can see why you're upset, but I do have a job to do. And it's not like I knew you and Molly were exes when I asked you to come on the show.'

Maybe not, but he still felt used. 'I've changed my mind. If I have to do this stupid chat, I want to talk to Jack or Sam,' he gritted out, naming his best mates. They'd be a nightmare, poking fun at him, but at least they wouldn't get him to admit to anything he wasn't ready for.

Rachel sighed and pointed to the sofa. 'Stop being ridiculous. This isn't a grilling, it's a chat with your sister who, despite what you might think, is looking out for you. And besides,' she added as she dropped down next to him. 'it could be a lot worse. What if Mum and Dad had actually agreed to come on and talk to you.'

'First, that was never going to happen. Second, the conversation would have been blissfully quick. And gratifyingly shallow.'

Rachel's face twisted. 'I guess you're right. It's not like they ever wanted to know how we were really feeling, did they?'

Some kids had parents who wrapped them in love and showered them with affection. Some had parents who didn't care what they did, or where they were. They had parents who fell somewhere between the two. Not bad parents, just distant ones, too intent on making each other's lives miserable to bother about talking to their kids.

'Am I like them?' The question shot out of him before he had a chance to stop it.

'What do you mean?'

'Molly keeps telling me I don't communicate, and she's right. I mean, fuck, look what a mess I made of things with Helena.'

Rachel wrapped her hand around his and gave it a comforting squeeze. 'How many times do we have to go through this? What happened to her wasn't on you. Some people are so lost in their own world, they can't be helped. You did all you could.'

'Did I?' The question still haunted him. 'If she'd fallen in love with someone else, someone better able to talk to her, would she still be alive now?'

'Stop it.' Rachel's hand tightened over his. 'You made yourself ill, torturing yourself with "what ifs", when it was all outside your control. Please don't go back to that dark place again. Professionals couldn't help her, so why in God's name do you think you could?'

Because I was supposed to be her rock. The person she could rely on to make things better. The words stuck in his throat and Rachel sighed, leaning into him.

'Molly's partly right about you not communicating,' she said quietly. 'You've never been one to share your thoughts or feelings publicly, but that doesn't mean you can't – or don't – talk in private when it matters. She saw you at your worst, when things were so painful you didn't want to talk about anything.'

He hung his head, taking a moment to process what she'd said. He'd moved on a lot over the last three years, but there were still times the guilt, the fear that he'd failed Helena, that he could fail someone else, threatened to strangle him.

The door opened behind them and Lauren walked back in with the camera crew. 'Are you ready for a friendly chat with your sister?'

'Friendly?' He thought of how he'd just spilled his guts in front of that very sister. Thank God the damn cameras hadn't been here a few minutes ago. 'You mean the one who's paid to lull contestants into *thinking* they're having a friendly chat, so they'll divulge information they would otherwise have been wise to keep to themselves?'

'Oh come on, you're smart enough not to fall into that trap.'

Rachel gave him a knowing smile and he felt a rush of nerves. Judging by the last few minutes, he was a long way from smart.

After checking lighting and sound levels, Rachel smiled at the camera. 'This is an unusual departure for me. I'm not here in the heart-to-camera room as the assistant producer on *The One*, but as Ben's sister. And we're going to have a chat.' His heart rattled against his ribs as she turned to him. 'So then bro, how are you and Molly getting on now? It looks like you've both got over the initial shock of being paired with each other and are starting to enjoy yourselves.'

All the other times he'd had a camera thrust in his face on the show, Molly had been by his side. It was worrying to realise how much he wanted her with him now. 'I'd enjoy it a lot more if we weren't filmed.'

Rachel rolled her eyes. 'But then there would be no show, and you'd never have met Molly again. I bet you wouldn't have liked that.'

'No.'

She laughed, giving him a playful prod in the ribs. 'Come

on, give your sister a bit more than that. You said before you're happy you were paired with her. Is that still the case?'

'Yes.' If Molly had been sat next to him, she'd have been shaking her head by now. And filling in a lot of the empty silences.

'I wonder if she's as happy to be with you, or if she still wishes she was with Duncan. That must be really weird for you, huh, knowing you're not the man she wanted to be paired with?'

He ground his teeth in annoyance. 'I thought you were here as my sister?'

'I am, and that's exactly what any sister would have asked.'

'We've been here for one week, there's another three to go. A lot can happen in three weeks.'

But only if you do something. Suddenly he was acutely aware that if he didn't, he was effectively handing her to Duncan on a plate.

'Of course a lot can happen, that's what's so thrilling about the show. It's intense, being in this bubble with someone it would otherwise have taken months to get to know to the same degree on the outside.' She gave him what could only be described as a devil-like smile. 'I mean, in three weeks you could be married.'

He stared at her, heart thumping. Was she trying to get him to admit his dislike of marriage, on a show where the aim was to force couples to do exactly that? 'Is there a question there, or can I go now?'

She shook her head at him. 'I just mentioned marriage because I know Molly has strong feelings about it, and I wondered if you'd got that far in your chats yet.'

With a creeping sense of dread, he remembered the conversation they'd had on the coach the first day, about why they were on the show. Him to help his sister out of a bind. Her to find her soulmate. No, to *marry* her soulmate. 'We've only barely passed the stage of her hating me,' he replied tartly. 'Talk of marriage is hardly relevant.'

He stood up, making it very damn obvious he was done. With a nod, Rachel told the cameras to stop rolling. 'What the fuck was that?' He demanded when the crew had left.

She sighed. 'I didn't mean it as an ambush. More as … food for thought. Because if you are really thinking of winning Molly back, you need to know her feelings on the subject.' She gave him a concerned look. 'And sort out your own.'

Chapter Fifteen

Family chat time over, the contestants gathered in the living room for Date Night. Natalie was there in full force. Molly could only admire a woman who felt so comfortable in her skin she was able to wear, well, *that*. A satin, fuchsia pink jumpsuit that proudly showed every bump, every wobble.

And damn if she didn't look amazing.

'Are you all excited for Date Night?' Natalie waved her hands in the air and did a little jig on the spot. 'This evening a chauffeur is going to drive each couple to a restaurant we've specially picked out because of its romantic setting. With only one week to go before you make the decision to stick with your current partner, or ditch them for someone else, it's the night you guys should really woo the hell out of your lady if you want her to stay with you.' She paused, taking a dramatic breath. 'And you ladies should woo the hell back if you don't want to lose your man.'

Everyone cheered ... everyone except Ben, who let out a deep sigh.

'Yeah, that's not going to happen,' Molly agreed, disappointment settling over her. She *wanted* to be romanced. Duncan had been really good at it, booking them into swanky restaurants, whisking her off for surprise weekends away, making a real fuss of her birthday. She missed that.

'You're not going to woo me?' Ben asked as they followed the other couples out of the room.

His palm rested against her lower back as he gently guided her past another couple. 'Obviously not.' Why was her heart beating so fast? 'Or vice versa. I mean, come on, it's you and me. Besides, you even sighed when you heard the word.'

'Only because I'm not going to be told to woo anyone.' He grunted. 'And that's a ridiculous word for it.'

'On that, we have a rare agreement. It sounds like the noise a ghost makes. You know, woo woo. Or a train.'

'I think that's choo choo,' he remarked dryly.

'It depends on the type of train,' she argued. 'Woo woo is a fast one, obviously. Your basic choo choo is a steam train.'

'I stand corrected.'

They halted by the front door where, two by two, couples were shown out to waiting limos. As she turned to look at Ben, she found herself staring into a pair of hazel eyes that shimmered with amusement. There was something more though, too. Something that made her stomach swoop.

Duncan had made her feel special, made her feel loved. But Ben had made her *feel*. And apparently he still could. Her reaction to him was visceral: a shift of her internal organs. A hard tug deep inside her that she could never really explain.

'Next car is yours.' Lauren waved them towards a sleek black car inching to the front of the queue.

'Hope you have a good evening, guys,' James called out as they walked to their limo. 'And if you can't get chatterbox there to talk to you, Molly, tell the crew and we'll come and find you.' He winked at Chloe who was standing next to him. 'You wouldn't mind a double date, would you Chlo'?'

Chloe's gaze skimmed over Ben and she gave Ben a sultry smile. 'Not at all.'

'Not going to happen,' Ben said under his breath as he opened the door for her before walking round to the other side.

'You don't like Chloe?' she asked when he'd climbed in, and okay, she meant James and Chloe. Chloe's name just happened to slip out first.

'I like her just fine.'

Molly felt an uncomfortable twist in her stomach. 'Does that mean you like her, or *like* her?'

He shook his head. 'Why are we even talking about her?'

'Because you said you didn't want her and James coming to join us,' she reminded him.

'Why *would* I want them to join us?' He blew out a frustrated breath. 'Do you ever remember a time when we had difficulty talking to each other?'

'Well, no, I guess not. Though to be fair I did do most of the talking.'

'Do you like talking?'

She rolled her eyes. 'That's like asking me if I like breathing.'

'Well then, it was a damn good combination, wasn't it? You talked; I listened.'

'You actually thought we were *good* together?'

He stared at her nonplussed. 'Didn't you?'

'I suppose so, but I figured it must have been all about sex from your side. When the fire died for you, you wanted out.'

'That's bollocks. The fire didn't die.' Irritation flared in his eyes. 'And how many times do I have to tell you that the only thing wrong from my side was the timing?'

She was starting to realise he was serious. 'What was it about the timing that was so wrong then?'

The lines either side of his mouth tightened, and a shadow crossed his face. 'My ex died a few months before you and I met.'

'Oh.' Her stomach dropped and her brain froze as she tried to grasp what he'd said. He'd been *grieving*? 'That's awful, I'm so sorry. But for God's sake, Ben, why didn't you just *tell* me?'

He turned to stare out of the window. 'I can't... I couldn't talk about it.' He exhaled heavily and when he finally glanced back at her, his face looked so tortured it made her heart ache. 'Can we shelve this for another day?' A deep breath in, and out. 'We're supposed to be wooing each other, remember?'

She desperately wanted him to open up, to help her understand why the man she'd fallen for so quickly, so acutely, had not just slammed the brakes on their relationship, he'd sent it to the scrap yard. But Ben was clearly hurting, and it wasn't fair to ask him to go back to somewhere painful only minutes before having a camera thrust in his face. 'I thought we agreed we weren't going to woo woo or choo choo. Instead we're going to have ... fun,' she settled on. 'We're in a limo, about to arrive at a swanky restaurant where the bill is already paid. Let's go and have fun.'

His returning smile was one of strained relief, yet mixed in with it was a fondness that sent her heart jumping into her throat.

After the conversation in the limo, Ben hadn't thought a fun evening was possible. Especially knowing there was a camera set on the table beside them, recording every word. But he'd forgotten what the real Molly was like when she was in full flow. And by real, he meant the Molly he'd known three years ago, before he'd stomped on her heart. Not the wary, hurt, angry version he'd spent the last week with.

'Come on then, tell me about this company Chloe says you sold recently.' Having swallowed her last mouthful of chicken, Molly settled her knife and fork onto her plate and studied him across the table. 'Did I mention she thinks you're, what was it? Oh yes. Mr Tall, Dark and Totally Delicious.'

'Is there a reason you're trying to push Chloe on to me?' He frowned as the realisation settled like a weight in his chest. 'Wait, this is about you wanting to swop partners, isn't it?'

Molly had beautiful creamy skin which flushed easily when she was embarrassed, like it was doing now. It also turned rosy after sex… He forced the unhelpful memory away.

'No. At least I don't think so,' she added hesitantly, screwing up her nose.

Reminding himself he still had time to change her mind, he took a sip of his wine and focussed on her earlier question. 'You asked about my company. I set up an app connecting people who want to hire unique spaces for weddings, or events, with owners happy to rent that space for a few days.'

'That's right, I remember you talking about the idea. We were at a restaurant overlooking the beach, the one that started life as a small church, and I said what an amazing place it was, and how it would make a great venue for a wedding.'

Nostalgia washed through him, yet Rachel's words from earlier rolled right alongside it. Had she been thinking about marriage even then? *To him?*

'Ben?'

'Sorry.' Shit, he couldn't think about that right now. This was his chance to remind her how well they used to get on, and he was damned if he was going to fuck it up by thinking too much. 'I replied that I had this idea to connect people who wanted to rent spaces that were original, via an app.' He made sure to catch her eye. 'You told me I should stop thinking about it and do it.'

An emotion he couldn't identify flitted across her face. 'And you took my advice.'

'I did.' He'd hit rock bottom after their split, but setting up the business had helped to drag him out of it. 'What about that idea you had, the one for making new clothes out of crappy old ones?'

'You mean my idea for *repurposing* clothes, *upcycling* them?'

'That's what I said.'

She gave an amused shake of her head, but then the laughter slid from her face. 'I never quite got round to it. I'm still doing that most fascinating of jobs, processing orders for car parts.' Her gaze drifted away from his and onto the table. 'At least they let me have a sabbatical so I could come on here.'

'Why didn't you progress it? It was a good idea.' He waited until her eyes found his again. 'I still have the jacket you made for me.' She'd found a couple of torn leather jackets in a charity shop and cut them up to make a vintage jacket for him.

'Of course you do. I can just see you wearing it.' She glanced pointedly at his suit. 'I'm sure it fits really well with the rest of your designer labels.'

'You know I loved it,' he retorted, inexplicably hurt. 'I used to wear it all the time.'

'Yeah, maybe.' Again her eyes darted away from his. 'But that was then.'

'You think I've changed?'

She sat back in her chair and shrugged her shoulders. 'How do I know? It's been three years since we dated. You've set up, owned and sold your own company in that time.' Her hand reached for her dessert spoon and she fiddled with it restlessly. 'You'll have gone out with lots of women too, I expect.'

The moment was interrupted as the waitress came to ask them if they wanted a dessert. Molly immediately shook her head, refusing to take the proffered menu.

Ben gave it a cursory glance before handing it back. 'I'll take a sticky toffee pudding, thanks.' When she'd left, he turned back to Molly. 'To answer your question, no. There haven't been lots of women.'

'Okay, well, it's none of my business anyway.'

She continued to play with the spoon and he felt a shoot of hope. 'Does it matter to you?'

'What? That you dated after me?' She shook her head dismissively. 'Of course not.'

It was hard to tell if she was lying because she still refused to look at him. 'After we split, I put all my energy, all my focus, into setting up the business. If I couldn't be in a relationship with you, there was no way in hell I could date anyone else,' he added, to be absolutely clear.

Finally her gaze jumped to his. 'Really?'

'Nearest I got to a hot date was a take-out vindaloo.'

'Funny.'

But a slow smile crossed her face. He wanted to ask if she was glad he hadn't dated, but this was all so fucking awkward when a camera was recording every word.

The waitress returned with his sticky toffee pudding and Ben glanced over at Molly. 'Want some?'

'It doesn't count if I'm sharing, right?'

He hated the hold Duncan still had on her. 'It doesn't count if I eat it all, either.'

'You wouldn't.'

He grinned. 'Want a bet?' Digging his spoon into the pudding, he scooped a big mouthful.

'Tell me it's awful.' Her eyes tracked the path of his spoon as she repeated his description of the chicken wings they'd shared on bowling night.

He devoured the mouthful. 'Definitely awful.' Reaching across to her place setting, he pinched the spoon she'd been toying with and scooped some more up. 'See for yourself.'

Their fingers touched as she took the spoon from him, and it was like an electric charge had zapped through him.

They carried on taking alternate mouthfuls until it was all gone, but he became no less sensitised each time their fingers touched.

By the time they were back in the limo, there was so much sexual tension hanging in the air, she'd have to be deaf not to hear it crackle.

Deaf, or still so into Duncan she was going to ignore it.

'Now we're away from the cameras, are we going to talk about this?'

'This?' Her voice sounded reassuringly as hoarse as his.

'You know what I mean.'

'Maybe I do.' Her exhale sounded loud in the intimacy of the limo. 'Lack of chemistry was never a problem for us.'

'You're single. I'm single. We have at least one more week together.' He raised a hand to her face, angling it slightly so she looked at him. 'Forget pretending, Molly, this is real. You know it, I know it. The question is, what are we going to do about it?'

'I don't know.' She drew in a shaky breath. 'I'm scared to do anything.'

It wasn't just her words. It was the tremble in her voice, the glisten to her eyes, that did him in.

She was right to be scared. What was he doing, tangling with a woman whose heart he'd already broken? She needed a man who could communicate properly with her, who wasn't afraid of opening up, of committing not just his heart, but *himself* to her.

Until he could do all of that, he had no business acting on the red-hot chemistry that still fizzed between them.

Ignoring the ache in his chest, he dropped his hand to his lap and turned to gaze out of the window at the dark night.

Chapter Sixteen

It was quiz night at HEA Towers and Molly was really looking forward to it. The Mr and Mrs style Q&A was her favourite part of the show as a viewer. When she used to watch it with Duncan, they'd often be in stitches over the responses because it was blatantly obvious some couples just didn't talk to each other. Or didn't listen.

'You guys are going to smash this.' Jasmine nodded towards Ben, who was chatting to Marcus. 'You dated before so you've got a head start on the rest of us.'

'She also dated Duncan.' Chloe gave Jasmine a sly grin. 'So maybe she can help you when you get stuck.'

Jasmine looked put out. 'Me and Duncan will be just fine. He's really into talking, you know? It's like he's interested in me and what I have to say.'

Molly did know, yet despite making her feel special, Duncan seemed to have severed ties with apparent ease. Just like Ben. *Just like her biological mother.* None of them had loved her enough to stay.

'Hey.' Maya pressed her arm. 'Are you okay?'

She squeezed her eyes shut, then blinked away the burn of tears and plastered a smile on her face. 'Absolutely. Can't wait for the quiz to start.'

A few moments later she got her wish as Natalie took hold of the microphone. 'Welcome to quiz night everyone. Now, as you all know, for a relationship to work, couples need to pay attention to each other. So as we head into the second week, this is the time we ask, who has been paying attention to their partner? Which couples have been talking, listening to each other? Shall we find out?' A chorus of cheers rang round the room and Natalie glanced down at her sheet. 'First up, we welcome Duncan and Jasmine, and Ben and Molly!'

Jasmine shrieked and Duncan strode over to her and grabbed her hand. As the pair of them made their way to the front of the room, Molly felt her skin tingle. A beat later, his deep voice echoed in her ear.

'Think we can make a run for it?'

She inhaled a nostril full of his expensive cologne, and the tingling increased. 'Worried you don't know anything about me?'

'I know plenty of things about you,' he murmured. 'How you liked to run your fingers through my hair when we kissed, how your skin flushed when you came—'

'Stop it.' She hated the way her breathing turned hot and heavy. He was right, that chemistry was still there, but chemistry could be ignored.

'I'm trying to make a point. Just because a couple might not be able to answer the questions asked, doesn't mean they don't know each other.'

'And just because a couple know each other's sex noises, doesn't mean they know each other either,' she snapped as they followed Duncan and Jasmine up to the front.

Four bar stools were arranged either side of Natalie and they perched on two on the right. Ben clearly didn't want to be there, yet you wouldn't know from the way he slid nonchalantly onto the stool.

'We'll start with a few warm up questions,' Natalie announced after they'd all settled. 'What does your partner do for a living?'

'At least that's one you might know the answer to,' Molly grouched as she scrawled onto the white board they'd been given for their answers.

'I don't think Jasmine is going to find it too difficult either,' Ben remarked dryly.

They all got the first question right, but when it came to the next one, it started to go downhill. 'What's your partner's favourite colour?'

Jasmine and Duncan shared a grin and both scribbled on their white boards. Molly looked at Ben, who shrugged and raised his eyes to the ceiling. Frowning, she wrote down her answer.

'Let's turn to Ben first.' Natalie turned towards him. 'Have you got an answer for what Molly's favourite colour is?'

'Green,' he replied with the conviction of a man who knew he was right.

Molly sniggered and showed everyone her answer. *Red*.

His eyebrows flew up. 'But you wear a lot of green.'

'You wear a lot of grey, but it's not your favourite colour,' she countered.

Natalie, watching their back and forth with obvious amusement, interrupted them. 'Can you tell us all what Ben's favourite colour is then, Molly?'

'Gold.'

Ben burst out laughing. 'What?'

'Gold,' she repeated, though she was now feeling a little less confident. 'You know, like the ceiling.'

'I'm aware what gold looks like,' he replied dryly. 'I'm just wondering how on earth you thought it was my favourite colour? Which is green, by the way.'

She glared at him, irritation bubbling as a pair of hazel eyes brimming with amusement stared back at her. 'You looked up,' she hissed under her breath as Natalie moved on to Duncan and Jasmine. 'I thought you were giving me a clue.'

His expression turned to bemusement. 'I was rolling my eyes. You know, expressing my disbelief at the trite question.'

Duncan and Jasmine got their answers right. Of course they did. And the next two. Molly didn't need Jasmine to tell her that Duncan's favourite colour was blue, to match his eyes, or that his favourite film was *The Terminator* and he was born in Luton. Because, guess what, they'd talked about that stuff.

It probably shouldn't be a surprise then that she didn't know Ben's favourite film was *Skyfall*, or that he was born in Leicester, because he didn't talk much. Nor, apparently, did he listen because he didn't know either fact about her, and she was pretty certain she'd have mentioned both at some point.

'They're making us look bad,' she muttered.

'Knowing each other's birth place hardly makes them a match made in heaven,' he tossed back.

Maybe not, she thought glumly, but it did say *something*.

Christ, how many more questions were there? Ben hated to lose to Duncan, but he hated answering banal questions even more.

'Moving on to the next question.' Natalie glanced between

them all, clearly in her element. 'What is your partner's favourite food?'

For God's sake. At least ask him something interesting. He quickly scrawled chips, but when Natalie asked Molly for her answer, it didn't match what he'd written. 'Since when did you love olives more than chips? Or actually, since when did you love *olives*?'

'Since she started taking care of herself,' Duncan answered for her, giving him a smug look.

'The question was what *her* favourite food was,' he retorted. 'Not what she thinks it should be according to her ex.'

Molly inhaled sharply. 'I don't need you deciding what I like or don't like,' she told him tightly. 'You got the answer wrong. Deal with it.'

Fuck. For a guy trying to persuade her to take another chance on him, he didn't need Duncan's smirking expression to know he was doing a piss poor job of it.

'Sorry,' he mumbled after Molly correctly revealed wings as his favourite food, and Natalie turned her focus to the other couple.

'What for? Getting the answer wrong? Or embarrassing me?'

'The last one.' He looked her in the eye, daring her to contradict his next words. 'We both know you prefer chips to olives.'

She sighed and looked away.

'Well, now we move to a more controversial question,' Natalie announced, after Duncan and Jasmine had got their answers right. Again. 'What would you say your partner thinks is your biggest fault?'

Finally an answer he was going to get right. He scrawled

down what he knew Molly would say, then took a moment to contemplate what annoyed him about Molly.

'Molly, let's go to you first. What do you think is Ben's biggest fault?'

'He doesn't communicate.'

When Natalie turned to Ben, he turned his board round so everyone could see what he'd written. *Communication*. At last Molly gave him a small smile.

'Well, it looks like you two have finally got another point on the board.' Natalie swivelled to face him. 'Same question to you, Ben. What's Molly's biggest fault in your opinion?'

'She doesn't have a strong enough sense of self-worth.' Molly's eyes widened to saucers at his answer and he guessed it was too deep a reply for this quiz, but tough. It was the one thing that really bugged him about her. It wasn't just because she let Duncan walk all over her, or because she actually believed the man was good enough for her, though both thoroughly pissed him off.

Molly turned her board round and he saw she'd written *talks too much*. 'You seriously think I believe that's a fault?' he whispered when Natalie turned to Duncan.

'Well, you don't talk that much, so I thought you'd find it annoying, having all that quiet, interrupted.'

'I prefer listening.' He made sure to catch her eyes. 'I especially like listening to you.'

Her breath hitched, and a blush bloomed across her cheeks. He wanted to enjoy the moment but Natalie was talking again.

'Duncan, what do you think Jasmine believes is your biggest fault?'

'I work out too much.'

Jasmine giggled at his answer and turned her board round. It read *spends too long in gym*. 'It's not like I don't appreciate the results though. Just that you disappear for hours every day.'

'It takes a lot of effort to look this good, babe,' Duncan answered, doing a pose to make his biceps pop.

Twat.

Apparently Jasmine's biggest fault was that she was too excitable, which Ben could agree with. She was definitely overexcited about a gym-honed body.

Mercifully their time was up and they were allowed to sit back down while the next two couples came up to answer a whole new set of inane questions.

'You guys did really well,' Molly said to Duncan as the four of them made their way back to their seats. 'We were rubbish.'

'Hey, don't put yourself down.' Duncan, who'd managed to sit himself the other side of Molly, gave her arm a patronising squeeze. 'It's hardly your fault. It must be hard being partnered with a guy who doesn't do conversation.'

'I suppose it depends on your definition of conversation,' Ben countered, annoyance simmering. He wanted to tell Duncan to get his hand off her, but as Molly had already told him, only she had the right to decide what she did and didn't like. And apparently she liked – or certainly didn't dislike – Duncan touching her. 'Is discussing your favourite colours a conversation?'

'It's called getting to know someone.' Duncan smiled at Molly. 'If we'd done the quiz as a pair, I'd have got all the questions about you right, too.'

Smug git.

Jasmine must also have been unhappy with Duncan because she interrupted him. 'It wasn't like we learnt all that about each other by chance though, was it?' She turned to Ben and Molly. 'Duncan's watched this show loads, so he knew they were going to do a Mr and Mrs style quiz. We spent the last few days genning up on each other.'

As the smirk slid off Duncan's face, Ben laughed quietly to himself.

He wasn't laughing when the results were finally revealed though, and Duncan and Jasmine won, with him and Molly languishing in last place.

'I know they kind of cheated,' Molly said when Duncan and Jasmine left them to go and collect their prize, a cocktail making kit. Presumably Duncan wouldn't be drinking from it. 'But we dated for two months. We shouldn't have come last.'

He studied her, noting the frown line between her eyes. 'Are you disappointed?'

'Of course, aren't you?'

'I don't like losing, sure, but only when it's a game that matters. I guess you need to ask yourself why you're not happy. Is it because you're naturally competitive, or because you wanted to make Duncan jealous?' He had to work hard to keep his expression bland. 'Or is it because you want to give us another go but think this quiz somehow proves you shouldn't?'

Those emerald eyes blinked and he wished he knew which one resonated with her most.

'If it's the latter, let me put you straight. You love penguins; you want kids, preferably at least two; your eyes light up when you talk about your parents.' Surprise flickered across her face and he held her gaze as he kept going. 'You hate your job but something is holding you back from moving on, and I think it's a lack of confidence which I don't get because you can talk to anyone and everyone. You love the arts, and doodle whenever you're in reach of a pen. You've somehow got it into your head that your body is less than perfect when in my eyes it's the most perfect body I've ever seen.' He watched her swallow and though she didn't look at him, he took some satisfaction in the way her cheeks reddened and a small smile hovered on her mouth.

'Sooooo, they didn't ask the right questions?' She said finally.

'So, it takes more than knowing someone's favourite colour and film to actually *know* them.' Her green eyes glittered back at him and he felt his heart swell. 'I think I know you more than you realise. And I want to get to know even more of you.'

Before she could answer, they were interrupted by Marcus and Maya, but he knew from the way she kept giving him sideways glances for the rest of the evening that he'd at least made her think.

Chapter Seventeen

Molly stared at the camera, recording every minute of their current failure, and then at the blank sheet of paper in front of her. Finally, she looked up at Ben, who seemed about as up for this task as she did.

Was she seriously considering giving them another go?

His words from the other night kept circulating round her brain, and now every time their eyes connected, she experienced a sizzle of awareness that was getting stronger day by day. But if she chose to stay with Ben, it probably meant saying goodbye to the chance of marrying Duncan.

Or could it mean saying hello to the possibility of marrying Ben?

And why did the butterflies in her belly flap their wings so much harder at the second one?

Shelving the thought, she tried to focus on the task they'd been given, running a stall at the fete they were all due to attend this afternoon. So far they had an empty sheet of paper.

'So, a quick sitrep.' She forced some energy into her voice

but bristled when Ben gave her an amused look. 'Didn't you use jargon in your company?'

'Not military jargon, no, but by all means, fire away.'

His lips twitched and she narrowed her eyes at him. 'Are you trying to be funny?'

'I wouldn't dream of it. Let's bite the bullet and get this done.' He made a visible effort to school his features. 'You were saying?'

Ignore him. Easier said than done when dry amusement looked so frigging sexy on him 'We've agreed not to sell cakes as it's boring and we can't cook.'

He looked over to where the other pairs seemed to be making copious notes. 'I bet they'll all be running off to the kitchen to make fudge and brownies.'

'At least they have an idea.'

'We have an idea.' He leant back against the lounger and she tried not to stare at his long legs, or the way his tanned arms flexed as he used them to pillow his head. 'You just won't agree to it.'

'Giving prizes for throwing ping pong balls into jam jars? That's so 1970s fete.' She screwed up her face. 'Next you'll suggest a coconut shy and guess the weight of a pig.'

He shrugged. 'Why not? It's simple and won't take us long to put together.'

'I'd rather be making brownies than trying to find a fat pig. And anyway, why should I agree to your idea when you won't consider any of mine? All of which were better.' Out of the corner of her eye she watched Duncan get to his feet and stretch out his hand to help Jasmine up. He waved away her efforts to pick up their full flip chart – the one covered in ideas – and instead hoisted it easily under his arm.

When she glanced back at Ben, she saw he was staring at her. 'What?'

A muscle ticked in Ben's jaw. 'You'd still rather be working with him?'

Was he jealous? And why did she like that thought? 'Jasmine probably persuaded Duncan to go along with her idea. Or vice versa.'

'And that makes it a good partnership, just going along with someone?' His gaze narrowed on hers. 'What happened to working together, combining brains, pooling ideas?'

'That's not what we're doing though, is it?' She retorted. 'We're throwing in ideas and the other person is dismissing them.'

'You say dismissing. I say we're challenging each other to come up with something even better.'

Duncan and Jasmine halted next to them on their way inside.

'Oh dear.' Duncan smirked at their empty flip chart. 'Looks like you guys need a bit of inspiration.' He winked at Jasmine. 'I was lucky I had this one.'

Jasmine giggled. 'He says that like it was all me. I mean, I said we should make fudge and wrap it up in muslin and cute little baskets, but he's the one who upgraded it to vegan brownies, then listed everything we needed to do to make it happen.' She put a hand over her mouth. 'Oh, I probably shouldn't have said anything.' She wagged her finger at them. 'No copying now.'

Ben looked at Molly. He didn't say anything, but then again, he didn't have to. His face said it all. *Told you. Fucking brownies.*

'Come on, babe, we need to get baking.' Duncan threaded

Jasmine's arm through his and the pair of them walked inside like something out of a Jane Austen novel.

'I hate that he calls her babe,' Molly said as she watched them go. 'He used to call me that.'

'You should hate that he called *you* that,' Ben stated, following her gaze before focussing his tawny gaze back on her. 'Molly is a lovely name, why not use it?'

'Babe is a term of endearment. It made me feel special.' Except why was Duncan using it for Jasmine? Was he really falling for her?

Ben gave her a long, level stare. 'You are special. You don't need a nickname to prove that.'

Her heart gave a delighted squeeze. If she was that special though, why did people keep walking away from her? 'Some of us need the reassurance. I think we should sell something,' she added quickly, determined to change the subject.

Ben didn't reply, just inclined his head as if to say go on.

'We haven't got time to make anything from scratch unless it's edible, which we've agreed is a no go, so we'd have to sell things that are already prepared. Like, I don't know …' She glanced around her. 'Can we dig up some plants from the garden?'

'I'm not sure the gardener would be too impressed.'

'And yet another idea you've squashed,' she muttered. 'What's the point? You're just going to wear me down so in the end we go with your stupid jam jar game.'

'Give me something better than stealing plants.'

God, he was annoying. 'How about we go to charity shops and buy things we think we can sell at a higher price? You know, like those TV shows where they raid flea markets to get stuff they think is worth something.'

'Or?'

She threw her hands in the air. 'Or how about you come up with something instead of sitting there like a lump of ... I don't know ... a lump of uselessness.' He raised a brow in that really annoying way she wished she'd never found sexy. 'Yes, that is a legitimate saying. It means you're even worse than a useless lump. And anyway, instead of being one, you could actually try to be *useful* and throw some new ideas in. Or hey, rehash some old crappy ideas if you want. Just give me something because we're floundering here.' A slow smile spread across his face and into his eyes, carrying with it a warmth that took her breath away. 'What's funny?'

'We could recycle some old, crappy ideas. Or...'

When he trailed off, she raised her eyes to the sky. Was there ever a more infuriating man than Ben? 'Tell me, oh wise one ... oh my God, that's it!' Her heart bounced against her ribs as she remembered their discussion in the restaurant the other evening. 'We could buy some old clothes and upcycle them.' It was frigging genius. But some of her enthusiasm dulled when she looked at her watch. 'Have we really got time? We'd need to raid the charity shops, decide what to match with what and then actually make something.' Slowly the practicalities of it all began to sink in. 'I don't even know if I can do this. I mean, sure, it's a great idea, but I sell car parts. I'm not a seamstress.'

'I have a jacket that says you are, and that you can do this.' Without waiting for her to reply, he leapt to his feet and started towards the house.

'Hey, wait. What about the flip chart? Making notes for what we need to do?'

Slowly he turned round. 'We need to buy clothes and find a sewing machine.' He gave a dismissive glance towards the flip chart. 'Do you really need to write that down?'

Well, okay then. She bounded over to him, having to take two strides for his one. It wasn't the Jane Austen show that Duncan and Jasmine had put on, and she was certain she saw the hovering cameraman smirk as she struggled to keep up, but Molly couldn't stop grinning. She was finally going to upcycle some old clothes and try to sell them.

What's more, Ben, Mr Businessman, actually believed she could do it.

Sitting in a deckchair at the back of their stall, Ben stretched out his legs and let his gaze wander away from the borrowed computer screen he'd been staring at and over to Molly as she crouched down to talk to the girl clutching her mum's hand.

The girl who was currently trying on a funky denim jacket with a flower-patterned collar that matched two new side panels. That hid a big rip.

Not only had Molly managed to transform eight adult denim jackets, she'd also turned five children-sized jackets into garments kids wanted to wear. Molly's gaze caught his over the curl-topped head of the little girl, and she grinned.

It was a grin he remembered from three years ago. Wide, smiling and full of happiness, it caught him right in the solar plexus. She was in her element here. All he'd had to do was riffle through charity shop rails for denim jackets and persuade his sister to find them a sewing machine.

'I've sold another one,' she squealed a few minutes later. 'We've only got two kids' jackets, one men's and two women's to go.'

'Plus ten more jackets in a box under this table.'

She pouted. 'That's mean, reminding me of what I didn't get round to doing.'

'I was reminding you what you still had to do.'

Her brow wrinkled. 'What do you mean?'

'I mean, if you want to make something out of them, I've made you a website you could sell them on.'

Her mouth gaped open. 'You're kidding.'

'I don't joke about business.' He slid the computer across the table and watched her face as she clicked on the links. 'I can tart it up, change stuff you don't like. And obviously when you get a proper catalogue together we'll need to upscale it.'

'When?' Her breath hitched. 'We?'

He shrugged, like it didn't bother him, but inside his stomach clenched. 'You don't have to do anything, but it's there if you want to.' His gaze locked with hers. 'And so am I.'

'Jesus, Ben.' She pressed a hand to her chest and all he could think was *lucky hand*. 'I don't know what to say.' Her gaze flew back to the laptop. 'You made me a flipping website, just like that?'

'Not just like that. It's taken me most of the afternoon.'

She rolled her eyes. 'You know what I mean. You can't set me up in business on a whim.'

'I haven't. The concept needs more work. A proper name, a plan, links to social media, turning into a more useable app, but I can help. If you want me to.'

'I don't know.' Her face still looked shocked. 'I haven't thought about it for so long.'

'I guessed as much.' His gaze skimmed over her top and jeans. 'Don't get me wrong, you could wear a bin liner and I'd think you were hot, but you used to wear your own creations. Why did you stop?'

'I ... umm, okay, that was a nice comment about the bin

liner. But to answer your question.' Her eyes darted away from his. 'Let's just say it took me a while to piece myself back together after we split. I didn't have the energy to think about designing my own stuff, never mind setting up a company. And then I met Duncan, and, well, I was happy again. I didn't need to do it.'

Annoyance shot through him. 'You were *happy* selling car parts?'

Those green eyes flashed back. 'I was happy being with a guy who made me feel like I was loved.'

She turned away from him and stalked back to the clothes rail. For the rest of the afternoon, he was left staring at her glossy mane of red hair. Never her face.

By the time all the stalls were packed away and everyone was starting to pile into the coach, Molly hung back, choosing to chat to Marcus instead of following Ben inside. Marcus, who was effortlessly charming. And funny, apparently, Ben thought bitterly as he watched them from his seat, Molly throwing back her head with laughter at something Marcus said.

'It looks to me like somebody's jealous.'

Guiltily he dragged his eyes away, only to find Maya smiling down at him from the aisle. 'I was wondering where Molly had got to,' he remarked.

Maya smiled and bent to whisper in his ear. 'Liar.'

'How do *you* feel, watching them?' he countered.

Maya sighed. 'I don't know. Maybe a bit miffed? That's how Marcus rolls though; he's friends with everyone. But I'm certain my feelings of jealousy weren't anything like as strong as yours.'

Great. Now he'd lost his poker face. But it was one thing losing it to Maya, he thought as she made her way towards the back of the coach. It was another losing it to Molly. Or that damn camera which had followed them all day.

Finally, Molly and Marcus climbed on board. He steeled himself not to react as she walked towards him. If she ignored him, if she strode past and went to sit with Maya and Marcus…

Relief washed through him when she slid in beside him. And God, that really pissed him off. He didn't want to react this way to a woman who didn't share his feelings.

She said she was scared, give her a break.

He cleared his throat. 'Do I have to worry about Marcus now, as well as James. And Duncan?'

She gave him a puzzled look. 'What do you mean?'

'Don't play dumb. You know what I'm saying.'

She bit into her lip, and he felt it almost as if it had been his teeth, nibbling into that soft cushion. 'Oh my God, you're *jealous*.' Her eyes lit up and her mouth began to curve. 'You're actually jealous.'

Excruciating didn't come close to describing how this felt. 'And that makes you *happy*?'

'Absolutely.' Her head bobbed, like she was suddenly so excited she couldn't keep still. 'I was so lost after you dumped me … no, don't interrupt,' she told him when he started to disagree. Again. 'That's how it felt. I didn't know what I'd done, how I'd got it so wrong. I started to doubt everything. And now, knowing you're jealous, even just a teeny bit, somehow it gives me something back. A control, I guess, that I lost when the person I'd set my heart on, the person I was starting to plan my life around, even though I know it was way too early for that, suddenly yanked it all from under my feet.'

Would he ever stop feeling like a shit? 'I'm sorry.' He

winced at the inadequacy of the two simple words. 'I don't know what else to say.'

'You don't have to keep saying that. I know you are.' She paused, and for once seemed to be thinking carefully before she spoke. 'You asked me why I stopped with the upcycling idea, and our split was part of the reason. I didn't just lose interest in things; I lost myself for a while.'

'Until you found Duncan,' he stated, careful to keep the bitterness from his voice.

'Yes. He helped me find myself again.'

'If he'd really done that, you wouldn't still be doing a job you don't like,' he pointed out. 'You'd have your own business by now.'

She rolled her eyes. 'Look, I'm really grateful for what you did, seriously, but owning a business isn't everybody's dream.'

'Neither is selling car parts.' She flushed with what? Embarrassment, anger? Either way, he'd been too blunt. 'I didn't mean that as a criticism of you. I just believe you're capable of so much more. I bet you know all about Duncan's personal training business, don't you? He even broke up with you so he could come on this show and promote himself. Now ask yourself how many times he asked about your work, your hopes and dreams.'

She opened her mouth, then closed it again. And finally turned away to talk to one of the girls seated on the other side of the aisle from her.

Chapter Eighteen

Molly was waiting outside the small lounge for their scheduled talk to the camera about the fete. She assumed Ben knew he was supposed to be here, but they'd not spoken since his snide remarks about Duncan on the coach.

'Hey.' She jolted when she saw Duncan striding towards her. He glanced quickly behind him, checking they were out of the camera angle, before bending to give her a quick kiss. 'How are you doing, babe?'

She reeled back in surprise. It had been over two months since he'd kissed her, and she didn't know what to make of it. 'Good, thanks. I'm waiting for Ben to do our "chat".' She mimed quotation marks.

Duncan laughed. 'Bet he doesn't do much of the talking. Hey, I meant to say, cool idea with the jackets. Didn't realise you were so creative.'

We went out for a year and you didn't find that out? Her mind reeled back to Ben's comments on the coach.

'Moll.' Duncan slid a hand under her chin, lifting her eyes to his. 'Are you okay, babe? Is that dickhead looking after you?

I noticed the pair of you tucking into fast food. You've got to promise to take care of yourself, yes?'

She waited for the reaction to his touch, yet her skin didn't prickle, her heart remained resolutely calm and absent of flutters. Even his words sounded more controlling than caring. Were Ben's digs starting to muddle her brain? 'What happens with me is no longer your concern.'

'Of course it fucking is.' Duncan's fingers curled around her jaw, and though it didn't hurt, it didn't feel right, either. It felt possessive. 'You're mine, babe.'

'Does Jasmine know that?' She answered tartly, taking a big step away from him.

He scowled and shoved his hands on his hips. 'I like Jasmine, she's fun to be with, but she's not you.' His expression softened. 'Come on, if we both agree to swop we could spend the next two weeks together.' He winked. 'We could end up as man and wife.'

'You'd do that? Marry me?' It was what she'd come on the show to achieve, so where were those frigging butterflies?

'You know I would. I mean, ideally I'd want to get the business going first, be sure I can support you properly. Call me old-fashioned but I figure it's my job to bring home the money, and my wife's job to raise our family. But if we're together next week, and planning our wedding? Why wouldn't we speed things up and take advantage of the free honeymoon?' He cupped her face again, blue eyes staring into hers. 'All I'm saying is, come and see me before you make your choice.'

'Everything okay, Molly?'

An arm slid around her waist, a hand settling just above the hip, and the butterflies in her stomach immediately decided to take flight. *This* touch felt not just right, but *wanted*. When she looked up at Ben, his eyes were a stormy swirl, his jaw snapped tight as he stared back at Duncan.

Her mind screamed that it was all sorts of wrong to lean against Ben, the man she'd tried to hate for so long, in front of the man who'd just said he wanted to *marry* her, yet despite that, her body swayed towards him. 'Everything is fine. Duncan was just saying how great he thought our stall was.'

Ben's arm tightened around her, drawing her closer to his side as he directed his next words at Duncan. 'You needed to touch her to do that?'

Duncan glared stonily back at him.

Molly wondered how she'd have felt if she'd come across Chloe, who was so obviously a huge Ben fan, with her hand cupping *his* face?

Her stomach knotted, and she had her answer.

'Well, this is a cosy gathering.' Natalie's voice boomed across to them as she marched up the hallway, Rachel and the camera crew following. 'Let's get this on camera.'

'Duncan was just leaving,' Ben said bluntly.

Duncan gave Natalie a genial smile. 'Happy to stay and have a chat with you all first though.'

'We're not having a chat.' Ben's voice had gone from flat to flat with a distinct edge.

Duncan laughed and turned to Molly. 'No fucking surprise there, eh?'

'Meaning?' Ben interrupted sharply.

Duncan flicked a glance at Ben before turning his attention back to her. 'What was it you used to say about Ben, babe?' He scratched his head, like he was trying to think, and Molly had a sinking feeling she knew exactly what he was going to say. 'I remember, you said dating him was like a giant guessing game where you thought you'd been getting the answers right, then bam, two months later you found you'd got them all wrong. "He wants to see me again, he likes me, right?"' He mimicked. '"He can't get enough of me in bed, he wants me, right?"' Embarrassment curled through her as Duncan repeated what she'd told him in the early days of their dating. 'I remember you being really shocked when I told you how I was falling in love with you,' he continued, talking to her but knowing exactly how much he was angering Ben. 'You said it was like a breath of fresh air to know where you stood.'

'And where was Molly standing when you ditched her to come on here so you could get more followers?' Ben retorted.

'That's enough.' She hated that her voice trembled, but anger and mortification were hard emotions to control. 'You're both talking as if I'm not here.' Stupid tears stung her eyes and she swatted them away. 'How dare you repeat private conversations?' she snapped at Duncan, before turning to Ben. 'And congratulations on telling everyone why Duncan tossed me aside, too.'

Humiliation burned through her as she pushed past them and headed for the stairs. She was dimly aware of Ben calling her name, but she ignored him. She had no interest in responding to a guy who'd just made her feel insignificant. Like a pawn in his one-upmanship battle with Duncan.

With tears blinding her eyes she ran up the stairs and flew down the corridor towards her room.

Every molecule in Ben's system cried out for him to run after Molly, but two things stopped him. Number one, he'd get the door slammed in his face right now. And number two, he had some damage control to sort out. Ignoring Duncan, he turned to his sister.

'Can we talk?' He waved towards the cameras. 'And without them.'

His desperation must have showed because she didn't argue. Instead she nodded and opened the door to the small lounge. 'Wait for me in there.'

Anger vied with self-disgust as he marched into the room. Christ, he was livid with himself. Not only had he allowed Duncan to wind him up, which was embarrassing enough, but he'd gone on to hurt and humiliate Molly, which was unforgivable.

'Ben?'

He whirled round to face Rachel. 'Did any of that get filmed?'

'Yes.' She put up a hand. 'And before you say anything, this *is* a reality TV show. Drama is what makes good television.'

'Even when it hurts someone?' Emotions were running too high for him to sit down, so he started to pace. 'And by that we're not talking about one of the confident *I want to be a TV star* contestants we all know make up most of the people here. We're talking about filming a woman who feels acutely vulnerable,' he added hoarsely, his voice nearly breaking as he pictured her face with tears rolling down her cheeks. 'A woman who's just been humiliated by two men she was once in love with.' His voice broke and he stabbed a hand through his hair, gutted he was one of them.

Rachel's expression softened and sympathy flooded her eyes. 'I think she was more upset with Duncan than with you.'

'And that's supposed to make me feel better?' He snapped. Her eyes widened, and as her gaze raked over his face, he felt suddenly naked, stripped of his guard.

'I was right, wasn't I?' she said softly. 'You are falling for her.'

Heaving out a sigh, he slumped onto the sofa and buried his face in his hands. 'I don't know.' He'd avoided admitting it to himself so far, but this desire to shove Duncan against a wall every time he saw him? To warn the man not to get within a million miles of Molly? Ben was kidding himself if he thought that was a normal reaction for him. 'I care for her,' he said finally. 'I don't want her hurt again.' And wasn't that the real kicker? He, the man who'd hurt her most, now suddenly thought he could protect her from being hurt?

Rachel's arm wrapped around his shoulders. 'I'll get them to delete the footage,' Rachel said quietly, 'if you promise you'll come and chat to us as we'd planned.'

'I will, but I can't speak for Molly.'

Rachel dug him in the ribs. 'Then I suggest you go and talk to her.'

He imagined her reaction when she saw him and his stomach churned. 'You'll get a better response than me.'

'Maybe.' Rachel rose to her feet. 'But this is a good test of whether you can man up and tell her how you feel. Which I presume, from your reaction to Duncan, is a lot more than the *I care for her* fob off you've just given me.'

He flinched. 'That's … harsh.'

'Is it?' She put a hand on his shoulder. 'I know you're still wracked with guilt over what happened with Helena, but you will never move on from it if you don't force yourself to let someone else in. And by that I mean not just let them into your heart, but into your mind, what you're thinking. This tall, dark and broody thing you've got going on works for a lot of women, but not for someone who believes she got you totally wrong.'

Thank You, Next

You said dating him was like a giant guessing game. Shame shot through Ben as he replayed Duncan's words. He'd been so besotted with Molly, he'd not once thought how his actions could have been interpreted. All he'd known was he wanted to see her, *had* to see her because she'd fast become the only thing that got him out of bed.

'What if I can't do it?' The question ripped out of him, leaving him feeling raw, exposed. 'What if I persuade Molly to give us another try and I let her down again? What if I'm just not cut out for a relationship with anyone?'

Rachel bent to hug him. 'How will you know,' she whispered into his ear, 'if you don't try?'

With his sister's words ringing in his ears, along with the name of the room Molly was in, Ben straightened his shoulders and set off to find her. He'd been here nearly two weeks, and was only now finding out her bedroom was along the corridor from his?

How the hell was he supposed to sleep at night, knowing that?

Heart in his mouth, he knocked on the door. 'Molly, it's me. Ben,' he added, in case she had lots of guys knocking on her door. And wow, that was a thought he didn't need right now.

He was hit with a wall of silence. Was she asleep? Just not interested in talking to him? He was gearing up to knock again, when the door slowly opened.

And his heart stuttered.

Beautiful, was his first thought, but he quickly followed it up with *achingly sad* as he noticed the red rims surrounding her glistening green eyes.

'I know, we still need to do our chat with Natalie.' She blinked and looked away. 'I was about to come and find you.'

'Well, yes, but that's not why I'm here. Not the only reason,' he corrected. 'Not the main reason,' he qualified, then swore. *This* was his best attempt at communicating? 'I came to see if you were okay. And to apologise. I shouldn't have said that about Duncan ditching you, it was crass. I was so intent on getting back at him, I didn't consider what I was saying. How it would hurt you.'

She nodded. 'It's okay.'

'No, damn it, it's not okay.' Frustrated with himself, he slapped a hand against the door frame. 'None of this is okay,' he added roughly, very aware of how close he was standing to her. And of the wall-mounted camera down the hallway. 'It's not okay that I upset you,' he told her more quietly, shifting so the camera only had a view of his back. 'Not okay that you thought dating me was one giant fucking guessing game.' His gaze dropped to her mouth, and his groin tightened in anticipation. 'It's not okay that all I want to do is follow you into your room and kiss the living daylights out of you,' he added, voice so gravelly he imagined he could make a ruddy path with it.

She swallowed, drawing his attention to her neck, and the parts he wanted to kiss after he'd finished with her mouth. 'You do?'

His heart pounded against his ribs as he reached to touch her lips with his fingertip. 'Would you let me? Despite what a git I've just been to you, would you let me kiss you?'

Her chest rose and fell. 'It's not fair to ask me that.'

'I don't feel fair, right now.' He felt churned up inside, aching, wanting.

Of its own volition, his body edged closer, his head dropping until his mouth was inches away from hers. Her breath hitched, but she didn't push him away. In fact she licked her lips, causing a sharp spike of arousal.

Fair. The word finally cut through his lust. Was it really fair of him to take advantage of this chemistry he knew they had?

With a groan of disappointment, he pulled back. 'Sorry.'

She nodded and glanced away. 'It's better if you don't flirt with me. You know I can't resist you when you do.'

'What if I try and earn that kiss?' He took a risk and ran his thumb across her cheek. 'Will you let me earn it?'

Her expression was wary, cautious. 'I'll let you try.'

'Good enough. And more than I deserve.' Feeling as if a weight had been lifted from his shoulders, he nodded down the corridor. 'Are you up for this interview now or shall I tell my sister to piss off?'

A little laugh escaped her. 'You can't do that. Being filmed, talking to the cameras, is all part of the deal.'

'Yeah, so she keeps telling me.' Molly closed the door behind her and they started to walk together towards the stairs. 'She also tells me I need to start talking to you,' he added. 'Telling you what I'm thinking.'

A small smile hovered over her lips. 'Yes?'

He nodded. 'So you should know that you didn't guess it wrong when we were together. I did like you, one hell of a lot, and I did want you.' He made sure to catch her eyes. 'I still do.'

Chapter Nineteen

Molly giggled as Ben stood on her foot. Again. Some men were meant for dancing, like James, and Marcus. And Duncan.

Some men weren't.

'Now I can see why you never took me dancing when we dated,' she whispered.

He glowered at her. 'Who in their right mind would choose to go dancing?'

'Err, me, for one. And loads of other people like me. Why do you think night clubs and dance studios exist? Oh and jazz clubs, party bars with dance floors, cocktail clubs with DJs...'

Whatever he'd been about to reply was interrupted by Natalie, who clapped her hands together to signal quiet.

'We're going to change things up now and try the rumba.' Natalie gave her trademark shimmy, the fringes on her vivid purple dress – it *was* ballroom – jiggling wildly. 'Rumba, of course, is the dance of luuuurve. And we're not just talking about a dance with steps to music, we're talking about a dance that tells a story of passion, of flirting, of longing.'

Ben exhaled heavily. 'Jesus.'

Molly dug him in the ribs, but she had to fight hard not to smile. The dance lesson they were having in the HEA Towers ballroom was so not Ben, but it was pretty frigging adorable watching him try. For once the man who was so confident, so comfortable in his own skin, was clumsy and stiff.

'So my dancing beauties, you need to listen hard to the professionals as they teach you how to connect with each other in this most intimate way,' Natalie continued in her dramatically husky voice. 'Remember, today is your last chance to work out if you and your partner have the sort of chemistry that makes you want to stick with them for the next two crucial weeks, or if you'd prefer to ditch and see if you can find that chemistry with someone new.'

If she ditched Ben, that someone *could* be Duncan. Of course it wasn't guaranteed, because any potential new match had to be agreed by Felix and Stephanie, but if two people both wanted to be together, it was unlikely the show would stop them, considering the viewers were routing for couples to marry at the end of the four weeks.

It's not okay that all I want to do is follow you into your room and kiss the living daylights out of you.

Ben's words flooded back to her. She didn't need a rumba to work out if she and Ben had chemistry. The bigger question was whether their chemistry was enough to make her want to give up the chance of being with Duncan. Maybe even of *marrying* Duncan.

Warm breath fluttered against her neck and she gave an involuntary shiver as Ben's deep voice whispered in her ear. 'If I have to impress my partner by my dancing, I'm fucked.'

Laughter burst out of her. 'Are you going to factor in *my* dance skills before deciding whether to stick or ditch?'

He raised his eyes to the ceiling. 'Hardly. I've already made my decision.'

'Oh?' And damn if her heart didn't jump, rattling against her ribs.

'You know I have.' He slid his hands into his pockets, expression deadly serious. 'I told you. I want to earn the right to kiss you.'

Something inside her swelled, and kept on swelling until she felt it break free and fizz round her insides. It was more complex than happiness, than pleasure. *Power*, she realised. She was used to pleasing, to hoping the other person liked her and yes, maybe Ben had been right when he'd said she gave her love away too freely. That's what happened when you wanted, really, really *wanted*, so much that it became a physical need, to be loved back.

Yet in admitting he wanted to kiss her, Ben had handed some of the power over to her. 'If you learn to rumba, it would go a long way towards earning that kiss.'

His eyebrows flew upwards. 'Are you toying with me?'

'Of course not. I mean, if you don't want to kiss me—'

'Fine.' He let out a huff of resignation. 'You earned the right to keep me dangling on a string.'

'Oh my God, you're my puppet.' She almost squealed at the thought of this big, brooding guy being at her beck and call. 'This is going to be so much fun.'

He narrowed his eyes, like he was all hard-nosed, but she was starting to realise that wasn't him. He might have dumped her, but he'd not done it as harshly, or as carelessly, as she'd first thought. And since they'd been on the show, he'd stuck up for her, protected her, even helped create a platform for one of her biggest passions, if she wanted to pursue it. Certainly that's how it had felt last night during their camera chat with Natalie. Sure, he'd done his usual strong and silent act for most of the interview, but when it had come to talking about the stall, his words had sent a bolt of pride through her.

'Trust me,' he'd said, speaking directly to the camera. 'Molly has a real flair for upcycling. She once made me a new jacket by using bits from the torn one I was going to throw out and another she bought at a charity shop. I still wear it.'

His comment had led Natalie to ask her if she did it for a living, and she'd not even needed to think of her answer. It had burst from her in a bubble of excitement, of anticipation and yes, of pride. 'I don't,' she'd replied. 'But I'm going to give it some serious thought.'

You're more than a seller of car parts. It's what Ben had been trying to tell her. For as long as she could remember, she'd been focussed on finding love, her self-worth resting on being part of a couple, but what if she didn't need to be in a relationship to be happy? What if she could find that happiness another way?

'Hey, where did you go?'

Guiltily she dragged her attention back to Ben. 'Sorry.' What were they talking about before she'd got so hugely, fascinatedly, sidetracked? 'Err, I was imagining pulling your strings. You know, your puppet strings. Do you think I need some training? Because I'd hate to jerk on the wrong one by accident.'

'You know exactly how to pull my strings.'

The rough edge to his voice sent heat scorching through her.

She was saved having to reply when the dance professional clapped to get their attention. 'I can hear some of you wondering, what makes the rumba that we're about to perform so sexy? Well, for me it's all about the hip action, especially from the men.'

Molly sniggered and glanced up at Ben. 'Do you think your hip action is going to be up to the task?'

His responding look held both amusement and heat. 'If I remember correctly, you used to enjoy my hip action.'

Damn it. The hard flip in her lower belly confirmed her memories – there had been zero complaints from her in that area.

'Gentlemen, I want you to walk slowly forward with the left foot, sashay to the side with the right, and then left again for the quick, quick steps.' The dance pro gave a quick demo, making it look fluid and ridiculously easy. 'Then you go backwards slowly with right, sashay with the left and then right again for the quick, quick steps. Ladies, you need to do the reverse.'

'What the fuck,' Ben said heavily, 'is a sashay?'

She had to work hard to hide her grin. 'Come on, you must remember that one. We did it,' she checked her watch, 'about an hour ago.'

'If I remembered,' he countered dryly, 'I wouldn't be asking.'

Was it wrong that she was enjoying his discomfort? 'I can't believe such an important piece of information passed you by. Here's a big hint. Step, ball, step.'

'Can I have the hint in English?'

Hands now on his hip, his tone had gone from dryly amused to mildly annoyed. Add in the fact his whole demeanour said *awkward*, and it was all too much for her. She started to laugh uncontrollably.

'You're enjoying this, aren't you?'

'Well, yes.' He scowled and she hiccupped out another

laugh. 'I meant I'm enjoying the dancing, not seeing you ... err ... flapping about like a fish out of water.' Another laugh bubbled out. 'Sorry.' She tried to straighten her expression. 'Aren't you enjoying it?'

'Definitely not.' His gaze snagged hers and when a fond smile slid across his face, it caused a slow sizzle in the pit of her stomach. 'But I'm enjoying you.'

The morning had been shite. Ben figured he'd put ballroom dancing lessons on his list of experiences never to be repeated. It would go right alongside breaking his arm, and roller skating, which had caused the aforementioned arm breaking.

The afternoon had been only marginally better, as it had involved heart-to-camera time – that was also going to go on the damn list once he was out of here – and watching back clips from the morning.

Bad enough that he'd looked like a total tool, his rumba dancing about as fluid as an unoiled robot. Excruciating that even Duncan in his too-tight pants had managed to appear more flexible than he had.

This evening though? Did it have possibilities? His gaze drifted to Molly, who was sitting beside him at the bar of the jazz club they'd all been ferried to. Her long red hair cascaded in waves down her back, and her sleek black off the shoulder dress displayed a sexy expanse of pale skin. He wondered if she'd ever looked more stunning.

'Molly.'

Her gaze swung from the dance floor, where she'd been watching several of the couples displaying the moves they'd learnt today, to him. 'Oooh, are you going to ask me to dance?'

His heart sank. Not only had he not been planning that, when he glanced at where Marcus was dancing like a pro, making even the usually tight-lipped Maya laugh, he knew even if he did ask her, he'd let her down out there. 'I was going to ask whether this was our last night together?'

'Oh.' Her eyes dipped to her cocktail glass, and the margarita he'd persuaded her to buy because who counts calories on a night out? Apart from obsessive online personal trainers. 'I don't know.'

He had to work hard not to flinch. 'You've not made up your mind yet?'

'Even if I have, I don't know if you have, so I can't say for certain if we'll still be matched together tomorrow.'

'I told you, I want to stay with you.' God, the thought of spending the next two weeks with anyone other than Molly. He'd have to escape over the wall.

'I know that's what you said, but...' She sighed and bit into her lip. 'Look, I don't want to go over old ground, but let's just say when it comes to knowing what's in your head, I've made mistakes before.'

'You know why I fucked things up last time we met. *I* was fucked up.'

'And now I'm supposed to trust you? Just because you tell me to?'

'No.' He ran a finger down her bare arm, receiving a jolt of satisfaction when she shivered. 'You're supposed to trust *this*. The connection we still have.'

Would she have denied it? Admitted to it? He'd never know because their conversation was interrupted by the arrival of the one person he didn't want to be in the same room as, never mind within a few feet of.

'You two not on the dance floor?' Duncan smirked over at him, black shirt so tight it was almost bursting at the seams.

'We will be.'

At his assertion, Molly's eyes widened to the size of dinner plates. *Sparkling green* dinner plates. 'You're really going to dance with me? Do that whole sashay thing, with all the hip action and everything?'

'Hip action, foot movement. Everything,' he confirmed, not having a clue how he was going to achieve it. '*After* we've finished our discussion.' He glared pointedly at Duncan, making it totally obvious he should butt the hell out.

'Hey, sorry for the interruption, mate, but I saw Moll watching us all dance, and I thought what a waste, because I know how much she loves it. I came to offer my services.' Ignoring Ben, Duncan slipped his hand round Molly's. 'What do you reckon, babe? We can show this lot how the rumba is really done.'

Jealousy snarled and twisted in Ben's gut like a wolf caught in a trap. It wasn't just that Duncan was touching Molly, but that he was doing it with a familiarity that reminded him they had history together.

'Err.' Molly looked to him and Ben wanted to tell her to wake up and smell the roses. The man wasn't worthy of holding her hand, never mind dancing with her. 'Maybe in a bit?'

'No problem, babe.' Duncan gave Molly's hand a quick kiss before letting it go. 'Remember what we talked about before. Come and find me later before you make your decision.'

A heavy silence fell between them as they watched him saunter off. Ben knew if he was going to have any chance of convincing Molly to stick with him, it was time to talk.

'I'm scared, too,' he admitted quietly.

Her gaze darted to his. 'Scared of what?'

'Scared of this connection we have. Scared of trying again.'

She gave a little shake of her head. 'I know why I'm scared. But why should you be?'

'You think it was easy, ending our relationship that first time? *Hurting* you?' Shit, opening himself up like this was hard. The words were in his head, but saying them out loud made them real, like he was yanking his insecurities out and serving them on a plate for her to laugh at. 'I might feel in a much better place now, but history tells me there's a chance I could fail you again.' His heart was hammering so fast he had to take a few breaths to calm it. 'Knowing that screws with my head like you wouldn't believe.' He nodded jerkily over to where Duncan was now pulling Jasmine onto the dance floor. 'But knowing you're thinking of ditching me to swop to him, screws with it even more.'

She looked at him curiously, but didn't say anything so he forced himself to keep talking, to say more than he was comfortable admitting. 'I hate that he calls you babe, that he knows your body like I do. That he's had a year of dating you when I only had two months which I threw away, and these last two weeks which haven't been nearly enough.' He felt jumpy, like his emotions were fighting, punching his insides and leaving him feeling raw and unbalanced. 'When you make your decision tomorrow morning, promise me you'll remember what we had before the split. There's nothing I want more than the chance to get that back. Build on it.'

Her eyes locked on his and he wished he could read her thoughts in them. 'Thank you for saying all that. For being honest with me.'

'Honesty is what you should *expect*,' he told her tightly, fighting to keep his emotions on an even keel. 'I'm sorry you don't feel I was honest with you before.' How damning to realise he'd not been, yet what could he have said? *Stay away from me, I'm bad news. My ex died because she couldn't talk to me. By the way, when can I see you again?* He'd been too desperate for the slice of heaven she'd given him and yes, too selfish, to risk driving her away.

Silence descended again. It was less heavy than before, but hummed with an awareness that pulled at his muscles, leaving them taut.

'So, umm, about the dancing.' She slid him a look that held both challenge and a question.

Slipping off the stool, he held out his hand. 'Be warned, we're not doing that,' he told her as he led her to the floor where Marcus and Maya were still *sashaying* the hell out of the music.

'What are we doing then?'

He pulled her abruptly into his arms, resting a hand on her lower back to draw her closer so that every part of her was slotted against every part of him. And he meant *every* part. The soft curve of her breasts against the hard planes of his chest. The heat of her core, against his fast-growing erection.

'This,' he whispered as they started to sway to the music. 'I'm going to use the opportunity as an excuse to touch you, to feel you pressed against me in case I don't get the chance again.' He eased back just enough to stare into her eyes. 'Is that okay with you?'

She looked up at him from under her lashes. 'Yes.'

Her head rested on his chest, and when he felt her body melt against him, his heart tripped.

They spent the rest of the evening dancing in the only way he knew how. The only way he wanted to dance with her, because sod the rumba, this was way more intimate. At one point he caught Duncan staring over at them, and he thought, *fuck you, I'm the one holding her now*. It was the only time his mind strayed from her.

When they finally climbed the stairs to their rooms, the air between them felt hot and sparky.

By the time they reached her door, he was a complicated mess of longing, fear and simmering hormones.

'I probably shouldn't admit this, but part of me wants to ask you in,' she said quietly, a husk to her voice that did nothing to quieten the ache between his legs.

'A big part of me wants to accept.'

She bit into her lip, a smile hovering. 'Big, huh?'

Unable to resist, he pressed his hips to hers. 'You know it.' Her breath caught, and when she pressed her hips back, he groaned. 'Don't tempt a man who's not had sex in way too long.' Because he couldn't *not*, he bent to kiss her, the press of his lips against hers too light, too brief, but if he sank any further, he knew he'd be lost. 'I'm going while I still can. Goodnight, Molly.'

As he walked back along the corridor to his room, he wondered if he would ever get the chance to kiss her again. To kiss her like he *wanted* to kiss her.

Chapter Twenty

Molly woke to a note slipped under her door. Heart racing, she rushed to read it, only to feel a surge of disappointment when she saw the handwriting.

Duncan.

Not the man she'd had the most vivid – and extremely erotic – dream about. The man she'd been a second away from dragging into her room last night.

Damn Ben for getting her so worked up she'd nearly lost her mind. And yet ... would it really have been so bad if she *had* slept with him? Wasn't she already in danger of falling for him all over again anyway? Even if, by his own admission, he might fail her again?

Pushing the thoughts aside, she opened the note.

You were meant to find me last night. Wise up fast, babe. Remember what that dickhead did to you. D x

Guilt slithered through her. While she'd been dancing with Ben, she'd totally forgotten Duncan had wanted to see her before they made their ditch or stick choices. Was the decision now out of her hands? Had Duncan assumed she was staying with Ben, so he was going to stick with Jasmine?

And did that even matter to her? Because it wasn't Duncan's face she saw when she closed her eyes at night.

I'm going while I still can.

Arousal flushed through her as she remembered Ben's final words to her yesterday. How his eyes had turned smoky, his voice holding a sexy husk that made her knees weak. The automatic response of a man who'd not had sex for a long time, as he'd admitted, or a specific response to her? He'd made it feel like the latter, but he'd always been so good at that.

She glanced at the clock on her phone and yelped. Time to get a move on. She was due in the orangery in ten minutes to meet up with the rest of the girls for decision time.

The options hummed through her as she got ready. They continued to bounce around her brain as she dashed down the stairs. Option one, stick with Ben, have stupendous sex, fall for him all over again. Live out her fantasy of walking down the aisle to him. She pressed a hand to her stomach, feeling the butterflies going crazy at the thought. Yet the most likely end to that scenario was her being turned down at the altar.

Option two, ditch Ben, ditch the fantasy, and be paired with someone else … who could quite possibly be Duncan. That path held the greater chance of love that was reciprocated, and of the ending she'd wanted when she'd agreed to come on the show. Marriage to Duncan.

Her pace slowed as she spotted Maya and Marcus ahead of her, holding hands. Wow. That was a dial up in their relationship.

Behind her someone cleared their throat, and she turned to

find Ben. He looked crisp and handsome in black faded jeans with a striped white and grey collared shirt buttoned loosely at the top. 'Morning.'

'Hi.' God, why was her heart so responsive when he was around? 'Did you … err … sleep well?'

His mouth curled at her awkward politeness. 'No. But thanks for asking.'

'No?'

He gave a slight shake of his head, then bent to whisper in her ear. 'Too many dreams featuring a hot redhead.'

'Oh.' She had no clue how to reply to that.

He looked over to where Marcus was giving Maya a seductive kiss before they each went separate ways, her turning left to the orangery and the rest of the girls, him to the right, to the sitting room where the guys were gathering.

'That could be us,' Ben murmured.

'You'd hold my hand?'

His heated gaze pinned hers. 'I'd hold every part of you as often as I could, for as long as you allowed me.'

With that, he turned to follow Marcus, leaving her standing in the middle of the corridor, her core aching, her cheeks flushed.

'Hey, are you feeling okay?'

Molly jumped at the sound of Chloe's voice. 'Yes, I'm fine.'

'Good, 'cos you look kind of hot and bothered. Hope you're not coming down with anything.'

Lust. 'Nope, all good.'

They walked together into the orangery where they were met with the buzz of female chatter. Natalie, dressed this morning on the more demure end of the spectrum in a pair of flared white trousers and a multi-coloured kaftan-like top, flitted between the contestants. The camera team were setting up and Rachel was busy working out where to sit everyone around the large oval coffee table. Their eyes met and Molly gave her an awkward smile, wondering if Ben had already told his sister of his decision.

As if she'd read her mind, Rachel walked over to her. 'I bumped into Ben in the corridor earlier. He told me you know what he's going to do,' she whispered.

I told you, I want to stay with you. 'I don't think any of us know for certain what we're going to say until the moment we say it.'

Rachel gave her a sad smile. 'I get it. Must be very hard to trust anything he says after what happened. But, though he might be really bad at articulating his feelings, he's not a liar.'

There followed a few minutes of shuffling and scraping chairs before they were all finally settled around the table, Molly sitting next to Chloe.

Rachel gave Natalie the nod.

'Okay, ladies, we've reached the midway stage of the show and with it comes decision time. Will you decide to stick or ditch?' She beamed, drawing out the moment as her dark gaze swept across the group. 'Let's start with you, Maya.'

'Oh, well.' Maya drew in a breath, then gave a shy smile. 'I've decided to stay with Marcus. We had a good night, last night.' A series of wolf whistles echoed round the table and Maya laughed. 'Stop it. It wasn't like that.' Then she groaned and put her head in her hands. 'Okay, maybe it was like that.'

Natalie whooped. 'Well, well, yours sounds like it's a relationship going in the right direction. Let's hope Marcus is thinking the same. I'll pop over to the men right after I've got answers from you all.' She turned to Jasmine. 'Have you decided to stick or ditch?

'Yeah, well, Duncan and me had a bust up after the fete. He

said I hadn't pulled my weight, left him to do everything, which was out of line because I made the freaking brownies.' She flicked her blonde locks back over her shoulder and glanced sideways at Molly. 'I thought maybe he was thinking of ditching me and asking to swop to Molly 'cos I know he still has feelings for her.' She shrugged. 'But he was all contrite last night, said he didn't want our journey to end yet, so I guess I should give him another chance.' Again she looked at Molly, and this time there was a triumphant gleam in her eye. 'I choose to stick with Duncan.'

Had *that* been why Duncan had approached her in the corridor the other day? He'd had a row with Jasmine and wanted to make sure he had a back-up option if she ditched him?

God, she really was naive when it came to men.

'Well, that's two of our original matches making it into the second week so far. How about you, Chloe?' Natalie shifted her focus and Molly felt her pulse start to race. It was her turn next.

'James and me might have looked good on paper, but we don't work in real life. I'm going to ditch him and take my chances on someone else.' She gave Molly the side eye. 'With any luck you guys will put me with Ben.'

'Okay, so that's a ditch for James, and a potential swop to Ben.' Natalie's eyes landed on hers. 'Don't keep us in suspense, Molly. Have you decided to ditch Ben and let someone else have a go with him? Or would you like to stick with him and see if you can make it work a second time around?'

Molly drew in a breath, her heart thumping at the significance of her decision and what it might mean for the next two weeks. 'I'd like to stick with Ben.'

'Seriously?' Chloe gaped at her. 'What happened to your pride? Didn't the guy already reject you once?'

Ouch, that flipping hurt. *Had* she lost her backbone, her sense of worth, even her common sense, by choosing to go down this road again? 'Thanks for the reminder, Chloe. But maybe I'm more forgiving than you.'

'Yeah, but there's a line between being forgiving and losing all your dignity, honey,' Chloe retorted. 'And I think you've just crossed it.'

Tears stung her eyes and Molly instinctively ducked her head so the camera wouldn't see how upset she was.

Would giving Ben another chance turn out to be the most stupid thing she'd ever done?

It felt like the worst meeting in history. A group of guys gathered round a table, ready to be interrogated not about their latest sales figures, but about their relationships.

'That's the seventh time you've sighed since you got here, man.' James gave him a wry grin. 'Something tells me you don't want to be here.'

'That or he's worried Molly's going to ditch him,' Duncan interjected.

He gave the personal trainer a bland look, though his stomach was pitching like a row boat on the North Sea in November. 'I'm not worried.'

'Maybe you should be.' Duncan leant back on his chair and folded his arms behind his head, no doubt so everyone could get a good look at his biceps.

'Know something I don't?' And damn, that hurt to ask, but

he'd rather take shitty news now, before the cameras started rolling.

Duncan couldn't hide his pleasure at seeing Ben rattled. 'Only that I told Molly last night I was going to stick with Jasmine, so you don't have to worry about her ditching you in the hope of getting me.'

Disappointment curdled in Ben's gut. Even if Molly had decided to stick, he'd never know if it was because she preferred him, or just made do with him because she couldn't have the man she did want.

But hell, if he managed nothing else this next two weeks, let him at least convince her she was worth more than the cocksure personal trainer.

Thankfully they were interrupted by Natalie – was that a tablecloth she was wearing? – who swept into the room, closely followed by the camera team and Rachel. As if there was some sort of sibling telepathy, her gaze swung to his. Silently he pleaded with her to let him know what Molly's answer had been, but she shook her head. Yet as she turned away, there was just the slightest curve to her mouth that gave him hope. Happy because he was going to get the answer he wanted?

Or amused to see him so bothered?

'Gentlemen,' Natalie began once Rachel gave her the go-ahead. 'Now is your turn to let us know your decisions – stick or ditch? If you choose stick, and your match has chosen stick, you'll spend the next two weeks deciding whether to marry them.' Ben's stomach clenched. He'd conveniently forgotten that's what they'd be gearing up to. But it was a worry for further down the line. *If* he got to spend the next half of the show with her. 'Any other combination, and you'll be dating someone new.' She looked around the table. 'Marcus, stick … or ditch?'

Marcus chuckled. 'Come on, I shouldn't even need to tell you. Obviously I'm going to choose to stick with the gorgeous Maya, if she'll have me.'

There was a beat of silence, and though Ben knew Natalie was doing it deliberately to ramp up the tension, if she kept him waiting like that, he might lose his breakfast.

'It's your lucky day, Marcus. Maya chose to stick with you, too. Whoop, whoop!'

Everyone around the table clapped, which Ben thought was really weird because it's not like Marcus had done anything. Then again, he had managed to persuade Maya to stick with him.

Slowly Ben raised his hands and joined in the clapping.

'Duncan.' Natalie swivelled her attention to the man next to Marcus. 'Are you sticking or ditching?'

'Sticking.' Duncan slowly let his arms down – probably because his biceps were proving too heavy to keep lifting. 'Jasmine and I are going all the way,' he added with what Ben guessed was meant to be a sexy grin, but looked like something he'd practised too hard in the mirror.

'Looks like you are,' Natalie confirmed. 'Jasmine said yes, too. So that's two out of two so far. Seems those matchmakers know their stuff. How about you, James? Going to make it three out of three?'

'Nah. Me and Chloe don't have a good vibe. I'm ditching. Bet she said the same.'

Natalie chuckled. 'You'd have won some money if you'd made the bet. So that's new partners for you and Chloe. Could be someone else from the house, or someone from the reserve list.' Her attention fell on Ben. 'How about you and Molly?'

'Stick.'

Natalie raised her eyebrows. 'We know you don't like saying much to the cameras, Ben, but how about a few more words.'

He huffed out a breath. 'I'd like to stay with Molly.'

'Question is, does she want to stay with him?' Duncan interjected. 'Then again, she knows I'm not up for grabs, so maybe it's better the devil she knows for the next two weeks. Or maybe she'll figure anyone else is better than Ben.'

Duncan's neat put-down sent anger fizzing through Ben, but even if he could come back with one of his own, there was no time because Natalie's eyes were on him.

'Ben.' She paused again, and his heart hammered so loud he was sure the microphones would pick it up. 'Molly chose to stay with you, too.'

Relief washed through him, and he hadn't realised how rigidly he'd been holding himself until he felt his shoulders come down from his ears and his fists unclench.

Further up the table, he heard Duncan mutter, 'Figures she'd settle for a guy she thinks still likes her, rather than risk someone new.'

So many things wrong with that statement, he thought angrily. The fact Duncan thought he knew Molly at all, never mind the dismissive tone, or the implication she was somehow desperate to be liked. To love and be loved. Yet it also niggled, because didn't he get that sense from her too, sometimes? Why else would she even have given Duncan the time of day?

And why else would she have fallen so fast, so hard for him, despite the fact he'd been battling demons he'd been unable to vocalise?

The moment Natalie wrapped up, Ben leapt to his feet. He needed to see Molly. Yet as he was about to leave, Rachel motioned for him to hang back. Frustrated, he shoved his hands in his pockets and waited impatiently while the rest of the guys filed out.

'I know you want to find Molly.' His sister put a hand on his arm, concern written across her face. 'But before you do, I thought you should know that she's upset.'

His insides cramped. 'What happened?'

'After Molly said she wanted to stick with you, Chloe basically told her she had no dignity, sticking with a guy who'd rejected her once.'

'Chloe should butt out of our business.'

'Of course she should. But you are on a reality TV show, so normal rules don't apply.' Rachel shook her head. 'She actually wanted you for herself.'

'Not even if hell freezes over.' He took a breath, tried to get his insides to settle back to some sort of normality. 'When are we due to have one of those damn camera chats again?'

'Later today.'

'Fine. I'll see you then.' He was about to march out, when he remembered his manners and turned back to give his sister a hug. 'Thanks for the heads up.'

'No problem.' Rachel paused, eyes searching his face.

'Out with it.'

'Okay. I'm worried, for both of you. Dating someone a second time around isn't an easy situation to navigate in normal circumstances. Add in cameras, a TV show, another ex, your history…'

'You wanted fireworks,' he told her grimly.

'I did. But not for anyone to get burnt by them.'

'What *did* you think would happen when you shoved me at the end of an aisle and asked me if I want to marry Molly?' He asked her bitterly.

Rachel winced, her expression full of guilt. 'I didn't think that far ahead.'

He nodded grimly. Maybe he shouldn't, either. After all, a lot could happen in two weeks, especially in the emotional soup of this show, with four couples – make that five now, thanks to James and Chloe both getting new partners – trying to work out whether or not to marry each other, all while living under the same roof.

Chapter Twenty-One

After the emotionally draining stick or ditch session, Molly made a beeline for the pool, which was where Maya caught up with her.

'Thought you might have escaped to your room,' the other woman remarked as she slipped elegantly onto the lounger next to her. What Molly wouldn't give to have a fraction of Maya's poise.

'I didn't want to give Chloe the satisfaction.'

Maya smiled. 'You know it was only jealousy talking. She was hoping to get a chance with Ben.'

'Some of that's true, I'm sure.' Molly sighed and picked at the frayed hem of her shorts. 'But some of what she said is true, too. In sticking with Ben, it does feel like I've put my pride on a dinghy and pushed it out to sea.' At least he'd kept his word and not left her totally humiliated by asking to switch.

'Well, clearly Ben wants to keep seeing you, too. Maybe things will be different for you guys this time.' She gave Molly a nudge. 'You must be able to imagine marrying him if you're willing to give him another try?'

Molly let out a long breath. 'I hate to admit this, but it was once all I fantasised about.'

'And Duncan? Did you imagine marrying him when you dated?'

'Yep.' Heated scalded her face. 'God, I sound like I'm just desperate to get married.' How mortifying to think she might have hurtled from one man to another because she was too afraid to be alone. 'Did you come on the show to marry?'

Maya pulled a face. 'Not exactly. I came on the show because I was fed up with bad dating choices and I figured why not let computers and experts take some of the risk out of it?'

'And you really think they might have got things right? I mean for you?' Molly added quickly.

A grin spread across Maya's face. 'What you're really asking is do I believe you and Ben are a better match than you and Duncan, and my honest answer is I don't know, but there's no denying the chemistry between you and Ben.'

It was back to that word again, yet chemistry hadn't been enough three years ago. 'What about the chemistry between you and Marcus.' Molly waggled her eyebrows. 'Seems things have – how shall I put it delicately – *moved* on?'

Maya giggled. 'In the end I figured I've only got two more weeks to decide whether to marry him or not, so I needed to get on and either ditch him, or fuck him.'

Molly stared at her open mouthed. 'And we all thought you were the quiet one.'

Maya laughed. 'You think anyone who goes on this show is quiet? We're all happy to run our mouths off now and again, or we wouldn't have chosen to be here.'

Thank You, Next

All except for Ben, who'd done it as a favour to his sister. A wave of sympathy washed through her and she vowed to be more understanding when they were interviewed this afternoon.

As if just thinking about him made him appear, she turned to see Ben step out onto the patio. He looked broodingly handsome, his expression thoughtful ... no wait, it was troubled.

She waved over to him, and Maya immediately stood up. 'I'm going to find Marcus. Congratulate him on his excellent choice of partner for the next two weeks.' She winked. 'Think on what I said. Now you've chosen not to ditch Ben, doesn't it make sense that you should—'

'I'll think about it,' Molly interrupted quickly as she glanced over Maya's shoulder and saw the approaching Ben raise his eyebrows.

'You should ... what?' He asked as Maya retreated back into the house.

Oh no. There was already enough sexual tension bouncing between them after last night. If she lobbed Maya's theory into the mix, she was going to spontaneously combust. Yet under Ben's scrutiny, she felt her cheeks burn.

'Ah.' The corner of his mouth turned up but he didn't say anything. Just eased onto the lounger Maya had vacated, looking all amused and sexy. God, he was sexy.

'What's so funny?'

His mouth twitched. 'Nothing.'

'Then why are you smiling?'

'It's not a smile.' His hazel gaze met hers. 'It's the look of a man happy that you're at least thinking about doing what I haven't been able to stop imagining.'

A few pulsing beats passed and she didn't know how to

respond, too embarrassed, too confused by her jumbled feelings.

Slowly his expression turned serious. 'Thank you.'

'For?'

'Choosing to stick with me. I know that can't have been an easy decision.'

'It wasn't.' It was pathetically easy, but she wasn't going to tell him that. *See, Chloe, I have some dignity left.* 'Don't make me live to regret it.'

An awkward silence followed her words, but Molly was too churned up to break it. The control she'd felt a few days ago felt like it had been handed back. She'd opted to stay with him. If that didn't send him a huge *I'm still hopelessly into you* signal, she didn't know what would.

'I'm sure it was easier when you found out Duncan was sticking with Jasmine,' Ben remarked finally, his voice strangely flat.

She twisted round to look at him. 'How did you … no, don't worry. Duncan told you that.'

Ben smiled grimly. 'He took great delight in telling me you knew he wasn't, and I'm quoting here, "up for grabs".'

'He put a note under my door last night. Reminded me to be careful about trusting you.'

His expression tightened. 'He seems very bothered by the idea of you and me together.'

'Of course he is, because he saw how bad I was after you broke up with me. He doesn't want me to go through that again.'

Ben looked pained. 'I hate that I hurt you. I hate that I could hurt you again. I wish I could sit here and promise that I won't, but I refuse to lie to you.' His hazel gaze pressed hers. 'What I feel for you is real, Molly. You *can* trust that.'

'Thank you.' Her heart felt a little lighter. 'I was supposed to see Duncan before I made my choice, but I forgot.'

'Ah.' A small smile hovered across his lips.

Silence stretched between them for a few seconds, along with that sparky awareness that made her ultra conscious of the fresh scent of his cologne, of the strong, capable-looking hands clasped loosely in his lap. Of the quiet way he sat. No fidgeting, like Duncan. Ben was reassuringly still, like he was content to just be there with her.

'So, potentially two more weeks together.' His eyes held a promise that sent her insides into free fall.

'Yes.' *Then we have to decide whether to get married.* Her heart thudded and she pushed the thought away, unwilling to ruin the moment. 'Wonder how many arguments we'll have.'

He smiled. 'Too many to count.' Heat replaced the amusement in his eyes, causing an answering arousal to coil in her belly. 'But maybe we'll find other ways to occupy our time, too.'

As the butterflies flapped excitedly in her belly, the next two weeks suddenly felt full of promise.

He would not miss this, Ben thought later that day as he followed Molly into the heart-to … bollocks, he was not going to call the room that. Not even in his head.

Rachel was stood behind the cameras, and when his eyes met hers, she gave him a sympathetic smile, as if she'd been able to read his mind.

'Well, if it isn't the former exes.' Natalie greeted them with the trademark beaming smile that seemed permanently fixed on her face. 'I'm not sure I'd have put money on you both choosing to stay together after that first meeting.'

'Ah, you mean champagnegate.' Molly turned and gave him an evil-looking grin.

'We've moved on from there. I hope,' he tagged on because he was well aware he was on probation. He needed to earn her trust, which he understood because he didn't trust himself, either. Not to be who she needed him to be.

The thought made him very uncomfortable as he took the seat next to her on the sofa. He'd come on this pressure cooker of a TV show because his sister had pleaded with him, not because he wanted to find love. Yet here he was, reunited with the woman he'd spent many hours thinking about during the last three years. He was enjoying the hell out of getting to know her again, spending time with her, but lurking in the distance was this artificial crux point. A day when he could be forced to make an impossible choice. Either marry her, something he absolutely couldn't do, or publicly humiliate her by turning her down. Something he absolutely couldn't do.

Fuck.

Hurting her once was careless. Hurting her a second time was unforgivable.

'Ben?'

Natalie's voice cut through his wayward thoughts and he blinked. 'Sorry?'

'It looks like your mind is somewhere else,' she replied dryly. 'Where is it?'

'None of your business.' He took in a deep breath, told himself to calm the hell down. Anything could happen in the next two weeks. Molly could get fed up with him and ask to swop, he could get voted off to give her someone new. His gut twisted, neither thought helping his peace of mind. All he could do was take it one day at a time.

Beside him, Molly sighed. 'Err, I hate to remind you, but you're on a reality TV show, Ben. What you're thinking is their business. And this,' she flapped her hands at him, 'This, Natalie, is what I'm up against. It's annoying for you guys, and for the viewers at home that he won't tell us what's going on in his head, but it's also really annoying for the woman he's dating. We're left in limbo land, wondering where we stand, which leads us to try and use his actions as clues.' She paused, turned to look at him. 'Which can result in making the wrong assumptions.'

Her eyes held a mix of emotions, and none of them helped to ease his discomfort. There was hurt still about what had happened, but also fear, presumably that they were heading that way again.

'It sounds like you might be regretting your decision to stick with Ben, Molly?'

A cold shiver ran down his spine, and the time between the question being asked and Molly opening her mouth to reply felt like two lifetimes. 'No,' she answered finally. 'There's nobody else in the house I'd rather be with.'

'Not even Duncan?'

Fuck, this was not helpful.

'I guess I still have unresolved feelings for Ben.'

As her quiet words settled over him, his chest tightened to the point of pain.

'And you, Ben.' Natalie's gaze swung back to him. 'I'll go back to the question I originally asked, which you clearly didn't hear. Was deciding to stay with Molly an easy decision to make?'

'Yes.' *Not enough.* He could feel his sister's eyes burning into him, willing him to get out of his comfort zone. To be as brave as Molly had been.

'Molly was the one who had the difficult decision.' His palms were sweating, his pulse hammering, but he forced himself to keep talking. 'When I first met her, I wasn't in the right head space for a relationship, but I started one anyway because I was selfish. And because she's gorgeous, funny and smart and I couldn't resist her. I ended up letting her down though. Hurting her.' Should he be saying this? Was he making things worse by reminding everyone what had happened? 'It takes a special kind of person to push past that and give a guy another chance.' He risked a quick glance at her and took encouragement from the softening of her expression, the warmth in her eyes. 'I heard someone say that Molly should have more pride than to stick with me, but that's bollocks. This isn't about pride; it's about heart, and Molly's heart is warm and generous. Maybe too generous, but I'm not going to argue. Not when it's given me another two weeks with her.'

When he'd finished his monologue, the room fell silent, punctuated only by a rustle of material as Molly crossed her legs. A cough from the woman behind the camera. Panicked, his gaze jumped to Rachel, who gave him a small smile.

'Well, thank you, Ben. That was quite a speech.' Natalie placed a hand over her heart. 'I've got to be honest, it choked me up a bit.'

'You and me both,' Molly said softly.

Her eyes shimmered and his heart flipped in response, as if it wanted to reach out to her. It was a dangerous sort of flip, because it told him he was sinking further into a relationship he wasn't sure he should even be starting. 'Can I go now?'

'And he's back,' Molly said, laughing. 'For a while there I thought there was an imposter inside Ben's body.'

'Of course you can go.' Natalie waved towards the door. 'Enjoy the next few weeks. We look forward to watching your progress.'

'What does she think we are, some sort of experiment?' he muttered as they started to walk back along the corridor.

'I guess we kind of are. Couples forced together in an artificial environment, monitored carefully, assessed after each trial. And you and I must be like a repeat experiment. Tried it once and failed, but let's give it another go and see if we get a different result.'

His heart somersaulted and he drew to a halt. 'Is that what we're doing, giving it another go?'

She stared back at him, her teeth biting into her bottom lip. 'I don't know. Maybe we're just having a couple of weeks with someone we know and still feel chemistry with, rather than risking two weeks with someone new and finding we can't stand them.'

'If we weren't here, if I'd met you again outside this show, I'd still want to date you.'

Her gaze flew to his. 'Really?'

'Yes, really.' It amazed him that she could think otherwise.

Her lips pursed together. 'But say this was a repeat experiment, and we wanted to get different results, we'd have to change some of the ... what's that word scientists use?'

'Variables?' He hazarded, trying to keep up.

'Yes, that's it. We'd need to change some of them.'

'I get the feeling you're now going to tell me what you want to change,' he commented dryly.

'I'm going to sound like a broken record, but you need to communicate more. And by that, I mean a *lot* more. Talk to me about how you feel, don't make me guess, even if you think this isn't working. In fact *especially* if you think that, so I don't feel like I'm walking off the edge of a cliff with a blindfold on.'

That's going to go well. Just look at what happened the last time you tried a relationship. He shoved the unhelpful thought aside. 'I'll try.'

Her gaze searched his. 'And what would need to change to make you less likely to ditch me and run?'

Every time, he thought wretchedly. Shame twisted in his gut, quickly followed by horror as he realised a wall-mounted camera was listening to every word. Taking her hand he led her back in the other direction, towards what he'd discovered was a small study. There he shut the door behind them and turned to face her.

Fuck, she was going to be the death of him, standing there with wary green eyes, freckles scattered across pale cheeks that looked so soft he ached to touch them.

'When we first met, it was intense.' He took a step forward and raised his hand, trailing a finger across those cheeks, feeling the bump of his heart as her breath hitched. 'I didn't know if it was real or if I was just running away from … from things.' Maybe one day he'd be able to tell her about it, but not now, not in a snatched moment. 'On some level I knew we were going too fast, too deep. It was why you never met my friends, my sister, but I couldn't stop. Being with you felt all-consuming, like if I paused, it would all vanish.' He paused and drew in a breath, afraid he wasn't making sense.

'Keep talking.' Molly's hand came up to cover his and he looked up to find her watching him carefully.

'It was only when I found those tickets, and I realised you were planning for us still to be together in three months, that I forced myself to take stock.' He rested his forehead against hers, hating himself all over again. 'I wasn't being fair to you.

In an awful way I was using you to forget what I was going through.' Her face twisted and she looked away, which caused a splinter in his chest. 'It doesn't mean I didn't have strong feelings for you,' he added roughly. 'If I hadn't, I would have found it much easier to call a halt on us.'

A long pause followed, during which his nerves felt as if they were being stretched to breaking point. Did she understand that there hadn't been anything easy or flippant about their time together? That he'd never intended to hurt her?

'And now?' She said finally, a vulnerability to her voice that ripped the splinter wider.

Gently, he cupped her face. 'I'm not running from anything.'

Chapter Twenty-Two

Molly clasped her hands together in delight as she looked out of the window. Admittedly it wasn't exactly turquoise, in fact it was definitely more grey than blue, but still…

'Look, we can see the sea!'

Ben glanced up from the notebook he was still scribbling in. Before it had annoyed her. Now she remembered this was who he was. Not a man who would chatter to her on the coach, but a man who would use the time to think, to put together plans. 'We're heading to Clacton, not the Caribbean.'

'It's still the seaside,' she protested. 'Waves, beach, ice cream, sand between our toes, seagulls pinching our chips. Oh and a pier, I think there's a pier. What's not to look forward to?'

He gave her a mild look. 'All of the above?'

She huffed out a breath. 'That's so negative. I'm sure you were more fun than this last time we dated. I seem to remember you being up for anything.'

His gaze locked with hers. 'Was I? Or was I just more into the ... activities we spent most of our time doing?'

A hot flush crept up her neck and over her face. Oh yes, she vividly remembered how their dates used to go. She'd spend hours agonising over which of her creations to wow him with, he'd come to pick her up. And three hours later they'd be undressed, in her bed, refuelling on pizza after a very *energetic* workout.

She was gripped by a sudden wave of melancholy.

'Molly?' He gave her a concerned look. 'What's wrong?'

'Nothing. I just remembered how happy I was then.' She bit into her lip, trying to keep her emotion in check. 'I can't actually recall ever being that happy before, or since.'

His gaze narrowed. 'Not even with Duncan?'

Embarrassed at what she'd just admitted, she turned to stare out of the window for a few beats before daring to look back at him. 'It was a false bubble though, wasn't it? You were enjoying the sex, the distraction. I was falling in love.'

He opened his mouth to say something, but then shut it again and sighed heavily. 'I told you.' He drew a hand down his face. 'My head was too fucked up at the time to make any sense of what I felt.'

But was he any more likely to fall for her this time round? Had choosing her just been an easy option to get him through the next two weeks?

The tannoy on the coach crackled into life, interrupting her dismal thoughts.

'Well, hello again, seekers of Happy Ever Afters.' Natalie's voice boomed over to them. 'Now we've moved into the second half of the show, the focus of our activities is going to change. Before, it was all about getting to know each other. Now it's all about deciding whether you want to marry the person you've been partnered with. Yes, that's it folks, you've got two weeks to decide if he or she is The One. Two weeks to decide if you want to say "I do" at the altar.' A mixed reaction echoed around the coach. A few gasps, a couple of giggles. Molly glanced at Ben, whose jaw was locked so tight she saw a muscle jump. 'With that in mind, this afternoon isn't just a trip to the seaside. It's a scavenger hunt where you'll get the chance to see how well you work together. Do you respect each other's opinion? Listen to each other or railroad over the other person's view because you think yours is more important?'

Ben shifted next to her. 'I've learnt from the Escape room,' he muttered.

Molly smirked. 'We'll see.'

'And now I want to remind you of the rules for this half of the show.' The coach fell silent and everyone, including Molly, stared back at Natalie, whose beaming smile was a strong indication she was enjoying their reaction. 'To increase the chance of genuine couples getting married at the end of the show, over the next two weeks not only will you still get the chance to ask to swop to another partner, the viewers will also get their say. If they don't feel you're heading for marriage, they can vote for you to be swopped to someone else, or even vote you off the show. We've set a threshold of votes for that to happen, but even if the threshold isn't met, depending on the number of votes received, we may decide to mix you up for an activity, if it's felt you'd have better chemistry with someone else.'

Molly shook her head, smiling. 'I love this part; it's so wicked. I mean it's exciting too, but wicked.'

Ben frowned. 'You think the thought of us being swopped is *exciting*?'

'I was thinking as a viewer.' She wouldn't be sitting on her comfy sofa watching the finale to this season, though. She'd be walking down the aisle, to the altar. Millions of people watching her. The potential for humiliation wasn't just huge. It was overwhelming.

Holy shit, what the hell had she been thinking, deciding to stick with Ben?

'Molly?' She turned to find Ben looking worriedly at her. 'You've gone pale. Are you okay?'

'Yes, fine.' *Just contemplating how I'm going to be able to hold my head up outside the show after being turned down at the altar by the man who's already dumped me once.* She turned to face him. 'You do realise if we survive as a couple, we're going to have to plan our wedding at the end of this?'

If her face had gone pale, his was chalky. 'It's beginning to sink in, yes.'

'I actually came on this show in the hope of getting married. To Duncan.' She let out a strangled laugh. 'Whereas you came on here just to help out your sister.' The more she thought about it, the more her stomach began to churn. 'We've come into this from two massively different perspectives. Do you even *want* to get married someday?'

His Adam's apple bobbed as he swallowed. She'd never seen him look more uncomfortable. 'I haven't spent much time thinking about it.'

'Whereas I've spent what is probably an unhealthy amount of time thinking about it.'

He didn't say anything for a full minute. Simply sat there, watching her, so many emotions crossing his face it was impossible to pin any of them down. 'We do have one vital thing in common,' he said finally. 'We both agreed we wanted to spend the next two weeks together.'

'I guess so.'

He searched her eyes, the brown and greens swirling, as if they were mirroring his troubled thoughts. 'Can that be enough for now? We've got time to work out the rest.'

She drew in a breath, forced her shoulders to relax. She was racing ahead to the end, when there was a whole middle still to look forward to. 'Yes, fine.'

He gave her a tight smile and shifted his focus back to his book. Silence descended between them, but it felt uncomfortable now. A major flaw had been exposed and it was hard to pretend it wasn't there. 'What are you working on?' He glanced up again, then back to his notes. 'Is it top secret?' she prompted. 'You're not allowed to tell me or you'll have to kill me? Or maybe you'll have to eat the notebook now, because I might sneak a peek at it later when you're not looking.'

He exhaled loudly. 'It's not secret.'

'Well then, come on, tell me.'

'I thought you were excited about seeing the sea.'

'I am, but we're not there yet, so you need to entertain me.'

He quirked a brow. 'Is that in the show rules? I have to entertain the woman I'm partnered with?'

'Totally in the rules. You should have a word with your sister if she didn't point that out to you. Very poor on her behalf. Now tell me what you've been doodling for the last hour.'

He sighed again. 'I've not been doodling.'

Finally, with great reluctance, he handed the book over to her. And her heart thumped when she saw the word upcycling outlined in a box, with arrows leading from it. *Vintage Style, Upcycled Chic, ReNew*. 'Is that... Are you...' *Don't assume anything, that's what got you in trouble last time.* 'Are you planning a new business?'

Another quirk of that brow and, damn, she wished it didn't make her insides go all squirmy. 'What do you think?'

'I think, maybe, you're planning *my* business?'

She'd meant it light-heartedly, but his face fell, his brow crinkling. 'No, nothing like that. It's your idea to do what you want with, *if* you want.' He nodded over to the notebook. 'This is just me doing a brain dump of everything you'd need to consider, if you wanted to pursue it. And if you wanted my help.'

She glanced over the pages, read words like register company, vision, business plan, budget. Then turned it over and saw more words, mind maps. 'Oh my God, Ben. This is ... amazing.' She willed herself not to read too much into it – setting up companies was what he did – but her heart couldn't help but turn a little bit mushy at all this effort on her behalf. 'Seriously. I process orders for car parts. I haven't the first clue about setting up a business, so when I do this, I'll really need some help.'

The corner of his mouth lifted. '*When?*'

'Yes.' Nerves battled with excitement. It felt important saying it out loud. More real than it had in her head. 'I did a lot of thinking after the fete, and I realised this is one occasion that you're right. I am good at upcycling clothes.'

'You are.' His smile was so encouraging, so fond, it made her heart flutter. 'And I like to be proved right.'

'I'll need to go back to my old job while I set things up, but I'm going to give it a try. Who knows, maybe I can be a business owner too.'

'I know you can,' he countered, voice so full of confidence, it made her feel a foot taller. 'The fete was your success, not mine. You're more than capable of doing it again, on a larger scale.' He looked back down at the notebook, then let out a slow breath. 'I hope whatever happens over the next few weeks, at the very least you and I will leave here as friends. And that you'll allow me to help you.' His eyes held hers. 'I don't want to lose you again.'

As her heart began to open up for him, like a flower responding to sunlight, everything she'd told herself about being careful felt like foolish nonsense.

Either Clacton-on-Sea was a hidden gem, a boast even its own tourist information didn't dare claim, or places felt very different when explored with someone who was … enthusiastic.

'Come on, next item to tick off is a photo of ourselves with something dodgy.' A broad smile lit up Molly's face. 'I know, we can do that at the pier.'

She grabbed his hand and started to tug him towards what looked to be a fairground on wonky looking stilts. 'You're right, that does look dodgy.'

She rolled her eyes. 'The pier isn't dodgy, it has *dodgems*. Get it? *Dodgy, dodgems*, it has to be close enough. This way we get to cross an item off the list *and* have fun riding them.'

'Even better,' he countered dryly.

Dodgems, piers, scavenger hunts. It wasn't him. *Just like marriage isn't you.* No, he wasn't going to think about that conversation in the coach. He had weeks … okay, two of them, to shift through his emotions and work out a way to talk to her about it.

Yeah, because he was so good at that. Discomfort rocked through him. He'd thought convincing her to give him another two weeks was the hardest part over, but his troubles were only just starting.

'It was named pier of the year in 2020.' Oblivious to his meltdown, Molly chatted away as they made their way along the seafront. 'If that doesn't say a pier not to be missed, I don't know what does. Ooh, look they have hot doughnuts. We have to get some.'

'This from the woman who wouldn't share wings with me two weeks ago.'

'Oh.' Her smile deflated. 'I forgot how bad they are for you. Maybe I'll just look at them. Smell them.'

She had to be kidding him. 'Why wouldn't you just eat one?'

'Err, didn't you hear the bit about them being bad for you?'

'I heard it, but it's not like they're part of your staple diet. If you want one, have one.'

'Yeah, it doesn't work like that. Not when you have a shape like mine.'

Anger simmered. What bullshit had Duncan been giving her? 'You mean like a real woman?' He took her hand, tugged her to him, then slid a hand over her bum, feeling himself harden. 'With curves I spend my nights fantasising about?' Her hips pushed against him, causing more pressing against his zipper, and he groaned. 'Unless you want to see me charged with lewd behaviour, you need to stop that.'

'Then stop fondling my bum.'

With a wicked smile, she stepped back and he looked away from her and out to the sea, willing his body to calm the hell down. 'Are you having the doughnut or not?'

'If you'll have half.' She threaded her arm through his. 'Because everyone knows a calorie shared, is a calorie that didn't really get eaten.'

Thank You, Next

He wasn't a fan of anything sweet, or sugary. 'Fine.' He nodded to the sign outside the kiosk. 'They come in threes.'

She shrugged, like it was a no brainer. 'Two for you, one for me. Sharing a bag is still sharing.'

Now he was eating two doughnuts he didn't want.

Yet when he watched her lick the sugar off her lips a few minutes later, he found himself utterly converted to the things.

Munching through her second huge bite, she eyed him curiously. 'Aren't you eating yours?'

'Yes.' His voice came out rough and he had to clear it before he could continue. 'But first I'll enjoy watching you eat yours.'

She grinned, and that didn't just hit his groin, it hit him in the chest.

'Molly, what on earth are you eating?'

Ben froze as he recognised the male voice. When he looked to his right, he found Jasmine and Duncan staring at them, Duncan with a horrified expression on his face.

Molly paused mid-chew, like she'd been caught stealing sweets from a kid rather than eating a blasted doughnut.

'Wow, there's like a billion calories in that,' Jasmine whispered.

Molly swallowed her mouthful. 'Half a billion.' She grabbed the bag from Ben and slid the other half of the doughnut into it. 'Not that it matters.'

'Of course it matters,' Duncan interrupted. 'Your health is important to me.'

Molly's expression softened and Ben was hit with a surge of jealousy. 'Don't worry, I've not forgotten everything you taught me,' she told Duncan. 'I'm just relaxing the rules a bit.'

'Well, don't relax them too much or you'll be back to how you were when we first met.'

Molly's cheeks turned a furious shade of red. 'What do you mean?'

Ben clasped his hand around hers, squeezing her fingers gently in a show of solidarity. He wanted to butt in and tell Duncan to piss off, but this wasn't his battle and Molly was holding her own.

Jasmine giggled. 'I think Duncan's worried the before and after video might be a bit shit. You know, like before and still before.'

Molly's hand went rigid in his. 'What video?'

Duncan looked daggers at Jasmine before raising his eyes briefly to the heavens. 'No big deal. I was hoping to make a case study of you. Thought you'd like it, be proud of your transformation.'

'And when were you going to tell me about this plan?' She inhaled sharply. 'Wait, that means you already have *before* photos?'

For the first time, Duncan looked uncomfortable. 'You remember us doing those exercises together, babe.'

'But that was for me. So I could see how unfit I was.'

'Sure, but I figured we could use it in a promo video when you reached your target shape.'

Molly's eyes widened, and her fingers gripped Ben's harder. 'What target shape?'

'The shape you wanted to be.' Duncan's focus shifted to Ben. 'The shape that would help bring back your self-confidence after he decimated it.'

A mix of both anger and shame roared through Ben and it took every ounce of his self-control not to lunge at Duncan.

'I thought you were giving me all this advice to improve my health because you loved me,' Molly said quietly, her voice wavering. 'Not so you could make some promo video out of me.'

As if he realised he was losing the battle, Duncan stepped forward and reached out his hand. Ben didn't know what he planned on doing with it, but he'd had enough. 'You don't get to put your hands anywhere near her,' he bit out, grasping Duncan's wrist.

Duncan snatched his hand back, his face like thunder. 'After what you did to her, you shouldn't be putting your hands on her either.'

And fuck, his self-control was slipping fast, but now the anger came with a heavy dose of gut-churning guilt.

'I *was* looking after your health because I loved you,' Duncan told Molly before Ben could gather his wits enough to deliver a stinging reply. 'I thought the videos would help show your transformation. Make you as proud of yourself as I was of you.' He shifted his hands to his hips. 'I'm not the bad guy here, Moll. About time you remembered that.' Turning to Jasmine, Duncan slipped an arm around her waist. 'Come on, babe, let's go somewhere less crowded.'

Silence echoed in their wake. Seagulls squawked above, waves lapped against the shore, chatter surrounded them, but between Ben and Molly there was only an awkward, tense stillness.

'What guy in love tries to get their girlfriend to exercise, to eat the right food, just so they can make a video to promote themselves?' Molly whispered finally. 'Shouldn't he have wanted me for who I was, not for the person he wanted to change me to?'

'I want you,' Ben told her hoarsely, wiping away a stray tear with his thumb. 'I want you for who you are now, and who you were when I met you. I hate that I ever made you feel I *didn't* want you.' But even as he said the words, guilt squirmed through him. He wanted her, yes, but could he ever see himself marrying her? And would she even want to be with him if she knew how badly he'd failed the last woman he'd been in a relationship with?

Her gaze fell to the floor. 'I seem to have an unfortunate track record of thinking people love me and then finding they don't.'

'You've been let down, Molly,' he told her roughly, his chest tightening viciously as he realised Duncan wasn't the only culprit. 'That's not on you.'

'Maybe.' She swallowed and looked down at the greasy bag of doughnuts in her hand. 'Do you think we can use these for the "something slimy"?'

He smiled, pushing his worries aside for another time. 'I think they can do slimy and doughy.'

'It's meant to be dodgy.'

'Doughy is two letters closer to dodgy than your dodgems,' he pointed out, enjoying her answering laughter.

Just when he thought the worse was over, he caught sight of Natalie, Rachel and the camera crew heading towards them.

Chapter Twenty-Three

Molly saw Ben's expression tighten, and heard his heavy sigh. Turning to see what he was looking at, her heart sank.

She didn't mind talking to Natalie, to the cameras. She didn't mind *talking*. But right now she felt horribly vulnerable. Duncan's admission about the video had made her question her judgement all over again. Had encouraging her to exercise and watch her diet been his way of showing her he loved her? The video a way to demonstrate his pride in what she'd achieved?

Or had he never really cared for her as much as he cared for his career?

'Oh dear, you guys don't look like you're enjoying your scavenger hunt,' Natalie exclaimed as she neared them. Today's outfit, a bold blue and white striped flowing dress, was surely chosen precisely because it looked like a deckchair. 'What's happened? Are you coming unstuck working together as a couple, like you did in the Escape room?'

Molly saw Ben having some silent brother-to-sister

communication with Rachel. If she had to guess, he was telling her to leave them alone. Rachel gave him a sharp shake of the head, which she didn't need to be a sibling to work out meant this was her job. Suck it up.

'We're working together just fine,' Ben replied, his jaw tight.

'We bumped into Duncan and Jasmine,' Molly told Natalie. 'And I found out Duncan was making a before and after video of me to show my improved fitness. He says it was because he was proud of me, but he did it without consulting me, which makes me wonder if anything with him was real.' She twisted her hands together. 'And that in turn makes me realise how bad I am at reading guys.' *People*, she amended silently, remembering her mum.

Beside her, Ben exhaled loudly.

Natalie turned to him. 'Do you have anything to add, Ben?'

'She should be blaming the guys. Not herself.' He nodded towards the end of the pier. 'Now please excuse us. We have the delight of the dodgems to look forward to.'

Despite her misery, Molly found herself spluttering with laughter. 'He hates them,' she explained to Natalie. 'I remember this one day when we were dating before, and I said I wanted to go to the fair. Ben told me he could think of a hundred better things to do.' Her belly fluttered at the memory. He hadn't quite managed a hundred, but it had been one heck of a valiant attempt.

'And I was right,' he cut in quietly.

The husk in his voice ensured everyone knew exactly what his suggestions had involved and she felt herself blush.

'How many more items have you got to do on your list?' Natalie asked, thankfully shifting the conversation along.

Molly glanced down. 'We need to find seaweed, a heart-shaped rock and partake in a water sport.'

'What?'

At Ben's worried look, she giggled. 'I've got a great idea for that. Something that will really show how well we work in a team.'

He narrowed his eyes. 'As long as I'm the one in the boat and you're the one on the water skis.'

Natalie laughed and waved them away. 'We'll get the cameras ready, good luck.'

They started to walk away but Ben stilled and turned round. 'How are the other couples doing?'

Natalie gave him a knowing smile. 'One couple only have two more items to tick off.'

He muttered something that sounded a lot like *fucking typical*, under his breath, but as they walked towards the fair at the end of the pier, and away from the camera, his body lost some of its tension.

She glanced sideways at him. 'Why are we heading to the dodgems?'

'I thought you wanted to go on them?'

'I want to beat the other couples more,' she countered, taking his hand and steering him instead towards the beach. 'Did you mean what you said back there?'

'About that fact you should blame me and Duncan rather than yourself? You know I do.'

She nodded, eyes out towards the sea. 'Sometimes I think it is my fault though.' Her voice faltered. No, she wasn't going to cry.

His hand squeezed round hers. 'Your fault, how?'

The concern in his eyes made her heart trip. 'There are people who must be easy to love, like … the purple chocolate in the Quality Street box. You know, the one filled with hazelnut and caramel. Everyone loves them. And then there are the people who are more difficult to love, like the toffee.'

He halted, turning to face her, his brow crinkled. 'You think you're the toffee?'

'Maybe? And I'm not saying that to get you to feel sorry for me, because just like the toffee, there will be people who love me, like my parents, well, my adopted ones. They love me.'

'You're adopted?'

Damn, why had she mentioned the word adopted?

'Molly?'

She took a step away. 'Sure, I'm adopted, but so what, loads of kids are, and my new mum and dad love me, so it's all good.' Making sure he didn't ask any further questions, she threaded her hand through his arm. 'Come on, we need to get those items crossed off.'

He resisted a moment, eyes searching her face, and she was afraid he saw more than she wanted him to. 'For the record, the toffee is my favourite.'

Her heart gave a joyful jump. 'You're kidding me.'

His eyes never wavered from hers. 'I never kid about Quality Street.'

'Umm, you said that about business,' she reminded him. 'When we were at that fete.'

'I'm allowed two things I don't joke about.'

'Sure, because you're such a laugh a minute about everything else.' But inside a little bubble of happiness floated in her chest.

'So what's this idea about the water sport?' he asked when they stepped onto the beach.

She grinned and ran down to the sea. There she pulled off her socks and trainers and rolled up her jeans. 'Come on. We're going to paddle. Nothing says water sport like two people paddling.'

He looked unconvinced. 'Where does the sport come in?'

'Come in and find out.'

She waited until he'd waded in, then took out her phone and snapped a photo of him a second after she gave him a gentle shove.

Dinner, cooked by Chloe and her new partner Liam, who was so ridiculously full on he made Molly seem quiet, had been average. Having food prepared by people who didn't know their way around a kitchen, then eating it with people he didn't particularly want to spend time with ... Ben added it to the long list of things he would not miss about this place when he left.

Sitting beside him at the table, Molly gave him a little smile, like she knew what he was thinking.

'What?'

She leaned in, and his Molly-awareness radar pinged into hypersensitive mode – *she smells so good, look at those awesome breasts, the curve of that bum*. Even being dunked in the sea wasn't enough to quell it. 'You can't wait to disappear to your room.'

'Not true.' It wasn't his room he wanted to go to. At least not by himself.

She gave him a shrewd look. 'You're up for the darts tournament?'

'If you're staying, I'm staying.'

'What brought this on? You normally disappear.'

'I'm not risking you being swopped to someone else.' The

thought of Duncan getting a day with her, maybe the rest of the show with her, filled him with fear. From the way the man kept glancing at her, Ben knew Duncan would use every opportunity he could to persuade Molly that he was still the same good guy she'd fallen in love with. The one she'd come on the show to marry.

There was that word again. Ben had spent two weeks convincing himself Duncan was the arsehole, but was he, really? Wasn't the real arsehole the man who'd convinced Molly to give him another chance, yet still hadn't told her why he wasn't a good bet? And who was utterly petrified by the thought of standing with her in front of an altar in two weeks' time?

Glad of the distraction, even if it was darts, Ben took Molly's hand as they walked with the others to the games room.

Molly, it turned out, was awful at darts, yet nobody would have guessed from watching her. Her face lit up every time she managed to hit the board.

'You're aiming for inside the circle,' he murmured when she leapt up and down after another enthusiastic effort.

'I know that, but first I have to get it on the board, and I just did that so go me.'

He couldn't argue with the logic.

When it came to Molly's next turn, it wasn't logic he wanted to argue with, it was James. The man suddenly appeared behind her, and by behind, he meant *right* behind, his body wrapped around her, her bum tucked against his groin. 'Here, Molly, you need to angle your shoulder, elbow and hand so it's at ninety degrees.'

Before he knew it, Ben had shot out of his seat. 'I'll show her.'

James laughed. 'Woah, feeling a bit possessive, are we?'

'Yes.'

His voice must have held an edge, because the room fell silent, all eyes on them. Included the blasted cameras.

James cleared his throat and stepped back. 'No worries. I just wanted to help.'

Ben took his place, slotting himself around her curves, and slowly felt his blood cool from the raging jealousy into a more manageable, heated desire. 'Sorry,' he whispered into the shell of her ear.

'What for?'

'I think I caused a scene.'

Her hair feathered against his chin as she nodded. 'It's okay. I'd rather have you show me how to do it.'

'Confession time,' he told her as he tried to straighten her elbow as James had shown her. 'I don't play darts.'

He felt her body vibrate with laughter as she took the shot, which predictably missed the board. As did the next one. And the one after that.

'You need a better teacher,' James yelled over.

Molly smiled. 'Or maybe the teacher needs a better pupil.'

'Nah, you need to be guided by someone with the right technique.' James waggled his eyebrows suggestively.

'She's never had an issue with my technique,' Ben countered, unreasonably irritated. James was being James, trying to provoke him. So why couldn't he let it slide?

'She just has an issue with how you play with her emotions, eh Moll?' Darts in hand, Duncan sauntered up to the throwing line. 'How you lead her on when you've no intention of having a real relationship with her.' He pinned Ben with his gaze. 'No intention of *marrying* her.'

For the second time that evening, the room went quiet.

You're a fine one to talk about leading her on, he wanted to fire back, but the truth of Duncan's last few words gnawed away at him, leaving a raw, angry wound. He wanted the relationship, desperately, but marriage? He was kidding himself and lying to Molly if he thought he could go through with that.

'I don't need you to fight my battles,' Molly told Duncan stiffly. 'You lost that right when you decided that being on this show was more important than being with me.'

Duncan looked put out. 'Come on, that's not how it went down.'

'It's exactly how it went down.' She turned to Ben. 'I'm going to call it a night. I'm feeling really tired.'

'I'll walk you up.'

'Maybe you were right and we should have disappeared to our rooms straight after dinner,' she said as they climbed the stairs.

'I don't think so.'

She darted him a confused look. 'You enjoyed the darts?'

'I enjoyed teaching you darts.'

'But you didn't; you don't know how to play … oh.'

They came to a halt outside her room and immediately the air turned thick with sexual tension. Standing in the way of the camera, Ben stared down at her, feeling his heart crash against his ribs. The top she wore was cut low enough he could see the curve of her breasts, and immediately his head filled with erotic images of what he wanted to do with those breasts. What he *had* done with them, before he'd thrown away that right. With a huge effort he dragged his gaze upwards, but that wasn't helpful because it landed on her mouth, on the lips he knew would be soft and yielding beneath his.

Angling his head, he bent to kiss her. A light, testing, press.

She moaned, or had it come from him?

'Fuck.' He dragged in a ragged breath. 'I don't know if I can walk away.' His eyes raked hers, seeing the same war going on in her. She wanted him, yet she was also scared. And damn if she wasn't right to be scared. 'Tell me to go.'

Her teeth settled into her lower lip. 'I'm not sure I can.'

This time he knew the groan came from him. 'I shouldn't be here, thinking what I'm thinking.'

'What are you thinking?'

There was a breathless rasp to her voice that tied him in knots. 'I'm thinking of all the ways I want to take you.'

'But?' She whispered, as if she sensed his internal battle.

'*But* I fucking hate that Duncan might be right. That I'll start something I'm not capable of finishing.'

'I've never had a problem finishing with you.'

The reminder only served to harden him further. 'That's not what I meant.'

She gave him a sad smile. 'I know.'

He should walk away. She needed to trust him not to let her down, and yet here he was, rapidly heading towards doing exactly that.

But. His legs wouldn't work. Instead of moving him away, they took a step closer, so he was pressed against her. 'Just one kiss,' he whispered, making a promise he wasn't convinced he could deliver on.

Her tongue darted out, wetting her lips. Then she nodded, and it was game over.

Years of abstinence, two weeks of simmering sexual frustration, being around Molly and not being able to touch her like he wanted to, surged to the surface and his mouth crashed down on hers, tongue seeking her heat as if it had never left, tasting, remembering, tasting again.

'Fuck,' he whispered hoarsely. 'I'd forgotten how sweet you taste.'

It was like coming home, yet experiencing the most thrilling night of his life, all rolled into one. Achingly familiar, but also his most erotic fantasy played out for real. With practised ease his thigh slotted between her legs, hands drifting from her face to smooth down her arms and then lower, to curve round her bum and pull her more tightly against him.

More. He needed more friction against his throbbing erection, more of her curves in his hands, the touch of her skin against his.

You can't do this. Not until you've been honest with her.

But his blood was too hot, his need too great and he dropped his hips, getting the friction he needed, feeling her heat through the fabric of his jeans.

Are you really going to blindside her again?

Damn it, he did not need his conscience interfering right now. With an anguished groan he drew away, breath coming out in shallow pants as he tried to get his libido under control.

Her husky whimper didn't help dampen the fire, nor did her look of disappointment. Before she could read anything else into his action, he took her face in his hands. 'I didn't want to stop.'

Her gaze jumped to his. 'Me neither.' She released a slow, choppy sounding breath. 'But it's good that you did. Really good,' she added, and it sounded liked she was trying to convince herself. 'You and me having sex would not be a wise idea.'

'Not what my body is telling me right now.'

She let out a strangled laugh. 'Nor mine. But my oxytocin levels thank you.' He frowned and she gave him a wry smile. 'I read it somewhere that women release nearly eight times more oxytocin than men after sex, and that makes us trust too quickly. At least that's what the article said, and that's not really helpful for me, so…'

'I get it.' More than she knew. With a heavy heart he traced a finger along her jaw, and around the sweet curve of her mouth before giving her a gentle kiss. 'Goodnight.'

As he walked back to his room, the ache in his body was nothing to the ache in his chest. Molly was so forgiving, so warm and open … but she was vulnerable, too. All that crap about the toffee. She thought she was hard to love, when in reality falling in love with her would be the easiest thing in the world.

And God, he was already halfway there, but she'd been right in the coach. They were coming at this from two hugely different perspectives. He wanted a chance at a relationship with her. She wanted a man who would be prepared to marry her, turn himself over to her. Tie himself to her legally. If he had no intention of doing that, he had to back off, now, or he'd be repeating all of his past mistakes.

Dating you was just a giant guessing game.

We're left in limbo land, trying to use his actions as clues. Which can result in wrong assumptions.

So far, his actions had put him on a path to meeting her at the altar.

Bleakly he realised there was only one real option left to him. He had to *talk* to her. Rip apart the darkest, tightly stitched up parts of him and open them up for her judgement.

The thought sent his stomach rolling.

Chapter Twenty-Four

Standing in the rear gardens of HEA Towers, Molly looked out across the giant inflatable obstacle course that had been hired for the day's activity. 'I thought this would be cool when they told us about it this morning, but now I'm not sure.'

Beside her, Ben scratched his chin. 'What part are you not sure about? Climbing up the inflatable ladders? Falling off the giant slide? Being hit by the bouncy balls?' He glanced sideways at her. 'Or trusting me to help you over it?'

Trust was the buzzword of the day. Marriage was about trust, so the day was designed to see how much trust they had in each other, as they would take it in turns to be blindfolded.

She desperately wanted to trust Ben, but there were parts of him she didn't know, parts he kept tightly buttoned up. He'd made it clear his body wanted her, but what was going on in his head, and in his heart?

'*Should* I trust you?'

He flinched and refused to look at her. 'You should trust that I don't want to hurt you.'

'Is that why you pulled away last night?'

She was pinned with a look from hazel eyes that swirled with emotions she couldn't identify. 'Yes.'

'You know we nearly got split up today.' The scavenger hunt had been aired last night. They'd come last, so a lot of people had voted to shake up their pairing, though not enough to make the threshold. 'I could be doing this with Duncan.' Most of the votes had gone to pair the two of them up. Were they right? Should she have chosen the man who'd openly spoken about marrying her, rather than the man who continued to make her play guessing games?

'I know.' He swore under his breath. 'Sorry, I realise I need to communicate better, but it's harder than I thought. Fact is, there are things I should have told you before I started kissing you.'

'Oh, okay.' *What things?* 'Is this to do with Helena?'

His jaw tightened. 'Yes.'

'You know what I loved about Duncan?'

Ben snapped his head round. 'He talked to you.'

'It's more than that. I knew where I stood with him. Even when he broke up with me to go on this show, he was upfront about why he was doing it.'

'Like he was upfront about the videos?'

She reeled back. 'Wow, you're not prepared to talk to me about subjects that are hard for you, but you're quite happy to raise things that are hard for me?'

His lids slammed over his eyes, and he muttered something under his breath which sounded like *what the fuck am I doing*, but she wasn't certain. Even if it had been, she didn't know if he meant what was he doing agreeing to clamber over inflatable obstacles, or what was he doing on the show. Or what was he doing with her.

When he turned to look at her again, his expression looked

haggard. 'Sorry, that was below the belt. I'm just ... I'm jealous of him, so jealous it twists me up inside and turns me into a colossal, insensitive prick. It's up to me to prove I'm a better choice. I know that.'

Silence stretched between them again, sticky, awkward. 'Have you done one of these obstacle things before?' she said finally, sensing they both needed a change of subject.

He shifted his hands into the pocket of his shorts. 'Not this sort.'

'You mean not the bouncy sort,' she filled in, wondering what he might look like on a rugged, military-style course. Sweat making his muscles gleam, those strong, sexy legs covered in splashes of mud, which he'd then have to clean off with a long soak in a shower. Water streaming down his chest as tanned skin slid over hard muscles...

Arousal coiled, tightening her core, making her knees week. Oh God, thinking like this was bad. Really, really bad. 'I've not done a course like this either.' She swallowed convulsively, trying to get rid of the tightness in her throat. 'I thought it would be shorter, somehow. More fun, less hard work.'

Molly heard a chuckle and turned to find Duncan had come to stand next to her. 'Come on, Moll, climbing over a few inflatable obstacles isn't hard work. Not now we've got you fit.'

We? What happened to him being proud of what *she'd* achieved?

Ben's hand curled reassuringly around hers, but his focus was on Duncan. 'Want to make this interesting?'

Duncan eyed him sharply. 'What are you thinking?'

'Loser does kitchen duty for the winners.'

'Hang on.' Molly tugged on Ben's hand. 'Shouldn't we discuss this before you go making bets on my behalf?'

'I thought you wanted to get out of kitchen duty?'

'Well yes, but...' Had he mistaken her for some sort of ninja? Reaching up on her tiptoes she whispered into his ear. 'We'd need to win. Against *Duncan*.'

Ben ignored her and held his hand out towards Duncan. 'Let's shake on it.'

Duncan laughed as they shook hands. 'Hope you like cooking 'cos you're going to be doing a lot of it.'

Molly watched him swagger off, then turned to find Ben frowning at her.

'You think we can't beat Duncan over a few plastic obstacles, even blindfolded?'

'It's not just you,' she pointed out. 'It's me as well. And it might have escaped your attention but this body is not made for flexibility, or speed, or skipping over hurdles.'

'Your body is perfect. Jasmine looks like she might fall over if we blow on her,' he added dismissively while she was still basking at the first four words. 'And Duncan has underrated how well we work as a team.'

'He has?' She had to fight not to giggle. 'I don't remember us working that well in the Escape room. Or the scavenger hunt. In fact I seem to recall they beat us.'

Ben's jaw set in a stubborn line. 'We've learnt since then.'

'You mean you're going to listen to me this time? *Trust* me?'

'Obviously.' His jaw jutted. 'Just make sure we win.'

Ben didn't know what had possessed him to make the damn bet. Actually that was wrong, he knew. He hated the way Duncan had talked down to Molly, insisting the course wasn't hard, that somehow he'd made her fit. And fine, he also hated the nicknames he used and the implied dig that he had a special relationship with her.

Buried beneath all that, like a dark cloud that hovered over him, was the knowledge he had to talk to her about Helena. Wiping the smirk off Duncan's face would at least help him forget that for a few hours.

'I'm feeling kind of nervous,' Molly whispered as they stood at the start line.

She looked adorable with her blindfold on, and Christ, those tiny sports shorts she was wearing made him hard every time he looked at her. 'Don't be. We've got this.'

She groaned. 'Please don't tell me you've been getting the lowdown on how to set a record time. Like your supposedly foolproof tips on the Escape room.'

'Of course not.' He'd tried, but the team in charge of the course had looked at him as if he was deranged. Apparently it was a fun, team building exercise, mainly hired out to companies.

'Go!'

To his shock, at the starter's instruction, Molly ran out in front of him. He watched in amazement as she began to clamber up the first obstacle like a blind Queen Boudica on speed.

Okay then, this was on.

They ducked, dived and scrambled over the course, Ben guiding Molly from behind, mainly so he could watch her bum.

At one particularly high climb up the slide, she huffed. 'Come on, give me a push.' Clamping down his baser instincts, he put his hands decorously on her hips and attempted to hoist her. 'Stop being a gentleman. Get your hands on my bum and give me a shove,' she shouted.

It was absolutely what was needed, yet when his hands made contact with the backside he'd been ogling all afternoon, the same one he had wild, erotic dreams about, his body totally forgot they were in the middle of a race.

'Ben!' Once over the obstacle, she ripped off her blindfold. Cheeks flushed, red hair coming out of its haphazard ponytail, she looked daggers at him. 'Stop daydreaming, put your blindfold on and get your arse over here.'

Quietly adjusting his hard-on, he tied on the blindfold, leaving a little gap because he wasn't stupid, and clambered up over the wall to join her, as instructed.

He couldn't have told anyone what the rest of the course involved. Only that every time she held his hand to guide him, every time she put her hands anywhere on him, he went willingly wherever she wanted him to go. All the while imagining those hands on him for another purpose. Undressing him, touching him, feeling him.

By the time they reached the finish line, he was a hot, horny mess.

'We beat their time!' Molly's arms wrapped around him, crushing her breasts against his chest as her laughter rippled in a breathy gush against his neck. 'Go us, we don't have to make dinner.' Still plastered against him, she drew back, whipped his blindfold off and peered up at him. 'Why aren't you more excited?'

'I am.' Unconsciously he pushed his hips closer to hers, and her eyes widened.

'Oh.'

'Yes. Oh.' Her lithe warm body rubbed against his, the fruity scent of whatever it was she washed her hair with streaming up his nose, invading his senses … it was the most exquisite torture.

'Should I move away, or...'

'*Or*,' he replied tightly, hands on her hips to keep her in place. 'Sorry. Just ... give me a minute.' Though he had no clue how he was going to solve the situation if he didn't get far, far away from her.

'I've got a better idea.' She slid round so her back faced him, her bum now against his groin which didn't help the situation one little bit. Taking hold of his hand, she whispered, 'stick with me.'

Frankly, he was at the stage where he'd follow her anywhere.

'Hey, impressive circuit,' Marcus called over as they shuffled past him and Maya.

'Thanks.' He pushed his hips against Molly and muttered, 'Keep going.'

She led them part way down the garden to a small summer house. 'We can wait in here while ... you know.'

They stepped inside and Ben found it impossible to take his eyes off Molly, and his mind off sex. How could he when they were now alone in an intimate space? And when she looked so fucking sexy, all dishevelled, glistening with sweat and dressed in those damn tiny shorts.

Sexual tension hung heavy in the air, a billion sparks pinging between them, sending prickles racing over his skin. When her gaze dropped to the 'tent' in his shorts and her teeth sank into her lower lip, he was done for.

With one step he drew right up against her again, his mouth zeroing in on hers, his hands reaching to clutch the bum that had been driving him mad all day.

He knew it was wrong. Anyone could come past, hell, even a camera crew. Plus there were conversations to be had, and Molly deserved more than a frantic fumble in a garden shed.

But fuck, he couldn't stop. The ache was too painful, his need too great.

And she wasn't pushing him away. Oh no, she was pressing her hips in tight circles against his erection, the friction sending spirals of pleasure coiling through him. Her mouth was eager, too, her tongue tangling with his, her hands running up and down his back before sliding to his buttocks, squeezing, eliciting a guttural sound from him.

'Should stop,' he muttered, his hand pushing under her T-shirt and finding smooth skin. 'Christ, I'd forgotten how soft you feel.'

'You're not soft,' she muttered, half laughing, half moaning when he pushed her against the wall and ground his hips into her.

This felt too good, his control shot to pieces. Determined that if he was going to come in his shorts like a hormonal teenager, he wouldn't be the only one falling over the edge, he broke away from kissing her mouth to drag off her T-shirt and push up her bra. 'Spectacular,' he whispered reverentially, dipping his head to kiss the skin of her cleavage, then further to take a rose-coloured nipple into his mouth.

'Oh God.' Molly's hands clutched at his head. 'More.'

His own needs were forgotten as he realised he had a higher need, a higher purpose. To make this incredible, sexy, responsive woman detonate in his arms. Three years ago he'd been able to do that, had almost enjoyed watching her release more than his own.

'Like this?' he whispered, moving to give her left breast attention while using his fingers to play with the nipple of her right. 'You used to love me playing with your breasts, didn't you?'

'Ben.' Her voice was muffled against his neck, her hips

thrusting mindlessly against the hard ridge of his fly. 'Oh God, oh God, oh God.' Suddenly she stiffened, then sagged against him on a long, strangled moan. 'Sooooo good.'

Satisfaction burned through him and he held her limp body tight in his arms, hearing her breathing slowly quieten, her heart begin to slow. Enough, he thought. Seeing the pleasure bloom across her face, was enough.

Chapter Twenty-Five

She'd forgotten how all-consuming, how overwhelming it was, being with Ben. Either that, or she'd pushed it out of her memory, determined to get on with her life, to embrace love, sex with another man. And sex with Duncan had been fine. Good, on occasions.

But with Ben ... how could he create such an erotic thrill with only his mouth on her breast, his erection rubbing against her core? Yet from the hoarsely muttered words in her ear, the sounds he made, it was like he'd been the one receiving all the pleasure, despite the fact she could feel his erection hard against her thigh.

Mind still fuzzy with passion, she reached inside his shorts to curl her fingers around his heavy length, re-familiarising herself with his shape, his feel. Remembering how flipping big he was. 'We haven't achieved our objective.'

He groaned, his breath whispering across her ear on a hot exhale. 'It's not going to go down if you keep doing that.'

'Condom?' And no, that wasn't a selfless request. The weight of him pushing into her hand, his big body taut with desire ... memories she'd tried to bury flooded back. She wanted to feel him move inside her again. Wanted the mind-blowing passion that only he seemed able to elicit from her.

Sod oxytocin, she *wanted* sex.

With a shake of his head, he drew back, his face a fascinating mix of contrasts; agony and bliss, disbelief and amusement. 'I was climbing an *obstacle* course.'

'Good point.' She gave him another long pull, and he grunted, dipping his head against her neck again. 'I'm on the pill though, so we could still, you know—'

'No,' he replied hoarsely. 'Don't get me wrong, I want to, more than you can possibly know, but if we have sex again, it won't be a fast fuck in a garden shed.'

'Summer house,' she murmured, stroking him again, enjoying the heaviness of him, the way he pulsed in her hand. Hearing his tortured breaths.

'Molly.' His lids fluttered closed.

His voice was rough, his body as taut as a guitar string, and liquid heat rushed once more to her core. 'Okay, then let me, you know, ease the pressure.'

He let out a strangled laugh. 'You don't need... It's okay.'

'It's *not* okay.' Reaching up, she kissed him, feeling her body respond again, her nipples tightening, her core clenching. 'Please, I want to do this. I want to see your face as you come in my hand.'

'Jesus Christ.' She watched his struggle to regain control, but then his shoulders sagged in defeat and he pressed himself further into her grip. 'Only if I can reciprocate.'

His hand disappeared into the front of her shorts, his fingers finding her so fast it was like they remembered the way. In an embarrassingly short time, he had her gasping again, her core tightening with pleasure, making remembering to keep stroking him increasingly difficult as he found just the perfect spot time and time again. 'Holy shit, Ben.' Arousal spiked and she cried out his name as another orgasm ripped through her.

With a quiet groan, he spilt into her hand.

'Shit. Sorry.' Swearing softly, he pulled away, his gaze dipping to the mess he'd made.

A muscle jumped in his jaw and in a flash the atmosphere in the little garden room turned from sensuous and intimate to cool and strained.

'It's fine.' *What had she done?* 'I can, you know, just wipe it on the grass.'

'You shouldn't need to … fuck.' He tucked himself back inside his shorts, eyes still avoiding hers.

Embarrassment flooded through her and she dashed outside to clean up, tears pricking her eyes as she bent down. Clearly he was regretting it already. She was so stupid. Why had she encouraged him?

'Hey.' She felt his presence as he crouched down next to her, his gaze settling on her face before he exhaled a curse. 'Come back inside. Please.'

Tugging her hand, he led her back into the summer house and sat down on the wicker sofa, lifting her onto his lap. 'This is what I should have done.' Carefully, like he was afraid she'd break, he pressed his lips to hers. Gone was the raw, mindless passion. This was tender, soft. A caress of her lips with his. 'Are you okay?'

She nodded, still unable to meet his eyes. 'Sorry if that wasn't what you wanted—'

'I believe it was quite obvious it was exactly what I wanted. What I *needed*.' He heaved in a breath, then feathered a kiss on the top of her head. 'I'm the one who's sorry. I reacted badly because I was … *am* annoyed with myself. I should have more control than that, but clearly around you, I don't.'

'I like that you don't,' she admitted, tucking her head onto his chest, finding the spot she'd always loved, where she could hear the steady pump of his heart. 'We still work, don't we?'

She felt his smile against her hair. 'We do.'

'But sexual compatibility was never our issue.'

'Compatibility of any type was never a problem. I always enjoyed you, in bed and out.' Another pause, and his hand shifted to stroke her hair. 'We should talk,' he murmured. 'Not now, but—'

'Maybe before dinner?' Was his hand stuck in her hair? Certainly it had stopped moving. 'Definitely before we end up in another summer house.'

'If there's a next time, and I hope to God there will be, it will be in a bed.' His hand shifted to smooth over the top of her legs. 'Meanwhile it would help me if you didn't wear those shorts again.' Pleasure fizzed through her, yet before she had time to enjoy his comment, he was cursing under his breath. 'Bollocks.'

She looked up and let out a yelp when she saw Natalie and the cameras heading their way. 'Oh crap.' Jumping off his lap, she patted at her hair. 'Do I look okay? I mean, do I look like we've just been sitting here talking, not like I've had two orgasms.'

Hazel eyes surveyed her face, and his lips twitched. 'You look gorgeous.'

'Really?' How was she supposed to protect her heart from him when he said things like that? And looked at her like he really meant what he was saying.

'Really.' He placed his hands on her shoulders and pushed her gently towards to the door. Just as she was about to step outside, he bent and whispered. 'Also like you've had two orgasms, and given me the best hand job I've had in three years.'

Her heart reared in her chest, bouncing against her ribs ... why three years? Because that was the last time they were together? She couldn't ask, because Natalie and Lauren were approaching fast, both with wide, knowing smiles on their faces.

Ben smoothed his hand down Molly's arm until he found her wrist, then wrapped his fingers around hers.

He'd not been wrong, flushed cheeks, hair coming out of its ponytail, she looked gorgeous.

And like a walking advert for spontaneous, outdoor sex.

All he could think was thank God it was Lauren and not Rachel. He wasn't sure he wanted to face his sister while he knew Molly's hands still held traces of his cum.

Guilt wormed again in his gut. He couldn't regret what happened, not when it had seemed easier to stop breathing than to stop holding her, touching her, exploding over her fingers. Still, the conversation they needed to have weighed heavily in his mind. The one he'd thrown out there to have later and she'd suggested having *before dinner*.

'It looks like we've finally found the missing couple.' Natalie's voice boomed over at them. 'And what, I wonder, have you two been up to?'

'Ben wanted to show me—'

'Nothing.'

Natalie's eyes swung between them, and a sly smile spread

across her face. 'Ladies first. What *did* Ben want to show you, Molly?'

Molly's cheeks went from flushed to overripe tomato and she bit into her lip. 'Err, he wanted to show me his … err, the…'

'Some ideas I've had for her company name,' he interrupted, half afraid in her flustered state she'd actually say the word cock.

Natalie looked taken aback, which probably explained why she didn't ask him why he had to take Molly to a summer house to show her. 'Is this the company you mentioned after the fete?'

'Yes, that's it.' Molly glanced at him with such gratitude, it made his throat lock up. 'I'm going to start a new business upcycling clothes. Ben's been helping me as he's kind of an expert in setting up companies, so for once I don't mind taking notice of what he says.' She let out the irrepressible grin he loved, and he hoped to God he'd prove as good at this as she thought. He couldn't bear to disappoint her again.

He listened with half an ear while she babbled on about why upcycling was so important and how she'd started off with jackets but wanted to have a full range of clothes and accessories, because who didn't want a handbag fused from three different types and colours of leather?

'Umm, thanks Molly.' Natalie interrupted the monologue, a wide smile fixed on her face. 'Interesting as your new company sounds, we really came to ask you about the obstacle race.'

'Ah, okay.' Molly gave her a sheepish grin.

'First, we wanted to congratulate you,' Natalie continued. 'Were you aware you two had the fastest time?'

'Ooh, did we?' Molly snuck him another grin. 'We knew

we'd beaten Duncan and Jasmine, but not that we'd come first. That should please Mr Competitive here.'

He stared back at her. 'What pleases me is that winning means we're unlikely to get split up.'

Her expression softened. 'The game was about trust. You trusted me to guide you over the course without hurting you, and I trusted you to do the same.'

'So you're starting to trust Ben again?' Natalie prompted.

Molly glanced his way and gave him a slow smile. 'It looks that way, yes.'

He forced a smile, every muscle in his body tightening. This was all hurtling ahead way too fast. She was talking about trusting him again and he was holding back vital information which would make her question what on earth she was doing with him.

But going back to that time was torture, agonising. He wasn't sure how to put it into words in a way that wouldn't make her hate him. And when that happened, the viewers would see their relationship disintegrate and vote for them to be split up. His chance with her would be over.

She'd probably be put with Duncan. By the end of the show she could be married to the man.

His stomach cramped and he felt the beginnings of a cold sweat but if she noticed he was even quieter than usual as they walked back to the house, she didn't say anything.

'Hey, we were looking for you two,' James called out as they passed the swimming pool. The man was stretched out on a lounger next to his new partner, Ella, his rangy body looking like it hadn't seen any sun in years. 'Rumours were, you'd gone off to shag.'

This was the last thing he needed. Pushing everything else to the back of his mind, Ben calmly reached for Molly's hand.

'You know what they say about rumours. They're a projection of the person who started them.'

James laughed. 'Well yeah, okay, you've got me there.' He leant forward and winked at Molly. 'Maybe I was imagining what I'd be doing if I went missing with you.'

'Imagining is all you'll be doing,' he retorted, which only made James laugh harder.

'Why were you looking for us?' Molly asked.

'We were planning a pool tournament before dinner and wondered if you guys were up for it?'

Molly glanced at him. 'Oh, well, actually we were going to—'

'Sure,' Ben interrupted. Disappointment flooded her face and shame rocked through him. He was being a coward.

'Great, let's meet at the bar in, what, twenty minutes?' James grinned, seemingly oblivious to the tension he'd just created. 'Maybe we'll have another wager on it, like the one you guys did with Duncan.' He chuckled. 'He's well pissed, by the way. Not sure he and Jasmine are talking now, after he basically blamed her for being useless. So, anyway, catch you in a bit.'

Molly was ominously silent as they made their way across the patio towards the house and he couldn't think of a way to break it. He knew he should explain himself, but he didn't have the words. Not yet. He needed more time to sort them out in his head.

'You said you were going to try,' she said eventually as they reached the bottom of the stairs. 'When I asked you to communicate more, you said you'd try.'

Her anger he could have handled, but the resignation in her voice cut him off at the knees. As if it was only what she'd been expecting. 'I know I did, and I *want* to try.' Frustrated with himself, he jammed a hand through his hair. 'It's just … I'm not sure if I can. I'm not good at talking about it.'

She nodded, once, her gaze scrutinising his before looking away. 'Then I don't know what we're doing.'

Fuck. He was going to lose her again, even without talking to her. 'Don't give up on me yet,' he said thickly, emotion clawing at him, making his eyelids burn. 'Please.'

Her eyes shimmered as she glanced back at him. 'You claim you only ditched me because you weren't in a good place, but how do I know whether you're in the right place now if you don't talk to me?'

He bent his head, feeling defeated. It was more than just his inability to communicate with her. Molly wanted a man who would bind himself to her. And he really, really didn't think he could go through that again.

Even more important that you man the fuck up and talk to her about what happened.

He steeled himself to apologise, to promise that he would, but Molly was already walking up the stairs. He was left with the sight of her perfect backside and the feeling he'd just let the most special thing he was ever going to come across, slip through his fingers a second time.

Chapter Twenty-Six

Molly usually loved theme parks. Crazy rides, fast food, everything dedicated to people having fun ... who wouldn't love to spend the day in one? But she wasn't feeling it today.

The atmosphere between her and Ben had been tense ever since his decision to play pool last night. And maybe he hadn't agreed they should talk that evening, but still, it had felt like a slap in the face. Like he had no intention of ever opening up to her. If that wasn't a giant STOP, DO NOT ENTER, DANGEROUS TO HEART sign, she didn't know what was.

Trouble is, she had an awful feeling it was all too late. That she'd gone and fallen for him again anyway. Or more likely, that she'd never fallen out of love with him.

The coach pulled into the car park and Ben cleared his throat. 'We're here.'

He'd tried to make polite conversation with her at the start of the trip, but given up when she'd turned away and pretended to be asleep. 'Oh goody.'

A frown furrowed his brow. 'I thought this was your thing.'

'Usually, yes. But today I'm not in the mood.'

His shoulders slumped and he exhaled a long, slow breath.

'Welcome to Thorpe Park!' Natalie popped up at the front of the coach, her voice a welcome interruption. 'Today is all about seeing how compatible our couples are. Are you a risk taker, a thrill seeker, desperate to ride Colossus? Or do you prefer to play things safe, take things easy? Perhaps just sit in the park and enjoy watching others? If your partner is one, and you're the other, is that okay, or will it prove frustrating?' She waved towards the park entrance, clearly visible through the front windscreen. 'Well, we're here all day so go explore and when you spot us, come and tell us how you're getting on.'

Molly snorted. 'Like that's going to happen.'

Marcus, sitting with Maya on the row in front, climbed to his feet and looked over at them. 'Which ride are you guys going to do first?'

'Colossus,' Molly replied. 'I thought we'd start off gently. Don't want Ben losing his breakfast.'

Marcus laughed. 'Oh dear, do I detect a bit of *incompatibility* between the pair of you already?'

Ben shifted to stand. 'No. I'm happy to do whatever Molly wants.'

He stepped aside to let her go in front of him. On one level she knew he was tall, but it was only in the confines of the coach that she realised quite how tall. As she shuffled towards the exit she wished she wasn't so aware of him behind her, the brush of his hips against her bum.

'Come on then, let's get this over and done with,' she said as they headed for the entrance.

He sighed heavily. 'Is it going to be like this all day?'

'You mean me being upset because you wheedled out of talking to me last night, and then taking that annoyance out on you by making you go on all the rides you claim you're happy to go on but I know you don't really enjoy? Oh and making sure to flag down Natalie for a good old chat every time we see her?'

Another deep exhale. 'Yes, that.'

'Very probably.'

'Then let's have a coffee first.'

She came to an abrupt halt. 'You've come to one of the best theme parks this country has to offer and you want to have a *coffee*?'

He nodded, his face unsmiling, his gaze unblinking. 'Please.'

He said the word softly, and a flutter spread in her belly. 'I hate it when you do that,' she grumbled.

'Do what?'

'You know what. Ask me in a way I can't say no. But fine, let's let the queues build up while we go and have a crap coffee, because theme parks are well known for their amazing cafés.'

Tension crackled between them as they walked towards the nearest café. After ordering a latte for her – she wasn't going to abandon all Duncan's health kicks but sometimes a girl needed calories – and an Americano for him, they headed to a free table at the back.

A taut silence filled the air as they settled onto their chairs. She was acutely aware of his eyes on her as she blew on the froth.

'Can we forget what happened yesterday?' he said finally, gaze dropping to his cup for a moment before looking back at her.

'Forget the obstacle course, which we won? Kind of hard to do that as the last time I won anything vaguely athletic was the bean bag race at primary school. Or forget our little happening in the summer house, which I thought we both agreed was pleasurable, but maybe you're regretting it now. Or—'

'I'm not.' His gaze seared hers. 'Christ, Molly, I could never regret that. But I do regret agreeing to play pool afterwards. It was ... cowardly.' He took a swig of his coffee, clearly trying to centre himself. 'The period of my life after Helena and I split ... after she died ... was very painful. Talking about it is extremely hard for me.' She watched his Adam's apple move as he swallowed. 'I wasn't ready to do it last night.'

'Fine.'

He gave her a wry smile. 'You think I won't ever be ready.'

'I think', she replied carefully, 'it doesn't really matter. We only have a short time left on the show, and then we're free to go our separate ways.'

His forehead scrunched in a deep frown. 'Is that what you want?'

How great would it be if she'd learnt to lie? 'No.'

His gaze locked on hers. 'Me neither.'

You've been here before. Her heart ignored her and did a neat flip. 'But we can't escape the fact that in just over a week I could be walking down the aisle to you.'

He swallowed, and he looked not just uncomfortable, but if he hadn't been a big, strong guy, she'd have said he looked *frightened*. 'I know. But let's not get ahead of ourselves. One day at a time, yes?'

'Okay.' She took a sip of her drink and ignored the warning bells telling her the longer she stayed with him, the more rope she gave him to hang her. 'So, Colossus first, then we hit, what? Stealth? Swarm?'

He visibly relaxed at her change of subject and eased back against his seat. 'You pick.'

'Are you sure? Because they can be quite frightening for someone who isn't used to theme park rides.'

'I don't scare easily.'

Unless it comes to talking about what happened with Helena. She swallowed the words. He'd apologised and she needed to let go. Besides, she only had to look at the way his jaw tightened and his eyes avoided hers, to know he knew exactly what she was thinking.

Stealth, Vortex, Nemesis, Inferno. It didn't matter what the ride was called, the experience was the same. Ben lost his stomach for a few minutes, then found it again once the ride came to a stop.

He didn't hate it. Just couldn't say he enjoyed the experience. Unlike Molly, who shrieked and laughed her way through every one of them. Did that make them incompatible? Of course not, because he would do anything to make her happy.

Really? Like talking to her properly, about the hard stuff? Marrying her?

Fuck, he hated his conscience. He gave the thoughts a determined shove. He couldn't solve anything now.

'You're like a big kid,' he remarked as the ride slowed and she finally stopped screaming.

She grinned, her coolness with him temporarily forgotten. 'It's not just kids who enjoy rides. Then again, if I did have a kid, it would be one heck of an excuse to go to all the theme parks.'

Kids. It wasn't something he'd ever thought about. He didn't see marriage in his future, but did he see kids? He glanced sideways at Molly as they walked off the ride. 'Do you want children, one day?'

She nodded slowly. 'Not just so I can go to theme parks, obviously, but yes. It would be a ... a privilege to have kids. Though not everyone seems to think that way.'

Her voice caught on the last sentence and he stared over at her. 'Molly?'

She shook her head, refusing to catch his eye. 'So, anyway. What's next?'

He slowed and placed his hand on her hip so he could draw her towards him. 'Talk to me.'

She huffed out a laugh. 'That's a bit ironic, isn't it, coming from you?'

His stomach plummeted faster than it had on any of the rides. Finally, he understood how difficult it must be, dating him. 'I've no right to ask, but I don't like seeing you upset. The only times I've seen that happen before now, I've been the cause. I hope that isn't the case this time.'

'No. And I'm not upset. It happened too long ago for me to still be affected by it, but sometimes it hits me when I least expect it.'

'What hits you?'

A shadow crossed her face and she stepped away from him, leaving his hands to fall uselessly by his sides. 'The memory of my first mum. The one who gave birth to me.'

'You said you were adopted,' he pressed. 'Do you know your biological parents then?'

'Not my dad, no, he was never in the picture.' Her voice sounded flat and she refused to meet his eyes. 'But I knew my mum, yes. For seven years.'

A feeling of unease settled over him. Sensing they needed privacy, he took Molly's hand and led her to a bench tucked behind a tree, away from prying eyes. 'What happened to her?' He asked as he drew Molly down next to him.

'Nothing, at least not that I know of.' She stared down at her hands which were now clenched in her lap. 'I mean, I assume she's still alive, but I wouldn't know if she was dead, because she just ... disappeared.'

'Disappeared?' His mind struggled to comprehend what she was telling him. 'Vanished?'

'Yep.' Her knuckles whitened, yet her voice was alarmingly flat. 'I was at school and I waited and waited, but she didn't show to pick me up. Eventually social services were called and they found a note at home. It said she couldn't be my mum anymore.' Her throat moved as she swallowed. 'She'd tried, she said, but she found it too hard.'

Anger surged inside him and he had to battle to keep it from showing in his voice. 'Of course it's hard, being a parent. God knows mine weren't great at it. But they didn't just give up.'

'Maybe yours loved you more than my mum did.' The way she said it, so matter of fact, made his heart ache. 'Or maybe you were easier to love. But it doesn't matter,' she added quickly before he had a chance to contradict her. 'Because I got adopted by my real parents, and they're amazing.' Her voice warmed and she finally raised her eyes to his. 'A lot of kids my age ended up in foster care but I was one of the lucky ones to get a second chance at having parents. At being part of a family.'

He was reassured by her smile, by the light that was back in her eyes; yet his mind was still stuck on her second sentence. *Maybe you were easier to love.* What a weight for a child to carry around, the fact that her mum had found it too hard to love her. 'Fuck, Molly.' His brain spun as he imagined how that trauma must have manifested itself as Molly, the abandoned schoolgirl, transitioned into Molly, the woman desperate to be loved. Insecure about where she stood. 'You need the words more than most people,' he said slowly as the realisation began to sink in. 'The reassurance that you're loved. That you won't be abandoned.' Pain jackknifed through him as he pictured her face as he'd ended things.

'I guess so, yes.' She gave him a sad smile.

With creeping alarm it dawned on him that it wasn't just words she needed. It was security. The type that came with marriage.

The alarm grew into stomach-cramping, cold-sweat-trickling-down-his-back panic when he realised how much damage he would do to her if he fucked this up *again*. She'd not just been let down by him and Duncan; she'd been let down by the one person who was supposed to love her unconditionally. Yet here she was, bravely talking about it, while he kept avoiding opening up to her.

'Ben?'

Her quiet question jerked him out of his tortuous introspection. 'Sorry, I'm just trying to get my head round it.' He lifted his eyes to hers. 'I don't know how you're not a complete basket case.'

She smiled. 'Some people would say I am.' Her gaze darted away and she bit the end of her nail. 'I don't think it's helped me when it comes to relationships. You once told me I gave my heart away too quickly, and I guess that's why.'

He thought back to that conversation. 'You told me you didn't expect me to understand your need to love. And be loved. No wonder you fell for a guy like Duncan.'

At the mention of the man's name, her eyes flashed. 'What do you mean?'

His insides gave a vicious twist at her defensive tone. 'He's nowhere near good enough for you, surely you can see that? He's shallow where you're deep, arrogant where you're totally unaware how amazing you are.' Ashamed, he hung his head. 'But I can't talk, can I? When I ended things, it must have felt like I abandoned you, like your mum had.'

She shrugged, but the careless gesture didn't fool him. 'It wasn't your fault you didn't feel what I did. I just *thought* you did; that's what hurt the most. Just like I thought my biological mum had loved me.'

'Hence the toffee Quality Street, not the purple one. Fuck.' He clasped her head, looked deep into her eyes. 'You're *not* hard to love. In fact, you're so fucking easy to love, it's not true. If people don't see that, the fault is with them, not with you.'

'Maybe I need to get better at choosing who to love,' she said quietly.

He swallowed down the emotion battling to erupt. 'Maybe you do.'

And if she had any common sense, he realised wretchedly, she would not include him on her list.

'Well, look who we've found.'

Natalie's voice crashed through his thoughts and he glanced up in horror to see her, Rachel and the camera crew advancing towards them. Protectiveness surged through him and he jumped to his feet, standing in front of Molly to shield her. 'Not now.'

Natalie faltered, and he whipped his head towards his sister. 'I'm asking nicely. Please don't film this.'

The desperation in his voice must have got through to her because she nodded. 'We'll catch up with you later.'

When they were out of view, he slumped back onto the bench.

Molly groaned and buried her face in her hands. 'You're going to look at me differently now, aren't you? Like I'm some sort of sad charity case who needs pity.' She angled her head towards him. 'That's going to really piss me off.'

'Hey,' he whispered, wrapping his arm around her. 'Looking at someone in a new light is inevitable, the more you find out about them. But you didn't do anything wrong.' *Unlike him.* The impact of what she'd just said ricocheted through him and his throat locked up, causing him to have to force the next words out. 'How can I feel anything but awe for you now, knowing what you went through? It didn't make you bitter; it made you even more determined to find love, which is incredible.'

Slowly she raised her head, her gaze searching his in a way that suggested she was trying to work him out. 'For a guy who can't do heavy conversation, that was a pretty good speech.'

He smiled, yet as he drew her tighter against him, his chest felt heavy, weighed down with knowledge that when he finally found the balls to have the conversation he needed to have with her, that new light he'd just spoken about would appear horribly murky.

Chapter Twenty-Seven

It was a beautiful day and the girls had chosen to sit by the pool and relax ahead of what Natalie had billed as 'a night on the town'. Their partners had gone off to play tennis.

'You're dead quiet today.' Chloe dipped her sunglasses to look over at Molly. 'You and Ben had a lovers' tiff?'

'We're not lovers.'

All of them – Chloe, Jasmine, Maya, Ella – burst out laughing.

'Well, what *did* you both get up to in the summer house then?' Chloe demanded. 'Whatever it was, you apparently came out all flushed and guilty-looking.'

Feeling it was safer to ignore her, Molly focussed back on her Kindle.

'I don't know what you're waiting for,' Chloe added, clearly not happy to let the subject of Ben drop. 'I'd fuck him if he looked in my direction.' Using a hand to fluff her glorious mane of dark brown hair, she elegantly rose to her feet and sashayed off to get herself a drink.

'So would I,' Molly admitted quietly when she was out of earshot. 'That's the problem.'

Maya frowned. 'Why is it a problem?'

'Because if I'm not careful I'm heading for a repeat of last time.' He'd said some really lovely things to her yesterday, but the conversation she wanted still hadn't happened. Last night, after the theme park, he'd studiously avoided her eyes as they'd been roped into playing Pictionary after dinner.

'Have you guys talked about the whole "at the end of this show we have to decide whether to get married" thing?' Jasmine shuddered. 'It's like, whoa, are you shitting me? Sure, it was the best part when I watched the show, but it's beyond scary from where I'm sitting now.'

'What's scary?' Chloe returned with a tall glass of clear liquid, rattling with ice cubes and slices of fruit. Could have been water. Could have been vodka and tonic or gin and tonic. Or just vodka, knowing Chloe.

'The thought of planning our weddings,' Jasmine repeated.

'Oh, well that's not a biggie for me.' Chloe prodded at the ice cubes with her finger. 'Liam's better than James, and I'm definitely going to have sex with him, but we've both agreed we're not getting married.'

'I really like Marcus,' Maya said slowly. 'But marriage?' She blew out a breath. 'Before I came on here I thought I'd be up for it if I met the right guy, but now signing my life over to someone else feels like a far bigger deal than I thought.'

'It's not about signing your life over,' Molly interjected, not happy with how that sounded. 'It's about committing to spend the rest of your life loving that person, no matter what.'

Jasmine giggled. 'It sounds so deep when you put it like that. For me getting married is more about agreeing to give your relationship a real go, you know? And if we did that on the show, we'd get this awesome free holiday in Hawaii.' She shrugged. 'If it doesn't work out, we just get divorced.'

'You think Duncan might want to get married?'

Molly was grateful for Maya's question, as it saved her having to ask it. It felt odd, listening to Jasmine openly discussing the possibility of marrying the man she'd wanted to marry only a few months ago. She was sure she should be more upset. Was she numb to it because of the artificial situation they were in?

Or was she numb because the prospect of marrying Ben had the butterflies swooping and dancing in a way they'd never done for Duncan.

'Duncan is a strong believer in marriage. I mean, I don't know if he'd be up for marrying me, but I know he wants to get married, have kids.' Jasmine laughed. 'He's kind of old fashioned that way. Wants the traditional family unit, his wife at home, looking after his kids while he works to provide for them.' She turned to Molly with a shrewd look. 'You probably know that though, don't you?'

God, this was weird. 'Yes.'

Jasmine looked like she was expecting her to add to that, but Molly kept her mouth firmly shut.

'So have you and Ben discussed what you'll do if you make it to the last day?' Jasmine pushed.

It was a stark reminder that this time next week, she and Ben could be planning their wedding. 'We've not talked about it yet.' Before anyone could probe any further, Molly determinedly shifted the focus. 'I love watching this show, and I've always routed for the couples, hoping they'll get married, but I'm with Maya. It suddenly feels like a huge step to take after only four weeks.' *But it's not only four weeks for you.* She'd been ready to take it with Duncan before the show. She'd wanted to marry Ben only a few weeks after first meeting him. What did she want now? 'For the viewers' sake, I hope we have at least one wedding in the house.'

As she finished talking, the hairs on the back of her neck pricked, and as if she had an internal Ben Knight radar, she noticed the group of four men had finished their match and were walking back towards the house. Dressed in black athletic shorts and a white polo shirt, Ben looked effortlessly sexy. He was chatting to Marcus, with James and Liam, Chloe's new match, trailing behind them.

Duncan had disappeared to the basement gym to do weights.

At that moment Ben glanced over at them and as their gazes collided, her heart began to race. It thumped even louder when he broke away from Marcus and began to head straight for her. His eyes never leaving hers.

'Holy fuck, that's hot,' Chloe whispered. 'Wish he'd look at me like that. Wish any guy would look at me like that.'

He came to a stop just in front of Molly, his gaze skimming over her halter neck top and shorts before heading down to her legs. When his eyes finally met hers again, they shimmered with such longing, her insides somersaulted, a riot of hormones, adrenaline and swarming butterflies.

Then he bent to kiss her and Chloe was right. Holy fuck.

'Can we meet up after I've had a shower?' he murmured against her lips.

'Sure.' Her voice sounded scratchy, like she'd not drunk all day.

With a single nod of his head, he strode off towards the house. Molly knew she wasn't the only one watching his long, runner's legs or the taut buttocks beneath his thin shorts.

'Looks like you're heading for an interesting afternoon,'

Maya murmured.

'You're definitely going to get fucked,' Chloe added with a wry smile.

Molly's heart clattered against her ribs. Sex with Ben ... God, despite knowing it would be a stupid move, she wanted it again. His hard body shifting beneath her, sliding over her. Thrusting into her...

The sound of laughter shook her out of her daydream and she looked round to find herself the centre of attention. 'That pale skin of yours does you no favours when it comes to hiding what you're thinking,' Chloe smirked. 'You're so turned on right now, aren't you?'

'Absolutely not.'

But to their further amusement, she pushed down her shorts, ripped off her top and announced she was going for a swim.

He was going to have the conversation he dreaded. Ben had made his mind up last night, while playing Pictionary – he'd even contemplated dragging her away and having it then, figuring it could be the lesser of two evils. But she'd seemed into the game, her face alive with laughter, and he'd been far too content to watch her than ruin the evening.

The time for putting it off was over though. Yes, he risked losing her, but there was a chance that, even after everything she was about to hear, she might still be interested in a relationship with him outside the show.

If he hurt her again, humiliated her, there was no way back.

A cold shiver snaked down his spine as he strode back out to the swimming pool. And his hands clenched into fists as he saw Duncan hunkered down, talking to Molly. Not only was the git too close, he wasn't wearing a shirt.

As he walked over to them Ben tried to remind himself Molly had liked his body well enough when they'd been dating.

Her gaze clashed with his over Duncan's shoulder, and she gave what could have been a guilty start, or was that his jealousy working overtime?

Duncan turned and slowly stood up. 'I'll see you later then. Babe.' The last word felt like a deliberate provocation.

With a cursory nod in his direction, Duncan strode off. In his wake, tension pinged between him and Molly. And damn it, there were far too many pairs of eyes pretending to sun themselves on loungers.

'Will you take a walk with me?'

Molly nodded and shifted to her feet.

'No going off to that summer house,' Chloe called out after them.

It didn't help the tension one little bit.

'Am I allowed to ask what that was about?' he asked as they headed down the steps from the pool area and onto the lawn. Spilling his guts was hard enough. No point doing it if her heart was still with Duncan.

'He apologised for not telling me about the video. And then...' Her cheeks flushed. 'He wanted to know if we'd had sex.'

'I hope you told him it was none of his fucking business.'

She didn't turn towards him, just kept looking straight ahead. 'In a way it is his business. Our split was only meant to be temporary.' Finally her eyes found his. 'We talked of marriage, Ben. If I hadn't followed him on here, we might have got back together at the end of next week.'

His heart lodged in his throat and he could barely squeeze the words out. 'He asked you to *marry* him?'

'Well, no, but he hinted at it. He wanted to come on the show to build his business, so he could support the wife and kids he was planning.'

Ben's stomach knotted, dread pooling. Duncan was offering Molly everything she wanted. How could he compete? What was *he* offering in return? 'What did he mean when he said "I'll see you later"?'

Her shoulders rose and fell. 'He wants to talk to me in private, which seems fair enough considering we only split because of the show.' Her voice turned quieter. 'We had a year together, and I can't forget how good he was to me. He took care of me, made me feel important. Every week we'd dress up and he'd take me on a proper date. He made a fuss of me on my birthday, and little milestones like our one-month anniversary. He made me feel *loved*. Considering you and Mum had made me feel the opposite, it was a really awesome change.'

His jealousy now felt selfish and pathetic beside the hurt he'd subjected her to. 'Can we sit for a bit?' He asked, nodding towards a bench.

With tension still vibrating between them, he slumped onto the seat and buried his face in his hands, trying to find his balance.

'I'm sorry.'

He jerked upright. 'What the hell for? It's me who needs to apologise.' It felt like it was all he'd been doing for the last few weeks.

'No. You've already done that, and we moved on. I shouldn't have thrown it back in your face like that again.'

'You should, because it helped me understand why you fell

for Duncan. It also told me what you need from me, and fuck, Molly, I don't think I can give you that.'

'Oh.' Her lids closed briefly over her eyes and her face seemed to crumple. Like he'd pulled the plug on the electricity cable giving her life.

He wanted to reach for her, smother her with kisses to reassure her how much she meant to him, but there was too much tension between them. Too much that needed to be said. With a deep exhale, he sat back on the bench, crossed his legs at the ankles and steeled himself for what he was about to say. 'I need to tell you what happened between me and Helena. Then maybe you'll understand.' His heart began to thump, his mouth to dry up.

She nodded, and her gaze roved over his face, seeming to take an inventory. 'I want that, you know I do because I've been pretty vocal about it. But only tell me if you're ready.'

'I'll never be ready to talk about this shit.' He could leave it at that, shelve the idea for a few more days. She'd given him an out, hadn't she? *But there's a fucking wedding at the end of the show. You absolutely can't let her be humiliated.* He inhaled, digging deep, trying to find his courage. 'You deserve to understand why I was such a wreck when we met. And why part of me is still a wreck, now.'

'Okay.' She gave him another study. 'You've got the look of a man about to dive out of a plane without a parachute.'

It was exactly how he felt. But she'd managed to tell him about her mum abandoning her at school without seeming to break sweat, so he needed to just fucking *talk*.

Heaving in another breath, he met her eyes, and faltered at the compassion he saw there.

How would she look at him after he'd told her?

Chapter Twenty-Eight

Because Molly was watching Ben intently, she saw a haunted look cross his handsome face. It cemented the realisation that he'd not been trying to fob her off when he'd told her talking about what had happened with Helena was painful.

She was a heartbeat away from telling him to leave it for another day, when he started to talk.

'I met Helena at university. I was like a moth to her bright, burning flame. She was beautiful, sure, but there was something else that drew me to her.' He paused, gave her a small, tight smile. 'In many ways she was similar to you. Lively, outgoing, gregarious. But where you're strong, she was more fragile.'

'Me, strong?' Molly gaped at him. 'If I was, I wouldn't have crumpled so heavily after you left me.'

'Don't. You picked yourself back up again. Opened your heart to Duncan.' His mouth tightened. 'A weaker person would have locked it up, preferring not to risk it again.'

How did he see things in her that she didn't? 'Thank you.'

'I'm only telling you the truth. But please, can we not talk about you and Duncan.'

His voice was strained, his body tense. Feeling the need to connect to him, she reached to squeeze his hand. 'You were telling me about Helena.'

He glanced down at their clasped hands and then drew them to rest on his thigh. 'I fell for her hook, line and sinker, so much so that when she said she wanted to get married, I went along with it. Even though I knew we were too young.'

'You were *married*?' Molly faltered. 'You talked about your ex … I assumed you meant ex-girlfriend.'

'No, ex-wife. But we're jumping ahead.' He drew in a breath, hand pressing down on hers against his thigh. 'I should have realised then, the way she seemed almost desperate to marry me, that there was something not quite right, but I thought it was just her way of demonstrating how much she loved me.' His fingers twitched. 'To be honest, I wasn't a fan of marriage. I'd seen how miserable it had made my parents, but Helena wanted it, and I was young and besotted. It was only after we married, that I realised there was a darker side to her. One she didn't want anyone to see, so she hid it by self-medicating. Unbeknown to me, while we were dating she'd moved from trying to mask her depression with alcohol and soft drugs, to regularly using cocaine. Her family was rich so getting hold of the money to finance her habit wasn't an issue. And we still had separate accounts after we married so I only started to suspect what was happening when her mood swings became more obvious. Of course I confronted her, told her cocaine wasn't the answer, that it was making her depression worse, not better, but she denied she was depressed.' He paused, raised his fingers to mime quotation marks. '"How can I be depressed now I have you to look after me?"' He exhaled in one, long, sigh. 'She promised to give up the cocaine but of course she didn't, and the more I tried to get her to seek help, the more aggressive she became.' His fingers tightened around her hand. 'Fuck, Molly, I was twenty-four and clueless. She needed someone who could talk to her properly, be patient with her. Not a guy who struggled voicing his own feelings.'

His voice was rough with emotion, his face tight with pain, and Molly's heart swelled, as if it had decided to go against her instructions and make room for him. 'I'm sure you did everything you could.'

'Did I?' In one sharp movement he let go of her hand and leapt to his feet. He started to pace restlessly. 'I tried contacting her parents, but she found out I'd gone behind her back and was livid. Said it was nobody's business but hers what she did with her life. And her parents were worse than useless anyway. As far as they were concerned, she was now my responsibility.' He drew a hand down his face and looked out across the lawn. 'I was lost. I didn't know what to do, how to help. Everyone kept saying it had to come from her, that I could only support her.' Finally his gaze found hers, his eyes a turbulent mix of brown and green. 'Have you any idea how hard it is to watch someone you love suffer and to feel utterly clueless about how to help?'

Unable to watch his agony, Molly rose to her feet and threw her arms around his waist. 'I'm so sorry, Ben. So sorry.'

His arms tightened around her and she lay her head against his chest, hearing the heavy thump of his heart. But a moment later he untangled himself from her arms and stepped away. 'Save your sympathy; I don't deserve it,' he muttered harshly, turning away from her to stare into the distance. Seeing God knows what.

Sensing he wanted to finish without any interruption, she reluctantly went to sit back on the bench.

'We were together for six years, married for three of them, but in the end I became so frustrated, I divorced her,' he continued, his voice detached, like it was coming from someone else. 'Nice of me, huh? She's at rock bottom and I washed my hands of her, like her parents did.' He gave a grunt of disgust. 'Part of me hoped it would jolt her into doing something, but another really selfish part of me didn't want the drama anymore: the fleeting ups followed by the hellish and all too frequent downs. I was twenty-six. I had my master's degree; I'd found a job. I didn't want to be married to an addict who only wanted me as an emotional crutch. I wanted to get on with my life. And I did, for a few months.'

His shoulders rose and fell as he sucked in a breath, and when he started talking again, his voice began to crack. 'I'll never know if she intended to kill herself, or if the overdose was accidental. I only know I wasn't able to save her.' He swallowed. 'I wasn't able to get her to seek help, or go into rehab. I couldn't even get to her in time when she phoned to tell me she didn't feel right. Her heart was racing; she felt too hot. I … I can still hear the panic in her voice. Like my mind is determined to remind me how much I failed her.' He blinked, turning his face away from her, but not before she'd noticed a telltale glistening of his eyes.

Her heart ached for him. 'You tried to help, but she didn't want to listen. You didn't fail her.'

He let out a low, humourless laugh. 'People have tried to tell me that: friends, the therapist I saw for a while. And there are days when I almost believe it.'

Her stomach pitched as she realised what she'd been doing. 'But then there are days when someone accuses you of being uncommunicative, and the doubts come flooding back.'

He crouched in front of her, hazel eyes raking hers. 'Do you understand now why I broke it off with you?'

'"It's not you, it's me",' she parroted, the words etched on her brain. 'I hated it, such a frigging cliché.' Yet slowly what he'd been saying these last few weeks began to sink in. 'It really wasn't about me, was it?'

'It really wasn't.' He bent his head, seeming to gather himself. 'I should have handled our split better, given you a proper explanation, but I was such a fucking mess back then. I shouldn't even have started anything with you; it had only been a few months since Helena died.' He gave Molly a sad smile. 'You were impossible to ignore though, and I was in desperate need of some of the happiness you were offering. But then I found those tickets, and I realised you were making plans for the future. It scared the shit out of me. How could I dive into another relationship when I'd failed the last one so catastrophically?'

His expression was so tortured, her eyes burnt with tears. 'Oh Ben.' Leaning forward, she rested her forehead against his. 'Thank you for telling me.'

'I was careless with you,' he said quietly. 'And I'll never forgive myself for it.'

'Well, *I* forgive you.'

His body stilled, and then his shoulders dropped and he heaved out a sigh before slipping back onto the bench next to her. For several minutes they sat in silence, him with his arm slotted around her. Her leaning into him, waiting for the tension to leave his body. When it didn't, she glanced up and found him staring ahead, his expression like he was still wrestling with something important.

'Ben?'

'I'm terrified of cocking things up again, of failing you, but I'm more scared of not trying. Of watching you slip through my fingers a second time.' He swallowed. 'But on the coach you told me you've spent an unhealthy amount of time thinking about marriage. Is it a deal breaker for you?'

She jolted, like he'd tasered her. 'I … I don't know. Maybe, yes. Why?'

He looked wretched. 'Because I really don't think I can do that again.'

'Oh.' Her heart floundered, the dream she'd nursed since she'd made the decision to choose Ben, now a pile of ashes at her feet. Yet when she looked into his red-rimmed eyes, she didn't see a man who didn't want to marry her. She saw a man who seemed to care deeply for her. 'I guess that gives me a lot to think about.'

That evening, the house was treated to outside caterers and a band. Ben sat with his arm across the back of Molly's chair, listening to her tell their table about the time they first met, wishing he knew what was going round in her head.

Were they over? Was she going to ask Rachel to swop her to Duncan now? And let's face it, his sister, the production team, they all wanted a marriage at the end of the show. If he wasn't going to supply it, why wouldn't they swop her to someone who might?

'So, you have a history of chucking your drink over Ben,' James summarised as Molly finished recounting their first meeting. 'It's a pretty corny way to pick a guy up but it certainly seems to work where he's concerned.'

'She didn't spill her drink over me the first time,' Ben corrected. 'The action of her knocking into me, caused me to spill mine.' He waited for her eyes to meet his. 'And she didn't pick me up. I went after her.'

Her brow wrinkled with a frown. 'You did? I mean, I started talking to you—'

'And I asked if you wanted a drink. Then I moved us from the bar to a quiet table. I sat close so I could stare into your eyes because I'd never seen eyes that green before. I touched you any opportunity I got; your fingers when I handed you another drink, a brush of my thigh against yours. When you didn't flinch, didn't move away, I shifted closer.'

Her breath hitched. 'I remember,' she whispered, her mouth so close he only had to move a few inches and he'd be kissing her. Was everyone else still listening or had the conversation moved on? He had no clue. All he could hear was her choppy breathing. 'But I was the one who suggested you bought me a drink,' she said softly. 'And who deliberately moved my stool so I could get closer to *you*.'

Her hand settled on his thigh and he had to stifle a groan. Was that a reflex, because he knew Molly was a touchy person, or was it deliberate?

'Oh my God, go and get a room,' Chloe exclaimed. 'There's like fireworks going off between the pair of you and it's making my eyes hurt.'

When he looked up he realised only Chloe and Liam remained at the table. The others had disappeared onto the dance floor.

Liam winked at Chloe. 'Come on, let's leave these two lovebirds alone and join the others.'

The moment they'd gone, Ben turned to Molly. The feel of her hand, the warmth from it, sent arousal scorching through him, making his trousers alarmingly tight. He swallowed to ease his throat, but no words came out.

'Don't give me time to think.' Her hand crept towards the place he really, really needed to feel it. 'Take me to your room. My room.' He held his breath, hissing it out again when her hand cupped him. 'Any room with a bed in it.'

He went from hard, to fully erect, a throbbing beast beneath his zip. 'Is that wise?'

She let out a strangled laugh. 'Definitely not.'

But her hand slid over him, as if she was reminding herself how he felt. 'Molly, what's happening here?'

'I don't know. But you opened up, told me the truth, so the oxytocin trust thing isn't a problem anymore. As I see it, I know exactly where I stand now, so while I'm thinking about what to do about that, there's nothing to stop us from—'

Ben lurched to his feet.

But he sat back down with a thump as he spotted Natalie, Rachel and the cameras heading purposefully in their direction.

'Shit.' Bad enough being filmed, but being filmed nursing a raging hard-on? And with your sister looking on? As subtly as he could, he tried to rearrange himself under the table. When he flicked Molly a look, he found her biting her bottom lip.

'If it's any consolation,' she whispered huskily. 'My knickers are—'

'Not helping,' he rasped, which made her giggle.

'Having a good evening?' Natalie's eyes swept round their empty table until they rested on him and Molly. 'It certainly looked like you were from across the room.'

'Yes, thanks.' Ben gave her a tight-lipped smile, which he

hoped she'd read correctly as *go away*. He slid his sister a quick glance, too, but she responded with a shake of her head which he interpreted as *no frigging way are you getting out of this twice in two days*.

'We haven't caught up with you this evening yet.' Ignoring his *please, bugger off* vibes, Natalie settled herself on a vacant chair and turned her attention to Molly. 'Are things as cosy between you and Ben as they look?'

'I'm not sure you'd describe it as cosy. We have a lot to work through, but he's started to open up, which I'm grateful for.' She slid him a smile. 'Plus he's great company, makes me laugh and I think we can all agree he's super-hot. It's hard for a girl not to have her head turned by him.'

Natalie laughed and switched her focus to him. 'And how about you, Ben? How do you feel things are going between you two the second time around?'

She wants something I don't think I can give her, but I'm certain another guy in this house can. The thought cripples me, but she's not closed the door on me so I'm not giving up. How the hell could he say any of that to blasted camera? 'You can see for yourself.'

Disappointment hurtled across Molly's face and he didn't need the shake of his sister's head to know he'd fucked up.

'When I say he's started to open up, maybe I was a bit optimistic.' Molly gave them a sad smile. 'Sorry, but I need to go to the loo.' She jerked her head towards Natalie. 'Please excuse me.'

His heart slowly sank in his chest as he watched the beautiful redhead in a shimmering green dress hurry away.

'You have some bridges to repair,' Rachel remarked coolly as Natalie and camera crew left, presumably to find another victim.

'No shit.'

She gave him a searching look. 'You've told her about Helena, haven't you? I was trying to work out if that was what you were discussing yesterday at the theme park, but it seemed more like you were protecting her.'

He sighed and rose to his feet. 'I love you, but what we were talking about is none of your business.'

He made to walk off, but Rachel put a hand on his arm to stop him. 'I could see she was upset, just as I saw you were upset today, talking to her on the bench. You can't blame me for being concerned.' Her eyes found his. 'I want to see you happy, Ben, that's all.'

'Yeah, me too.' He stared in the direction Molly had walked off. 'But it feels like one step forward two steps back at the moment. And being on this show is not helping.'

'I can see that. But I can also see that without this show, you wouldn't have met Molly again.' She tugged at his arm, forcing him to look at her. 'The algorithm, our matchmakers, they put you with Molly for a reason. And they were right.' Her expression softened. 'You've fallen in love with her, haven't you?'

He'd known for a while, but hearing it said out loud was terrifying. 'Is it that obvious?'

'It is to me. But maybe not to the person who's only just learning to trust you again.'

'You mean the same person who came on here to get married. To Duncan,' he added bitterly.

'If she wanted Duncan, she would have chosen to swop after two weeks.' Rachel gave him a tight hug before stepping back. 'You need to decide whether you love her enough to offer her the ending she really wants. Or whether your view of marriage is so blinkered you're prepared to let her go and see her get married to someone else.' She smirked. 'Potentially a man in a too tight tuxedo.'

He ground his teeth, but couldn't fault her neat summary. With his mind a jumble of thoughts, his body an angsty mess of hormones and his heart weighed down with emotions he needed to work through, Ben strode off to find Molly.

Chapter Twenty-Nine

Molly stared at herself in the mirror and took a few deep, calming breaths. Okay, she could do this. Walk back out with a smile on her face. Ben was ... Ben. He'd not had a personality transplant just because he'd finally told her why he'd been so messed up when she'd first met him.

But he *had* opened up, and now she knew he had hang-ups and insecurities too. She also knew he didn't want to get married.

A band wrapped round her chest, tightening so much that for a moment she couldn't breathe. *Was* it a deal breaker? It should be. Giving up on her dream of love, locked into the security of marriage, just for that fluttery feeling in her chest every time she looked at him? For the fizz she felt in her blood when he was near her, like she was filled with champagne?

That was madness.

Yet how could she give him up now, when she'd not yet had a chance to explore what they could be together this second time around?

It was too soon for a decision like that.

Pep talk done, she opened the door to the downstairs ladies and stepped back out into the hallway, only to see the object of her thoughts barrelling towards her. Without a word, he grabbed her hand and manoeuvred her against the wall. Then stepped right into her personal space, his eyes dark and stormy.

'I'm falling in love with you.'

Her heart somersaulted. 'You are?'

'It should be obvious, but you need words, so I'm giving you the words. But I refuse to tell Natalie and the camera crew that before I've told you.'

Oh God. She could barely breathe, her insides a mess of overexcited, flapping butterflies. 'I'm falling for you, too.' *I've fallen*. No, for her own sanity she had to keep part of herself back from him.

'Yeah?' A deep, satisfied smile crept across his face and the storm left his eyes, replaced with a burning smoulder that fanned flames of desire everywhere it touched. 'You've never looked more gorgeous,' he told her hoarsely as he cupped her face. The warmth of his palms caused goosebumps across her skin. 'And I've never wanted to kiss anyone more.'

'Do it.' Her voice sounded so rough she had to clear her throat and try again. 'Stop talking and do it, please.'

He chuckled, sending her hormones into a crazy jig. 'You're asking me to *stop* talking now?'

'Oh, shut up.' On a huff of frustration she wound her arms around his neck and jumped him. Literally jumped up and anchored her legs around his waist.

'Whoa, okay.' His hands immediately went to grasp her hips, securing her in place as he pushed her back against the wall. Now his erection, hot and heavy, was exactly where she needed it. And his mouth was doing exactly what she wanted from him, tongue diving into her depths, lips sucking and nibbling and driving her mad. 'This better?' he murmured, the husk in his voice sending another jolt of arousal through her.

'More.' She wriggled, needing more of his mouth, that hot, dirty tongue as it continued to explore. More friction from the hard, pulsing length of him.

He groaned. 'That's... Shit, Molly. Keep doing that and we're going to have sex right here, right now.'

'Yes.' Automatically her hands went to his fly, her fingers frantic. Only Ben, she thought dimly. Only he had ever turned her on so much that she didn't care about anything else but having him slide into her, those hips racing, his fevered breath hot in her ear.

A hand clamped down on her wrist. 'Fuck.' He let out a guttural sound as his chest heaved. 'We can't do this here.' Lifting her hand to his mouth, he dropped feather-like kisses into her palm. 'Public hallway. Cameras.'

'Oh.' Her head was still spinning, her body so hypersensitised that even the press of his lips on her palm caused a tightening in her core. 'My room?'

He let out a pained sounding laugh. 'Yes, God, yes. But...' He gave a few short thrusts of his hips, just enough to let her know his predicament.

'Okay, we need to take a breath.' She let out a disgruntled moan as he lowered her feet to the floor. 'Think about ... other stuff.'

Another throaty laugh. 'What do you suggest?'

'Umm,' she bit into her lip, and he grunted.

'Don't do that.' His hot gaze skimmed her face, and dipped down to her chest. Then he exhaled heavily and slammed his eyes shut. 'You need to go. I can't... Nothing is going to go down while you're still here.' His lids blinked open and his next words were whispered in her ear. 'Not while you're looking all flushed, your mouth like the perfect resting place for mine. Your nipples hard and waiting for my tongue.'

She'd forgotten, she realised as arousal scorched through her. Forgotten how the man who didn't talk about his feelings, could talk so easily about sex.

'Okay.' Legs shaky as a new-born lamb, she eased away from the wall. 'I'll, umm, go then. To my room.' As the madness of lust slowly ebbed away, the insecurities kicked in. 'And ... err, wait for you?'

'If you think for one moment I'm not going to follow you,' he growled, 'I've not been making myself clear enough.'

She took in the smouldering stare, the wound-up stance, and started to smile. 'Nope, perfectly clear. For once I can totally tell what you're thinking.' On a laugh she started to fan herself, and though it was in jest, she wasn't kidding about how hot she felt right now. 'I'll leave the door unlocked.'

Ridiculously, *impossibly* aroused, she darted towards the stairs.

Her stomach dropped as she spotted Duncan heading towards her.

'Hi.' Did she look like she was about to have sex? 'I'm ... err ...off to bed.' Her scalp prickled, her face felt so hot.

'I'm glad I caught you.' He took hold of her hand, and it felt wrong, but she didn't know if that was because she was about to have sex with another man, or if her body had decided Duncan was not the right man for her, even if her mind hadn't totally closed off the idea. 'Where's your head at the moment, babe?'

'What do you mean?'

'I mean, do I still have a chance with you? All that stuff about the videos, I know you were upset but it wasn't like I deliberately set out to mislead you. Just that I figured you were doing so well, I was so proud of you, it seemed like a great idea to build on that.' His blue eyes pressed hers. 'Hell, Moll, I still love you, and I'm willing to marry you at the end of the show, if that's what you want. But if you don't want that, you need to let me know, so I can see if I can work things out with Jasmine.'

Over Duncan's shoulder, Molly caught sight of Ben turning the corner towards them. Her heart flip-flopped, giving her the answer to where it stood, even if her head was still wavering. 'I think we've been matched with Ben and Jasmine for a reason. We should be focussing on them. Goodnight, Duncan.'

Scampering up the stairs, she raced to her room, all thoughts of Duncan vanished the moment she shut the door behind her. All she saw was Ben's smouldering gaze, all she heard was his growling promise to follow her up here.

Oh God, he was on his way. Should she lie provocatively on the bed, or sit all cool and confident on the armchair? Bed, she decided. That was where she wanted to end up. But as she started to clamber onto it, her heels caught in her dress. Bugger. Shoes off, that's what she should have done first. As she frantically tried to extricate her heel from the hem, she heard the door burst open.

Ben's heart crashed against his ribs as he thrust open the door to Molly's room. He wasn't sure what he expected to find; Molly had never been predictable. Add that to the fact he'd spotted her talking to Duncan as he'd walked round the corner, and Duncan's smirking, *we were just discussing weddings* reply to his unasked question ... yeah, he had no idea what he was walking into.

He certainly hadn't anticipated Molly in some sort of contorted yoga pose in the middle of her bed.

But Christ, she could make any position look sexy. He couldn't say if it was the red hair tumbling round her shoulders, the high flush on her cheeks, or the way her breasts were cushioned, like two pale, soft pillows, within the V of her dress. His gaze dipped back up to her face and his heart stuttered. *That's* what did it for him. The expression on her face, like she didn't know whether to die of embarrassment or laugh out loud.

'Crap, this wasn't how you were meant to find me.' Amusement clearly won and she began to giggle. 'I was shooting for alluring with a heavy dose of take me now, but I've caught my frigging heel in the hem of my dress. If I ever try this again, I need to take my shoes off first.'

'Or maybe just take the dress off. Leave the shoes on.'

Her gaze jumped to his and her cheeks flushed. 'That's another option.'

Arousal bumped up against an overwhelming feeling of fondness, the combination causing an ache in his chest as he walked up to the bed and gently turned her ankle so the heel of her silver sandal slipped out. His gaze travelled up and down her body. 'I feel like a starved man at a sumptuous wedding buffet. I don't know where to start.'

Placing his hands on her calves, he skated them all the way up, over her hips, along the silk dress covering her breasts, and right up to her face. Cupping it, he bent his head and kissed the mouth he spent far too much of his time staring at.

Her lips parted immediately, letting him in, and he sank inside, tasting her from every angle. Unlike their previous

Thank You, Next

fevered kisses this was slow, deep, sensuous. Lust still simmered but he'd put a cap on it for now. They had all night. He didn't want a frantic coupling. He wanted to make love to her.

Pressing kisses along her jawline and down to her collarbone, he slipped his hands behind her back and tugged at the zip of her dress, easing it down.

Her body rippled in a gentle shudder. 'I crashed and burned with alluring, but I guess the *take me* part worked?'

'Oh, I'm definitely taking you.'

He watched, captivated, as the silk flowed off her shoulders, leaving him with the sight of her breasts pushing against the delicate lace of her bra. Breasts he spent an uncomfortable number of hours dreaming about.

Breasts that fell like perfect pear drops into the palm of his hand, he amended after unclipping her bra. 'For the record, you nailed alluring, too.' He ran his thumb over the soft skin, then sucked on a nipple, making her gasp. Satisfaction flooded him and he transferred his attention to the other breast.

'Ben?'

'Hmm?' Distracted was not a strong enough word. Bewitched was closer.

She tugged at his jacket, trying to pull it off his shoulders. 'I want to see you.'

Deciding he needed to see more of *her*, he gently pushed her down onto the bed, then slid the dress over her hips, past the shapely legs and the killer heels, and onto the floor.

What a vision. Pale skin, rosy pink nipples, a smattering of lace covering the place between her thighs that he needed to reacquaint himself with. Now.

With a final look of appreciation, he gave the sexy lace a gentle tug and discarded it onto the floor with the dress. Then he dived into the heat of her, nuzzling, tasting, relishing her moans, the way her thighs pressed against the side of his head, locking him in place.

'So good,' she breathed. 'So frigging good … oooh.' She shuddered as he found exactly the spot he'd been searching for. 'Holy cow, that's it. Just there. Oh my fucking God…'

Her hips catapulted off the bed and he watched with satisfaction as tremors rippled through her as she came, and came, her head thrashing from side to side against the pillow.

Finally she raised herself up, eyes soft, expression dreamy. 'You haven't lost your touch.'

Am I better than Duncan? He crushed the thought. There was no room in this bed for anything else but Molly, her sexy as fuck body, and him.

A determined look spread across her face and she reached for his jacket again. 'Clothes, off. This is the part where you actually *take* me, yes?'

His mouth felt dry as dust. 'Yes.'

Scrambling to his feet, he started to shrug off his jacket, only to get distracted again when he felt the zipper of his trousers slide down and her hands slip into his boxers to drag both them and his trousers down, past his hips. 'Damn. This only works if you take off your shoes.'

He bent to help her, hastily whipping off his socks too, because no man wanted to be left in only his socks.

With just his shirt to go, his fingers fumbled with the buttons as her hand captured his throbbing erection, sliding up and down his length, making him groan as she brushed against the sensitive head.

'He's not forgotten me, has he?' She murmured, her lips feather soft against the heat of his skin.

'You were the last person who touched him,' he croaked

out, then wondered what the fuck he was doing, talking about his dick like it was a person.

Slowly her hands came to a stop, and when he looked down at her, she was gazing up at him, her eyes wide. 'You've not had sex since me?'

'No.' Before she could ask any more questions, he picked her up and almost threw her onto the bed. Then he quickly tore open a condom from his wallet and sheathed himself before climbing on to join her. When he gazed down at her, the tenderness he saw in her eyes sent a rush of emotion hurtling through him. She was letting him back in, not just to her body, but to her heart.

The responsibility of it bore down on him, yet he could no more move away now, than he'd been able to the first time they'd made love all those years ago.

'What are you thinking?'

Her softly voiced question pulled him out of his head. 'I'm thinking that last time I was in this position, I was so weighed down with guilt I had to shut my eyes. I knew it was too soon for me, that I'd end up hurting you. And I did.'

'I don't regret it,' she whispered, her eyes locked on his. 'If I had the time again I'd still choose those two months. They were the best of my life.'

His heart tripped. How could she be so open with him? 'You deserve more. I want to give you more. I want to give you all of me this time.'

She gasped as he sunk into her in one smooth, forceful stroke, as if his body knew the way. As he began to slide in and out in long, rhythmic thrusts, he kept his eyes pinned on hers, watching as the pleasure bloomed across her face. 'I missed this,' he whispered, his hips picking up the pace as his own needs began to batter at his control. 'Missed feeling your tight heat surrounding me. Missed watching you come undone.'

Her eyes widened; her breath began to unravel. 'Oh, oh.'

'That's all you've got for me?' He croaked, body surging into her now, his attempt at control abandoned.

Her mouth opened again, and she chanted his name over and over as her orgasm raced through her.

With a deep, satisfied groan, he gave one, two, three more pumps, then he was gone, lost in his own pleasure, shudders rolling through him as he came.

Chapter Thirty

The days were flying by. Yesterday they'd been kayaking, which had been awesome until they'd fallen in. The look on Ben's face as she'd turned round to look at him too quickly would be forever etched in her memory. Not horror, or anger, or even surprise. Oh no, he'd stared at her with a kind of tender resignation. Like he'd absolutely expected them to end up in the lake. Something that had become clear when Marcus had come over to them afterwards and laughingly handed Ben a ten-pound note.

'You bet Marcus we'd capsize?' She'd asked, part impressed, part insulted.

He'd given her a wry smile. 'You and me, in a boat. Did you really think there'd be any other outcome?'

She'd not been able to contradict him, because that's who they were. Mismatched, some of the viewers had commented. A couple who rubbed each other the wrong way. It was why there were always a steady number of votes to split them up. Yet the threshold hadn't been reached, because there were an equal number of viewers who saw what she *felt*. When they rubbed together, the sparks, the chemistry ... it was phenomenal. Addictive. They could be arguing one minute, but the next he would have her pinned to the wall, her legs wrapped around his waist, his mouth attacking hers.

Apparently, their heated interaction in the hallway the other day had sent viewing figures soaring.

Molly wondered what those viewers would think if they knew how much hotter things got behind closed doors.

Yet despite the clamour for more steamy moments, the production team had decided the voting pattern was sufficient to warrant shaking their pairing up and teaming her with Duncan to do the maze this morning. She couldn't even blame them, because if she'd been a viewer, she'd definitely have voted to put the other two ex-lovers together. See whether there were still sparks between them.

'Have you and Ben talked about your wedding then?' Duncan asked as they made their way along the labyrinth of hedges.

His blue eyes weren't as bewitching as Ben's hazel eyes. They didn't make her so stupidly giddy that she lost herself in them. But they were concerned, caring. They were the same eyes that had helped her through the bleakness of her break up with Ben. 'He doesn't want to get married.'

Duncan halted. 'Whoa. That's ... wow. Why the hell not?'

'He has his reasons.' And she thought she understood them. He'd only seen a dark side of marriage. Helena had wanted to marry him so he could look after her, pull her out of her depression.

'He doesn't want to marry you, or he doesn't want to get married?'

'Doesn't want to get married.' Yet if he met someone he absolutely couldn't image living without, would he be prepared to open his mind to the possibility? *I really don't think I can.* It wasn't a hard no, though maybe it was a hard no for her?

Duncan started walking again, signalling for her to take the left turn. 'How do you feel about that, babe? You always wanted marriage.' He smiled sadly. 'Remember how excited you got when you thought I was proposing that day I told you about the show?'

Embarrassment flooded her. 'I remember.' She didn't feel like the same person she'd been then though. Being on the show had given her a lift, a confidence boost. She'd proven she could handle herself in front of cameras, face whatever task was given her. At the fete, her upcycled clothes had been a huge success, impressing Ben so much he'd promised to help her set up a business.

This Molly felt she was capable of running one.

This Molly was capable of making a man like Ben – confident, smart, drop-dead gorgeous – fall in love with her. And okay, he didn't want to marry her, but wasn't the fact that he thought she was worth loving impressive enough?

'I meant what I said the other day.' Duncan took her arm and steered her towards the path on the right. 'It's not too late. Tell the producers you want to swop to me, and I'll tell them the same.' He smiled down at her. 'We could be one of their success stories, babe. The couple who get married at the end of the series.'

She laughed, remembering how invested they'd been as viewers, desperately hoping at least one of the couples got their happy ever after. Yet as his words settled over her, she remembered their last conversation. 'You said if I wasn't going to marry you, you were going to try and work things out with Jasmine.' She turned to face him. 'Duncan, do you really want to marry *me*? Think about that carefully. Not whether you want to get married, but whether you want to live the rest of your life with *me*.' Feeling a wave of affection, she touched his cheek. 'I appreciate the offer, I really do. And the me who joined the show would have jumped at the chance. But this me … I'm not sure if that's the right way forward anymore. I'm worried we both wanted the marriage, more than we wanted each other?'

His eyebrows crunched together. 'What do you mean?'

'You talked about wanting a family, a wife you could support so she could have your kids. Maybe that's your dream, Duncan. Not marriage to *me*, but marriage to someone who'll give you that.' Raising onto her tiptoes, she pressed a light kiss on his cheek. 'Let's talk again, but whatever happens, know that I really care for you, and I'll be forever grateful to you for loving me at a time when I thought nobody ever would.' Feeling a ball of emotion rise in her throat, she swallowed it down and pointed behind them. 'Now, I think we've been doing this maze all wrong. We need to go back and take the path on the left.'

He shook his head. 'Nah, you're rubbish at directions, remember? Don't worry, I've got this. Let's keep going.'

She shook her head, experiencing a sudden pang of longing for the man she should have been in the maze with. Ben argued with her, disagreed with her. But he never put her down. 'You go your way and I'll go mine. I'll see you at the exit.' She smiled. 'I'll be the one sitting on the bench, waiting for you.'

Ben looked down at his towelling robe and sighed, possibly for the hundredth time since they'd arrived at the spa a few hours ago.

What was he doing in a spa? Fuck knows. After lunch they'd been given the opportunity to choose their own date – something about how this would highlight another of the key foundations of marriage, compromise. He couldn't remember seeing any of that in either his own or his parents' marriages.

It wasn't even as if compromise was specific to marriage. It was essential in any relationship. Not that he'd needed to compromise today though. The moment Natalie had mentioned the option of an afternoon at a spa, Molly's eyes had lit up so much, agreeing to it had been a no-brainer. He'd even gone along with 'the mud thing', and the massage. His exact words had been 'I'll do anything, as long as I don't have to spend the day in white towelling.'

His capitulation might have had something to do with the anguish of seeing her walk off with Duncan to the blasted maze a few hours earlier. Or the relief when he'd watched her come out without the man.

Or maybe he just loved seeing her happy.

The thought buzzed around his brain, causing a few sparks in his subconscious, but those sparks died when he realised he wouldn't be making her happy in a few days' time. Not when he turned her down at the altar.

'It isn't white.'

Molly gave him a cute smile, the one where she was trying not to laugh but her eyes were so bright it was impossible for him not to know how amused she was.

'It's a robe.' There had been a choice of white or brown – mink, the lady had said, as if it helped. 'You've got me sitting here in a robe, waiting to have a facial, having just had a salt body scrub.' He might as well cut off his balls and hand them to her.

'But just look how sexy you are.' Her gaze travelled the length of him and he couldn't lie, his ego swelled at the appreciation in it. 'You've got all the women going ga-ga over you.'

'Most of the women here are twice my age,' he pointed out. Three years ago he would have left it at that, assuming what he was about to say next was obvious. Now he was learning to state the obvious. 'And you're the only one whose opinion matters.'

Her expression turned soft, and he was fast discovering there was a tremendous satisfaction in knowing that sometimes he got his words *right*.

She reached across her lounger – yes, they weren't just in twin robes, they were sitting side by side on ruddy *loungers* – and whispered. 'I think you look sexy.'

It wasn't the glimpse of her cleavage, or even the husk of her voice. It was the promise in her eyes that had him finding his trunks embarrassingly tight. 'That's nothing to how sexy you look, but we need to change the subject.'

She gave him a smile that was part siren, part *I'm about to giggle*. Unable to help himself, he put his hands on either side of her face and gave her a brief but thorough kiss before gently pushing her back on her lounger. 'What's after the facial?'

'We've got our couple's massages.' An image of a naked Molly spread out on a table flashed across his mind. Not helping. But then she picked up the leaflet they'd been given when they arrived and started to read it. 'I still don't know whether we should go for the hot rocks, or a clay wrap, or just a full body massage. And we need to decide Swedish or Shiatsu, Thai or deep tissue. Or we could do an aromatherapy massage.' She let out a long, delighted sigh. 'So many decisions. And after that, we have pedicures.'

And now his libido was back under control. 'I'll do hot rocks, clay, Swedish, whatever. But I'm drawing the line at a pedicure.'

She wriggled her toes, which should not look as sexy as they did. 'Don't you want to give your feet a treat?'

'No. However, I do plan on enjoying your primped and polished feet later.'

She giggled, but any further conversation was interrupted as they were escorted by a staff member to the treatment room. There they were shown two tables swathed in towels and asked to lie down. He'd just climbed onto his when there was a knock on the door. His stomach hurtled south as his sister stepped inside, the camera crew in tow.

He was never going to live this down.

'Getting ready for your facials, I see.' Rachel struggled to school her expression into one of consummate professional, and not of smirking younger sister about to see her brother exfoliated. 'Are you having fun?'

'So much fun,' Molly answered, leaning back on her elbows on the massage table, beaming smile firmly in place. She was like a kid who'd been told she could spend the day in a sweet shop and eat everything she saw.

'And you, Ben?' Rachel's mouth started to twitch.

He gave her a hard stare. 'About as much fun as you'd expect.'

'Well, don't mind the camera crew. They'll keep out of the way. You just lie back and … err … enjoy.' And now his sister was biting the inside of her cheek, her eyes bursting with silent laughter.

'Oh we will,' Molly replied as he reluctantly got into the

supine position beside her. 'Just think, our faces are going to be like a pair of babies' bums after this.'

It was clearly too much for Rachel. She let out a huge roar of laughter, before slapping a hand over her mouth. 'Oh shit, sorry. It's just, seeing Ben ... no, never mind ... ignore me.' Fighting more laughter, she waved towards the two women therapists. 'Start whenever you're ready.'

One of them began to waffle on about cleansing, exfoliation, massage, creams, steaming and ... a face mask? He was going to get a fucking face mask?

'What have you got me into?' He hissed under his breath at Molly.

She smiled sweetly. 'You'll thank me later when we're all exfoliated and polished. And relaxed, so very, very relaxed.' She winked. 'And maybe a bit sleepy, too. So sleepy we might have to go to bed early.'

Immediately the thought of his sister sniggering in the corner, of the cameras watching him have God knows what done to his face, became minor irritations. Yet as he anticipated his evening, lurking in the back of his mind, encroaching too near to be dismissed, was the knowledge his time with Molly was soon going to come to a crashing end.

Chapter Thirty-One

In a couple of days, the show would be over.

In a couple of days, she would be walking down an aisle.

In a couple of days, she could be *married*.

But not if she stuck with Ben.

Her heart floundered in her chest, telling her everything about how it was feeling right now, yet she couldn't ignore that her original aim of marrying Duncan was still a possibility.

Was she really going to let this false bubble she was living in with Ben stop her from achieving it? *I'm worried we both wanted the marriage, more than we wanted each other.* She'd raised it as a question to Duncan, but it was one she needed to answer for herself, too.

'Pink or yellow.' Chloe pursed her lips. 'Or red, maybe?' She spread the photos of the floral arrangements onto the table. 'This is ridiculous, planning a wedding I know I'm not going to go through with.'

Molly was sitting with Maya, Chloe and Jasmine, all of them trying to choose their wedding flowers. It was just one of a whole list of things the producers had given them to sort out in the next couple of days.

'But you don't know what you're going to say until you actually get to the end of that aisle,' Jasmine insisted.

'Err, no way am I committing myself to a lifetime of Liam, and only Liam,' Chloe protested. 'Not even for a free holiday in frigging Hawaii. And anyway, this is so sexist, us girls sitting here choosing flowers while the guys bugger off and play tennis.'

'I hear you.' Maya flicked through the book they'd been given. 'But I guess in the guys' defence, they'd arranged to play before they knew what we'd be doing this morning.'

'Duncan will be here after his gym session,' Jasmine chimed in. 'Before he left he told me he thought we should go for pink though, so that's cut down the choices.'

Molly froze. He was actively planning his wedding to Jasmine, yet at the same time saying he wanted to marry *her*? 'Ben wouldn't be much help even if he were here.' She forced herself to keep the conversation going. 'He'd just tell me to choose whatever I wanted.'

Chloe gave her a thoughtful look. 'At one point I thought I was going to get a shot at him, but he seems to be all over you right now. Bet you're fucking like rabbits, yeah?'

'Chloe!' Maya rolled her eyes, nodding towards the cameras in the corner of the room. 'That's between Molly and Ben.'

'Why? We all joined this show knowing we were going to have any relationship talked about and scrutinised.'

'I'm enjoying being with Ben,' Molly replied quietly, trying to ignore the way Chloe had tagged *seems to be* and *right now* onto the bit about him being all over her.

'But are you going to *marry* him?' Jasmine asked, in

between carefully noting down the codes for the arrangements she liked. 'That's what we're all supposed to be here for, isn't it? To get married.'

'It's certainly why I came on the show,' Molly agreed.

Maya raised an eyebrow. 'Is that a big hint that you're going to say *I do*?'

If Ben was standing at the altar, what would be the point? He wouldn't say it back. Yet if Duncan was the man waiting for her, would she really still want to marry him? Especially as he was lining up a reserve bride? 'I'm just saying when I came on here, I really wanted to get married.'

Maya frowned. 'Why?'

Molly couldn't remember ever being asked that question. 'It's the certainty of it, I think. The security of knowing that you've found someone who's not only promised to stick with you, no matter what, but they're willing to make that promise legally binding.'

'Yeah, but married couples break that promise all the time,' Jasmine argued. 'For me marriage is all about kids. I think it's easier for them to have the same surname as their parents, and it kind of gives them a bigger official family, you know? It joins his family and mine. Plus my mum wants to buy a fancy outfit and my dad wants to walk me down the aisle.'

Maya laughed. 'All good reasons. For me, getting married is the ultimate expression of love. Living with someone is like hedging your bets, playing it safe. Marrying them says I know I'm never going to meet anyone I'd rather spend my life with.' She gave a little shrug of her shoulders. 'To be honest, I'm not sure I'm there with Marcus yet.'

Is that what Ben was doing with her, Molly wondered, hedging his bets? Waiting for someone better to come along?

With a sigh, she looked down at the bouquet images. 'I'm going for red.'

Everyone made their decisions, and then the floral arrangements were taken away and in their place trollies were wheeled in, filled with cake samples.

Natalie clapped her hands together in that way she had that was part school teacher, part showman. 'Now we come to the best part of wedding planning, choosing the cake. In HEA Towers we don't have a wedding meal after the ceremony, as not all your weddings will end in marriage.' She paused to mime wiping tears from her eyes. 'But we hope you'll all want to celebrate the end of your time here with cake and champagne, so find a trolley and get sampling.'

'Bet the guys turn up now,' Molly muttered.

Rachel, who'd come to stand next to her, laughed. 'We just passed them in the corridor.'

'Was Duncan with them?' Jasmine asked, frowning. 'He told me not to choose without him.'

Molly could have saved her the worry and told her Duncan's idea of the perfect cake was one made with carrots, oats and yoghurt.

Was he part of her past now?

And what about the man who'd just strolled into the room, hair still damp from the shower? Where did he fit into her life? Dressed casually in faded jeans and a navy polo shirt, one hand loosely in his pocket, her heart swooped as she watched him walk over to her, long legs eating up the distance.

'Hey.' The quick kiss he pressed to her lips woke all the butterflies in her stomach. 'Looks like we missed the flowers and made the cake. Some would say that's a result.'

'Some would say that was planned,' she countered, which made him laugh.

'Not sure how helpful I'd have been.'

'But you can force yourself to eat cake?'

'I'll try my hardest.' He bent to whisper into her ear, causing her to inhale a lungful of freshly showered male. 'Then can we get out of here?'

Damn those sparks of arousal that skated down her spine. That made her crave his touch, his attention, crave *him*, like she'd never craved anyone. 'Probably.'

He grinned. 'Let us eat cake.'

Sex with Molly: outstanding. Sex with Molly in the middle of the afternoon: unbeatable. Even on a stomach full of marzipan, Victoria sponge and white chocolate. He could have predicted she'd insist on trying every sample, even though he'd attempted to persuade her the first one was fine. It wasn't like it mattered; they weren't actually getting married.

'We have to come up with a list of people we want to come to the wedding,' Molly murmured, breaking through his thoughts.

She was half lying on top of him in the bed, his bed, this time, because he'd argued they might wear the bedsprings out on hers. He'd only been half joking.

'We really have to invite people to a wedding that isn't going to happen?'

'The wedding will happen. What might not happen is the marriage.' She shifted, moving away from him and onto her back, creating a physical distance yet also, it felt, an emotional one.

'Might not happen?' Unease rippled through him. 'You're

not still hoping we'll get married, are you? Because I told you—'

'You won't marry me. I know.' Her eyes avoided his, and that unease became full-blown alarm. 'But Duncan told me if I asked to swop to him, he would marry me.'

What the fuck? He wanted to wrap his hands around the man's thick arms, shove him against the wall and ask him what the hell he was playing at, trying to pinch Molly from under his nose. 'That bastard plays dirty.'

'You think it's a game?' She snapped back. 'You don't think he could actually want to marry me because he loves me?'

Instantly contrite, Ben sat up. 'Shit, I'm sorry. Of course he could love you. I've told you, you're very easy to love.' Emotion jammed his throat and the next words came out scratchy. 'Damn it, Molly, *I* love you.'

Her emerald bright eyes searched his. 'But not enough to marry me.'

'That's not fair.' The pressure on his chest felt suffocatingly heavy, like someone was standing on it. 'You know my views on marriage. It's unhealthy, binding yourself to someone else, making them responsible for you, for your happiness.' Helena's face flashed through his mind, her eyes full of hope, her expression so trusting as she told him she was alright now she'd married him. As if *he* could save her. 'Relationships should be partnerships, supporting each other, being there for each other. But not being *consumed* by each other.'

'Marriage doesn't mean that to everyone,' she stated quietly, the pity in her eyes cutting him to the quick. 'Maya said it was the ultimate expression of love. A public declaration that you're never going to love anyone else like you do the person you're marrying.' She gave him a sad smile. 'She said living together was just hedging your bets.'

Christ, that sounded awful. And not how he thought of it at all. 'Is that how you feel?'

She bit into her lip, eyes darting towards his, then away again. 'You know what happened to me with my first mum. I guess being rejected like that didn't just make me need the words, it made me need the legal promise. The security of knowing I won't be abandoned at the drop of a hat again.'

'Shit, Molly. I don't know what to say.' Emotions swamped him. Fear he was losing her, panic he couldn't do anything about it. 'Can I hold you? Please?' She hesitated, and his heart went into free fall, but then she gave a small incline of her head. As he bundled her into his arms, a little of his fear subsided when she didn't resist him.

Holding her tight, feeling her body snug against his, he cursed fate that the two women he'd fallen in love with had both needed more from him than he could give.

'With your mum,' he asked after a while, 'did you have any warning she was going to leave?'

'None that my seven-year-old self picked up on. I caught her crying a lot, yes, but she'd wave my concerns away and I figured that's what adults *did*. That morning she made me pancakes, which was usually a weekend treat, so maybe I should have realised something was off, but at the time I just thought it was my lucky day. Then she dropped me off to school like normal.' Her body shifted as she burrowed further into him, her voice turning quieter. 'Turns out it wasn't my lucky day, after all.'

His chest squeezed painfully. It was so totally fucked up that a mother could do that to a child.

'Maybe there were more signs that she wanted to leave me, signs I should have picked up on,' she whispered after a beat. 'Because it turns out I'm not great at noticing them.'

His stomach plummeted. 'I bet you're looking for those signs now.'

She exhaled a breath. 'Every frigging day.'

Guilt slammed through him like a runaway train. How could she ever be happy with him if she spent every day expecting him to blindside her again?

'I'm in love with you, Molly. And I don't want what we have to end when we leave the show. I want to continue seeing you. Be in a committed relationship with you.' It felt like his heart was breaking down the middle. 'I wish I'd met you before Helena, but I didn't and now … fuck, I'm terrified what I can offer isn't enough, but it's all I'm capable of giving you right now.'

There was a long, humming silence, filled with unspoken words. When she finally did speak, it did little to ease the pain in his chest. 'I know,' she whispered. 'I know.'

Chapter Thirty-Two

It was the day before her wedding. And that was surely a sentence to send a flutter of nerves through any bride. Even one who wasn't going to actually get married.

Yet the man she'd decided to walk down the aisle towards, loved her.

She'd chosen the uncertainty of a relationship with Ben over the certainty of marriage with Duncan.

Stupid decision? Very possibly.

'Molly?'

She snapped out of her head and turned her attention back to Rachel, who was showing her and Ben the proposed setting for their wedding. The ballroom.

'What do you think? We can make an arch of the red roses you chose, which would look great against this backdrop.' Rachel waved towards the gold-framed paintings and deep red walls.

It looked like the perfect venue ... for someone else's wedding. 'Umm, can't we do it outside?' The day might not be destined for happy ever after, but Molly figured it might end up being the only wedding she'd ever have.

Rachel looked at Ben, who gave one of his characteristic shrugs. 'Whatever Molly wants.'

'This is *our* wedding,' she reminded him. It was one thing letting her choose, another being so detached he didn't seem to care.

'But it's not.' He slotted his hands into his jeans' pockets. 'It's us putting on a show in front of the cameras.'

She tried to remind herself he was being practical. 'I'm still going to be wearing a bridal dress. I'll be walking down the aisle to whatever music we finally agree on, holding a bouquet of red roses which I chose so it wouldn't clash with my hair. My parents will be here, and my best friends. We're going to eat cake and drink champagne, even though we won't be cutting the cake as man and wife.' Damn it, why were eyes starting to prick, her voice to sound shaky?

'Hey.' He strode over to her, eyes full of concern as he tilted her chin so she had to look at him. 'What's wrong?'

'Nothing.' She sniffed.

The corner of his mouth lifted in a wry smile. 'Use your words, Molly.'

'Funny.' Out of the corner of her eyes she could see Rachel and the camera crew watching them. *Filming* them. God, this was embarrassing. 'I know I'm being stupid,' she whispered. 'I know I should see this like you do, one final thing to endure before you get to escape, but ... but I'm actually sad this is all coming to an end. And I'm sad I'm about to have a wedding without any of the joy.'

A deep furrow bisected his beautiful eyes. 'It doesn't have to be joyless. It can be a ... a celebration of our month here.' He kissed away a tear that had slid down her cheek. 'I bet there aren't many people who thought you and I would make it this far after our first meeting.'

'Me included,' she mumbled. If only the word wedding wasn't so aligned with marriage, wasn't so aligned with where she'd wanted to end up.

'All the time in the world,' Ben's softly spoken words nudged her out of her head.

'Sorry?'

His thumb caressed the curve of her cheek, eyes warm and understanding on hers. 'That's the song I think you should walk down the aisle to. A reminder that there's a life waiting for us outside these four walls. A life where we can make plans, do what *we* want to do. All at a pace of our own choosing.' He planted a soft kiss on her lips. 'A life where I spend every day making sure you know how much I love you.'

But it's not enough to marry me.

She swallowed the words. He'd explained his reasons and she'd accepted them. If she was choosing Ben, she was choosing a relationship without a safety net.

Rachel cleared her throat and Molly felt a deep sigh rumble through Ben. 'We know you're still there,' he said dryly.

'Good. Would you like to share with the viewers what you've been discussing?' She turned to Molly. 'You looked quite upset there.'

'I'm a bit overwhelmed this is all coming to an end,' Molly admitted, keeping to part of the truth. 'I've had such a fabulous time on the show, and I don't want to leave.'

'And is that how you feel, Ben?' Rachel asked, with a glint in her eyes.

He gave his sister a long-suffering look. 'No, Rachel. It isn't how I feel. I'm looking forward to not being followed around by you guys.'

She rolled her eyes and waved the cameras away before turning back to her brother. 'As unbelievable as this may sound, I'm looking forward to not following you around, too.' She pointed towards the door. 'Why don't we head outside and you can tell us where you'd like your wedding to take place.'

'Does it really matter?'

Yes, Molly wanted to scream at Ben, *it matters to me*. She knew it was the sentimental side of her, rubbing up against the practical side of him, but to hear him treat their day as such a chore, was hurtful.

'Talking now as your sister and not the associate producer,' Rachel said to Ben as they walked towards the French doors. 'Have you spoken to our parents about coming to the wedding?'

He shook his head, his expression hardening. 'I didn't see the point.'

Molly's heart sunk even further. Hadn't he just said they should treat it as a celebration? Certainly, *she* wanted her parents there. She wanted them to meet him.

'Well, it's your decision, so fine,' Rachel answered, glancing over at her brother as they walked past the swimming pool and down the steps onto the main lawn. 'Who are you going to invite then?'

Ben stared straight ahead. 'I've only invited Jack and Sam.'

Rachel pursed her lips. 'Doesn't sound like much of a wedding list.'

Ben halted and turned to face his sister. 'It isn't much of a wedding. Sorry to put a pin in your happy ending bubble but we won't be saying "I do". I respect that you love the show you work on, but putting couples through a sham of a wedding so you can provide viewers with some *will they, won't they* drama under the banner of entertainment? It fucking stinks.'

His eyelids slammed shut and he heaved in a breath, only opening them again once he'd let it all out.

Tension pinged through the air following his outburst, and Molly didn't know where to look. Ben had been tearing a strip off his sister, yet it felt like he'd been ripping into her, too. 'Umm, anywhere outside is fine for our wedding, our sham wedding,' she corrected, tears stinging her eyes again. 'I've just realised I promised to meet the girls to … err … try on our dresses.'

She heard Ben curse under his breath before saying her name, but she needed time away from him. Ignoring his plaintive look, she hurried inside.

And slapped straight into a wall of muscle.

'Whoa, where are you running off to?'

Duncan put his hands on her arms to steady her.

'Nowhere.'

He scanned her face, his brow furrowing. 'You look upset, babe. What has that bastard said now?'

'I'm fine.'

'Yeah, that's a lie. You think I can't tell if you're upset after dating you for over a year?' He sighed. 'Look, I'm glad I bumped in to you. I know you turned my offer of marriage down, but it's not too late to rethink it.'

Molly didn't want to hear this. She'd made her decision, and yet … there was something about the way Duncan was looking at her now, all soft and caring, that reminded her she had been happy with him. Until Ben had come along. 'You can't mean that,' she whispered.

'Why not? We were good together. No dramas, just you and me, rubbing along happily.' He smiled. 'You can rely on me to look after you, babe. I'll give you the security you need.'

It was what she'd always longed for, yet something about the way he said it, grated on her. He meant well, but needing someone to look after her, like she was weak, like she couldn't look after herself? Was that how he saw her? How *Ben* saw her?

No. She remembered the discussions they'd had about her starting her own upcycling business. The way he'd looked at her with such confidence. *The fete was your success, not mine. You're more than capable of doing it again, on a larger scale.*

Ben saw the woman she wanted to be. Duncan only saw the struggling, heartbroken woman she'd been when he'd first met her. 'And Jasmine? Isn't she expecting you to marry her?'

He shrugged. 'I like her, sure, but I want to marry you.'

'You can't keep saying that. You're confusing me.'

'I've got to keep saying it, babe. By tomorrow, it will be too late.' He reached for her hand. 'Look, I get it, everything's too much right now. Why don't you come with me. I've got just the thing to take your mind off things.'

'Does it involve alcohol?' She really, really needed a drink.

Duncan studied her for a moment, then nodded. 'I guess I can deviate off my schedule for once.' He laughed. 'Come on, let's go and get smashed.'

It was probably a terrible idea, but it was also exactly what she needed.

Chapter Thirty-Three

Ben's heart crumpled as he watched Molly dash off into the house. He'd royally fucked that up.

'I'd call it wedding night jitters, but apparently it's all a gimmick,' Rachel remarked sourly, which didn't help lift his mood

'Don't,' he retorted tightly, his temper right on the edge.

She must have heard the warning in his voice because her chin, set at fight mode angle, relaxed a fraction. 'The thing is, you might hate this show and all it stands for, you might hate marriage and all that stands for, but Molly doesn't.'

'I know.'

'Marriage to people like Molly, to people who go on this show and who watch it' – she stared pointedly at him – 'and those who work on it, it's like the holy grail of love. The place we all want to end up when we meet the person of our dreams. Our soulmate. The one we can't live without.' She stared him right in the eye. 'You once believed in it too, or you wouldn't have got married.'

'I got married because Helena wanted it, not because I believed in it,' he protested.

Rachel's expression hardened. 'So you were prepared to compromise for Helena, but you're not prepared to do the same for Molly?'

'That's not... Hell, do you know what you're asking me?' Anger coiled in his gut. 'Helena depended on me and I let her down. I married her, sure, but I still wasn't enough for her. Still wasn't able to give her what she needed.' He jammed a hand through his hair. 'You think I'm not acutely aware that the same would happen with Molly? That I am, actually, not nearly good enough for her, either?' His voice cracked. 'You think I'm not totally and utterly aware of how I could break her, like I broke Helena?'

'No.' Rachel's arms appeared around his waist, her hug tight. 'You take that back right now. You didn't break Helena. You tried to fix her, but you couldn't because she was the only one who could fix herself. Molly doesn't want to marry you because she needs you to fix her, or even to take care of her. She's only needs you to love her.' She let out a small sigh. 'But fine, we've had this argument about marriage before and I know you're not going to change. So you need to make tomorrow about ensuring she's not humiliated. If she's not going to come away from it married, at least make sure she knows how much you love her. That way, when you cock up – because let's face it, that *is* going to happen – but at least when it does, she'll know it's just a blip. She'll still believe, absolutely, that you won't leave her, won't break up with her like you did last time.'

Won't abandon her. Ben added the words quietly to himself. Christ, Molly deserved to be worshipped, put on a pedestal. At the very least, to know she was the centre of someone's universe.

He straightened his shoulders, nodded at his sister. 'Use the opportunity tomorrow to make sure she knows she's it for me. Got it.'

Rachel smiled. 'Good. And now you can help me choose the perfect place for you to do this while you give her a chance to cool down.'

'Okay. Thanks.' He bent to kiss the top of his sister's head, like he'd done many times before. 'And sorry for mouthing off like I did. I might not like the show, but I know a lot of people do.'

'And do you know why that is?'

He gave her a wry smile. 'There are a lot more fans of marriage than I realise?'

'No. Irrespective of your views on marriage, the show deals with probably the most important decision we ever have to make in life. Is this person I'm dating The One?'

He didn't need the ache in his heart to know the answer to the question.

The bigger question was whether, by not marrying Molly tomorrow, he was going to lose her.

It didn't take Ben long to decide on the perfect place for his and Molly's ... ceremony, he decided. A ceremony where he could publicly let her know how he felt.

Yes, that made sense to him now.

He also gave Rachel a list of things he wanted for the outdoor venue, and a final request to collect an item from his house.

Then he headed inside to find Molly.

He tried the kitchen first, because it was the main hangout, but there was no cute redhead in sight. Just Marcus and Maya, chatting easily as they made themselves what looked to be a pitcher of something alcoholic.

'Hey, Ben.' Marcus looked up from where he was slicing cucumbers. 'You want to join us for a glass of Pimm's?'

'Maybe later. I was looking for Molly.'

Marcus glanced at Maya, and something unspoken passed between them. 'I think she's playing pool.'

He felt a ripple of unease. 'Okay, thanks.'

After another silent communication between them, Maya cleared her throat. 'You should know she was upset when we saw her.'

'I know. That's why I need to find her.'

'You should probably also know that Duncan *did* find her. And that's who she's playing pool with. Against James and Ella.' Maya's eyes lifted to his. 'And this is the second pitcher of Pimm's we've made. They polished off the first one.'

The unease of earlier turned into full-blown fear. Muttering his thanks, he marched off to the pool room. Had he done the unthinkable, and pushed Molly back into Duncan's arms?

His first thought when he burst into the pool room, was thank God. Molly wasn't sitting on Duncan's lap, or taking part in any of the terrifying scenarios that had played through his head.

She was bent over the table, cue in hand, all her focus on the balls in front of her.

'Ah, Ben.' James waved him over. 'Come and join us. Have you seen your girl in action on the pool table? She's been hustling us.'

'I remember she was good.' He walked over slowly, aware of Duncan's eyes following him. 'Beat me a few times.'

The ball Molly had been eyeing up, sailed into the top left pocket. She looked up and grinned at Duncan, which made Ben's hands curl into fists. 'Good shot,' he said, loudly enough that she could hear, hoping his voice sounded steadier than he felt.

She jolted, clearly unaware he was there. 'Oh … umm … thanks. Did you and Rachel agree on somewhere for our … err … the…?'

'Ceremony,' he filled in. 'We did, yes.' She nodded, teeth sunk into her lower lip, and he hated the tension he could feel even from this distance. She was relaxed with James, with Duncan, but not with him? 'Can we talk?'

'She's got a game to finish first.' Duncan uncoiled himself from the chair he'd been sitting in, like a minder, protecting his client. A boyfriend protecting his girl.

Ben's fists tightened so much his nails dug into the skin.

'I do.' Molly nodded carefully, like she was worried her head was going to roll off her neck. 'I'm showing them how to play pool.'

'So I hear.'

She gave him a cautious smile before bending down to line up her next shot. After helping himself to what was left of the Pimm's, he leant against the wall to watch. It hurt to see her with Duncan, but maybe he needed the reminder of how easy it would be to lose her, if he didn't buck up his ideas.

'Did you hear, we're on stag and hen dos tonight.' James's voice cut through his morose thoughts.

'We're not in our couples?'

'Nope. Apparently we're not allowed to see our prospective brides now until the wedding. Some stupid Victorian superstitious shit if you ask me. Then again,' he glanced around, saw Ella was standing by the pool table with Duncan and Molly, and whispered. 'I need to get away from Ella. This wedding crap is driving me nuts. I really think she's going to say *I do*, even though I told her I won't be.'

Ben winced sympathetically. 'Maybe you need to be clearer, just to be sure.'

'Yeah, won't harm. Last thing I want is for her to be humiliated like that. What about you, mate? You had the wedding discussion with Molly?'

'Yes,' Ben replied distractedly, his eyes on her as she laughed at something Duncan said.

James proceeded to rattle on about the joy of having a stag do without having to get married, but all Ben could think was how much he'd miss Molly tonight. And how important it was he made things right between them before tomorrow.

Finally, finally, Duncan sunk the black and the game was over. Ben thought his jaw would break as he watched Duncan give Molly a celebratory hug, but he forced himself not to react. It was one thing her knowing how important she was to him. Another being overly possessive.

Still, he wasted no time slotting his arm around her waist at the first opportunity. He was about to lead her out of the room when Rachel popped her head inside.

'Can you all come to the sitting room, please. We want to tell you what's happening tonight and the schedule for tomorrow.'

Damn it. As the others trailed out, he gave his sister a pleading look and she mouthed, 'You've got three minutes.'

He suspected three hours wasn't long enough for the apology he needed to make, but before he could even get the opening words straight in his head, Molly was talking.

Thank You, Next

'You don't need to look so worried, Ben. I'm sorry about earlier. I got a bit over-emotional and let all the talk of flowers and cake go to my head like you said I would. But I'm over it now and everything is absolutely fine. Hunky dory, in fact.' As he tried to keep up with the constant stream of words, he wondered quite how much of the Pimm's she'd drunk. 'We aren't getting married, but that doesn't mean we're splitting up. That's it, isn't it? We're just rolling along, seeing where this takes us. Tomorrow is about us saying goodbye to the show, but not necessarily goodbye to each other, even though we're both going to be saying no to each other at the altar.' She gave him a tipsy smile. 'No more blindsiding Molly. She knows exactly where she stands. On her own two feet.' A little giggle burst out of her, that sounded like a hiccup. 'Yep, I've finally worked it out and I realise I don't need anybody to marry me, because you know what? I'm absolutely fine by myself.'

Why did what she was saying sound so cold, so *not* what he wanted, when it was exactly the message he'd intended to convey? 'This is okay with you, then?' He searched her eyes and found her gaze slightly unfocussed and unwilling to lock on to his.

'Of course. It's ... sensible. And very grown up.'

He couldn't work out if she was happy, or sad, or just drunk.

'Molly.' He placed his hands on her face and gently tilted her head so her eyes were forced to meet his. 'Tomorrow *will* be a special day for us.'

'Yes, maybe.' A frown appeared between her eyes. 'You don't even want me to meet your parents, Ben.'

He reared back, stunned. 'You think that's because of you? Christ, Molly. I don't get on with my parents. Haven't really spoken to them since I buggered off to uni at eighteen.' The three minutes were slipping away, and he was no further forward. 'Look, when I was ten, I caught my mum having sex with the neighbour. I blurted it out at the dinner table that evening, and both my parents were horrified. Not in what I was saying, because apparently that was common knowledge, but that I was saying it at all. I was told what they did in private wasn't any of my business and to keep my thoughts and feelings to myself in the future.' He gave her a wry smile. 'Probably didn't help my whole *unable to communicate with other human beings*, issue. And the fact that Dad was the laughing stock of the neighbourhood, that he lost his dignity, his self-respect, all because he couldn't easily untangle himself from his marriage, probably didn't help my whole anti-marriage stance.' He waited for her eyes to meet his. 'But it's the only reason I don't want them here tomorrow. Rachel keeps in contact with them. I don't.'

'Oh.' Her expression held both sympathy and a glint of understanding. 'Looks like I'm not the only one slightly screwed up by a genetic parent.'

'You're not.' He angled his head. 'So you don't have to worry about my parents. Do I need to worry about Duncan?'

She blinked and glanced away. 'It's you I won't be marrying tomorrow.'

His heart stuttered. She was just restating what they'd agreed, but it sounded awful the way she said it. Like she was turning him down. Turning down a life they could have together.

Before he could press her more on what she meant though, they were interrupted by a knock on the door and his sister's voice. 'Three minutes was up two minutes ago.'

Swearing under his breath, he bent to kiss Molly. 'I'll see you tomorrow then?'

She nodded. 'Better go, or you'll have no family members at our "ceremony".'

The flat tone in which she said it made him wonder if it was the right word, after all. 'I thought calling it that was less liable to result in a kick in the nuts than sham wedding.'

'You're right,' Rachel's voice interrupted from the other side of the door. 'But if you don't get your arse in the sitting room right now, your balls will still be in danger.'

Molly sniggered and gave him a little push. 'Better do as you're told.'

He took a second to tuck a strand of hair behind her ear. Another to drop a final kiss on her mouth. Then took her hand as they walked to the sitting room, Rachel snapping at their heels.

Chapter Thirty-Four

It was the morning of her wedding. Holy shit.

Lying flat on her back in bed, Molly blinked up at the ceiling, willing her heart to stop racing.

A groan came from the body lying under the duvet beside her, and immediately she sat up, her pulse hammering ... but then the body giggled. Not Ben then.

'We're getting married in the morning.' The body began to sing, off-key, then started giggling again. 'No, wait, we're getting married ... *this* morning. How the fuck did that happen?'

Molly was more interested in how the frigging heck Jasmine had ended up in her bed? As she tried to comb through the cobwebs in her brain, a voice came from the floor.

'You're having a wedding, Jas. I doubt you're getting married.' Maya, sensible, straightforward Maya, who was somehow lying on a mattress on the floor with...

'She's definitely not getting married.' Chloe nodded over to Molly. 'Duncan's still into Molly.'

All eyes were on her. 'Umm.' Molly shifted uncomfortably

before giving Jasmine an apologetic look. 'He did offer to marry me.'

'Oh my God.' Chloe's eyes boggled. 'Did you say yes? Are you marrying him today, not Ben?'

Jasmine cleared her throat. 'Hate to be the bearer of bad news, Moll, but Duncan is going to marry me. We agreed. That's why he was adamant on what he wanted for the wedding. For us it's going to be real.'

Whereas Ben hadn't been bothered about the details at all. For him, the wedding had always been a sham. 'I guess we'll find out when you meet at the altar.'

'Are you really planning to say "I do" to a guy who's also toying with marrying someone else?' Chloe asked Jasmine, her expression a mix of disgust and horror.

Jasmine pursed her lips and gave Molly a calculating look before turning back to Chloe. 'I've only got *her* word for that. And the way I figure it, marriage is about trust, yes? So if Duncan's there at the end of the altar, and prepared to look me in the eye when I stand next to him, then I'll know my answer.' She sat up, blonde hair in a mess, make-up smeared. 'And anyway, whatever happens we're still putting on dresses, getting our hair and make-up done, oh and our nails, and drinking loads of champagne.'

'I second that.' Molly flopped back on the bed. They were all so different, but last night, over cocktails and hours of dancing to nineties pop music, they'd somehow managed to bond. 'Does anyone remember why we all ended up sleeping in my room?'

'You started getting all whiny about wanting to find Ben,' Jasmine replied, giving Molly's ribs a quick prod.

'We decided the only way to stop you making a tit of yourself and getting caught by the producers sneaking down the corridor to his room, was to lock you in yours,' Chloe added.

'And guard you,' Jasmine added, then frowned. 'Which somehow turned into us dragging Maya's mattress in here.'

'Yeah, because Maya then said she wanted to see Marcus,' Chloe added. 'So we told her she had to be under guard, too.'

'I did not say that.' Maya stuck out her chin defiantly until they all stared back at her. 'Okay, maybe I said that once. Right at the end of the evening when I was tired and drunk and overly emotional.'

'I'm sure I took a photo of you.' Chloe grabbed at her phone, then winced. 'Err, didn't you say your family was turning up at nine o'clock, Jas?'

'Oh, fuck.' Jasmine pushed back the duvet and groaned as she attempted to stand. 'Who said they wanted to drink loads of champagne today? I think I'm going to be sick.'

'What time is your wedding?' Molly asked Chloe as Jasmine staggered around, looking for her shoes.

'Twelve o'clock.' Chloe shrugged. 'It's not like me and Liam are headed for Mr and Mrs, but I can't wait to see my mates, and my parents. Plus my kid sister is excited to be a bridesmaid, even though I told her this is just a practice for when I have a proper wedding with a guy I'm actually in love with.'

I'm in love. The words kept bouncing around Molly's head. 'What if that guy said he loved you, but he didn't want to marry you?'

Chloe scrunched up her face. 'Then I'd ditch him and find someone else who did. I mean, if he's not prepared to compromise and give me something I really want, would I want to stick with him anyway? Does he actually love me at all?'

Molly's stomach churned. Chloe was saying everything she'd thought. Yet had Chloe ever really been in love? *I'd ditch him and find someone else who did* was easy to say, but once the heart was fully entangled with someone, it seemed impossible to untangle it. Molly *had* found someone else prepared to marry her. Yet still her heart ached for Ben.

'I hate to break up this enlightening chat, but we need to get a move on,' Maya interrupted. 'By my reckoning, we have Chloe and Liam at twelve o'clock in the orangery, Duncan and Jasmine at three o'clock by the pool...

'It sounds like some weird Cluedo game,' Chloe interrupted, making them all laugh.

'Let's hope there won't be any daggers,' Maya added drolly. 'Me and Marcus are at one o'clock, in the ballroom. When are you and Ben?'

'Two.' Molly placed a hand on her belly and felt the butterflies starting to flap. 'Somewhere outside. I let Ben choose.'

Maya's eyebrows flew up. 'You didn't want a say in where your wedding was going to take place?'

'We're calling it a ceremony.' Yep, that silenced the butterflies. 'And we'd had an argument at the time, so I kind of waltzed off and left him and Rachel to it.'

'You two are pretty fiery together,' Jasmine remarked. 'Were you that way with Duncan?'

'No,' Molly admitted, thinking back to their time together. Were she and Duncan more compatible? Or... 'I think maybe with Duncan I was trying to be what he wanted me to be. With Ben, I'm just myself.' A fiery, spontaneous woman who talked a lot, and had zero filter, who liked to eat, to drink, and wasn't overly bothered how skinny she looked in her leggings.

'You should always be yourself.' Jasmine flicked her hair

back over her shoulders. 'If the guy doesn't like that, then tough.'

'I heard you went white-water rafting for your last date with Duncan. Was that really what *you* wanted to do?' Molly asked softly, watching as a flicker of uncertainty crossed Jasmine's face. 'You don't need to answer that, but promise me you'll think about it before you go down the aisle.'

Jasmine nodded, then picked up the tight sequined dress she'd worn last night and started wriggling into it. 'Good luck girls. May the day end how you want it to.'

Maya and Chloe followed Jasmine out a few moments later and suddenly the room was quiet. As she lay back on the bed, Jasmine's parting words hummed through Molly's mind.

How *did* she want the day to end?

Ben glanced around the garage where Rachel had stored the things he'd requested for their ceremony this afternoon.

Would Molly see a thoughtful gesture, his attempt at making it clear how much he understood her, loved her. Or would she see a pile of crap?

'Love you to bits, bro, but are you sure about this?' Jack, long-time friend from school and acting today as best man and grumpy painter, threw down his brush. Then proceeded to wipe his paint-streaked hands across his shirt. 'Most women want glamour at their wedding. Not junk.'

'Hey, it's artful junk.' Sam, his other school mate, second best man and more genial painter, scowled over at Jack. 'At least the stuff I've painted is.'

'Isn't there some saying about not being able to make fancy purses out of pigs ears?' Jack pointed at the wooden ladders they'd just been painting green. 'I reckon it would be easier than making a wedding arch out of fucking stepladders.' He gave a despairing shake of his head. 'What's happened to you, man? Have you been taken over by aliens or something? First you agree to come on some reality dating show, now you're painting crap for a wedding you don't want to end in marriage but for a woman you do want to impress the hell out of even though you ditched her three years ago?'

Ben played the words back and realised it was all factually accurate, even though there were some subtle, yet important, additions. 'I only agreed to come on the show to help my sister out. We're not painting crap; we're upcycling. And while you're correct – we won't be getting married – I do want her to leave today knowing that I love her.'

'And rather than marry her, you're going to do that by making her stand next to a couple of stepladders?'

'Hey, you forgot the bit about her walking down to them on old rugs lined with jam jars,' Sam added unhelpfully.

'Jam jars containing tealights,' he corrected. Then wondered if Jack was right, and he *had* been implanted with an alien brain a few months ago.

Feeling suddenly weary, he slumped onto one of the crates they were about to turn into seats. Or was it tables? Fuck, his head was swimming, and not just from the hangover after last night. Weddings that might or might not end in marriage, cameras, friends and families drifting into the house, flowers arriving by the lorry load… Was any of that why he was feeling so unbalanced today? Or was it that he'd not seen or spoken to Molly since he'd watched her and the rest of the women disappear off in a coach for their collective hen do yesterday?

What was she thinking now? Was she weighing up

Thank You, Next

Duncan's concrete offer to marry her, versus his dubious-sounding *ceremony*?

'Hey.' Sam gave his leg a kick. 'There's more painting to do. No shirking on the job.'

Heaving out a sigh, he climbed to his feet. 'You guys aren't operating under a hangover,' he muttered as he bent to pick up his brush. Was green the right colour? It wasn't even her favourite. He'd thought it would match the outdoors, and fine, her eyes too but that sounded like something his alien counterpart might think. Now he looked at it though, white was surely the colour that said wedding. Or, wait, she was having red roses, so should they paint some of this stuff red? No, he had cushions in red. That was enough wasn't it? Or maybe it was too much, and she'd only want the flowers to be red...

'So what was the stag do like, then?' Jack asked, thankfully curtailing his spiralling colour doubts.

'Not what I'd have chosen.' Ben was a 'drink down the pub with a few close friends' sort of guy. No fuss, no bother. Nightclubs with weird cocktail combinations, being forced to either dance or stare at people dancing because it was too damn loud to hold a conversation... It wasn't him.

'That's because we weren't there,' Sam said smugly.

He couldn't deny it. He liked Marcus, had grown to tolerate James. But it took more than a few weeks for him to feel comfortable enough around someone to want to spend time with them.

Except for Molly. From that moment she'd nearly tumbled into his lap, he'd wanted to be with her, even though he'd known it wasn't a good idea.

They finished painting the two stepladders and then started

on the other single ladder he'd planned to place over the top of the other two to create the arch.

The one Molly would join him in front of.

'Have I mentioned how weird this feels, going to a wedding where I know the bride and groom aren't going to actually get married?' Jack said, breaking what had been, up till then, a productive silence.

'As best men, maybe we should do something when you say no to getting married?' Sam added. 'Like apologise to the guests?'

'There'll be nothing to apologise for. We'll both give our answer at the same time, so it will be clear it's a joint decision. Nobody is getting humiliated,' he added, just to hammer the point home.

'Right, so you both say no. Then what?' Jack prompted.

'Then I'm going to make it clear that while it's a no to marriage, it's not a no to Molly. I'm going to admit how I feel about her, and formally tell her I want to continue our relationship away from the TV cameras.' He hadn't finessed the words yet, which had caused knots in his stomach all morning.

'So what, like a declaration of love?' Sam asked.

'Yes.'

Jack, the bastard, burst out laughing. 'Ever thought you could do that by agreeing to actually marry her?'

Ben exhaled in frustration. 'Come on, you know why I can't do that.'

Jack stared back at him. 'Can't, or won't? Because from where I'm standing, there's no legal reason why you can't. The only thing stopping you is some crap hang-up from the past that it's high time you cast off.'

Put like that, it made him sound selfish. He could marry

her, but he wouldn't because ... because? The reasons began to blur as he recalled the conversation with Rachel. Molly didn't need him to fix her. Hell, Molly didn't need fixing at all. She was perfect as she was. And more than capable of living her life without him, building her business, gaining even more confidence. Moving on from both him and Duncan.

'Okay, so instead of showing her you love her by marrying her, you're doing it by ... this.' Sam waved his brush towards the stepladder, splattering paint everywhere. 'You'd better pray she likes it.'

The knots in Ben's stomach tightened.

'And pray the frigging ladders don't fall on her as she walks through the arch,' Jack added, giving them a look of distaste.

Ben was about to point out she'd be standing in front of the arch, not walking through it, when Rachel popped her head round the door. 'You guys need to up the pace. It's nearly lunchtime and I want you finished by 1pm to give us chance to set it all up.' Her gaze fell on the stepladders, and then down to the rugs which now weren't just old and threadbare, they were decorated with paint spatters. 'Somehow I imagined you creating a ceremony with less junk and more...Wow.'

If the knots in his stomach tightened any further, he'd not be able to eat the bloody cake he'd spent half an hour choosing. 'That would have been a helpful discussion to have yesterday.'

Rachel gave him an apologetic smile. 'Sorry. I'm sure she'll love it. I mean upcycling is her thing, yes?'

She was passionate about upcycling clothes, but had he taken that too far? Given her a ceremony that was *tatty*?

Fuck, what message did that send her? 'Let's forget this. It was shit idea. We'll have whatever arch they used this morning...'

Rachel strolled over to him and put her hands on his face. 'Stop. She's going to love the fact you put some effort into this, even if she doesn't actually love … this. Besides, it's too late to change your mind now. All the weddings need to be different and this is very … err … different.'

She gave him a bright smile, one clearly meant to convey everything was going to be okay but actually, because it looked forced, conveyed the opposite. Then she turned heel and disappeared, leaving him with his half painted junk. And two mates trying not to laugh, but failing miserably.

Chapter Thirty-Five

Molly slipped her dress on in the bathroom and then stepped into her room to give her parents a twirl.

'Oh my goodness, you look stunning.' Her mum wiped at her eyes. 'That dress is perfect for you.'

'Perfect,' her dad mumbled in agreement. He was quieter than her mum, but his expression always said it all. And right now, it was doting.

Molly stared at herself in the mirror. She didn't look like a traditional bride, but then again, this wasn't a traditional wedding in any sense. Still, she'd decided to be true to herself and go for a dress she would have worn if she'd actually been getting married. So while the others had chosen from a bridal shop, she'd dived into the second-hand shop next door. Using the sewing machine she still had in her room from the fete, she'd combined the red corset from one dress with the long, cream skirt of another, trimming the edges of the asymmetric hem with red lace. It was funky, different. The type of clothes she used to wear, when she'd first met Ben.

The type of clothes she was becoming confident enough to wear again, she thought with a dollop of pride.

Her mum came up behind her. 'Molly, sweetie, we've been watching the show. I know they edit things in a way that builds the excitement, but it does seem that while this Ben loves you, he's not a fan of marriage.'

'He's not.'

Her mum slid an arm around her waist and squeezed. 'Is that okay with you?'

Anybody else asked, she could lie. But she couldn't lie to the woman who'd opened her heart to a lost seven-year-old girl. 'I'm trying to work out my feelings. Ben's been burnt in the past by marriage and he's made it clear it's not going to be on the cards for us.'

'But you've always wanted to get married.' Her dad, protective as always, watched her carefully.

'I know, and I still do.'

'So what is going to happen today?'

The concern on her mum's face made tears leak down Molly's cheeks. 'Don't worry, Mum. Whatever happens, I'm going to be fine. I promise.'

It didn't feel like an empty promise, either. For the first time since she could remember, she truly felt in control of her own destiny.

Her mum touched her cheek and smiled. 'I know you will, my dear girl. You have always been so much stronger than you gave yourself credit for.'

'And one day I'll walk you down the aisle to a man who not only loves you for the special woman you are, but who also wants nothing on earth more than to marry you,' her father said gruffly, wrapping her in his arms from behind.

'Oh, Mum, Dad. You're going to have me walking down

Thank You, Next

the aisle with panda eyes.' She wiped at her eyes, trying desperately not to cry. It didn't matter that she'd not been wanted by her biological parents. And it wouldn't break her if Ben didn't want her, either. She'd lived through both scenarios already, and survived. Besides, she was wanted by this couple; she *was* loved. 'I don't think I tell you guys often enough how much I love you both.' Her voice cracked but she pushed on, needing them to hear it. 'I'm so grateful you chose me to be your daughter.'

'Oh goodness.' Her mum let out a shaky sounding laugh. 'Now you're going to start me crying.'

'Is this where I tell you both you'll make beautiful pandas?' Her father smiled, but the roughness of his voice betrayed his emotion.

Molly laughed, relieved at the dial down in emotion.

'I meant to ask, what happened to Duncan?' Her mum asked. 'Has he had his wedding yet?'

'Duncan and Jasmine have their ceremony after ours.'

Her mum searched her eyes. 'So there's still time to change your mind and marry him?'

Molly smiled. 'Look at you, acting like a typical fan and hoping for the happy ending.'

A loud tap on the door saved her from any further discussion on the subject. 'It's Rachel. Are you ready to go downstairs?'

Her parents looked at her, and Molly nodded, even though inside her belly was a quivering blancmange. 'I'm as ready as I'll ever be.'

She opened the door and Rachel took a step back, her gaze skimming up and down before resting on her face with a satisfied smile. 'You look amazing, Molly. Ben will be swept off his feet.'

She tried to imagine Ben – pragmatic, no nonsense Ben – being swept off his feet by anything. 'I'll settle for him not making a comment about me being unable to find a top to match the bottom half.'

Rachel smiled. 'I'd like to think he has more charm than that, but maybe that's what they mean by the triumph of hope over experience.' She turned to her parents. 'I feel I should introduce myself properly as I'm not just Rachel who works on the show. I'm also Rachel, sister of Ben, and fellow wedding guest.'

They all shook hands, the cameras remaining far enough away that they didn't feel intrusive.

'We're looking forward to meeting him,' her father remarked, with just enough coolness to make Rachel's smile falter.

'How are you feeling?' she asked Molly, her smile back in place.

'Honestly, I don't know. Nervous, definitely.'

'Well, your friends are waiting downstairs for you.' Rachel led them down the stairs towards the sitting room. 'I'm sure they'll help you relax.' She winked. 'And I'll see you next when you're walking down the aisle.'

The moment Molly stepped into the room, her three best friends squealed with delight and ran over to her, wrapping her in a four-way hug.

'Oh my God, Moll,' Penny exclaimed. 'You look amazing.'

'I can't believe we're all going to be on *The One*!' Ava squealed.

'You mean you can't believe we're going to Molly's wedding,' Emma added dryly.

'And we're going to be on *The One*!' Ava chimed in.

'*And* we're going to meet Ben Knight.' Penny fanned

herself. 'I hope you realise you're walking down the aisle to a fan favourite. Viewers have been going mad for him. Not just because he looks like a frigging model, but because of that brooding "I say very little" vibe he's got going on.'

Molly smiled, but inside, her belly had gone from quivering blancmange to a wriggling bag of eels. It wasn't just the thought of walking down the aisle to Ben.

It was the uncertainty of what would happen when the wedding was over.

In his room, Ben gave his collar a firm yank, much to Rachel's annoyance.

'Stop it. You're going to make your tie all squiffy.'

'I'm not sure about it.'

Rachel gave him an eye roll. 'I told you, Molly's gone for a red theme, so this will match.'

'It looks ridiculous with the jacket.' A suit, that's what he should have worn. Charcoal grey, Italian. Not leather. 'I look like a confused cowboy.'

'Stop being a baby.' Rachel gave his red tie another tweak, then ran her hands down the lapels of his jacket before stepping back. 'You look very handsome. And almost good enough for the bride.'

His heart skipped a beat at the mention of Molly. 'You promise me she's okay?'

'She's better than okay. She looks stunning.'

'She'd look gorgeous in a bin bag. I meant, does she look happy?'

Rachel nodded. 'Maybe a bit nervous, but when I left her she was being made a fuss of by her friends. And her parents are lovely, though I think you've got a bit of work to do to win them over.'

'I'm sure.' He tugged again at his collar, causing his sister to give him a dark look. 'I'll be glad when all this is over.'

'Getting jittery at the thought of seeing Molly walk down the aisle towards you?'

'No.' He heaved in a breath, forced his heart to steady. 'I hate that I haven't spoken to her since yesterday, and even then, we didn't leave on the best terms.' He thrust a hand through his hair in frustration. 'I don't know how she's feeling, and that's twisting me up inside. Doesn't help that next time I see her, it will be in full public glare.'

'Which is entirely my fault, I know.'

He gave her fingers a gentle squeeze. 'But if you hadn't strong-armed me onto the show, I wouldn't have got back with her.' He gave her a wry smile. 'Any chance I can sneak off and say hi to her before we meet by the stepladders?'

Rachel elbowed him in the ribs. 'Not a chance. Your sister might give in to that pleading look, but your associate producer wants the drama of you two meeting at the altar on camera.' She winked. 'And those stepladders have been sprinkled with HEA Towers wedding dust. They now look less like they've been pinched from a decorator and more like a rustic outdoor wedding arch.'

'Thank God.' He heard a tap on the door and the rumble of two male voices outside. 'Looks like the rest of my wedding party has arrived.'

Nerves jangled as he opened the door.

'If it isn't the groom.' Sam clapped him on the back. 'How are you feeling now, mate?'

'Like I want to be somewhere else.' Somewhere private. With Molly.

Jack laughed and gave him a similar thump before taking a step back and squinting at him. 'Nice jacket. And I love the way you've matched the red tie with the red paint in your hair. Classy.'

Because he knew these guys, he didn't immediately run to a mirror. Instead he turned to Rachel and raised an eyebrow. Eyes brimming with laughter, she gave a small shake of her head. Enough to reassure him Jack was talking shit. 'At least I haven't got red paint on my trousers.'

To his immense satisfaction, Jack immediately looked down.

'Enough of the schoolboy pranks.' Rachel hurried them out of the door. 'We need to be in place before the bridal party start walking down.'

'Down where?' Sam asked.

'We've set everything up in the garden,' Rachel answered. 'Molly wanted an outside wedding, and Ben decided it should be by the summer house.'

'Oh yeah?' Jack gave him a quizzical look. 'Any particular reason?'

He was thankful he'd given up blushing a long time ago. 'I thought Molly would find it quaint.'

'Umm.' They headed out across the pool area towards the back garden. 'Wouldn't be because something happened in there, then?' Jack prompted. 'Aside from you discussing company ideas, I mean, which seemed the obvious thing to do in a summer house. With a gorgeous woman. Who looked very flushed when she was interviewed.'

'You've *watched* the show?' Ben asked, aghast. He'd assumed the audience were people he didn't know and would never meet.

'Of course we have,' Jack replied. 'You were in it.'

'We even put bets on what happened in that summer house,' Sam added, causing the pair of them to cackle like schoolboys.

'Fuck off.' It was all he was capable of, because ahead of him he could already see the upturned crates, the rugs lined with tealights that led to the arch of painted ladders which thankfully looked a lot more elegant than when he'd left them.

He wasn't getting married, but tell that to his heart which was beating like crazy. Would what he'd done with the setting, what he'd say to her when he finally got her alone, be enough to convince her he was worth sticking with? Or would she go and hunt down Duncan, whose wedding, Rachel had informed him, wasn't until *after* theirs.

Or maybe she'd focus on her business and put all the relationship drama on hold until a man who truly deserved her turned up. A man who'd marry her in a heartbeat because what sane man wouldn't want to put a ring on her finger, make it clear to every other man that she was taken?

'I spy the cameras and the bridal party.'

At the sound of Rachel's voice he snapped his head round, making Sam and Jack laugh. 'Molly's here?'

'Not yet. We're going to film friends and family getting settled first, then Molly will arrive.' Rachel paused. 'Her dad's going to walk her down the aisle, but he wanted to meet you first so he's escorting her mum over, then going back for Molly.'

'Sounds like you could be in trouble,' Sam murmured.

'Nah,' Jack cut in. 'I caught a glimpse of him and I reckon Ben could take him. He's got height and age on his side.'

'Thanks.'

As the group neared, Ben walked towards them, his heart pounding. He nodded in the direction of what he assumed where her friends before halting in front of the woman with silver blonde hair and a polite smile, and the man with salt and pepper hair and a stern look.

'You must be the man who broke our daughter's heart.'

So her father was a man who didn't pull his punches. 'I am. But I won't make the same mistake twice.'

Ben had no clue what thoughts were going on behind the pale blue eyes that stared back at him, but a beat later, to his intense relief, her father offered his hand. 'If she decides to keep seeing you, I look forward to getting to know you better.'

If. The word sent a cold shiver through him. 'And me you.'

They shook hands, and he bent to give Molly's mum a polite kiss on the cheek.

'I hear you chose the setting,' she remarked glancing over to the junk yard/rustically romantic wedding venue, depending on your perspective.

'Yes.' He desperately wished Molly was here. She'd ease the awkward tension and smooth out his sharp edges. 'I tried to capture what I thought was Molly.'

Behind him, Sam and Jack started coughing, loudly. Annoyed, he turned to glare at them, only to find they were giving him wide-eyed stares, nodding jerkily towards the … fuck.

'I didn't mean … I wasn't inferring Molly is in any way not perfect…' He paused, drew in a breath. 'I know Molly is a big fan of upcycling,' he finished lamely.

His stomach plummeted as her father frowned. 'And?'

His collar felt like it was strangling him. 'I thought she might … enjoy this.'

Her mother stared over at where her daughter would soon been walking down the aisle. 'Enjoy having the guests at her wedding sit on crates?'

No response came to mind. All he could think was how badly wrong he'd got everything.

'Good heavens, are they stepladders?' Her father was staring at the makeshift altar.

Of course. No wedding should be without a set. As his misery intensified, he was saved a reply when Rachel slid an arm around his waist before addressing Molly's father. 'Thomas, we could do with starting on time, so if you wouldn't mind going to find Molly?'

'Ah, yes, of course.' He ambled off and Ben was left with Molly's mum, and a crushing sense that he'd made the worst first impression on record.

He turned to say something to her – he didn't have a clue what, just something to break the awful tension – but his heart jumped in surprise when she smiled and patted his arm. 'Don't look so terrified. You know our daughter better than you think.'

Chapter Thirty-Six

Molly sucked in a breath and smiled at her dad. 'Let's go.'

She took his arm and carefully walked down the steps to the gravel path winding round the side of the back garden. 'Where are we heading?'

'You'll find out soon enough,' her father murmured, eyeing the trailing cameras warily.

'Don't worry about them; you get used to being filmed. Most of the stuff isn't used.' Her pulse scrambled as she saw a glimpse of … something ahead. 'Ben chose to have it by the summer house,' she stated softly, memories of what happened there making her heart flip flop.

Her father looked at her, but thankfully made no comment.

The closer they got, the clearer the scene became. 'Are they … stepladders?'

'That's what I asked.' Again she felt her dad's gaze on her, this time full of concern. 'What are you thinking? Because if that bugger has in any way disrespected you—'

'He hasn't.' A wide grin spread across her face. 'Oh my

God, he definitely hasn't, Dad. He's...' Damn it, tears welled in her eyes again. 'He's somehow managed to come up with exactly what I'd have chosen.'

'Oh, okay.' She felt the tension leave his body. 'You're still planning on saying no, though?'

I want to say yes. For the first time, that thought drowned out all the others. But it was stupid, because Ben wouldn't be saying *I do*. 'I think so.'

'You think?' Her dad came to an abrupt halt. 'I thought you said he won't marry you.'

'He won't.' She swallowed, trying not to listen to her heart, which was jumping up and down in her chest and saying, *wow, look what he's done, the care and thought he's put into it. See how well he knows you.* The butterflies in her belly began to flap manically.

This wasn't the work of a man who would bail on her. It was the work of a man who *loved* her.

But she wanted marriage, didn't she?

Want, she realised. She'd said want, not need.

'I'm glad you're still thinking clearly.' Oblivious to her epiphany, her dad began walking again.

'You don't like him, do you?' she asked sadly.

'It's hard for me to forget what he did to you.'

'I know, but I've forgiven him for it, and so should you.' She pressed a kiss to his cheek. 'His reasons for ditching me were good ones, Dad. Trust me on that. And it wasn't all on him, because he did try and contact me, but I deleted his messages without reading them.' What would her life be like now if she'd read them? If they'd met up again a year later. Would they still be together?

Her thoughts scattered as they drew closer, the sight in front of her demanding all her focus. Their guests were seated on crates, furnished with plush red cushions. The aisle between the crates was covered with rugs, all different, but the colours a blend of reds and browns. The edges of the rugs were lined with flickering tealights, set in jam jars. At the end of the aisle was a magnificent arch made of green painted ladders, entwined with red roses and white voiles which fluttered in the breeze.

And in front of the arch, standing with his back to her, was a tall, dark-haired figure, a leather jacket stretched across his broad shoulders ... holy cow. Emotion ploughed through her as she realised it was the jacket she'd made him.

As if he sensed her, Ben turned, and when their eyes met, her heart nearly exploded out of her chest. His mouth curved upwards, the smallest of smiles, but combined with the adoration on his face, it was like being wrapped in a warm, fuzzy blanket of love.

She was no longer the toffee. Her parents, the ones that counted, loved her. In his own way Duncan had, too. And even though he didn't want to marry her, *Ben* loved her.

It was more than enough.

Just then the music started, and as she heard Louis Armstrong singing 'We have all the time in the world', she almost melted.

'Ready?'

Swallowing down the boulder of emotion in her throat, she nodded vigorously. 'Definitely.'

Joy suffused her as her father led her slowly down the aisle. She was glad of his support because her legs felt unsteady, yet despite that, she suspected she'd have raced down the aisle and into Ben's arms if her dad hadn't been there to hold her back.

Hazel eyes watched her all the way, so intense, so mesmerising, she couldn't possibly glance away.

When they reached the makeshift altar, her dad squeezed her hand once and then stepped back, she assumed to sit next to her mum, but she couldn't look. All she wanted to do for the rest of her life, she realised with absolute clarity, was to gaze into this pair of swirling brown and green eyes.

'You look unbelievable.'

Ben's husky voice sent delicious shivers skating down her spine. Smiling, she gave him a careful study, taking in the leather jacket that still moulded perfectly to his trim form, the red tie and matching red rose in his lapel. His chiselled jaw was freshly shaved, and the utter handsomeness of the man caught at her throat, even as those magnificent eyes held her captive. 'You look very dashing.'

He smiled, but it didn't quite reach his eyes. 'Is this…' He nodded towards the flower-entwined ladders. 'Is it okay?'

That's what was worrying him? 'It's better than okay,' she reassured him. 'It's perfect.'

A real smile split his face and she found she was unable to do anything but smile back. For a few moments they just stood there, grinning like fools.

The registrar cleared her throat. 'Molly, Ben, are we ready to start?'

'Oh yes, sorry, we were just catching up.' She beamed, feeling so happy it almost hurt. 'It's been soooo long since we saw each other,' she added, giving Ben a sidelong glance and receiving a soft laugh in return.

'Well, if you're both ready, let's start.' The registrar glanced over her shoulder. 'Who gives this woman to be married to this man?'

Oh shit. She'd forgotten her dad would be asked to give her

away. She turned and gave him a beseeching look and he nodded, but his expression remained severe. 'I do. As long as he promises not to hurt her again.'

Ben went rigid.

Ooookay. It could have been worse.

'Now, as you'll be aware I'm going to ask you both to deliver your responses to my question at the same time.' The registrar caught her eye and smiled kindly. 'Do you, Molly Harris,' – he turned to look at Ben, whose jaw muscle was jumping, he was wound so tight – 'and do you Ben Knight, take each other to be husband and wife, respectively. To live together in matrimony, to love each other, to honour, to comfort, and to keep each other in sickness and in health, forsaking all others, for as long as you both shall live?'

Ben's hand gripped hers, and when he squeezed it, warmth flushed through her and everything else seemed to melt away. There was just her and the man she loved. The man who made her hormones dance, her body sing.

The man who, with just a touch, could make all her jittery molecules realign.

She didn't need the paperwork. She didn't need the public promise. Didn't need marriage at all. Taking in a deep breath, she turned to Ben and smiled. 'No.'

But just as the word left her mouth, she heard him speak loudly and clearly. 'I do.'

What? A gasp escaped her – or was that from the guests?

Frozen in shock, she stared back at him. 'That wasn't what we agreed.'

'I know. I thought...' He swallowed convulsively. 'I've got this wrong, haven't I? Fuck.'

Clearly agitated, he looked around at the cameras, and as she watched the most confident man she'd ever met begin to tremble and retreat into himself, she grasped his hand. 'Come with me.'

Ben stumbled as Molly almost dragged him out of the way of the cameras and the shocked eyes of the guests, and into the summer house.

The place he'd brought her to orgasm with his fingers, where she'd taken him in hand, her soft hands wrapped around his dick.

Fuck.

If he'd had his revelation then, instead of while he was standing at that blasted altar, would he have still had a chance with her?

There were not enough fucks in the world for what had just happened.

He wrenched the door of the summer house open and lurched to the small sofa, burying his face in his hands.

'What on earth, Ben?'

He jolted upright, gaze raking her pale, stunned-looking face. He wanted to get down on his knees, beg her to change her mind and marry him. But he was also angry, damn it. At himself for not having this discussion with her before he publicly humiliated himself. And at her for leading him to think she wanted to marry him, when it was clear from her horrified expression at the altar that it wasn't the case. 'You're choosing Duncan then?'

His tone was far too harsh for a man who should be pleading with her to choose him instead.

She slid her hands onto her hips. With her flashing green eyes and mismatched dress that should look odd but managed instead to look uniquely gorgeous, just like her, he'd never been more in love with her. Or felt she was more out of his reach. 'Why do you say that?'

'You said you wanted to get married. You clearly don't want to marry me, so I assume Duncan is the lucky man.' He couldn't keep the bitterness out of his tone.

'Whoa.' She put up her hands, as if trying to calm a wild animal. And he felt wild, untethered, unhinged. Like his whole life had been turned upside down. 'You told me this wasn't a wedding; it was a *ceremony*.' She emphasised the word. 'Did you really expect me to still say "I do" after you've spent the last two weeks telling me over and over again how anti-marriage you are?'

His anger deflated, and with that no longer there to focus his mind, his heart splintered 'No.' He lifted his gaze to hers. 'But I hoped you'd be happy that I changed my mind.'

Her expression softened and she slipped onto the sofa next to him. 'Who said I'm not?'

He told himself to ignore the dart of hope. 'You didn't look happy. You looked—'

'Shocked,' she filled in for him. 'Because that's how I felt.'

He let out a strangled laugh. 'I blindsided you again, and I promised I wouldn't do that.'

'You did.'

She gave him a level look, but when her lips began to curve into a smile the hope began to blossom. 'Do you...' It was a struggle to speak through the boulder of emotion that had lodged itself firmly in his throat. 'Do you want to marry me, Molly?'

Her eyes searched his, giving nothing away. 'Before I answer that, let me turn the question back on you. Do *you* want to marry me? Or are you doing it because you're afraid if you don't, I'll marry Duncan?'

He huffed out a laugh. 'That was definitely part of my thought process.' He'd been given a chance to convince her. Now was not the time for half measures. 'I love you, Molly. I want you however you'll have me. For as long as you'll have me.'

The green in her eyes glittered and for the first time he began to think maybe he hadn't completely wrecked his chances, after all. 'Go on.'

He inhaled a deep breath, dug deep into the feelings in his gut, his chest, his heart, and tried to find the words to match them. 'My aversion to marriage was never about you. There was never any doubt in my mind that I wanted to spend the rest of my life with you. But Helena thought marrying me would be the answer to making her happy, and it wasn't. *I* wasn't.' He took a risk and brushed a thumb across the soft skin of Molly's cheek. 'I couldn't bear the thought of not being the answer for you, either. Of letting you down.' His heart leapt when her hand came to rest over his.

'What changed your mind?'

'I haven't changed my mind, not entirely.' Christ, it hurt to say this, but he had to get the words out, make sure she knew everything. 'I'm still scared shitless that I won't be enough for you, that I'll be less than you're hoping for, but Rachel helped me to see that this time round it would be totally different.' He wrapped his hand around hers and drew it against his chest. 'You don't need me to fix any parts of you. You're fucking perfect already.' He gave her a wry smile. 'Then Jack reminded me that saying I couldn't marry you was bollocks. The only thing stopping me, was me. And that made me question why the hell I wasn't plotting to bind you to me as close as was humanly possible, why I wasn't planning to put a ring on your finger to make it clear to everyone that you were mine.' He raised her hand to his mouth, kissed her knuckles, and felt his heart thump against his ribs as he looked into her eyes. 'Are you mine, Molly?'

The smile she gave him was one he would never forget. It radiated love, happiness and a promise for the future. 'Yes, I'm yours, Ben. I have been ever since I met you the first time.' With her free hand, she cupped his face. 'But I don't need to marry you.' Though his heart jolted, the warmth of the fingers that gently pressed against his face helped to reassure. 'For a long time I was so terrified of being alone, of being left again, that I was consumed by the idea of legally tying myself to someone.' She smiled into his eyes. 'But the confidence I've gained from coming on the show, from being with you, has made me realise I don't need a man to take care of me, to provide for me. If I have to live by myself, it's okay. I can have a good, happy life knowing I'm loved by my adopted parents, by my friends. And that I have a purpose, which I hope will be upcycling clothes, but who knows? Something else may come up. The important thing is, whatever is in my future, I can deal with it.'

Knowing the journey she'd been on, his heart filled with pride, yet he still didn't feel on firm footing. 'Am I in your future?'

Her laughter filled the summer house. 'After the wedding you just designed for me, you'd better believe it.'

Suddenly he was the one needing words. 'What are you saying? Can you spell it out for me, because all I heard was you don't want to marry me, but I might feature in your future?'

She wriggled out of his hold and clasped both hands to his

face. 'I don't need to marry you, but I love you to pieces and I *want* to marry you. If you're still offering.'

'Yes, fuck … yes, a million times yes.' Heart untethered now, bouncing around his chest like a helium balloon, he wrapped his arms around her and kissed her. And kissed her again, until they were both gasping for air. 'I'm going to put you in charge of organising it though,' he whispered between feathering kisses along her jaw. 'Because I had no clue what I was doing, as is patently evident. Jack and Sam ribbed me so much this morning when we were painting the ladders I told Rachel to find me somewhere else to hold it. She refused.'

Molly moaned, tilting her head so he could kiss down her neck. 'Well, I'm glad she refused, because it's exactly what I wanted.' She grinned. 'And it's even better now I know you were painting it this morning when I was trying to recover from my hangover.' Suddenly she leapt to her feet, almost upending the sofa. 'You know what, sod it. Let's do it now.'

'It?'

Her eyes sparkled, her face radiated such joy it nearly slayed him. 'Let's go back out there and get married.'

Chapter Thirty-Seven

Endorphins buzzed through Molly as she tugged Ben's hand, pulling him off the sofa.

'You want to get married now?'

She nodded vigorously, excitement fizzing through her. 'Yes.'

He looked adorably bemused. 'You don't want to wait and do it properly? You know, seats instead of crates? A real altar? No cameras?'

'You're really checking whether I want to get married to the man I love, on the world's best dating show, surrounded by the people most important to me, in a unique setting you spent hours putting together?' Her face felt like it was going to crack, her smile was so wide.

'Okay then.' He looked so handsome in that moment, and so *happy*, her knees started to buckle. 'But first things first.'

Just as she thought she couldn't get any weaker, he bent to kiss her.

It was gentle at first, his lips warm and caressing. But then his tongue dived between her parted mouth, and he let out a guttural noise as his hands settled on her hips, drawing her against him, deepening the connection.

Within seconds he had her pressed against the wall of the summerhouse with all the urgency of a man who wanted more than a kiss.

'Please tell me we've got time to consummate this marriage before the vows,' he said hoarsely.

'Yes.' She pushed herself more firmly against him, rubbing against his erection, making both of them groan.

He lifted her up, but just as her legs wound around his hips, there was a knock on the door. 'Rachel here.'

Molly felt Ben's body go rigid and then his chest rise and fall as he heaved out a sigh.

'Everyone else is too scared to come and check on you,' Rachel continued through the woodwork. 'But I figured the fact you're both still in there together is a good sign.'

Ben's eyes blinked shut and he rested his forehead against hers, his breath hot and heavy. 'Get lost,' he mumbled to his sister.

'I've got a TV show to film,' Rachel shouted back. 'So not happening.'

'Fuck.'

The clear frustration in his voice, in the hips that were still giving slow pumps against her core ... the whole ridiculousness of the situation, that this was happening in the middle of her wedding, with TV cameras waiting for them to come out of the summer house they'd already had one other X-rated encounter in. It was too much for Molly. She burst into giggles.

Ben's eyes snapped open. 'You think this is funny?'

'Umm, sort of?' She wriggled, giggling again when she

heard his frustrated huff. 'I think the consummation will have to be done the traditional way. After the wedding.'

'I think I hate my sister,' he muttered darkly, thrusting his hips once more before exhaling a deep sigh and slowly lowering her to her feet.

'Err, hello? Is anyone going to tell me what's going on?' Rachel again.

Molly gave Ben a big, sloppy but very quick, kiss. 'I'll go and tell her the happy news. You ... err ...' She glanced down at the huge bulge between his legs and felt another ripple of giddy arousal. 'Is it bad that I want to lick my lips?'

'Jesus.' He dragged a hand through his hair and turned sharply away from her. 'I'm seconds away from telling my sister to fuck off and pinning you against the wall again.' She watched his shoulders rise and fall. 'Go. I'll be out in a minute.'

'Okay.' Her heart doing a happy dance, she flung her arms around him from behind. 'I heard it helps to recite the alphabet backwards.'

He grunted. 'Knowing I'm about to get married in front of TV cameras should do the trick.'

He was a private man, who'd never wanted to get married again, yet he was about to marry her very publicly because, she suspected, he knew that was what she wanted. Feeling a fresh wave of love for him, she kissed his broad back. 'Thank you.'

He twisted his head round. 'For?'

'Stepping out of your comfort zone, for me.'

His face softened. 'I'd do anything for you. Haven't you realised that yet?'

It was too much. Now he'd learnt how to use his words, *he* was too much. Tears began to spill down her cheeks.

'Can one of you please come out and tell me what the hell

is going on?' Rachel again, a hint of desperation to her voice now.

'See you at the altar?'

Ben smiled. 'See you by the stepladders.'

When she stepped outside, Rachel gave her a long, careful study. 'How are you doing?'

'I'm good.' She twisted her hands, feeling that rush of excitement again. 'I'm better than good. I'm about to get married.'

Rachel's eyebrows shot up. 'Today? Now?'

Molly grinned. 'Can we have a Take 2?'

'You can have as many takes as you like.' Rachel put a hand to her mouth, eyes brimming with joy. 'Oh my God, I don't believe it. This is so exciting. I'm so happy for you, for me. For Ben.' She wrapped her arms around Molly in a giant hug, then stepped back, laughing. 'You know I'm talking as Ben's sister now, right? I mean obviously this is great for the show, but you're getting married. To Ben. You'll be my sister-in-law.' She closed her eyes briefly, drawing in a deep breath. When she opened them again, she gave Molly the most spectacular smile. 'You are exactly who he needs. I'm just really amazed he had the sense to see that.'

'Hey.' Ben came out of the summer house and gave his sister a mild look. 'Haven't you got a wedding to film?'

Rachel rushed to hug her brother. 'I'm a guest at this one, remember. But we'd better get back to everyone before they send out a search party. Why did it take you so long to come out of there, anyway?'

Ben slammed his eyes shut and let out a long-suffering sigh.

Molly burst out laughing.

Thank You, Next

'Do you take Molly Harris to be your wife, to live together in matrimony, to love her, to honour her, to comfort her, and to keep her in sickness and in health, forsaking all others, for as long as you both shall live?'

In the end, they were the easiest words he'd ever had to say. 'I do.'

Their small congregation whooped and cheered, and Molly's smile almost blinded him. As the registrar continued the service, as rings were exchanged, the final pronouncement that they were man and wife made, Ben wasn't even aware of the cameras filming them. All he knew, all he cared about, was that Molly's eyes were overflowing with happiness.

'You may kiss the bride.'

Molly bit into her lip, eyes dancing. 'I think you already did that in the summerhouse,' she whispered.

He gave her a tender look. 'I think I'm never going to turn down an excuse to kiss you.'

As her eyes softened, he did just that, though this time he kept it PG rated.

More cheers sounded in his ears while he kissed her, and when he raised his head, he found they were being showered in ... something.

'Oh wow.' Molly picked a few petals off his jacket. 'Dried rose petals for confetti. You thought of everything.'

The devil on his shoulder said keep quiet, take the credit, she might repay you big time tonight. His conscience told him starting married life off on a lie was a huge no-no. 'I was the stepladders, the crates, the rugs. Basically, the junk. Rachel was the flowers, the drapes, the confetti. Basically, everything that says romance.'

'But you set the theme.' She planted a light kiss on his lips. 'And you married me.'

'No.' He tucked a stray strand of hair behind her ear. 'We married each other.'

He was about to dive in for another kiss, when he felt a tap on his shoulder.

Jack and Sam stood there, grinning like fools. 'Hate to break up the party, but don't we get to kiss the bride too?'

'What rule is that under?'

'Best mate rules.' While Molly laughed, Jack wrapped her in a big bear hug. 'I can see why he married you today. Bet he figured if he waited and you met me, he'd have no chance.'

'Hey,' Sam interjected. 'She might prefer me.'

'Jesus.' Ben watched as his wife – his frigging *wife* – was wrapped in another monster hug. 'That's enough.'

Sam chuckled and let Molly down. 'Just saying hi to your brave lady wife.'

That seemed to set the flood gates opening and everyone wanted to come and shake his hand, or hug Molly, or in the case of Molly's friends, hug him. There was laughter and ribbing, especially about the length of time it had taken them to come out of the summer house. Then they all wandered leisurely back to the patio where they drank champagne and cut into the cake – as man and wife.

Molly's dad raised his glass and gave them a sweet toast, welcoming him to the family, which made Molly's eyes glisten and him choke up.

As he watched her envelop her parents in a hug, then laugh with Rachel as if they'd known each other all their lives, he thought how stupid he'd been to be so afraid of something that now felt so *right*.

'Oh my gosh, our first marriage of the day.' Natalie – who

looked a bit like a wedding cake herself in a lacy, tiered pale pink frothy number – dashed towards him, drowning him in chiffon as she reached up to hug him. Then she moved off to find Molly, dragging her back over and pointing to the camera crew. 'Mr and Mrs Knight, this is so exciting. You need to come and tell us all about it.'

This was why he'd rather have married her after the show, he though wryly. 'Not happening, Natalie.'

She pouted. 'Come on, think of all the viewers who've been on the edge of their seats this whole series, wondering if you'll ever be smart enough to marry Molly. They want to know what made you decide to say I do.'

Before he could tell her that the only person who needed to know that was Molly, he felt his wife's arm – yes, it was no less astonishing the second time he said it – slip through his. She smiled up at him and gave his bicep a reassuring squeeze. 'Natalie, can I just have a minute with my husband?'

His belly gave a long, slow flip as the last word settled over him. And then his system went into overdrive as she shifted to smooth her hands possessively down his tie, her eyes shimmering with something that made his heart race. 'Rachel said they're going to ferry us all to a fancy restaurant so we can have a proper wedding meal with our friends and family.' Her hands pressed against his chest, and his groin tightened. 'I told her that would be amazing, but first we'd both like to change.' Slowly, very slowly, she licked her lips. 'She said that was fine, she'd keep our guests entertained while we ... changed.'

'Does this changing involve getting naked.' His voice dropped an octave. 'At the same time, in the same place.'

She nodded, expression all serious, except for the wicked glint in her eye. 'As we're husband and wife now, I think that would be ... appropriate.'

He grabbed her wrist. 'Then what are we waiting for?'

She glanced over at Natalie. 'We just need to do this one quick interview first.'

'You're using sex to blackmail me into talking to the cameras?' he asked, part aghast, part twistedly impressed.

'I might be, or actually Rachel might be because she had this kind of evil look in her eyes when she offered to look after my parents while I showered and change *after* I'd been to the heart-to-camera room. And she definitely emphasised the word after.' As his face paled at the thought of his sister being this devious, Molly grinned. 'Anyway, it's not important. All that matters is, if we do this really small thing, we then get to have honeymoon sex.' She slapped a hand over her mouth. 'Oh my God, I totally forgot, the couples who get married win an all-expenses paid honeymoon in Hawaii. *We're* going to Hawaii.'

He could look forward to that, later. For now he was far more focussed on the honeymoon sex remark. 'Five minutes,' he said, turning to Natalie. 'Five minutes and then we're done with the cameras.'

Natalie beamed. 'Five minutes.'

And that's how he found himself, on his wedding day, talking to a camera, and through it, to apparently millions of people who had become addicted to the love story between him and Molly.

'When did you decide you were going to say I do?' Natalie asked him.

He glanced at Molly, who grinned back at him. 'I decided I wanted to spend the rest of my life with Molly several days ago. I just hadn't planned on getting married, until today.'

Molly rolled her eyes, which of course Natalie picked up on. 'You look like you don't believe him, Molly.'

Thank You, Next

Without waiting for her reply, he shrugged off his jacket and started to tug his shirt out of his trousers.

As Molly's eyes widened, Natalie began to fan herself. 'I'm not complaining, but what are you doing, Ben?'

He lifted the shirt and showed Molly the tattoo he'd snuck out to have done yesterday. The one of her initials, on the other side of his chest to those of Helena's. He'd had to pay over the odds for it because the artist had recognised him from the show – unbelievable – so he'd felt compelled to tip heavily to make sure he kept quiet until after the show had aired.

Her eyes welled and she gave him a wobbly smile. 'You did that, even after I made you have a facial and his-and-her massages?'

'Yeah, because that's when I knew for certain you were it for me.' He gave her an adoring smile. 'Nobody else would have got me in that place.'

In a flash she leapt into his arms and began kissing him. Dimly he was aware of Natalie clearing her throat. Of her muttering something about them clearly starting their honeymoon early. Of bodies shuffling out.

Then he heard a click as the door closed behind them.

Slowly Molly raised her head and grinned. 'Thought that was quickest way to end the interview.'

'I love your thinking.' He brushed back her hair, smiled deeply into her eyes. 'I love you, my wife.'

'And I love you, too, my husband.'

Epilogue

One year later

Molly flung open the door and greeted their visitors with a beaming smile.

'You look amazing, Natalie.'

The presenter was dressed today in a vivid purple jumpsuit – a bold statement which suited her down to the ground.

'Thank you, honey. You know me, a shrinking violet.' She winked, and Molly laughed before turning to give Rachel a hug.

'Hey sis-in-law.'

Rachel tutted. 'Not today, I'm working. I hope that brother of mine is all set to talk to us.'

'You know Ben. He's chomping at the bit, can't wait to get in front of the cameras again. Only yesterday he was saying how much he misses that heart-to-camera room. He used to really love spilling his feelings in front of you guys.'

'My wife', came Ben's dry voice from behind her, 'is talking bollocks.'

Molly turned and gave him a mock glare. 'My husband is rude.'

'Oh, this is magic.' Natalie waved a hand towards the camera crew. 'We need to get this on film,' she hissed, before turning back to her with a bright smile. 'Please, carry on.'

Ben briefly raised his eyes to the ceiling before facing his sister. 'I blame you.'

'I'm not going to take responsibility for your wife talking bollocks. I do shoulder some of the responsibility for Molly being your wife.' Rachel smiled sweetly. 'But as that was the best thing that's ever happened to you, I reckon you owe me.'

He heaved out a breath. 'You know what I meant.'

'What, you mean you blame me for these guys?' The two men lugging cameras inside gave a self-conscious wave. 'You won't even notice them when we sit down. The pair of you are just having a catch-up chat with Natalie about the last year. You're our success story, so suck it up bro.'

'Maya and Marcus are still together,' he pointed out, then glanced over at Molly. 'And Duncan and Jasmine are married with a baby.'

She knew Ben had worried when she'd heard the news, but all she'd felt was happiness for Duncan. He'd got what he'd wanted, a wife and family to look after. As she'd gone on to tell Ben, she'd got what she'd always wanted, too. Her soulmate.

'Duncan and Jasmine didn't marry on the show,' Rachel countered, dragging Molly out of her daydream. 'You're our golden couple.'

Ben briefly closed his eyes, as if the idea of it pained him.

The cameras were set up in their open plan kitchen/living room/garden annex/study/place they spent all their time. Molly shuffled next to Ben on their corner sofa, and Natalie sat opposite them.

Thank You, Next

'So how is married life?' She asked.

Ben looked at Molly. Expecting his lack of response, she grinned and shook her head. 'You're going to answer that.'

'Why?'

'Because I used to do all the talking and I think the viewers should see how much you've changed.'

'I haven't.'

A giggle burst out of her at the look of frustration on his face. Truth was he *had* a changed, in the only area that counted, the only part of him she'd wanted to change. He talked to her all the time about how much he loved her.

'Let's start off easy, Ben.' Natalie gave him a bright smile. 'I know it was a year ago now, but how was Hawaii?'

'Good. A least, what we saw of it.' He gave Molly a sideways glance, amusement lurking in the hazel eyes she still got lost in.

Amusement and heat, she corrected as a flush crept across her face. 'Hawaii was amazing,' she said brightly. 'We went to Pearl Harbour, swam with turtles, had a helicopter ride over an active volcano and ... err...' Ben raised an eyebrow, giving her that sexy, wryly amused look that never failed to send her pulse soaring. 'Well, you know, sun, sea and ... umm ... sand. Lots of sand.'

Laughter chased across Ben's handsome face and she gave a silent fist bump. Making him laugh was one of her favourite things to do. That and making him gasp, and groan...

'And how has life been for you since you've come back from honeymoon?' Natalie asked.

Molly again turned to Ben, who shrugged. 'I answered the first question.'

She rolled her eyes. 'Okay, fine. Well, life's good, actually. Really, really good.' She paused and gave Ben another glance.

'Should we tell them about the business? We should, shouldn't we?' Thrilled to have the chance to talk about her second passion, after Ben, she faced Natalie again. 'We set up this business together called Shabby Chic. The name was actually my idea. I figured it encompasses exactly what we're trying to do, which is turn shabby items, you know, the clothes and furniture people give away because they're old, tatty or out of date, and turn them into chic clothes and furniture that everyone wants to buy.' She glanced back at Ben, saw he was watching her intently, his expression so adoring it brought a lump to her throat.

'We run it together, mainly from this room actually, because it's so bright in here, and lovely to look out at the garden. It really helps when you're trying to be creative, you know? Sorry, am I rambling? Probably I am, but I'm so excited about this business. It's not just working on something I really love… I mean, upcycling clothes versus selling car parts. It's like a dream come true.' She reached to squeeze Ben's hand. 'But it's not just what I'm doing, it's who I'm doing it with. Working with Ben, his drive, his ambition, it's incredible. Every day is like an adventure. I'm learning so much from him, but also learning so much about him. About myself, too.' She laughed. 'Sorry, I've gone off tangent. Where was I? Oh yes, I was saying we run it together. Ben already ran his own business before he met me, so it made sense for us to split our responsibilities so that I'm in charge of our products, you know, what we sell, and he's in charge of how we sell it.' She frowned and looked over at him. 'That's how we said to explain it, isn't it?' She waved a hand at the cameras. 'But I guess you guys don't really care about the details. You're more interested in whether we have rows, but honestly, we've found this rhythm.' She laughed. 'You know, thinking about it, we probably work well together because we don't actually see much of each other. In the early days we were both at home because I was making the clothes, but then things took off so we had to employ people to help, and now we have a workshop where we make things, so that's where I spend most of my time. We've branched out into jewellery and we're starting to make furniture, too.' She giggled. 'That was inspired by Ben's stepladders at our wedding.'

She glanced again at Ben, saw he was still watching her, but now along with the adoration, there was amusement.

'You let me do all the talking again.' She raised her hands in the air and looked to Rachel and Natalie. 'The viewers should hear from him, too, shouldn't they? You should make him say something.'

Natalie laughed. 'Molly's right. How is married life from your perspective, Ben?'

He slid Molly a look, gave a slight shake of his head, but the love in his eyes melted her heart. 'It's perfect.'

'That's so sweet, Ben.' Natalie smiled. 'But can you give us just a few more words?'

He sighed. 'Look, all people need to know is I love Molly. This marriage didn't happen because we were taken in by the show and the cameras. It happened despite all that.' He turned towards her, his gaze riveted on hers. 'My sister lured me onto the show by telling me I would meet my perfect match. For once, she was right.'

Oh, wow. A lump rose in Molly's throat. 'What he said,' she managed hoarsely, reaching for his hand.

His eyes blazed back at her for a few humming minutes, before he turned back to Natalie. 'And now we're done. You guys have interfered enough in our relationship. From now on it's just Molly and me.'

Acknowledgments

I have a confession to make. Before writing this book, I hadn't really seen any reality dating shows. Not because I didn't want to, but because my house is dominated by men who would rather stick needles in their eyes than watch one. So when I was discussing this next book with my agent, and she suggested the hero and heroine meet on a dating show, I was unsure how I could write it. But then she sent me a list of dating shows to watch. After I'd gorged myself on *Married at First Sight*, *Love Island* and *Love Is Blind*, I was hooked on the idea. Not only was it an intriguing set up that gave me ample sources of tension and humour to explore, but it also meant I could disappear off to watch TV in the afternoon all under the banner of research. So I'd like to say a huge thank you to the fabulous Hannah Todd for the idea for this story, her help with plotting it out, her ever present enthusiasm and encouragement which is a joy to work with - and for getting me addicted to dating shows!

I'd also like to thank the team at One More Chapter, and in particular my editor, Charlotte Ledger. This is the ninth book I have written with Charlotte and I have loved working with her on every single one of them. She knows exactly how to get the best out of both an author and the story, always challenging for it to be better, and yet in a way that motivates and inspires. Even when her suggestions continue onto the next page, and the one after that, and the one after that, as was the case with this book! So thank you Charlotte for pushing me to make Molly and Ben's story as good as it could be. And an even bigger thank you for taking a chance on me all those books ago.

Thanks also to the rest of the One More Chapter team who work seamlessly behind the scenes to catch my plot holes, my misspellings and my poor sentence construction to shape this book into something ready to be read. And for giving it such eye-catching packaging.

This is also my chance to thank the friends and family who have been there for me during my writing journey – ten years since my first book was published and they're still cheering me on. The roll call includes my lovely mum-in-law Anne, my sis-in-law Jayne, nieces Maddi, Tiggi and Gracie, cousins Shelley, Karley, Kath, Kirsty and Hayley, Auntie Jan, friends Charlotte, Sonia, Jane, Carol, Tara and Priti. And a special thank you to my dear mum who sadly has dementia now and can't read my books anymore, but still asks about them.

I'm not sure where any of us writers would be without the amazing book bloggers who are kind enough to read and review our books, so a massive thank you to everyone who's given me a shout out on social media, taken part in a blog tour or just taken the time to read my books. Your support is priceless. Including, but definitely not limited to: Rachel Gilbey, Anne Williams, Maelia Cybéle and Claire.

Finally, the most important thanks of all go to YOU. I am so grateful that you chose one of my books to read and I hope that whether you love dating shows like Molly, or don't want anything to do with them, like Ben, you'll enjoy their love story.

ONE MORE CHAPTER

YOUR NUMBER ONE STOP FOR PAGETURNING BOOKS

The author and One More Chapter would like to thank everyone who contributed to the publication of this story...

Analytics
James Brackin
Abigail Fryer
Maria Osa

Audio
Fionnuala Barrett
Ciara Briggs

Contracts
Sasha Duszynska Lewis

Design
Lucy Bennett
Fiona Greenway
Liane Payne
Dean Russell

Digital Sales
Hannah Lismore
Emily Scorer

Editorial
Arsalan Isa
Charlotte Ledger
Federica Leonardis
Bonnie Macleod
Janet Marie Adkins
Jennie Rothwell

Harper360
Emily Gerbner
Jean Marie Kelly
emma sullivan
Sophia Wilhelm

International Sales
Peter Borcsok
Bethan Moore

Marketing & Publicity
Chloe Cummings
Emma Petfield

Operations
Melissa Okusanya
Hannah Stamp

Production
Emily Chan
Denis Manson
Simon Moore
Francesca Tuzzeo

Rights
Rachel McCarron
Hany Sheikh Mohamed
Zoe Shine

The HarperCollins Distribution Team

The HarperCollins Finance & Royalties Team

The HarperCollins Legal Team

The HarperCollins Technology Team

Trade Marketing
Ben Hurd

UK Sales
Laura Carpenter
Isabel Coburn
Jay Cochrane
Sabina Lewis
Holly Martin
Erin White
Harriet Williams
Leah Woods

And every other essential link in the chain from delivery drivers to booksellers to librarians and beyond!

If you're not a ten on Sophie's spreadsheet, you're never getting her between the bedsheets...

No aspect of Sophie's life goes unrecorded in her Excel spreadsheets, so when she accidentally sends it to her entire contact list instead of just her best friend, Sophie has a lot of uncomfortable explaining to do.

First on the list? Dr Michael Adams. After a disastrous first date, Michael scored a '3' on Sophie's 'love life' tab, but when she shows up to apologise for sharing his result with the world, he issues an unexpected challenge: ten dates to prove that love can't be calculated by an equation or contained by boxes on a spreadsheet.

Sophie isn't someone who's used to thinking outside the digital box, but there's something about Michael that makes her want to take a chance...

Available in paperback and eBook!

NOBODY PUTS ROMCOMS IN THE CORNER

Kathryn Freeman

Not an expert, not even close, not in any of this. But nobody will try harder than me to make you happy.

Sally is a classic romantic and Harry is a classic cynic, but when a drunken bet leads the new flatmates to (badly) recreate 'the lift' from Dirty Dancing, and the video goes viral (#EpicRomcomReenactmentFailure), they both realise there's potential financial benefit in blundering their way through the romcom lexicon for their suddenly vast social media following.

Now, as Harry and Sally bring major romcom moments to new life – including recreating that classic diner scene – their faking it turns to making…out and suddenly they're living a real life romcom of their own!

But like all the greatest love stories, the road to happily ever after is paved with unexpected challenges for this hero and heroine…

Available in paperback, eBook, and audio!

Dream job. Dream house. Fake fiancé.

A year in a gorgeous Italian castle…

When Anna Roberts' life implodes, an online search leads her to an ad for the ultimate dream job – management of a gorgeous castle on the shores of Lake Como, accommodation included. The only catch? Anna can't do it alone…

…With the last man on earth she'd choose!

The castle owners will only accept a couple as caretakers, which means Anna needs a man on her arm at the interview. Enter her neighbour, Jake Tucker.

Pretending to be a couple is difficult … but pretending the tension simmering between them doesn't exist is quickly proving impossible!

Available in paperback and eBook!

Welcome to the Beach Reads Book Club. Where love is just a page away...

When Lottie Watt is unceremoniously booted out of her uptight book club for not following the rules, she decides to throw the rulebook out the window and start her own club – one where conversation, gin and cake take precedent over actually having read the book!

The Beach Reads Book Club soon finds a home for its meetings at Books by the Bay, a charming bookshop and café owned by gorgeous, brooding Matthew Steele, and as the book club picks heat up, so too does the attraction between Matt and Lottie.

If there's anything Lottie has learned from the romances she's been reading, it's that the greatest loves are the ones hardest earned.

Available in paperback, eBook, and audio!

MR RIGHT ACROSS THE STREET

Kathryn Freeman

'Amazing chemistry!'
Julie Caplin

Mia Abbott's move to Manchester was supposed to give her time and space from all the disastrous romantic choices she's made in her past.

But then the hot guy who lives opposite – the one who works out every day at exactly 10 a.m., not that Mia has noticed thank-you-very-much – starts leaving notes in his window… for her.

Bar owner Luke Doyle has his own issues to deal with but as he shows Mia the sights of her new city he also shows her what real romance looks like for the first time.

When he cooks up a signature cocktail in her honour, she realises that the man behind the bar is even more enticing than any of his creations. And once she's had a taste she knows it will never be enough!

Available in paperback and eBook!

Not an expert, not even close, not in any of this. But nobody will try harder than me to make you happy.

Sally is a classic romantic and Harry is a classic cynic, but when a drunken bet leads the new flatmates to (badly) recreate 'the lift' from Dirty Dancing, and the video goes viral (#EpicRomcomReenactmentFailure), they both realise there's potential financial benefit in blundering their way through the romcom lexicon for their suddenly vast social media following.

Now, as Harry and Sally bring major romcom moments to new life – including recreating that classic diner scene – their faking it turns to making…out and suddenly they're living a real life romcom of their own!

But like all the greatest love stories, the road to happily ever after is paved with unexpected challenges for this hero and heroine…

Available in paperback, eBook, and audio!

ONE MORE CHAPTER
YOUR NUMBER ONE STOP FOR PAGETURNING BOOKS

One More Chapter is an award-winning global division of HarperCollins.

Subscribe to our newsletter to get our latest eBook deals and stay up to date with all our new releases!

signup.harpercollins.co.uk/join/signup-omc

Meet the team at
www.onemorechapter.com

Follow us!
@OneMoreChapter_
@OneMoreChapter
@onemorechapterhc

Do you write unputdownable fiction?
We love to hear from new voices.
Find out how to submit your novel at
www.onemorechapter.com/submissions